OVERBOARD

IVY NGEOW

ISBN 978-1-913584-00-9

A Leopard Print book

First published in Great Britain in 2020 by Leopard Print Publishing

"Beyond all the things is the sea."

- Seneca

1
YOU

A LIGHTNING BOLT SPLIT the night sky.

For a few seconds it looked like daytime. Thunder roared. Going to shore was an immediate threat.

When pulling down air, the down drafts of rain caused thunderstorm winds which blew outward from the centre of the rainfall area. Sailing had taught you everything you believed in. You repeated the affirmations like a chant: *if you don't know what to do, do nothing, Keep Calm and Shut Up, screaming wastes energy, discretion, the better part of valour, patience, virtue, fools rush* etc.

The boarding ladder tore off like the paper on a burrito. Fenders, warps. Sea water crashed onto the decks, its white surf breaking on the bathing platform. Tossing out an anchor wasn't a good idea because you were in a wide body of water and had lost all visibility. Although the severity of storms and timings were unpredictable, once the winds changed, everything would stop. It was *not* an emergency yet. *Screaming wastes—*

A window broke free and blasted straight at you, sudden

as a slap. It missed. Maybe it was a line of storms, common in the tropics. You felt the sensation of falling again and again off the waves due to the exceptionally large troughs.

The only thing left to do was to chop the throttle. You grappled in the wet darkness with various wooden fixtures such as the cargo hatch and capstan to get to the cockpit like some mime artist. The boat was being tossed like a salad due to the rogue waves coming at it in all directions. Any boat could capsize in sea-state 9. The aim was to avoid broaching, or running into the backside of a wave, but actually which was back and which was front? Was there a down and up too?

With no visibility, you couldn't negotiate an inlet on a lee shore. You couldn't even go outside now or radio for emergency rescue services as you'd be risking electrocution. Stainless steel towers, railings, ladders. All unsafe. You should only hold onto wood. At the helm in the cockpit, something heavy and sharp landed on you. There was no pain. The hit was so great it was numbing.

Under you was a vast darkness. Above, there was sun, or there seemed to be, not yellow, just a glint. It might not even have been daylight. In a couple of hours, you would be back on shore, making coffee and eating the croissants still inside the larder of the stainless steel kitchen, thinking, phew, that was a bad night.

No. You are deluded.

Everything was spinning. The waves shuttled you back and forth. Your head kept falling forwards as if something had gone in your neck, weakened by the impact when you were hit by that sharp, heavy thing. What was it? There was a feeling of being just about to faint, doll-like, head lolling, unable to look up. Wanting to fall asleep without even feeling drowsy.

Your head dipped down when you could no longer hold it up and you glanced at the dials on the polished mahogany dashboard as though seeing them for the first time. One needle indicated several hundreds, another many thousands in another dial but several hundred and many thousands what? The digital system was no use, it was all dark, gone. You slid away from the cockpit, weak, and instinctively latched onto the upholstery and wooden frames, still avoiding the metal posts and grab rails.

The boat was not sinking, so that's good, right? You know the rule: if we're not sinking we must be floating—

AN EXPLOSION. IT WAS in the engine room. It was not daylight, nor was it the illusion of sun. It was just white, so white it was black. There was no sea, or sun, just the inexorable wetness from the rain and waves. You landed onto the deck as the boat's hull arched like a mountain. It was like a waterslide which carried you off at great speed. Sleep came during the white and wakefulness during the black. Your head felt light and did not loll any more-

Everything alternated black and white, the time interval between could be seconds or hours. You were on fire. You clung onto something to put it out—

WHEN YOU OPEN YOUR EYES, something is in your hand. It is white. Your fingers feel the smooth rough texture. It must be a piece of paper. You must have been gripping hard as it's crumpled now. There are green curtains around and where they part, grey walls beyond. When you look back at your

hand, it's holding the edge of a sheet, not a sheet of paper. Sheet and sheet. Well, close.

Within reach is a small metal grey nightstand with wheels and a glass jam jar of orange chrysanthemums on it. Now there's a cheerful colour, the only thing of colour because next to the jar is an empty diaphanous plastic medicine cup, as small as a shot glass. On the ceiling is an arrow with a word on it in a scribbly script font you can't read. What's the arrow for? Where is it pointing to?

Just then, there is a knock on the door, and you hear voices in another language, one you're familiar with but now can't place. The door opens with a quiet click and a woman appears. She must be a nurse because she is in uniform, and pushing one of those mini basket trolleys on a stand.

Inside it is the stuff for taking your temperature and your blood pressure. 'Good afternoon. You're up.' Oh it's afternoon. You watch her. For a few minutes you forget about your hunger.

Her English is good and she is big-boned. She is wearing a light blue hijab. Still from her face alone you can see that she is in her mid to late thirties and average-to-not-very-good looking. You have a hawk eye for the ladies and can discern from a distance the appeal of a woman, hijab or no hijab. It is more a sixth sense than 2020 long-sightedness. Another thing not taken away from you: your eyesight. You must have been a creative and visual person and still are. Although you do not consider her attractive, she must be a damn sight more attractive than you are now.

'The doctor will be coming to see you in about an hour when he completes ward round.'

She pushes up the trolley stand and takes your temperature and blood pressure. She makes her recordings and a note of the time on the clipboard at the end of your bed after she glances at her watch which is safety pinned to name tag on her uniform. It is in a foreign script. You cannot read it. She picks up the empty medicine cup and leaves the room with the trolley.

After she's left, you are afraid to fall asleep for fear of waking up somewhere else again. You run your tongue along your teeth and you only now become aware the gums are exposed. You feel dizzy when you shut your eyes, like when you go to bed drunk, and the whole room spins when your eyes are closed.

THE NURSE RETURNS WITH A TRAY. Dinner, she says. You look at it. You know it's Thai food from the smell. Fish sauce. Lemongrass. Garlic. Ginger. It is pungent and fragrant. Your eyes water just from the smell. Coconut jasmine rice. You cannot tell what it is from its semi-solid nature. The inside of your mouth feels like a sponge. There is an intense ache when you open your jaws. It gives you a shock. You can't chew. But you are hungry. So far so good.

Outside it is already dark.

Don't worry about the time,' she says. She must be an experienced mind reader. 'You had an accident,' she says, 'and now you must rest.'

You are the luckiest man alive and eating Thai food. And not paralysed. After the sumptuous meal you feel drowsy. Or maybe it is the medication. You want to go back to asleep. 'Don't fight sleep,' the nurse says. 'It's normal to be sleepy after an accident. Some fishermen found you off the coast of Southern Thailand near the port village of Laem Sak.'

The wires. You look at the ceiling again. The arrow and

the word in a scribbly font. It's Thai. You hear a long low sound and look up. You try to glance at the outside world through the darkened windows though there is nothing to see. She puts the tray down and draws the curtains. 'It's a ship's horn.'

You are near the coast. She has told you the name of the village but it's now gone.

The nurse pushes the meal trolley to you and set up your cutlery. She comes to the side of your bed and begins to straighten the sheets.

'You're imagining things. You mustn't worry.'

She brushes back the hair from your forehead. 'We need to cut your hair.' She looks this way and that, side to side like she is a hairdresser imagining what styles would suit you. 'It's getting in your eyes.'

You feel like a boy again in a barber's chair. In your present state, do you actually need to be presentable?

'I am finishing my shift now. I am going home. The night shift nurse will clear your tray, do your teeth and take your blood pressure later on. You're lucky you have some teeth left. Good night.'

THE ROOM SEEMS DRAB and the lights hurt you. You know it is a hospital. It looks like one. The ceiling is in panels, painted white. It has criss-crossed battens also painted white and reminds you of the mock Tudor style in great swathes of Surrey. To make a terribly uneven interwar surface seem less terrible and more even, one put criss-crossing battens and painted the lot to mimic a lesser yet grander period in history. You don't know why but you know all this. You are interested in buildings, in light, composition.

Each panel is not smooth at all like a plaster ceiling. These panels you supposed, make it easy to access the pipe work and electrics beyond. It is strange to imagine there are services alive and kicking beyond the room that you are in, air conditioning ducts sighing, coughing, heaving and contorting. To provide acoustic buffering, you supposed, in case of patients screaming and wailing, the ceiling is pock-marked like a cake by its currants. You bet spiders come out of the bigger pockmarks. You feel hungry. You must be getting better. Hunger is a sign of life, of being alive.

This is a nightmare. It must be. This can't be real. All things considered you are calm and not as shocked as you'd like to be because you are kind of restrained now by your injuries. You must have had a positive streak. You'd like to tear all this off and jump out of the window or at least just open the door to take a look what on earth is outside in the corridor. But all of that is impossible right now as you can't move very much.

You check your hands, everything is there. The fingers. Legs, toes, body, all moving, though slowly and with a concrete weight you do not recognise. When you feel your face, it is completely covered in bandages except for the eyes and forehead. There are holes for your mouth and nostrils. Hair. It's there, coming out of the bandages. It feels long and greasy on your forehead. It's in your eyes. Good. You haven't lost anything that you are aware of. You hope this is true, as you are unable to check your genitalia because you have been mummified. All of it'd better be there.

You see the fluorescent tube lighting above, tautly suspended from stainless steel wires.

2

PHOEBE

Battambang, Cambodia

H E HAD BEEN JUMPY before he left, 'high'. She dreaded to think he was coked up.

It was the industry, not him, she told herself. He was working hard when he went out of contact.

'I'm sorry we are shutting in a few minutes,' said the woman in charge of the internet café. Only the name was grand – Opera Café. Four stone-age black PCs in a row were supported by one-time doors with sawn off former RSJs as their "desk" legs. There was a sign to say they were on Opennet which was cheaper and faster than Online or Ezecom. She read it blankly while her rage simmered. Why couldn't he just send a one-liner saying he was OK? She needed just that one email. She did *not* require any live streaming, feeds or social media with the slow ADSL service on offer.

'How many?' Phoebe sighed.

'About ten minutes. Nine.'

Phoebe Wong's 18 month old iPhone 5s was at the Apple

Fix Mobile Repair because it was unable to search for the carrier or the signal. She had not heard from Greg for four days. It was and it was not unlike him. It was usually the other way round. If he had not heard from her, she would be receiving 2,000 missed calls. There was no need to panic yet, she assured herself. His phone was dead and he had not emailed.

She logged out as it was not worth trying tonight. She tried to call Greg again but there was no reply. The phone was off and if only she had tried ringing him about three days ago, or daily. But they did not have that kind of relationship. The British valued and respected privacy and independence. "Don't like to bug people," they'd say. They needed their 'space' — a Western concept invented to mean 'no verb required'. For example, if someone (to be fair, that would be Greg) started a question beginning with 'Could you just—'. You must complete it with 'OK'. No verb was required. There was an unspoken rule already in place called marriage.

What Greg had been up to or what the shoot entailed in Singapore she had no idea and mostly didn't want to know. Most of his contracts required non-disclosure agreements (NDAs). He was working for the 'insalubrious, debauched and very wealthy' in his words. In her mind, this translated as 'job involving top class recreational drug use'. Her throat had been tight as she'd shuffled into the internet café in an alleyway off the village square that evening.

When one was on a grown up gap year, or Groggy, the theory was that one did not actually want to be connected all the time. That was the theory. Phoebe was a graphic designer and Greg was portfolio careerist meaning photographer, videographer, influencer, blogger with compound streams of income and contracts. Those were just his official jobs. Now she shivered to think what unofficial mission he was on when he went silent.

Someone like him, a 'slashie', with multiple life-work work-lifestyles was always a 'cool' guy, an enigma, a rogue, which was why she was attracted to him in the first place. He'd also decided for her that she should have a safe 9-6 job as an employee, that she should then quit it to travel and to volunteer with him in Cambodia and through all this she should inform him where she was at any point in time. The same rules did not apply to him. If she at all disagreed, demurred, or even just asked where he was he would lose his temper and storm off.

Groggy meant the chance of a lifetime before you were way past it, living the life of a middle-aged selfless volunteer, on the philosophical process of self-discovery, living the dream, giving the gift etc. Yet what she was actually experiencing was often the opposite. Mild frustration and stress that nothing worked properly, quickly or to her London time and metropolitan system of thought.

The bureaucracy and sexism mostly blew her mind but she kept her cool. Being Chinese, she was used to being repressed and controlling her entire range of emotions, from rage to utter delight. You never displayed anything unless you were sure that you should, and who the hell was ever sure?

Hot, with 93% humidity, Battambang had been the highlight of the trip for Phoebe. At the Community Education Centre, some of the children were orphaned but seemed as happy, polite and innocent as any other children. The children's home provided them with a safe place to develop. Learning how to eat thriftily was part of the street food concept and part of being brought up Asian.

Lok lak is one of Cambodia's simplest dishes – just

cubed, stir fried beef with red onions on a green salad. The dressing of lime juice, salt and Cambodian Kampot pepper was the pièce de résistance of this economical dish.

Phoebe felt she had only just got to know Cambodia. Greg on the other hand had been actively running his travel blogs for a year. His income from blogging had been helpful for their day-to-day existence while volunteering as groggys. It also didn't hurt that he was attractive-looking, tanned, grey-haired with green eyes and full lips for those paid partnerships on Instagram.

When they'd first arrived, it had been rejuvenating wandering through the old city, exploring the well-preserved early 20th century French colonial architecture, riding on mopeds, drinking fresh local fruit juice from street vendors.

Phoebe was now experienced at haggling in markets, an Asian skill that had been lost to her as she grew up in the West. And temples in Asia were like cathedrals in Europe. 'They're all the bloody same,' remarked another volunteer once.

She had a local Metfone SIM only deal but waited to use free WiFi as, like any Londoner of Malaysian Chinese descent, she'd been brought up frugal and knew how to save money by spending money, spend money by saving money, the difference between the two and the variations in between. At her 41 years and with the experience they brought, she should understand the gradients between throwing away money and actually making money.

∼

TWO DAYS OFFLINE was hell even for a middle-aged luddite.

Outside of major cities, network coverage on the four networks — Metfone, Smart, Cellcard and qb — was weak.

It was his duty to at least let her know where he was, wasn't it? Communication was poor, between them and in this country. This was not London.

The landlines destroyed during the Khmer Rouge era had yet to be replaced, and the lack of phone lines not only hindered business but also kept Internet access costs high everywhere except Phnom Penh and Siem Reap. A grizzled ex-pat from Liverpool had told her in the queue at the Phnom Penh post office it had only been a few years since mail destined for Cambodia had to be collected in Bangkok.

Volunteering taught you patience. You could not really put that on your LinkedIn profile. She often gave up when trying to upload a Wordpress blog post. Blogging became an encumbrance, a millstone, something you could give up. She wanted to give up. She wanted to scream. But who would hear her? She buried her head, hands over ears.

'Feebs?' A familiar voice called out.

She took her hands off. After she gave up on the ancient PCs, she was relieved to see her best friend there, a fellow volunteer called Trish who had become very close friend and always cheered her up even though they had an age gap of 20 years between them. Trish was a tough Yorkshire lass with short hair, tattoos on her calves and back and a big smile. Her makeup-free skin was dewy and radiant even after a long day. Even her tattooed calves were taut and smooth.

'Hey!'

'Hey. Whatcha doing here?'

'Nothing as you can see,' Phoebe said in a controlled manner. Suddenly, she felt her mask fall apart. She choked back on her tears, unable to speak.

'Oh no, what's happened?' Said Trish. She put her arms around Phoebe straightaway. 'Tell me.'

Phoebe shook her head. She did not know what to say. Her tears fell and her face was scrunched up. Trish reached into her pocket and handed Phoebe a tissue. She wiped her tears and calmed down.

'Wanna grab a beer?' said Trish.

Phoebe looked at her watch. Yet another Asian habit. You don't say yes or no until you have checked the time.

'Greg's missing.' Phoebe could only manage to bring up those two words.

THE PETITE BUT SQUARE-JAWED woman police constable said something in Khmer. The woman next to her said, 'She wants to know what you and your husband were doing in Cambodia when he went missing.' Where should she begin? Phoebe had to think before replying to the interpreter. After all, she had decided, after 5 days, she had to go to the local police station to report Greg as missing. She paused and sighed.

When they'd asked themselves 'what are we living for?', she and her husband Greg realised they were living – no, hoping - for a change. 'We needed it,' she told the interpreter. She wanted to say more, but decided to keep it to herself.

Phoebe already knew they wouldn't get it here where everything was a matter of life and death and how. Every month in the Sunday Times, there was yet another article about how people are living longer now in the West, and even longer without children.

The life you lived from 0 to 40 had to be repeated from

40 to 80. Middle-aged middle-class couples or singles without kids went on Groggys. It was what you do these days when you had it all, had done it all and had been everywhere.

They'd sold their six-year-old VW Golf (so handy for Ikea trips) and put everything in storage. They tastefully decorated their three-bedroom garden flat in Balham in greys and taupes and mink (the colour, not the animal) after they'd had enough of ogling at interior photos on Houzz and Pinterest to get ideas.

This was their career make or break. Nowadays employers wanted to know if you bled for the poor or for a cause and all for free. There was even a section for it on LinkedIn. 'What I did for free'. They bought a one-year open return ticket. They rented out their flat to childless professionals, younger versions of themselves.

'OK,' said the woman police constable. 'So you are not here to make money or to work.'

'No. I mean yes.' She knew they wouldn't get it. People were so poor here that no one would go abroad on their own expense and work for free or "volunteer".

Phoebe and Greg had never understood money. This was the most important and biggest thing they had in common. To them, you either have it or you don't. Step One. If you don't, you worked like mad to earn it. If you did, then Step Two: you worked so it didn't run out. You travelled, spent it all until the first instance and you repeated Step One.

There was not enough to save when you have to carry out the two-step cycle. In London. Their only nest egg was the flat in Balham and their inheritance when her parents died. Greg's had already passed away after long illnesses.

'Constable Chantrea wants to know what Greg's occupation is,' said the interpreter.

'One of his main jobs was being photographer for the wealthy which gave him access to several sidelines doing commercial digital agency work too.'

'He had many jobs?'

'Yes.'

'Like what? What other jobs did Greg do?'

'Blogging, selling ad space on his blogs, influencing, reviewing.' The interpreter had several attempts at translating the terms. Eventually the WPC understood, as indicated by her nods.

'Constable Chantrea asks if you know where he went five days ago,' said the interpreter after an awkward pause.

'No. He said Singapore but I don't know where. He was always vague about where he was going exactly and what he was doing. It was just work.'

'What about the client he was working for? Do you know who they are?'

'No.'

Greg had repeatedly explained that "the bastards", meaning his clients, were loaded and liked to do expensive things but all in secret. The more loaded, the more private they were. For they knew the only thing of value in this world was your own privacy. Everything else was just shopping.

There was a longish conversation between the WPC and the interpreter who then said, 'They have to look at immigration records to see where his passport has travelled through. They will investigate the next step. If you hear from him, of course, let her know straightaway. That is all she needs from you now.'

He was now just another missing person which the

police had to look for. For his substance use and abuse he could be arrested. Phoebe bit her lip and decided against divulging the information that Greg was known for going on benders. He had disappeared for days before. Lost weekends and Ibiza crushers. He enjoyed being lost without her.

'They have his photos, description and the last outfit you recall him wearing,' said the interpreter. 'And you say Chelsea tattoo on left calf?'

'Yes. But I don't have a photo of that. It's a single blue lion.'

3

DOMINIQUE

"The first thing we do, let's kill all the lawyers."- William Shakespeare, Henry VI, Part 2, Act IV

A SCAFFOLDER SPAT. HE had a hair band, a bob hairstyle and longish Gap shorts; almost too feminine for a building site, and more like a 'cool' student in Nutrition or Fine Arts at UCL. She started wondering what he was like in bed but when she looked closely she saw that his clothes were very soiled.

Even the word scaffolding was a cough, a splutter, guttural, sharp. She was forty-seven years old, sitting with the Office Angels A3 cardboard box of all her possessions from the office and on her lap the last of her Pret salads. She forced herself to think about the scaffolder to take her mind off her redundancy.

Tomorrow would be the start of homemade salads. Sitting here on a bench in Paternoster Square where everyone was anonymous, you could be rich, poor, working, not working. She was sitting there deciding whether she should throw the whole box away without looking through it or to take it home.

Instead of going straight into the office car park keycard access where her silver year-old Mercedes GM Roadster was parked, something must have made her step into the Square. She needed fresh air (a metaphor for thinking space — there was no actual fresh air in central London, she knew that).

She needed to work it out, like an ordinary human, not some legal nut. It was cathartic. It was like she had been put on a drip and something was draining away from her, though she didn't know what but it felt better. Life slowed down.

She watched so many people doing so many things. She overheard people on their phones in five minutes at least five snatches of conversations and those were only the ones in English. There were more in other languages.

'I wanted to get your advice on something...'

'It was lovely. So yeah we flew to Nice and drove down to Monte Carlo... EasyJet...'

'No, the script was already done. That's what I understood...we had to change part of...'

'If they could get they arse in gear by Monday, it would be ideal. If if if. I reckon we got it covered...'

'It's just cost. What about mobility issues... no, I know... but the point...'

When she looked at her watch it was only ten minutes, but it felt like hours. But this was the way London operated, quickly and on so many levels. Life went on regardless of her news. London was a turning unending system of gears. All the conversations she heard were more than those between her husband James and herself.

He'd moved to work in Singapore in 2008 and she hadn't wanted to go with him. *Then*. He came back about four times a year during term breaks to see her and Daphne. He had no interest in her or her job. Because she'd refused to move with him, it had become a sore point, a stalemate. It could not be brought up.

Now indeed circumstances had changed. She thought about him, with a new optimism. She could now join him and move there. Now was the time. Losing her job meant she could press re-start. Have a fresh new beginning in Singapore with James. Work on their so-called marriage. Get a new job through LinkedIn.

Daphne was in boarding school and would fly to Singapore every holiday. It *was* possible. *Anything* was possible. She would have told him that very day only because of the time difference, it was too late. It was 4pm in London and 12 midnight there.

Suddenly, all these fantasies floated away. Such ideas were just to give her a bit of positive outlook and light relief only. Would he even welcome her? Dominique was feeling everything, something, nothing. Rage, pain, frustration and of course, the shame of redundancy. It could also be the inexplicable sudden perimenopausal rage followed by instantaneous exhaustion.

The 'sitting-in-the-open-air' drug started to do its job. She felt drowsy. Was it already June? Wow, half a year gone, already. Everything was already testing. Despite the harsh sunlight it must have been fifteen degrees. She got up from the bench and headed for the carpark.

Originally the silver Roadster was not hers. She already had a 1959 Mercedes 190SL Roadster in ivory (nicknamed The Sheryl Crow as the rock star had the same model) sitting patiently in her garage at home awaiting a few little jobs to be done. This was the real star, the show-stealer.

It was a gift to her from James fifteen years ago at their wedding, the same colour as her dress. A few things had gone wrong. Mostly body work. Rust in the chassis and/or the body due to the "double-wall" construction and poorly designed drain holes that were forever clogging.

'All the usual stuff with a classic car,' said Reggie, her mechanic in a specialist garage in Hertfordshire. Neither Reggie nor the tiny garage had changed since WWII.

But it was worth fixing up the Crowmobile. She preferred vintage models of the rock'n'roll or Hollywood era. She learnt and grew with each restorative process since her wedding. The parts had to come from Japan and the USA so a classic car taught you patience.

Did you really need Zen and meditation when you could ride in the Crowmobile? Quite apart from it being a work of art, it had exceptional road handling. Individually mounted wheels on the front axle and double-wishbone suspension with hydraulic shock absorbers.

Cars were like children. You did not want another one but sometimes they came along and you cried. They were so beautiful and cute you'd have to love them anyway. James had bought the silver Roadster last year on a whim, just to drive about in London.

She did not want another beast especially a modern one but what the hell. It had a powerful 921 and 928 engine: 105 horsepower at 5,700rpm. The availability of parts for restoration made it a laboratory of love.

After the initial toy-buying thrill wore off he lost interest. So now she drove it around at the comfortable London speed limit. Sometimes she did have an orgasmic buzz, a hum of utter perfection, if she ever went over 80mph on the motorway. Speed was not freedom. It came at a price. Just like a top job.

When they'd made her redundant, it was really irritating that they told everyone she was leaving. Why did they say that? They made the leaving sound like she'd quit.

There was never an opportunity to explain herself because the necessity to finish off what she was or had been doing with a red face, pack up and leave was greater and far outweighed the necessity to clarify to her now former colleagues. In any case, the higher up one was, the greater the fall and the quicker one must get up and out. Those pawns who served their notice? Notice was for little people. She'd got a big cheque, and she had not properly considered the zeros.

Better if she left quickly. Every minute lost was a kilo of dignity. Blame it on Brexit. There was no hashtag, no come-uppance, no punchline. She considered a haircut or some bigger treat — a trip to the Bahamas to her favourite resort, The Ocean Club as in the One and Only Ocean Club. A Balinese massage followed by a sushi lunch at Dune, Jean-Georges Vongerichten's breezy sea-view restaurant.

Her usual $1700 a night suite would be ready for her in about ten minutes from when she called them. There was no fuss, they knew her by her name, her voice, her telephone number, there was no internet booking or security check nonsense. There was no need to bring the "card you paid with" or print outs with QR codes.

It was like family. She got a 'modest' suite by her standards but she liked the informal nature of her visits to the Bahamas. She looked forward to the meticulously-kept lawns, the spectacular stretch of sea and mediaeval statues in courtyard-style tropical gardens. She could be there. One sleep away.

After leaving the square, she called her best friend Lucy when she was driving.

'Lucy, you won't believe it. They fucking made me redundant. No, no, I did not see it coming. Yes, can you imagine it? Now. Listen. The Ocean Club. Fancy it?'

SHE GOT HOME AND started packing, deciding she could buy it all there if she had forgotten anything. Lorraine, her PA, brought her a light meal and a bottle. She was going alone. Lucy could not be expected to say yes on such short notice.

Netflix and her phone would keep her company. She set her alarm as she had to be at the airport at 0755h the next day to check in. When she got to check-in she could have a think and discuss her decision to move to Singapore with James if she could get through to him.

She slept really badly that night due to her shock, the drinking, the loneliness and also the excitement of going to the Bahamas. When you were lonely, the thrill of doing something different (like losing your job and going abroad within 24 hours) was shockingly pleasurable.

She still felt the blood rush to her head. It was like being a child who out of the blue had been allowed to stay up until midnight. She felt queasy with excitement. This could be her last holiday before Singapore.

Why not take the risk? She thought. And if not now, when? Losing her serious, stable and safe job had brought out the rebel in her. Partly it was her own vanity and ambition, but it was her name too. Names had everything to do with your life choices, if you subscribed to Freakonomics theory.

What kind of a name was Dominique when you were

not even French, Algerian or Afro-Caribbean? Quite simply, it sounded like 'dominant'. It was even a place in the Caribbean, just about. Her name meant 'Of the Lord' and surely therefore all-controlling, all-powerful? She believed it influenced her performance at school, in her career and even her ambition.

Her parents had named her after the main character Dominique Francon in *The Fountainhead*, the novel by Ayn Rand. As she grew up, she became more and more like her fictional namesake, never giving people what they want. She gave herself what she wanted, which had to be something she also despised.

It was part of the perversion and luxury of being a Dominique. She'd grown up in Holland Park. Her father was a wine merchant and her mother had never really worked but was some kind of expert on 18th century French literature. They were obsessed with all things French. Dominique had been fluent in it from childhood. She did not want to turn into her mother, someone who was self-indulgent, bilingual and did not work.

She felt a brief stab of guilt in the limo when she went to the airport when she did not get a chance to tell Daphne she would be away for a short break. Her mind was in turmoil. She Whatsapped her PA Lorraine and the housekeeper Ellie on a group chat. Daphne was in boarding school and would not even know if she disappeared for a few days.

Dominique took the 0955 BA 0253 Business Class. 9 and a half hours later, it arrived at Lynden Pindling International in Nassau, at 1415. After clearing customs and immigration and then claiming her luggage, she met her usual limo driver, Caruso. He turned onto John F Kennedy Drive, down Prospect Ridge Road and along West Bay Street to Lakeview Drive and finally onto Casino Drive.

It was a comfortable, familiar sight — all of it. She recognised landmarks on the 40-minute drive. This had to be one of the most beautiful beaches in the world. She slept in the afternoon. Had a lobster and Chablis dinner on the terrace framed by fairy lights, bougainvilleas and scented with night frangipani. Unable to concentrate on the book she'd brought with her, she slept some more.

The next day, she returned to her suite at the One and Only Ocean Club, after breakfast on Paradise beach and a rather long and sticky walk. She tore open her new cheap treat (only £ 46.00 for 75ml), Clinique's Moisture Surge 72-hour Hydrator from the duty free lounge in Heathrow's Terminal 3. It promised to hydrate, soothe, highlight and prime, the 'ideal post-sun 5-minute mask'.

She applied the Hydrator and lay down on the chaise longue in the garden-cum-courtyard by her private pool. She had about half an hour before the masseuse would turn up for her deep tissue appointment. Dominique set the 5-minute timer on her phone and shut her eyes, feeling rather blank and numb.

A temporary respite from the world of work. She had already been on LinkedIn this morning, checking out some rôles. She'd banked the cheque before she got on the plane. They only paid her a piddly £175,866.41 in redundancy for her years of employment there. Not enough digits in *that* number, no way. She hoped that TXWF went bust soon. That new Partner had been wanting to get rid of her for a year and made her life hell.

Imagine waking up and only having three things to do; eat, drink coffee, do yoga. This must be what other mums did all day. No wonder they didn't want a job. What incentive was there? She could even become a vegan. You don't need much energy to eat, drink coffee and do yoga.

She used to wake up at 4:55 am to 30 or 40 things to do; email and bureaucracy from clients, clients of clients, clients of clients of clients, Partners, ex-Partners, colleagues, the housekeeper, the PA, the school, the dental surgery, the builder, the PTA and so many more before actual 'work' began.

She looked at her 18-month calendar and waited for the bings and bongs of reminders from her phone. She was just about to rinse off her 5-minute Hydrator mask when her iPhone rang. Who was it? It had to be Lucy or Lorraine calling her.

'Mrs Laney-Sambrooke?' the trill of a man's voice. 'It's Martin Pelland. I'm calling from HSBC Singapore.'

She listened. He seemed to be saying a string of incomprehensible words.

'I am in the Bahamas. I can't hear you very well.' She composed herself. Then her mind went blank.

She heard a repetitive sound. She forgot what intermittent sound it was that kept chiming. Then she remembered that the five-minute timer in the bathroom suite was going off to remind her to remove the Hydrator mask.

'Can you wait a second?' She went into the bathroom, put the phone down and rinsed it off. 'Yes. Yes, I am back. What are you saying? Can you repeat-'

'A body has been found, police say.'

'Can you repeat that?'

'A body. It had washed up to shore. The police contacted HSBC this morning. Mrs Laney-'

'Yes. Yes, I am here. What are you saying?'

They were calling all the way from Singapore so it must be serious.

'We require you to identify it.'

'But who is it? What body?'

A pause. 'Mrs Laney-Sambrooke. I am calling you about your husband James.'

'But-but who are you?' Dominique said sharply.

'I am Martin of HSBC.'

'Yes, I know that. You said. But I- don't know you and I have never... heard of you. James never- mentioned-'

'I'm a senior partner. I work with James.'

'I'm sorry, this must be a mistake.'

'Do you know anything about what happened in the last week?'

Dominique was gasping short breaths. She just could not reply. They had no idea that the last person to know anything would be his wife. He was 53 years old. He had bought himself toys, new playmates and now it was over.

How come none of them knew what happened to him or cared? He was not thirty. He would have a heart attack if he even went on a bender for ten minutes. You heard of those bankers who do crazy things on coke and one even murdered his whores, Jack the Ripper-style.

Did she worry when she didn't hear from him? She didn't know anything so how could she worry?

'Since the Vesak Day long weekend, he has not turned up at the office and we haven't heard from him. We were concerned. We think he was sailing as he often takes his boat out. Vesak Day was Tuesday 29th May. Yes. It's a bank holiday here. But last night, Tuesday 5th June, a body washed up on the coast of Penang. That is, our night, your day.'

'Yes,' she bleated, accepting that they were trying to accommodate time differences into her mental space like she had never heard of time zones before.

Suddenly there was the doorbell. Shit! It was really loud. Who the hell was that? Oh, she remembered then, it was the bloody masseuse arriving. She did not know how to get to the door. Her legs had turned semi-liquid. The bell rang again.

'...the... door,' she whispered. Her voice had completely gone.

'The police will be in touch shortly,' Martin said. 'I'm really sorry, but I had to let you know first.'

Dominique was shaking.

'Do you want to identify it?'

Not really, but what choice had she?

'HELLO? HELLO? MRS LANEY-SAMBROOKE?'

She was sweaty and cold. Her mouth was paper-dry.

'Can you hear me?'

How could they sound so polite so kind and calm when they were talking such shit.

'We could not contact him. We tried to call but it went straight to voicemail.'

You do not call someone who is dead — they won't answer, she thought grimly. For she'd assumed that, preparing herself for the worst already. They would not ask you to travel thousands of miles if they were not sure themselves.

If she had to travel directly there from the One and Only Ocean Club, it occurred to her that she only had the Hydrator, her toiletries bag and four sets of bikinis with her. She could not stay on here any longer when she had to go and identify a body.

How could she sleep now? She considered calling the Resort private doctor for prescription meds. Of course, since they already knew her no questions would be asked. She could get any meds, in London or abroad. Heaven knew she needed them right now.

Many things went through her mind like white blinking lights and she wanted to pass out. The doorbell stopped ringing. The masseuse finally went away assuming she was asleep, or out and had forgotten about the appointment.

IN THE VAST CREAM-PAINTED wood bathroom, she keeled over. She had to hold the frameless glass screen enclosure of the shower for support. Her stomach heaved in waves.

Her healthy vegan organic low sugar matcha and chia seed low fat breakfast came up through her throat and nose and splashed over her toilet like a tsunami, leaving the sharpest burning feeling in her mouth. Martin was still talking but she could no longer listen. She dropped her iPhone onto the marble floor and it clattered like a chipped mug.

Yes, can you imagine it? Now. Listen. The Ocean Club. Fancy it? To her horror, her mind was playing tricks. The words she had said to Lucy just the day before rang out like a schoolgirl's taunt.

4

YOU

THE DOCTOR COMES IN. He could be Chinese. You look at the doctor's name tag. You strain to see.

When you look around, objects near you are often out of focus or taking a while to become clear, like you are behind a grainy film screen.

'So how are we doing?' he says. You think he has said 'we' but he may have said 'you'. It is the beginning of those nightmares where you open your mouth and nothing comes out. Nothing comes out. You arch your jaw like a cat and start to speak again but there is no sound.

'Your vocal cords have snapped. You cannot speak now, and please don't try. And you suffered multiple injuries and burns.'

You listen, speechless in both senses of the word.

'We have scheduled some surgery to fix this. For now, you will have to write down what you want to say.'

He thrusts a little blue notebook and cheap ball point pen into your lap, like it's a desk. Yet you are hardly mobile.

You will manage a question, if only a spidery scrawl. You want to write *how long have I been here?* But those six words will not form. You think all your fingers work as they seemed to when you tested them, but now they cannot and will not move.

They are fixed in some grotesque kind of sylph-like ballerina's hand position as though you are in an arthouse play. They cannot even grip a pen. You're sure you are not paralysed and now something has happened and mind over matter doesn't matter. Your mind tries again and they just will not move.

'Ah yes. You have... Don't worry,' the doctor says, reading your mind. 'It will come. Some parts of your brain are still recovering. You will be holding a pen very soon. Tomorrow you will be writing an essay!' He is trying to make you feel better, to give you hope that you will improve so quickly. You do not laugh, you cannot. Is it even funny?

You are tightly bound or as tight as they can manage and have no idea what has happened to you, or even what injuries except what they've told you in passing. Even if they did tell you the day before or the day before the day before, you may have forgotten due to the state you are in and the amount of medication.

You believe you must be in good hands, intensive care in a good private hospital where the care is constant and of top quality. When the staff speak perfect English then that is your only gauge of the service you are getting, though of course, you could be totally wrong. You can't speak and you can't write.

SOME DAYS PASS AND you still cannot hold a pen. The nurse gives you a generic tablet but there is no internet, she warns you.

'Just for you to type messages to us, or write. Let's find the app. They say there is an app for everyone,' she says.

After tapping away, she returns you the tablet. '1 for yes, 2 for no, 3 for I don't know, 4 it's about something else. OK? Multiple choice questions. Easy.' You type 1, your first word. I need a cigarette, you think. How will you type or draw this?

You wait until she is locked into eye contact with you. You hold out two fingers in a Victory sign with your right hand and put them to your mouth.

'You want a cigarette. Of course. I didn't even know you smoked. Well done for remembering. We need to get you in a wheelchair to take you outside. You can't smoke in here,' she chuckles. 'Not since forty years ago.'

It seems to take a very long time but a male orderly comes in with the nurse and they transfer you to the wheelchair with seeming ease, like removing a cake from an oven and setting it down without a scratch.

You are given a pair of sunglasses as you get used to the light. You are a mummy with shades. A yummy mummy, you think, amusing yourself with your own very English joke. There will be a lot of internalising now.

You weep after dinner. You completely lose it. That feels like the first real meal you've ever had. You are hungry and you know that it is Thai food. But why do you like Thai food so much? Are you close to something? You are strongly connected to the food and you crave it every day. Thai food is your favourite food and you know it. You recognise every dish that has been served.

After eating, you feel very light-headed and sweaty. Your gums sting. You want to pass out, your breath hot and fetid. You almost certainly have a fever. Panting, you press the call button. It lights up red. You try to throw the handset onto the floor but it springs back as it is on a retractable cable.

Why won't they fucking come now? *Now*. A sense of panic fills your throat.

IT'S MORNING. THE HIJABI-WEARING nurse comes in with a colleague and they move you to a wheelchair so that they may change the bloody sheets. Not swearing. They are actually heavily-stained. You have such bad diarrhoea now and you dislike the nurses having to change your soiled sheets – although, of course, they have seen it all before. You are sweating and turning. You have returned to the black and white flashes. It is black when you seem to wake up and the white is when the fever so high it makes you pass out.

'THEY THINK IT'S CLOSTRIDIUM DIFFICILE,' says your usual nurse whom you now recognise. 'We don't know how you got it. Maybe through some kind of contamination.'

You do not understand what she is saying.

'The doctor will come in to see you in an hour,' she says. There is an awful amount of waiting in hospitals. You think it is only the NHS but it must apply to any hospitals. You surprise yourself that you remember general things from long ago, like the NHS, Thai food, time, what one hour is, day and night, curtains, panelled ceilings of Surrey. You must have had a job, or still have one.

They talk to each other in their language so you do not understand.

You are taped up. The entire face, head, neck, body. You can move one arm at a time. It feels very stiff and heavy. But you can touch your bandages. So you may as well touch them and the openings again.

Your mouth bandage opening is large enough for eating some semi-solid mush. You ate something yesterday. What was it? Maybe it was not yesterday but a while ago. The meals have melted into each other and each day.

Where is abroad? Where are you come to think of it?

'I would love to travel but I have never been anywhere,' says Minus Hijabi to you. 'I read so much as a child and I have been around the world in books.'

You read and can read.

On the boat you must have seen lots of beautiful things,' Hijabi added. 'It was a beautiful boat. I saw the photos in the papers.'

You'd really like to see the papers she was referring to. But there is time. She only just told you that her name was Saadiya.

After an hour, another hour, and another. You think you do enjoy waiting. You are a patient patient. Only time can reveal more time.

'Do you know who was on the boat with you?'

You type 3.

She leaves with her colleague with the sheets and bedding in the laundry bin trolley. You feel very nauseous and dizzy from your fever and fall asleep again until the next awakening.

5

PRZEMEK

HIS NAME MEANT CLEVER or ingenious. Indeed, he had a flying start in school.

Prze- ("przez", before) and -mysł ("myśleć", to think). It might mean a man who thought before he acted, a considerate, intelligent person.

Something happened in his teens. His father left his mother and four children. Przemek left school to do odd jobs before someone suggested London.

You could stand in a street corner and then bingo, you had a job. His English was as good as anybody could get in Poland, at least without studying English formally. He'd make it, easy. And he'd make it look easy.

He started doing odd jobs with his friend but he decided to enrol for courses in the evenings, living in a bedsit in Ealing. He wanted a pet that would and could not love him in return. Dogs and cats wanted affection but the pet that would not require love would be a reptile. Since childhood he had been fascinated with pythons.

This was a real step up for Przemek. He had been searching in specialist pet shops, eBay and Preloved for a few months before he decided on a female Burmese in Dagenham, about 8.5 feet long. He got there in his van.

It was love at first sight. He found her tame, friendly if you could call that kind of behaviour friendly. If she were used to being handled, she would be referred to as friendly. He spoke to her in Polish straightaway.

This was incredible, what a princess she was, he thought. She was copper, reticulated, shiny as sequins. She had a cute diamond-shaped head and nice eyes. He willingly paid 80 pounds, very affordable, as he made that in an hour. He was excited to take her home. She was all muscle and bones. It relaxed him to hold something that was so tense, a workout in itself.

A job in London and a Burmese called Montse. He wanted that Catalan name long before he had her. Short for Monstserrat, meaning 'serrated mountain', it was perfect since he originally wanted the name 'Monty' if it was a boy. A friend that was low maintenance was cool.

HE MET ANDREIA AT a job he was working at. He was still doing his Level 2 City and Guilds' evening training for gas safety. She also had an unpronounceable name to match his and also had to simplify and shorten it in order to live in this country. Though he had changed his to Premeck to make it easier for customers (who said it sounded like Primark). Staff at Plumbase, Plumb Center, Benchmarx, Screwfix, Wickes, Tool Station (which he now preferred due to the wider range) and so on became familiar with him not just by sight but by name.

The counter staff were likely to be Polish themselves. There were days, even weeks, when he would not come into contact with any English-speaking people. He enjoyed working out when he was not at work or in school. He was a 5' 8" or 172 cm, well-proportioned, a slight golden boy who looked like a life-sized Oscar statue. Since he came to Britain he became quite fluent in metric to imperial conversions as both were equally common in the building industry.

At first it was all sex with Andreia and no language was necessary. It was either love or lust at first sight. How do you know which? Unless you could age by about 25 years, for you could only know through time. She was petite with the tiniest waist and firmest ass.

Malagasy people were descended from Indonesians and Africans two thousand years ago. But then all of us were from Africa at some point in the past. You could see the Asian ancestry from her gently sloping dark green Chinese eyes, a hazelnut complexion and full mouth like a night flower in bloom.

Within three months she convinced him to leave his bedsit in Ealing and share her flat in Battersea Rise. It used to be called the poor man's Chelsea but now it was hipster nappy valley. It was a big move for him to leave his wood-chip-walled and single light bulb bedsit with dodgy electrics. There was something about her that was animalistic, tribal, brave (she didn't mind Montse).

Montse was cool with anyone, (why not, since she was cold-blooded) and she lived in her tank. She was also quite a big girl already, when Andreia invited Przemek to move in. Snuggling with Montse was out of the question. Apart from the fact that snakes were bigger than fish in a tank, essentially the concept was the same, they looked at you, you looked at them. You fed. They ate. You left them alone. They left you alone. Job done.

Andreia spoke a few languages including Malagasy and French. To add to this exoticism, she had also been to some high-class French school back in Antanarivo called the Lycée Français and picked up English and Italian.

Her family were considered bourgeois. Her father was like an ambassador or something and she did tell him what he was exactly but he had forgotten already. She was qualified as an interior designer in Paris and through some contacts started working on luxury projects in London and Paris.

They were both 24 and had plenty of time to crank up their careers, though for Przemek it would never be a career or a profession. It would remain a trade.

People were disdainful about sex but you might as well be disdainful about the ego, vanity, dreams. He should know well. After all, he was a lay philosopher. He did not need any more reality than at work and at his night school.

What he liked, *loved*, was to escape, via Cartesian mind-body dualism. His body was somewhere and his mind was somewhere else. It was otherwise a fancy concept for existential daydreaming.

Montse was not a daydreamer, he was sure of it. She did not know any better - that was a positive aspect of having a pet reptile. Andreia could come and go, being neither predator nor prey.

ANDREIA'S SPACIOUS GARDEN FLAT in Battersea Rise was in a large Victorian villa style terrace house chopped up into flats in the 1980s. The garden was at least thirty metres long. He moved in one sunny, cool Saturday morning in May.

The landlord had done it up all nice, in taupes and

greys. A few IKEA pieces of furniture and some charity shop junk furniture painted emerald green and grey plus one feature junk item painted in a bright yellow colour called Trumpet, and it was good to go.

Rose gold accessories brightened the flat. He knew nothing about interior design and wanted nothing to do with it. However, being a central heating engineer only having Level 3 left to do to be fully gas safety qualified, he could at least make sure they'd always have hot water and heating.

The landlord and Andreia were pleased that he was handy. Anything that should and could be fixed would be fixed. Showers, taps, electrics, leaks, coat hooks.

Everyone was handy in his family. He had three siblings and two of them, a sister and a brother, were in the UK too. His sister was an artist and his brother a cellist with the Polish orchestra. When they arrived in the UK, his sister became a cleaner and his brother a builder.

England was a place for transforming economic migrants, or rather a place for economic migrants to transform. If you could re-skill, learn English and a technical trade, you were sorted, whether or not you returned home. His sister would not be cleaning forever.

If art was your calling, you eventually had to return the call and say 'no thanks'. It was no way to make a living. His sister had had to re-train in something else, and she had chosen Cognitive Behaviour Training (CBT). She had just completed Level 2.

His brother had friends who had settled here with Polish girlfriends and had children. Their children even had English names like Edward, Oliver and Thomas. They got the names from the engines in Thomas the Tank Engine. If you needed names, this was where you went. Even girls' names. Emily, Annie and Clarabel, and Mavis.

Przemek was home a lot with Montse, his constant companion. He worked from 8 to 5 and very sharply he would knock off. Andreia had an opposite life to him. She started later, more often than not at 10 or 11 for coffee meetings with clients or suppliers.

She had suddenly got very busy and worked late, regularly going to networking events and weekend design exhibitions or trade shows at Olympia, Earls Court or O2 with fellow professionals. She was trying to get her own contacts for private commissions so as to leave her employment in Chelsea Harbour in some firm.

He was now paying double the rent he had been. But she said she'd get him more jobs. Big contracts beyond his dreams.

He spent a lot of time doing what he did in Ealing, working out or reading with his beer and working on the garden on weekends. He had ideas about turning this into a kind of tropical sanctuary for Andreia. A lush landscape reminiscent of the dense and fragrant flora of Madagascar.

When the handsome couple checked out bars like Rise 46, Adventure Bar, The Lighthouse, The Schoolhouse, they attracted admiring and envious glances. When he got dressed up, drunk people mistook him for Leonardo di Caprio.

The hedonism of the 1920s was something that fascinated and mystified him. He liked his freedom, or rather the freedom of the fantasy. He was lucky. He had his martini glasses refilled by the manager without any hesitation or arm-twisting. He was Gatsby, he was Baz Luhrman, except Przemek would live up to cocktail names and there was no broken heart.

Andreia was empress of Battersea, like Rihanna, all proud pout and eyes, glossy hair, nails and skin. They were both fit and slim and in their prime, glowing with a dewy radiance that celebs who could afford to would try to buy, but would never have.

They had what young people had, a 1920s carefree existence, uncertain but lived with passion. They had their anonymity, their innocence. They laughed because they were happy, as children laughed. Unlike Leonardo or Rihanna, they were not media machines.

Who wanted private jets, recreational drugs or Hollywood mansions when you could have youth, beauty and money for your night out?

On account of their easy-fit, easy-care looks and interest in the 1920s, Przemek and Andreia had been seeking speakeasy bars in London, a secret magical world recalling the Prohibition days in the United States, of illicit drinking dens, jazz and swing time music.

They had been to Chelsea Prayer Room in Kensington to hear muted trumpet solos, smooch to stride-style piano music in one-two, learnt dancing, marcel-waving, quiff-slicking, shoe-shining, show-stopping. They had Lindy Hopped to *Ain't Misbehavin'* and *Five Foot Two Eyes of Blue*. They tangoed to *La Cumparsita* and *Nochero Soy*.

Here was a strange oxymoron: which came first, him happy or her happy? Six months into the so-called honeymoon period, the sex was petering out. She was tired from her work and looked forward to just eating her salad, chilling with a glass of wine and falling asleep. It bugged him and he did not know how to bring it up.

He was not articulate or conversation-friendly. He became rock hard just thinking about salsa dancing with her. "All good things come to an end" went the hopeless saying. But Andreia seemed happy enough.

What was the difference between happy and happy enough? Did that mean he was also happy as an indirect effect of having made someone happy enough?

He thought of his singleton nights before he moved in with Andreia in Battersea. When not working out in the Ealing Nuffield gym, he'd stayed in his flat, with Żywiec beer by his side and Montse in the tank, he'd busied himself studying philosophy.

To be left alone, reading and sipping an icy beer uninterrupted, and without a furry animal trying to massage your thighs or drip warm breath all over your feet, was a real luxury.

And one evening as he waited on the sofa for Andreia to come home, he would have to say that time alone and time with Andreia each had pros and cons.

Reading was pumping iron for the mind. Sex was pumping iron for youth. 'What should I do?' he asked Montse in Polish. 'Should I have another beer or wait until she comes home?'

Just then a text came in. It was from Andreia.

6

PHOEBE

IN THE OPERA CAFÉ she received an email from the hospital. How did they get her email address?

She put her hands over her mouth. Had her heart stopped? No breath came out. They said they had tried to call but they could not get through. He'd had an accident but he was alive in a hospital. She could not believe it. They'd found him.

She gripped the RSJ legs to steady herself. She would have to fly out as soon as she could to the hospital in Southern Thailand. They gave the coordinates. He could not speak.

There would be no use in calling him as his vocal cords had been ripped by the accident and he was waiting for his op. Of course, she replied straightaway. She would be there as soon as she could.

She realised her face was wet and she was weeping. She checked the time. It was night time, so it was daytime back in London. Her mother Eva had warned her about the dangers of the gap year. She opened Skype, logged in and called her mother.

As usual they spoke at cross-purposes, like each was having a conversation with herself. Although they were trying to communicate, Phoebe felt like they were each speaking in a different foreign language.

It did not help that her mother's English was not perfect, despite having lived in the UK for more than 40 years. The Skype call quality was clearer than the conversation, which was not saying much.

'Many people had accidents on their gaps years, young or old.'

'It's gap.'

'That's the shop.'

'No. Mum, listen, you just never hear about it because you don't know them, they are not celebs-'

'Why can't he have a normal job like anybody else?'

Her mother was being Chinese again, so she held her breath for a second. 'But this is not a celeb, this is Greg, mum.'

'Anyway what is "gap"? Why people even want to do it?'

'We've been through all this. It's something that both of us want to do.'

'No Asians do such dumb thing. I think it must be Greg want you to go on mad trip. In the old days you lucky to get job and hang onto it for life.'

'There is no such thing as a job for life in these times, mum.'

'Now people throw it all away in order to do things like jump off a mountain while tied to elastic band, trust every-thing, one's entire existence, past present future, on this elastic band.'

Phoebe did not mention her sister Bethany. The name could not be brought up by anyone. Bethany never did anything mad. She was as safety conscious and as low risk as a girl could be. She did not even ride a bicycle.

Her mother and her would be thinking the same thing of Bethany, how life was short, ending too soon, taken away, robbed and so on, all the hackneyed phrases. The anniversary of her death was always a sombre and excruciating day. Bethany was now simply a ghost who would haunt Phoebe's family forever.

IT WAS NIGHT AND she was being eaten alive by mosquitoes at the internet café, still trying to book flights when another email came.

The hospital had written to say that the patient was running a high temperature, had a serious infection, was delirious *and* they were doing tests right now, so no visits were possible for a few days until the fever came down.

Phoebe considered what her mother had said earlier. Trish came into the cafe.

'Hey.'

'Hey.'

'Do you want to grab dinner?'

'That would be so great. I was about to book the flights.'

'So you called your mum?'

'Yes.

'And?'

'And you know. Same-same.'

Her mother could be kind yet without being understanding at all. Yes, this *was* possible for an Asian person. Phoebe was a BBC (British-born Chinese). She had never been surrounded by Asians until she was here in Asia.

Now Phoebe had become aware that her mother was expert at what was impossible for a white person. They were the other way round. A British person could be understanding but unkind. Phoebe was in purgatory while she awaited further news and now she was not even able to book her flights.

'At least he is OK?' Trish didn't sound sure.

'You think so?' Phoebe was even less sure than her friend.

'He is alive and you'll see him soon.' Trish put her arm around Phoebe.

'Yeah,' she wiped at her own tears absently, like a child who'd been picked up after falling over.

'Couldn't they give him paracetamol or antibiotics or something to bring it down?'

'I am sure they are doing all that.'

'What else are they doing? What tests?'

'I don't know... anything. I just- I can't even-'

Trish gave Phoebe a hug and Phoebe returned it. She had been so busy gripping the rusty RSJ legs as though they were smooth and silky pets, she had not realised where her arms were.

Phoebe achieved nothing that day other than making a few children happy with what they designed in their art club. She did not even book her flight, just endured a phone call with her mother and been savaged by mosquitoes because in her stress and anxiety she'd forgotten the repellent.

'I am here to rescue you.'

'I know. Thank you.' Phoebe smiled through her tears.

'What do you feel like eating tonight?' asked Trish.

'Let's go to that Mlob Chan place by the river.' Phoebe

loved the name, it meant "shade of the nutmeg tree". 'I really fancy a prahok with kroeung.'

'You're doing fine,' said Trish. 'You've been so brave, Feebs. You've just got to trust that they're doing a good job. '

7

EVA

S HE HUNG UP FROM her Skype conversation with her daughter. She let go the edge of the grey Corian worktop that she was gripping.

She swallowed hard.

She was in her kitchen with its Fulham-style metro brick tiled white splashback. Cooking was her passion. She loved her kitchen, appliances and gadgets. Most Chinese women her age did, after all. She was fastidious.

She was proud that she cleaned the whole house herself, and better than any cleaner ever could, or would. She kept it sparkling, immaculate. Not a speck of dust even on usually unseen top edges of pictures or door panelling. She would clean until there was nothing left to clean and then it upset her that the cleaning was complete. It gave her hope and motivation.

Yet, now, looking around her, she couldn't see what it was all for or what mess she could possibly be making as she was only cooking for herself and Robert. She checked the Neff oven clock before calling Robert at his lab at the University.

Should she call him or wait until he got home that night? But she needed to tell him straightaway. What could be more urgent than their son-in-law being in an accident?

'Phoebe did not want to worry us so she did not inform us that he had been missing for 5 days,' she said in Cantonese. She thought if his colleagues were listening in, at least they would not know what was being said. 'And now they found him.'

'What?'

She repeated what she'd said. Robert listened in silence. Eva could tell her husband was shocked by the news because normally he was impatient and he'd always interrupt her.

They'd never got on with Greg but he was now very ill, and he was still family. Their shared grudge was normal, no one could ever be good enough for their daughter, Phoebe. No one. Unless he was a prince, a world-renowned cardiologist or top criminal lawyer of Chinese origin.

'Where?' He said finally.

'In Thailand on a beach. Phoebe told me, but I forgot the name. They checked immigration data.'

'He's... alive?'

'He's alive.'

Robert was silent again.

'But very ill. He's waiting for surgery.' She knew what he was thinking. 'They know it's him because... because of the Chelsea tattoo... the other crew members are dead.'

'How many?'

'I don't know. That is all Phoebe said.'

'What was he doing? Why was he found on a beach?' Robert spoke, it seemed, a lot more than she expected.

'He was filming on some yacht.'

'A yacht?'

'Yes.'

'What yacht?'

'A luxury yacht. They found a wreck 5 km off the coast of the village where they found him. On a beach.'

'What was the name of the yacht?'

'Dearest, I only know everything through Phoebe. I am waiting for her update tomorrow or so.'

'I have to go. Bye.'

Eva hung up. She sighed and rubbed her temples. Her hands shook. She didn't like it when she felt 'like this'. She stopped trying to rub her temples. They felt greasy with sweat.

A headache was coming on. It was because of Greg that Bethany was not here today. She could not stop Phoebe from marrying him. One bad thing after another. What did she see in him?

He was alive. It was not fair. She felt sick. She rushed upstairs to Bethany's old bedroom, the door of which was always shut. She entered and threw open the window to air the room. She slumped to the floor and leaned her back against the bed.

The June sun came through the window. This still was the best bedroom in the terraced house, enshrined and untouched, south facing with a view of the rear garden.

Eva was not here for the view. She closed her eyes and took deep breaths, comforted by the memory of her daughter. She used to tell Bethany stories from home sitting in this very position while her daughter sat cross-legged next to her.

She did not believe in ghosts. How much better if she did, for she would indeed be sitting with the ghost of her child and never be lonely again. Always stories, always a child, always here.

She sat still for a long time until, even with her eyes shut, she felt the clouds move and obscure the sun coming in from the sash window.

8

YOU

THE DOCTOR SAYS THE tests results are inconclusive. That means they have to do a few more tests. It is not Clostridium Difficile (C. Diff). They cannot do the throat surgery.

The bandages can come off in two days though.

'You are healing well from your head injuries.'

'Your wife has been informed and will be coming as soon as you are ready and feeling better.'

'Keep drinking fluids though.'

'You are at risk of dehydration.'

Everyone who comes into your room says something different. It is like a rehearsed script and you are in a play where you have a silent role.

They tell you that someone was on the boat with you or maybe more than one person, but how do you know this is true? You have to just trust them to tell you what is the truth or what they think is the truth. They ask you questions when in fact they are telling you what to say. Still they persist and ask you again.

'Do you remember who was on the boat with you?' He asks the same question as the nurse.

You type 2.

You are pleased that you are able to distinguish the questions. It's difficult: they ask not exactly the same questions each time, but almost.

The Chief Inspector comes in. He is so short that when the door opens, you do not realise he has come in. You can't see him. You just see a camp-looking skinny guy with a quiff and chains, like he's been clubbing all night.

'A wreck has been found,' says the Chief Inspector through the camp translator. 'We're looking at the immigration records now.' There is a moment of distraction when you look at the translator's pointed boots, tight black jeans, colourful bracelets. One earring.

'When you hear the word wreck, do you remember a terrible storm?'

You listen. You have no choice.

'I have a first in English from Bangkok University, ' he says. 'What I'd like to do is work abroad. I'm only doing police work for pocket money.' He cleared his throat and continued. 'Tour guiding, been there, done that, it was pathetic and repetitive.'

The Chief Inspector frowns and coughs, not enjoying the discussion being waylaid by the translator. Then he introduces himself. It is a long and unintelligible name, that is, long and unintelligible to you because it is foreign and your brain is not exactly firing on all cylinders now.

'So on Sunday 3rd June you were found on the coast off Krabi, in the Ao Luek District, 5 km from the wreck,' says the translator. The Chief Inspector mumbles something. 'He says to show you the photos,' says the translator.

'We have now gone through the immigration records.

Saturday 26th May you set sail from Singapore in a luxury yacht. On Tuesday 5th June, a body was found in Penang. Male. We are currently waiting for it to be identified. We are looking for more survivors or bodies. There were 4 of you who set sail from Singapore. Therefore, there are two still missing. Thai women.'

You listen attentively, unable to add anything.

'Do you remember the storm?'

You type 3 on the tablet. You type 2 also.

∼

YOU HAVE BEEN TRANSFERRED to another hospital. They did say where but you have now forgotten. The bandages have come off. Your hair is damp and greasy. First, a nappy change. Second, a hair cut.

These modern hospitals amaze and surprise you. You only have to think: 'maybe I need a haircut'. A barber appears. He shaves you with a scary traditional cut throat razor. There is no mirror.

Busybody nurses, including the friendly Muslim nurse, are giving instructions. You are shown a mirror at the end of it. You don't know what instructions these are because you end up with a crewcut. You look like a runaway convict.

After the haircut, both they and you notice the burn wounds all over your face and skull. They change your dressing before you see any more of Frankenstein's monster. It is not a good look. Some stitches have melted away, some have not. Some are deep and long, some shallow. Not just a pretty face!

There is a special privilege you can only experience while staying in a hospital. You can take a piss and smile discretely, while eating or watching FOX News. This moment is made possible by the wearing of an adult nappy or "pampers" as they are known here. The convenience comes with a heavy price. The changing of the soiled diaper is designed to strip every last shred of self respect and dignity you have.

You lie there on the bed naked as a toddler while two nurses examine your bare groin for nappy rash and roll you over to inspect your anus for evidence. They then clean you and lift you to slide the nappy from under to be tied and velcro snugly.

The nappies come from a seemingly bottomless shelf on the trolley. You are changed at the slightest hint of soiling or discomfort, about every two hours.

After you have a fall while trying to go to the toilet yourself, you are banned from going to the toilet as you did not call for help. 'You have just had a double-fracture, what are you trying to do?' Therefore, you are forced into wearing a nappy.

You are living from day to day now. Sometimes you lie there and panic. You are covered in cold sweat. You struggle uselessly. You cry. You are at the mercy of these nurses. You will live and die in their hands.

Without them you would have fallen flat on your face more than once and not been able to get up until the morning. You remember that you have broken both legs. They keep telling you like you are senile.

You can type now. You can say more than 1, 2 or 3 to them. But you can only type very slowly. You are frustrated and give up quickly. Your brain hurts when you do more. They don't have the time or the patience to sit with you.

You may need handling like a child but you are not actually their child. Who can wait while you type out a fifty-word statement? The moment they come in they take away the tablet to perform the undignified task of changing your nappy or checking for bedsores.

'Put that thing down, Greg,' they command. 'The inspector and the translator will be here any minute.' This is the first time you have heard your name. Light. End of tunnel. All that. It has been many weeks.

The nurses know. They know everything. At any sign of struggling, gasping, grunting, they fetch the medication.

The translator says, 'The Inspector has informed the Cambodian British Embassy. Your wife Po-ebay in Battambang will come and meet you when you are better.'

You have a wife? You listen patiently as though this is some kind of radio play or soap opera.

'You are Greg Strickland. You are 53 years old. You were born in 1965. You are white British. You were found on Sunday 3rd June by kind local people in the village of Laem Sak who brought you here. You have been in hospital for 7 weeks and 2 days, 9 hours and 56 minutes. It is Tuesday 24th July 2018 today.'

They are repeating the dates to you because you have forgotten it all. You listen to the young man prattle on. You start to shake again with cold, clammy fear.

They observe you and speak to each other in Thai. The inspector gets out a laptop from his case. He powers it up and shows you photos of a wreck. A boat which is in tatters, damaged and unrecognisable in parts.

You see the word *Achara* on the side. You want to shout, but you can't. It feels tight and painful on your chest and throat. You pant silently.

'Po-ebay is very distraught. Your wife,' says the translator. The inspector nods as though in agreement. 'She's coming to see you. We have not mentioned to her that you don't remember a thing. That will upset her. Don't worry, she is

OK. When she arrives we are hoping it will all come back to you - or at least more than what you remember now.'

'You were volunteering in Cambodia. You were working on a luxury yacht?' You stop listening because you cannot take in any more. This radio play needs to be continued on another day in another episode.

You feel tired and your brain aches. Your throat is on fire. You will be well soon and out of here. No more nappies or bedsores.

Physio has started since they know you can't wait to take a piss yourself without these women supporting your arm, groin, and holding your willy. They are as strong as trees. Do not underestimate the ability and the power of a woman, they say.

You've just got over an infection. You are about to go under again for this throat surgery. And then speech therapy. One intervention leads to another. It's called being institutionalised. You want Po-ebay to come quick and take you away.

So much for your endless patience. What does she even look like? Why do they show you photos of the past or what they want you to help with but they never show you the photos of the present?

You are listening to their meandering questions which they seem to answer themselves. You see them merely as your key to escaping this place.

You have had enough. By all accounts you have had the best hospital food. You have been craving Thai food from the instant your eyes open and that is what you got. 'It is like God has answered your prayers,' says the friendly Muslim nurse.

Who is God? What is God? You want her to not speak, not preach. Since you cannot speak and now cannot be bothered to type. You hate writing or typing, it must be because you are a visual person, a photographer, didn't the inspector say? You start to feel rage when she speaks of 'God'.

After the infection, a blood clot, after that, circumcision because the foreskin got infected too due to being bedridden or some more bugs. Anaesthetic creams, nappy changes, no voice, double-fractures. You are getting sicker, not better.

You are comforted by the sight of stainless steel wires on the ceiling. Every night you look up at them. You focus on the wires a little longer but soon you are drowsy and you fall into deep sleep. In a week Po-ebay will be here.

9

DOMINIQUE

APHONE WAS RINGING constantly. It woke Dominique up. She must have passed out.

It was not her iPhone. It lay there, like her, lifeless and shiny. Oh yes, some spilled tablets too. It was the hotel phone ringing. She was lying on the marble bathroom floor. She crawled to the bathroom receiver next to the toilet.

'H-hel-' she stuttered in a hoarse sigh.

'Mrs Laney-Sambrooke? Are you all right? We have been calling you because you missed your massage appointment?

'Uh.'

'If you are in now would you like your masseuse to return?'

How many minutes or hours had passed? Hours? She looked at the iPhone on the floor and pressed the activate button. Only 45 minutes and thank God she woke up in time.

'Mrs Laney-Sambrooke? Are you there?'

'Uh.'

'Are you all right?'

'No...' she whispered.

'We'll send a doctor straightaway. Hang in there.'

She dropped the plastic receiver.

She had had to arrange for her subcontractors (Lorraine and Ellie) to do the actual organisation of flying out to Singapore straightaway but she would have to micromanage all of it.

Had she and James lived in a different time and place, for example if they had been teenagers in a mixed marriage in India, they would have gotten along just by being practical – working, bringing up children, working even more. The children would have grown up, would have looked after them, they would have aged, then died. This would have meant a meaningless life for her.

But what is a *meaningful* life then? Because people lived in a complex modern society formed of Western liberal secular values, it was more important to *not* be practical. Don't just put up with it. The social pressure had always been to bring meaning to life, to assert and exert oneself to free up something else that one wouldn't otherwise have.

One had the choice to do this since people only have one life and freedom. As for Dominique, a big earner herself, no one had more freedom than she. She was not a penniless or poorly educated housewife.

She lay back down on the cold hard floor.

The phone was ringing again. Now she really was confused. She opened her eyes and looked around. It was the iPhone this time. She climbed up to a sitting position and leaned on the rim of the toilet bowl. She answered the call.

'H-hel-'

'Mrs Laney-Sambrooke.'

She was pretty sick of hearing her name so many times

today. It just confirmed to her that she really was who she was even though she'd been convincing herself it was all not true.

'Uh.'

'This is Detective Sergeant Mohd Ismail calling from Marine Operations Force Investigation Unit in Penang.'

They had simply made a mistake. Lucy would be gobsmacked. None of this was true.

'The Malaysian Maritime Zone teams have found a body that matches the missing person that is your husband. His face is disfigured and unidentifiable, his body, fingers and face partially eaten by fish and seabirds, his jaw broken, but he is wearing some items which you should take a look at. Either in person or in photos.'

'Uh.'

'He is very bloated fortunately.'

'Huh? Fortunately?'

'Well, his ring and watch stayed on, stuck to the knuckle, even after he lost his fingertips.'

She retched again. At least she was already holding the rim of the WC pan.

The doorbell rang and rang. The door then opened. Two people came in through the bedroom into the bathroom where Dominique lay, the doctor and an assistant housekeeper or someone. They must have used their own master key to get in when she did not reply. They helped her to her feet before supporting her to the bed.

'POOR JAMES,' SHE SAID to the doctor when she came to. 'He must have really struggled as he was a strong swimmer and he just loved the sea.' She sipped the tea they made for her.

She lay under the bedding, still clutching a face towel that she had been holding onto since vomiting.

'We will help you make any arrangements that you need. You have enough medication for a week. You should be OK.' He made some notes while the assistant counted and packaged up pills in a small envelope. 'Here's a medical letter too, if you need it.'

She nodded.

'Don't worry, we know you here. Call us if you don't feel well or if you need anything.'

She had not been more than 24 hours in the Bahamas but now she had to be on the move again. She wiped her tears with the face towel she was holding and not a tissue. The tissues were useless, small and thin. She had so much to cry about. They left her to rest. She heard the door shut.

Be practical, Dominique, she said to herself again in a harsh voice. Pull yourself together. Chin up. You're doing great.

She checked the time difference and called Lucy.

'Lucy, oh!' she gasped, 'oh my god, you won't believe it,' her voice was so shaky it was vibrating.

'Hey didn't you just arrive? What's happened? Darling. Oh god. Tell me.'

Dominique started weeping and could not speak because she was trembling hard and could not even hold the phone. She hung up. 2 minutes later she felt calm enough to call Lucy back.

'Listen. You won't believe it. James is dead.'

'Fuck, no! Oh my god. What? Are you sure? Oh sweetie. I will come out and meet you. I am sorry I didn't say yes yesterday.'

'No! You can't. Uh. I have to go to Penang. Can you imag-

ine? He's had some accident. They want me to go and identify him.'

'Oh God! This is just awful. I can't believe it-'

'Uh-'

'Oh sweetie. How are you doing? Are you OK? What are
you doing right now? Who is helping you?'

'Look, got to go,' she whispered. 'Thank you. Lots of love.
Call you again when I get there.' She was shaking again
when she put the phone down. Now she had called Lucy,
she felt ready to call the others. First, Lorraine and Ellie.
The last person she managed to speak to was Daphne and
though she decided she did want to speak to her mother,
she could not get through. She would try her mother again
when she got there if she was awake enough after the flight.

She must have slept and woke up and slept some more.
It was the medication. She was not even aware whether she
should be eating anything. She was in no mood - and
neither was she ready - for lunch at Dune, a place which
always reminded her of the early days when she and James
first came here more than 12 years ago, before Daphne was
born, and they fucked in the cabaña.

She remembered it with guilt and sadness. She had
wanted everything; a top career, a top husband, a beautiful
child, a few investment bags, sports cars and what she
wanted she got. All of it. Having great sex was not and had
not been on her list of prerequisites for a successful life, or
what she would deem successful. Didn't someone famous
say that everything is about sex except sex itself which is
about power?

After wasting an entire day with her own chilling
thoughts, tears and calls to London to micromanage
Lorraine doing her flight bookings, it was time to get to the
check-in.

She was light-headed from an entire day without a single meal at the Dune restaurant or a swim in her new red bikini or yoga in the cabanas or cocktail or a beach massage. It was like a nightmare you could not wake up from, you were trapped in paradise and but you were in hell.

Dominique checked the flights bookings Lorraine had made. It looked like it had been complicated. There was one thing you could not subcontract in this life and that was flying. Only *you* could carry out the flight yourself.

She called Daphne again from the airport departure lounge and both sobbed and listened to each other sobs without speaking. She was at her boarding school in Brighton so Dominique had to pick a time when Daphne was not in class and had her phone switched on.

She did not know how to break it to her so she decided not to. She just said daddy was very ill. No words were even possible. There were indeed worse shocks than losing your job.

DOMINIQUE ARRIVED AT PENANG INTERNATIONAL, a zombie. Two airlines, four countries, 28 hours' flying time, a 2220 departure. Heathrow at 11.55 the next day. Gatwick within 3-and-a-half hours. Gatwick-to-Qatar and the cream on the cake, the flight to Penang.

No 5-minute Hydrator would work even as a placebo. It might as well have gone in the bin at any of the airports she had just been through. It only served to remind her of her own vanity and foolishness. How could a £46 pot of cream save your face?

For the first time Dominique was not in the mood for shopping. The shock helped float her like a ghost through all these mundane activities. Before arrival, she had already changed out of the clothes she wore in Nassau and into one of the Chanel outfits, since swimwear and T shirts would never have done.

Lorraine had organised for Dominique to pick up a couple of Chanel outfits at Heathrow T3 (without passing through the terminal). Amie, Heathrow's personal shopper, would make sure everything was the right size and curated for an upsetting trip.

A couple of pairs of CC classic ballet flats, Chanel stud earrings, a WOC (wallet on chain) which was a burgundy-lined wallet in black grained calfskin caviar leather on a gold chain, a couple of ruffle silk tops and lightweight, crease-free black trousers.

Lorraine had arranged for a black Mercedes to pick her up from the terminal and take her to the morgue at Penang hospital in Georgetown. There was no one from HSBC, just a Malay-looking driver with her name on a placard. Red tape was waiting. She was so exhausted she could barely move her eyes to look at the driver.

This was not CSI, you didn't go into a cold windowless basement where bodies were kept in freezer drawers. After the customary identity checks and form-signing to make sure Dominique was indeed James' wife, she was sitting in a living room (that was funny, 'living' room as opposed to dead room?) with nondescript beige sofas and big windows with views of palm trees and spiky bushes.

Dominique was thinking this could be the perfect setting for a porno flick when her daydream was suddenly interrupted by the chief medical examiner and morgue attendant, Siti Haslinda, a Muslim woman in a hijab.

'Thank you for coming out so quickly. I understand that this is a difficult time. I know you have been travelling-' She had an A4 sized envelope which she handed to Dominique, who did not take it. Siti Haslinda turned the envelope over and pulled out a wad of photos altogether, face down.

Dominique did not reply. She looked down at the white backs of the photos. She was not listening to the Chief Medical Examiner's voice tailing off. She just wanted the woman to cut the crap. Why prolong the agony? She needed them to get on with whatever they had to get on with as she felt and looked like hell.

These people were just spieling the same clichéd nonsense that they reeled off to every family member who turned up here. She felt really nauseous and wanted to vomit every few minutes. The strong smell of disinfectant hung everywhere, layered with the cloying heavy stench of the morgue attendant's perfume.

'OK. What we're going to see is quite unpleasant so I'd like to minimise the shock for you.'

Dominique barely nodded. Background music was either non-existent or of such elevator quality as to be beneath even the most bored person's notice. She looked in vain for a crescent and star, a cross or a Dharma Chakra wheel on the walls, doubtless they did not want to risk offending the bereaved. Like Dominique, they'd be struck by this absence, and perhaps offended, too.

'If you can't look at the body, please look at the photos.' Siti Haslinda calmly explained. 'I just want to clarify something. If you positively identify James today, we will be signing it off. Part of his face is missing including his jaw.'

Dominique could not even look at Siti Haslinda. Her eyes remained downcast and hovered over the backs of those photographs. She flipped over the first of the photos as fast as ripping off a waxing strip.

10

PRZEMEK

H E HAD THE MIDAS touch, Andreia said. Since they'd met, her freelance business had been booming.

In the evenings he had to now contend with watching Montse swallow. He was spending an increasing amount of time on his own, or rather, on his own with Montse.

Andreia was out for drinks and nonstop socialising with new networkers, fellow professionals, designers, attending talks and lectures. He did not like this kind of people at all, soft hands, soft life. He had been to these things with her and felt like he had sailed into space. He did not know what they were talking about and he was not interested in design, networking or marketing.

Once Andreia had introduced him to a garden designer, but there was nothing much to say after "box trees, yew trees, not hedera helix, not sansevaria, my favourite is red cordylline australis." Most of the girls that he'd known back home would have called him a catch.

But here he did not know how to mingle, chat, or use Latin and French words as though everyone knew what they meant. His "skills" were philosophy, snake-rearing, 1920s dancing and sex.

Andreia had never made any disparaging comments about his reticence and on the contrary had been kind, friendly and keen to introduce him to yet more of these types and these dos.

He was uncomfortable. He bowed out, preferring the company of his books and snake, just as it had always been in his Ealing bedsit. Like Montse, those people were predators. Could he see *himself* as a predator too? But who would be his prey?

THE GARDEN WAS OVERRUN with squirrels. Or should he say infested? In these situations, he always asked himself, what would Leonardo do?

Everything that he made an effort to plant or to make was damaged and eaten. Even the garden seats and table legs were bitten to pieces. They were savage. He tried all the usual deterrents. Even "invested" £29.99 in sonic rodent repellent.

What did it do? Nothing but give him a banging headache for weeks due to the high-pitched ringing. It was like having tinnitus except it was outside the house, not in your head. It made the garden looked like it had been dug up by moles, so unpleasant you could not go into it, let alone check if the squirrels were still there.

After about two months of hassling the manufacturer and the seller of this item, he only managed to get a partial refund due to improper use, which was, they said, the fact that there were no rats and the setting was too high. The damage got more and more unreal.

They ate all the tulips he planted, the vegetables. The garden was pitted and dark as a rotten plum. They destroyed everything and quickly too. It was just no use. They ate the nuts and seeds he put out for birds. They finished this entire ration at one go, in minutes.

Przemek watched. If he even ran out they glared at him. They were neither shy, nor fearful. They just feasted before his eyes. No birds came. Even the bird feeder, which Przemek himself had fashioned out of chicken wire and bits of sawn-off log, was bitten to pieces and lay in tatters.

Przemek looked online for yet another way to exterminate the squirrels. His search must have triggered off ads. Normally he hated ads, but one caught his eye for pest control air rifles. He did not need a licence if the muzzle energy is under 12 ft lbs. Good.

Even the words air rifle had a shade of riffing on air guitar, something fantastic, capricious and coated by fairy dust. Maybe he could be a real sharpshooter with an air rifle. Choosing the actual model was a tough decision because there were just so many. He read through forums to find what people said. He hit 'translate' to make it quicker.

Further nights of searching led him to make his choice. It was the Sheridan Silver Streak and it arrived wrapped in thick brown paper and a big red bow, like he was Elmer Fudd. There was something caricature-like in what he is about to do after all.

The .20 Calibre air rifle because it was more accurate than the lightest, the .177. The .20 could be used for both bulls-eye target shooting and for pest control. He'd have to practise.

For pest elimination, he needed to get one that was around 700 fps. A pellet gun's power depended on its calibre and powering mechanism. All pellet guns were powered by compressed air but he would choose the most common method – spring piston.

This would have the natural satisfaction of cocking shot after shot with consistency. It had to be something that was as accurate as he was.

He practised after work with a few timber offcuts rather than tin cans which would have been much too noisy. He didn't want the neighbours to start complaining. In London you were never far from neighbours. Success came. With a swell of pride, he became aware that he must have been a sharper shooter than he'd thought, all along.

Soon Przemek was feeding squirrels to his pet. His muscles were achy from pulling the trigger. He relaxed by watching the simple mechanical action of Montse's muscles constrict to digest the meal.

While it was low maintenance, Descartes would say it was just a beast that was being maintained, like a vintage motorcycle or the motor of a machine. Watching the pulsing of muscles move the squirrel down the food chain and the digestive pipe, like plumbing, was quite satisfying. It was a hideous animal. There was a fine line.

Ugliness was just beauty with vulgarity.

ANDREIA GOT HIM TO price up a job for draining down the system, moving pipes and replacing some radiators in six bedrooms and four receptions in an enormous property in Holland Villas Road. It was like worth 12.7M she said, as if it would impress Przemek. Who really cared about other people's money?

She had put together a team of contractors. There was a complicated round of tenders and costing plans in the previous three months. Przemek won the contract for the mechanical and electrical subcontracting.

'Your quote was approved by the client before she had to travel,' Andreia said. 'Which is great news as it means we can start now with the messy stages while she isn't there.'

Przemek was keen on getting there and spending all day to 'crack on with it' as they say in England. It made him laugh how it sounded like Krakow. He made his own healthy lunch to save time.

He did not like Greggs because it meant meeting hostile English builders whose jobs he seemed to have stolen, or so they often told him. He was self-conscious about his accent. Also he was not keen on bacon rolls, steak slices or whatever it was builders ate.

And Polish cafes were where you'd end up meeting Polish builders, very competitive too. He seemed to have also stolen their jobs, somehow. They were cliquey, tending to look you up and down to work out if you had more work or less work than them. He was now neither a true Polish builder nor an Englishman, so what was he?

Looking after an inanimate predator made him rational, tolerant and benevolent. All those Spinozan cliches *You are what you eat, the glass is half-empty or half-full*, etc. originally stemmed from Descartes.

Spinoza had been a lens grinder before he died of tuberculosis at 44. So what did he know? Przemek's glass was half-empty and no matter how Andreia refilled it, it felt drained.

PRZEMEK WAS QUEUEING FOR 9 rolls of piping and 42 valves at

Screwfix. There was nothing to look at in Screwfix unless you needed new workboots or safety goggles.

The music was top 40 or X Factor nonsense with female voices belting out words and muffled orgasmic noises you could not and did not want to hear. He closed his eyes and thought of muted horns, tinkling piano and deep thumps of a double bass.

He missed the 1920s Speakeasy evenings that Andreia and him had used to go to back in the spring, when he'd first moved into her Battersea flat.

Andreia was hankering after expensive furniture, since she'd started purchasing it for her clients. A desk that cost 1200 pounds. 'That is dirt cheap,' Andreia told him. 'It's all gold and black lacquer, what do you expect?' Nothing, he expected nothing.

When she got back in the evenings, she was on the iPad drooling after new shoes or furniture. She grumbled about the smallness of the flat, forgetting there were only two of them, and that this was London.

She wanted to buy a house, but it was hard to get a mortgage these days. Then there was the awfulness of IKEA flat-pack furniture, the landlord, the trips to the Clapham Junction ASDA...

Did he notice that she mentioned getting a mortgage with him?

He had not noticed.

'How can you not notice? The banking crises, Brexit, Trump.'

She rolled her eyes. He was not pathetic, he was apathetic. He was rich in other things, such as thoughts, gardening, squirrel-sniping, cherubic good looks like his doppelganger Leonardo and of course heating and plumbing.

He'd like to see her bleed a radiator or fix an H11 error on a Worcester Bosch.

One of these contracts would last him the following six months to a year. He and his team planned to work top down in on the logic that the waste, debris and the routing would be travelling top-down too.

He'd start at the top with the girl's room and the spare bedroom, first floor, ground floor and the basement. The last was obviously a man's study, messy, full of guitars, being ripped out and turned into a gym or exercise studio for the client or the client's wife.

He had never met them and probably never would. Andreia and the main contractor arranged everything.

It was a bit close to home – they were now both working on the same property. He collapsed in bed after 'handling' Montse, picking her up a few times after she'd had dinner, lifting her and lowering her like a movable gym weight with resistance.

He replaced her in the tank. Sometimes he needed to think about plumbing routes before he fell asleep – he couldn't figure out whether it was because it was very interesting or very dull.

Whenever he fell asleep, she was still 'working'. Thinking, making notes, talking about her business. She did not care if anyone, i.e. he, was listening or not.

She was deeper and deeper into the "sickness" that was business. He found himself drifting more and more towards the world was now his alone, the 1920s delusion.

With any spare minutes he had, watching Montse eat dinner twice a week, cleaning his filthy site boots (which obviously could take a while though most people did not even think about this when he was knee-deep in their shit), making simple Polish meals, he would slip into his fantasies, as easy as silk.

1930s playboy, Irish thoroughbred tycoon, Greek philosopher or French aristo, whatever took his fancy. He was a soul from another time, trapped in a Polish plumber's mind and body.

Even when there was time, it never seemed to be the right moment to tell Andreia of his stupid fancies and they ended up talking about having to go and queue in the Apple shop in Westfield to fix her MacBook, or even about his van requiring a service soon.

Montse did take up physical, mental and freezer space. They did not exactly have a huge kitchen. She was only being tolerant. There was regularly a gasp of terror or surprise or groan when a squirrel was thawing, twice a week.

Przemek guessed it did not look very appetising and there was also a historical stigma associated with the sight of a dead rodent, microwaved or not. Back home in Madagascar, Andreia said all reptiles were pests. You had to kill it before it killed you.

Why could he not have a cute pet dog, like a King Charles Cavalier which they could flaunt around at weekends in the chi- chi suburb of Battersea, amongst the double decaf chai soy latte drinkers on the pavement?

SOMETIMES HE HAD TO have a wank too.

Przemek had never been a big TV fan, unlike Andreia. She knew exactly what to watch or follow and when. She had the line-up of the line-up. She used to find all sorts of series for them to get into on their nights in before his studies took over.

Nowadays they were unable to watch anything in the evenings. Of course they *were* both exhausted. She would fall asleep. There was no greater demand on yourself than being an unformed, uninformed fighting spirit. Ah, Youth.

It occurred to him many times his fondest memories were of his time in that Ealing bedsit with Montse just doing his Pearson Btec Level 2.

His brain had wanted to explode from studying. 8 hours a week for 10 weeks, part-time, costing £475 for the English for Speakers of Other Languages course. Everyone said ESOL. In 10 weeks, he was competent.

But he wanted to be better than competent. He wanted to write, joke, watch movies without subtitles, be able to understand slang even when shouted at a million decibels in a pub. He was now progressing to the next course, the IELTS.

He needed a holiday. Przemek had booked their summer trip to Poland. He could not go for too long due to Montse and work. He wanted to indulge himself; get a hair cut the way he liked it (and how they knew he liked it) and to buy cheap vintage Prohibition-era clothes.

He was hoping to seek out old friends, eat proper comfort food. He missed his mother's gołąbki (minced pork with rice, onion, mushrooms, wrapped in white cabbage leaves), śledź w oleju z cebulą (herring in oil with onion) and kotlet schabowy (breaded pork cutlet).

The nearest London equivalent to kotlet schabowy was pork tonkatsu at Wasabi on Euston Road where he was working on a small office block. These were all simple poor men's meals but he craved them.

The boys back home who wanted to make that move to

UK but had not had the courage to yet – they would be in his local, the Absynt bar in Kazimierz, Krakow, a timeless bohemian joint.

At the very last minute, Andreia said she was unable to "come with".

'Oh no, Andreia,' Przemek said. 'I was looking forward to you meeting everybody. They all want to meet you.'

'I- just- can't. I have to go to France for a new project. I'm sorry, I was looking forward to it too.'

'Is it because Poland is not France?'

'Look. It is not that. I've got so much work on. I- I travel so much for work that I don't need a holiday.'

He listened.

'The last two months you have been going back and forth to Kazakhstan for some boutique hotel project and you told me you were working constantly, even in Stansted departure lounge. I never see you.'

'I can't do anything about that,' she snapped.

11

PHOEBE

THEY LISTED GREG'S FULL list of injuries and ailments.

Third degree burns. Broken jaw and left arm, ruptured spleen, stable pelvic fracture, rib fractures, collapsed left lung. 18 bones in total.

She knew that she had to bring him back to Battambang to care for him, but she was not a doctor or nurse so was that even a good idea? What was the healthcare and medical support even like in Battambang? Or come to think of it, at her family home in London?

Her mother used to be a nurse. But Phoebe would be lucky to get two ibuprofens from her mother. She was as uncaring at home as she was caring in her profession. She had become quite hardened. Moving to the UK and shift-work might have done it. She had no more to give at home.

She had only just got used to the routine. A groggy's days were long and the nights were short. This was part of the groggy's wake up call. Phoebe had found it hard getting used to

1. living in a basic flat with bunk beds, two flatmates and
no WiFi

and

2. being woken up at 4 am by pulsing beats from backpacker
bars.

Balham had spoilt them by being all estate agents, Farrow and Ball paint and organic vegan cupcakes.

After falling back into light headache-y sleep at 5 am, she was woken up again, this time by chanting monks and bell-dinging from a temple somewhere. She *was* able to make herself go back to sleep again, just like a sleep-walking mother.

At 6 am she was woken up for good by the last call of a crowing rooster. She missed her skinny latte from Caffé Nero. Instead she had rice congee for breakfast. Phoebe had almost forgotten the wholewheat bran, organic green tea matcha powder and fruit that she was used to.

She took a shower. At least the showers in Asia were electric; constant pressure, instant hot water, no ancient combi boiler panting and pumping out each drip. One up to Asia.

Phoebe now had a taste of what it was like to be a super-minority. Although Trish and Matt were 21 years old and first-time gap year volunteers who genuinely had never done anything, they made her feel welcome, without boundaries.

It was the unspoken school rule that while you were abroad, you looked out for and looked after each other, like fellow immigrants in a new city.

Phoebe didn't feel too well that morning. It could be the lack of sleep. Or too much alcohol. They didn't tell you in the welcome pack booklet that a 41-year-old could not drink or think like a 21-year old. The young were invincible.

She was tired, greasy-haired and had a metallic taste in her mouth. Whenever Phoebe stole glances at Trish, she realised the gap year was the great leveller, not motherhood.

Phoebe felt unorganic, processed, past it, yet had been put into accommodation with someone half her age. That was because they didn't think there was a barrier, or if there was, *get over it.*

At 8.15 am she was ready and walked to the bus stop amidst smiles, laughter and general jolliness from both adults and children. They waved hysterically.

She was not even that pretty now with her red streaked hair cut short and her tanned no makeup face. What a change from working in Soho and all that effort to look designery, bohemian and – well, yes - effortless.

Phoebe was often mistaken for 38-year-old Fan Bing Bing from that terrible Marvel franchise, 2014 X-Men: Days of Future Past. Trish had said she looked like her when she'd moved in. Google told her the rest.

Hello Hello Why Why you come. People shouted at her on her way to the bus stop. They didn't understand why she had left the civilised west to come here when she was middle-aged and deserved a comfortable easy life. They could be direct.

She got a Khmer coffee. It was a bit too sweet as it was tar black with layer of condensed milk at the bottom. She jumped on her moped for the journey to the community education centre. When she arrived the children had already started their lessons because school began at 7 am and finished at 12noon in Cambodia.

Children grabbed, mobbed and hugged her. It was like being invaded by dwarf paparazzi. *Teacher Teacher!* They all smiled and called with tremendous adoration and affection. Phoebe had to high-five each of them until her palms were nearly bleeding.

But her heart softened with each smile. Phoebe spent the whole morning marking, handing out books, writing on the boards or reading to the class.

The class sizes were huge, about 40 to 50 per class. She thought the local teachers were just the best teachers. They had no resources except themselves. They taught with their voices, eyes, their hearts and souls.

Normally lunchtime was deafening. But now Phoebe found the volume distracting and soothing to her current state of mind. Phoebe was not used to children and occasionally had to take paracetamol.

Her head ached in the racket of children chanting times tables, playing skipping games, reading, singing whatever songs they were supposed to be practising and calling out to get her attention, all at the same time.

Phoebe and Greg had been keen on children. It would have been his way of getting her to be all his. There was a small gap in history about 5 or 6 years ago, a gap she could not even remember herself, that was like a crack of first daylight through the trees, when they'd tried to have children, it being her last chance. It didn't happen.

It had seemed convenient to forget trying. The NHS didn't cover fertility treatment at her age so they would have had to stump up 12 to 20 thousand pounds for private IVF.

Did they want children that bad? Probably not, so they spent it on a new extension with bifold sliding double glazed doors instead.

~

AFTER SCHOOL, PHOEBE WENT to the children's centre to help with homework classes, teach English, computing, art, crafts or some recreational activity. She had to help prepare dinner, chop fruit and wash clothes for the children.

5 pm. Goodbyes. High fives all round again. At 6 pm Phoebe took the moped back to her local area, ghetto beats, sunset.

You were never alone as a Groggy. How could you be? She'd met friendly faces and had dinner with them at the local bar, chatting, drinking bottles of Angkor, the local beer.

She felt guilty that Greg was not around, breathing down her neck and checking on her. Secretly she enjoyed her Newfoundland. Her own private Idaho.

She trained local children and adults to earn livelihoods through education and vocational training. In the evenings, dancing and drinking was for the young. Trish and Matt joined her in her local bar. Their evening had just begun whereas Phoebe's had ended.

She had her iPhone back and was therefore contactable at all times. With a heavy heart, she glanced at the notifications and the email had come. She needed to make sure she was reading between the lines and that what they mean was Greg was OK.

It was taking a long time to re-read and process the email. This time she had remembered the mozzie repellent.

The hospital said they had to transfer Greg to another hospital because it was taking too long for him to receive his throat operation and they were not equipped with either staff or facilities. She was shaky.

What did they mean not equipped? She had been born and raised in London, on the NHS, a child of immigrants. Her father was a neurosurgeon and her mother an ex-nurse.

She did not understand or trust an email from a hospital in some village in Thailand, though she knew she must.

What choice had she? Phoebe told herself she was just being paranoid, or even racist. She stared at her phone, and bit her lip, re-reading until it was seared into her memory. She swallowed hard. Things must be getting worse for Greg.

Another hospital. Where and for how long?

WHY HAD THEY NOT emailed her? Late nights had become early starts. Phoebe felt queasy off and on. Anxiety did that to her. Back in London she had been eating only organic low fat, low carb, low GI food but when you were away from home, you threw caution to the gale force storms.

The irony was she had a 'rich' diet, as in, nutritionally, because she was technically 'rich' being from the West, compared to Cambodians. Here she was on a poor person's diet as that was all there was: white carbs, deep fried food every day and even coffee with a knob of melted butter in it.

The health risks extended to getting a moped. On top of that, she knew this food was bad for her but had no right to be critical of the local food. She had come here to live as a local. The last thing she wanted was to act all spoilt like some snobster from London.

Phoebe waited in the clinic looking at the wall clock. It was evening after a whole day at the Children's Centre. But there was a long queue and she needed something to settle her stomach.

She was still feeling nauseous, and the metallic taste in her mouth, which had been making her thirsty, despite drinking so much water, had made her feel under the weather. She felt homesick.

She wanted to be back in her own dim bedroom in Balham, with its white Ikea Billy bookshelves and her clothes drying on the folding rack and a draughty single-glazed sash window, its cords painted so stiff it could never open.

She was too old and too tired to do this gap year thing. What were they thinking? Who were they trying to impress? Now Greg was in hospital and she was exhausted by the sun, the intense heat, the long days, the volunteering, the drinking. Everything.

Trish took her there on her Honda Dream 125 c.c. moto, short for moped or motorbike. In the waiting room, Trish sat next to her but Phoebe said nothing to Trish.

You couldn't tell a young person that you were too old to do this. What would the young person say? There was nothing to say because it was all true. There was nothing to read here as the papers and magazines were all in Khmer and had been vandalised or torn or were at least 12 years out of date.

Trish just looked around her and smiled periodically into the stares of the other patients.

'Not long to go,' she said to Phoebe reassuringly, as though she knew.

'Fohb! Fohb!' A voice called from reception desk.

'Oh I think that's you,' said Trish. 'Let's go,' she said at first, then she hesitated. 'Do you want me to go in with you?'

'Oh no,' she waved dismissively, 'I will be fine.'

WHEN SHE CAME OUT, she looked faint. She sat back down in the waiting area, her face in her hands. She shook her head. Her shoulders quivered. Trish handed her a tissue.

'When he asked you when was your last period, what did you say?'

'Well I said I was not sure. I don't even get my periods any more.'

'Why? You are not that old? Are you?'

'He laughed and said my periods stopped because of malnourishment and overwork here after leaving the healthy lifestyle of the West, and to be precise, West London! Apparently that can happen.'

'Oh yes. To Olympic gymnasts though, not to the likes of you and me. No wonder you have lost weight. Greg will be thrilled about the news though.'

'Yeah but I am 41 years old. I am a geriatric mum.'

'Don't say that, people have children much later these days.'

'How do you know?'

'I see them. Mums with grey hair pushing strollers around.'

'Those are the grannies. Not mums.'

'Come awwwn. Feebs. Let's get a drink. Let's celebrate.'

'I can't drink any more. Won't do the baby any good. I shouldn't even have been drinking the last two months!'

'You can have a diet coke or something.'

'OK,' she said. 'No! I just remembered. It's full of chemicals!'

First of all, volunteering must be a walk in the park compared with parenthood. Everyone she knew said this and everyone she knew who was her age had already been there done that.

They suffered and complained (and those who didn't complain showed it in their facial and body expressions, which was far more unsettling) but she knew that was just to make her feel good about not having children.

Secondly she would break it to them after the obligatory third month. They would break out in insane grins and the usual welcome to sleepless nights, the first 25 years were the hardest and a string of tips, advice and truisms would follow.

Thirdly, she was not even sure she wanted children now. Greg was fancy-free, nearly broke and if she dared to admit it, irresponsible. It was possible that children would ground him and make him become a doting father.

Ten years ago she was up for it to risk it and experiment, but right now, she was actually happy being flatmates with a 21-year-old who could outdrink Greg, who rode her moped with a brrrrm and a yelp and was as innocent as a child.

'Have a juice. Or is that full of sugar?' said Trish. 'Come on. Don't be so silly. You can leave volunteering, like, next week even, and go back to Balham with Greg. It will be wonderful, so, so wonderful.'

Phoebe didn't answer and tried a fake smile on her friend.

12

DOMINIQUE

'MRS LANEY-SAMBROOKE... IS it Laney, sorry, or is it Sambrooke?'

'Laney-Sambrooke. Actually. No. No. I am not a Mrs. I mean I am a Mrs but I did not take on his name. I mean, I have kept my maiden name.' Something told her this was the most number of words she'd be saying all day.

'OK,' said Siti Haslinda. 'The authorities are almost always certain of the body's identity by the time they ask family, friends, acquaintances and colleagues, to make it official.'

'OK.' Dominique touched her brow, she was perspiring despite the air-conditioning.

'Which allows them or us, rather, to prepare the identi-fiers accordingly. If you wish to take this further and request for DNA testing, we can talk about that.'

Dominique took deep breaths, counting to 7 with each intake and each outtake.

'Yes,' said Dominique, 'I am sure I'd want to.'

'No problem. There is a chance the body in question

could have been carrying another person's ID, or wearing clothes that aren't theirs. But unless the body is a John or Jane Doe, this shouldn't be much of a mystery. So please take your time to view the photos at your own pace. I will leave you to it.'

Dominique noticed that Siti Haslinda had discreetly moved a bucket with a lid, a packet of wet wipes, a jug of water, a drinking glass tumbler and a box of tissues next to the sofa and coffee table. It must be what happened.

Identifiers either were sick and/or hysterically sobbing. What you needed during a crisis: tissues, wet wipes and a bucket. Dominique was left in the room to work up the courage, with no toe-tapping detective leaning over her shoulder.

She was told earlier that mostly decomposed, damaged or missing parts had *not* been photographed, such as, his lower face, legs and thighs. She was relieved and surprised to discover that photos that *had* been taken were not graphic or gruesome in nature.

They only showed the areas necessary for identification. The feet. The gold ring still on his finger. The appendectomy scar. Hair.

The feet she was not so sure about as she had not seen them since 2008 when he left for Singapore. He usually came about 3 to 4 times a year at least to spend some time with Daphne so he liked to return for her term breaks.

However, he skipped a trip this year. Even when he did come back, she had only seen him in slippers or socks or he was fully clothed complete with footwear and coat. The rest she was sure about.

The hair was the right colour, a bit greyer than she remembered but she had not seen it in about 8 months as he had not returned to London in that time.

It was his watch, but of course it could be anyone's watch. He had the certificates somewhere with the serial numbers. It was a standard diving Rolex, the Omega Seamaster, therefore not the top of the range, but it was the one James used to wear.

The deal clincher was really the gold wedding ring. It was so tight it looked welded around the finger stump which bulged around it. There could be no one who would or could wear such an ostentatious ring except maybe Jay-Z to the Grammys.

The Cartier Panthère 18K solid gold, shaped like a spotty panther's face with its mouth open and fangs bared, had eyes of blazing green emerald just like James's, the nose was black onyx and the head entirely encrusted in diamonds. He wore it everywhere.

She was surprised that the fishermen who found the man did not try to get it off the bloated corpse as they could have lived on the proceeds of it for the rest of their lives and the next generation's.

They must have thought it was a replica. Dominique knew her husband and herself better. Neither would wear a replica of anything. They would rather go bare. This they had had in common.

She looked at photos of his outfit. There were three photos of his dark green slim fit mesh polo T-shirt. One of the left breast showing the classic Ralph Lauren embroidered logo in red, one of the front which really showed nothing but the collar detail with the two buttons but the front was mostly torn, damaged or ripped by fish and seabirds and one of the back collar showing the label.

Also there were three photos of his once-white shorts now completely stained by blood and diesel. The photos were of the details and the label. They were also Ralph

Lauren. He had no toes or fingers left, and hence there were no photos of those, said Siti Haslinda.

She had not seen him for 8 months and so had no idea what he was wearing these days. She thought it had been only about 5 minutes looking at the photos but it could have been 15. Her mind started to drift like jetsam on the tide.

Her face was wet with tears which dropped onto the buzzer. She rang and rang it. Her hands were shaking hard and she only just became aware of them. She could hardly exert pressure on the buzzer.

She made several attempts before she could pull out several tissues and blew her nose. Her fingers were cold and weak, but she was calmer than she thought she would be under the circumstances: shock, no sleep, and the now trivial-seeming redundancy.

Siti Haslinda came in with a sheet of helpful links for contacts to grief counselling back in London should Dominique feel she needed it. 'Are you OK? Are you OK?' she kept saying.

'I'm fine,' Dominique whispered without looking at the sheet of links.

'Not too bad, then.'

'No.'

'Are you OK?' Siti Haslinda repeated.

'Yes,' Dominique said, but only to stop Siti Haslinda asking the same question over and over.

She was light-headed and her eyes had glazed over.

'Do you wish to see the—'

'No. I don't.'

'Shall I call you a taxi?'

'No, thank you. I have my car and driver waiting outside. We need to get to my hotel.'

'Wait here, please. I will get the papers for you to sign and of course, his— his—'

'His ring and watch.'

'Yes.'

'Not the clothes.'

'No.'

She looked at her own simple but bashed Tank Solo Cartier watch 3:45pm here was 7:45am in London. Therefore, it was high time she called Lorraine and Ellie.

On trips, she would never take her other Cartier, the Baignoire dress watch in 18K pink gold, diamonds and silk fabric worth 22 thousand pounds. She had two more watches: her special Van Cleef & Arpel iconic Alhambra and the basic Tissot Flamingo Black for everyday workwear.

She could see all the jewellery they owned the instant she saw his ring and watch, they were their joint prize possessions, yet now they floated before her like debris. Her throat was dry and she clutched at it.

Siti Haslinda poured her water from the jug, she drank all of it and it was refilled. She looked briefly at the papers. She hesitated. She ticked the box pending DNA testing results.

Every few seconds, it hit her that she was not in the Bahamas. She was in a morgue in Penang.

She wanted to be taken to her hotel quickly so that she could have her meds and lie down in the dark. The photos, the forms. Yet nothing was a louder wakeup call than the sight of his Panthère ring. He was now gone. It symbolised everything that was him: ambition, greed, power.

Siti Haslinda came back with a clear plastic bag and the contents. She said, 'the watch still works.'

Dominique was mute. She floated like a veil. She wanted

a whiskey but she knew better than to ask a Muslim for one. She neither knew where she was going to next nor the next day. This was the strangest holiday she'd ever been on. Four planes over two days.

'The DNA tests—' Dominique said.

'Yes?'

'I want them done.'

'We will need samples from you to do a match. A comb, razor or toothbrush. He has been deceased for more than a week but bone matter may be intact. Please courier the items to me ASAP.'

She was guided out of the building in to the sweltering late afternoon heat, to where her driver was waiting. She saw very bright lights and momentarily felt light-headed again. As she took her next step, her legs folded over.

The last thing she saw was her own hand dropping the plastic bag of luxury goods, and being on the floor glancing up at Siti Haslinda's cheap plimsolls. 'Are you OK?' she shouted repeatedly as she rushed over. Dominique blacked out.

10,000 POUNDS. THAT WAS the cost of repatriation "quote" from the British High Commission. Dominique's mother would want to be at the funeral. Her mother adored James. It was the reason she had been so keen to see Dominique married to him.

It was the wedding of the century. Her mother wanted to ensure that Dominique would never suffer a day without a handbag or starve to death. Since Uni, Dominique had had a knack for picking the penniless.

Her previous boyfriends had been drummers or poets or

such "types". Her mother knew that even though Dominique was a professional woman in her own right and not an uneducated housewife, there was no harm in marrying money. Like for like. Tit for tat. Ashes to ashes.

The death had been reported to the British High Commission in Kuala Lumpur. There was so much paperwork to deal with, she had no time for reflection or grief.

Partly this was because she was still in denial that James was gone for good, although he'd left her many years before. Just when she had decided to move to Singapore to join him.

Her planned new start in life was more than jeopardised. It was finished. James's soul had been destroyed long ago in the financial world and now his body had followed at last.

She registered his death, bought a UK style death certificate, which amounted to a visa for the deceased. But she baulked at the zinc-lined hermeneutically sealed coffin costing several thousand pounds which prevented exploding, popping open or exuding toxic odours and germs during the flight home.

Furthermore, to get authorisation to remove the deceased from the country she needed yet another certificate – the certificate of embalming. None of these certificates came cheap.

Daphne would be having a nervous breakdown and she would be grieving quite enough without the added shock of seeing the coffin. It made sense to bury or cremate him in the country where he had died. She chose cremation.

However, it would have to be after they obtain his DNA. Dominique did not believe in bereavement counselling. Neither did James if he was alive.

It felt like a business trip — taking care of business and

for Daphne's sake, with a brave face and even braver, bigger steps. The whole week since arrival had been eaten up by administration and costs. Dominique did not like to dwell on the morbid.

Before she could apply the adage – time is the healer and so on, she had assumed an armoured air of indifference against the clawing talons of loss and grief. They could tear out your eyes and your heart.

DOMINIQUE SPENT TWO NIGHTS at the Straits Suite in the Heritage Wing of the Penang Eastern and Oriental after picking up the ashes and their own 'passport'. It gave her a sense of calmness now that the decision had been made and James was in a tin, like a new caddy of tea.

It was very poignant that they were travelling together for the last time. His final voyage home, to the UK, was with her. She had wanted this so much, hadn't she? To have and to hold.

The Heritage Wing was the original one, dating from 1885. When she was last in Penang, three years before with James, she'd stayed in the same suite. It had Moorish minarets, a soaring echo-dome lobby, khaki-clad doormen and pith-helmeted bellhops.

Some of the world's most celebrated writers, artists and politicians had stayed here. The personalised check-in by the butler made it delay-free. He handed her a folded cold towel on a silver tray with a cocktail menu.

She could either have her beverage at the bar or in her suite. She chose her suite. She could not leave the suite in her state, mental or physical. The thought of perching at a bar left her shaking.

She looked at the cocktail menu and chose a Sidecar. There was no mood which could not be improved by the arrival of a cocktail from a personal butler.

After sunset, on the windy hilly rockface road to the beach with its sharp hairpin bends, Dominique was reminded of the scenery in South of France on driving holidays. The sea glittered, its deep blue almost black.

THE 12:15 BUSINESS CLASS SilkAir flight from Penang landed at 13:50 in Singapore. Once through arrivals, a driver called Tim was ready to drive her to the Shangri-La.

The hotel was right next to her deceased husband's 7-bedroom 3,200 sf serviced penthouse apartment on Orange Grove Road. Dominique had to make do with the Premier Balcony Suite in the Garden Wing as her usual Horizon Club Deluxe Suite in the Tower Wing was occupied by a K-Pop band.

Set in 15 acres of lush greenery and still next to Orchard Road shopping belt, it was Singapore's Champs-Élysées. The Shangri-La was her favourite hotel in Singapore.

She barely had time to step into the spa, or any of the 11 restaurants and bars in the resort. She was here on duty. She had to attend to James's mess in his apartment.

Standing in his vast lounge, she was bewildered. She looked around his stuff. Antiques. Vases, a chest, a console table, Chinese pots or urns, modern art. Seven guitars. She retrieved his comb, toothbrush and razor from his vanity.

She needed to get these quickly to the lab in Penang. She shuddered, remembering that she'd wanted to move here to be with him, just days ago. She did not realise she was weeping until she felt her face was wet.

She was floating in a dream, one surrounded by drivers, concierges and bellhops. A dream of living like a fugitive from suite to suite. She had already forgotten The Bahamas.

Though only a few days had passed, it was a blur that seemed to have happened years and years ago, in another time, when she was innocent and young. After what she had just been through, she now was ready for anything, even clearing out his things and going through his paperwork.

Her phone rang.

'Huh-hello.'

'It's Martin.'

'Who?' She wiped her tears, as if he could see her.

'Martin Pelland. HSBC.'

'Oh. Yes. What can I—'

'I want to make sure you are OK. You got into James's apartment, then?'

Well obviously, she thought. 'Yes, I did. I'm fine. Listen, I've got to go.' What on earth did he want?

'Do you want me to pick up some dinner and a bottle for you or something? I know you're busy.'

'No,' she said. 'I mean, no, thank you.'

'What are you doing?'

'I'm clearing James's stuff. I have to send his personal items for lab testing.'

'I can help you with that. I can courier them to the lab for you. Tonight itself. Just leave it with the concierge. I'll pop by in less than an hour. No need to come out.'

'Thank you so much.'

'It's no problem.'

'Actually, could you not come? I don't really want to go downstairs now. I've too much to do.'

'Leave it with the concierge. He can courier that for you under account.'

'Fine. I can handle this myself.'

'Wait, Mrs L—'

'I've got to go, bye.'

She sighed and blew her nose, after disconnecting him.

13

YOU

YOU CAN DO SO many nifty things now. Even rotate 180 degrees. Physio has been going well.

Tomorrow is your throat surgery. The day has come at last. You are in a new hospital now. It is much bigger and more modern.

You have said goodbye to Saadiya for a few days. You can type *goodbye* and *thank you* on the tablet. She has taught you how to form the words and it is not long before you are saying things to her. She never types back; she always speaks instead.

'Do you want to read anything? I'll get it for you.'

The papers. You type.

You type *no books.* They take too long and make your eyes and brain hurt. But that in itself is too long to type. She misunderstands and thinks you mean why aren't there any books and where are the books?

You re-type *I mean I do not want books.*

She goes out and comes back with the Bangkok Post, an English-language paper which you read from cover to cover.

Then you realise it is two weeks old.

YOU HAVE ARRIVED BACK at the original hospital. You have a new bed now. The old one has been taken. You are now sharing with three others in the room. This means you must be better. You are feeling rather encouraged.

'British Embassy is getting a new passport made for you,' says Saadiya.

You are glad your insurance is taking care of all this. 'Your wife has started the ball rolling,' Saadiya says. You feel choked up. Everything is progressing as it should.

You open your mouth wide and try to say ah. Nothing comes out. Didn't Saadiya say 'when they first do it, you won't be able to speak immediately. It will still take a while for the vocal chords to warm up and take control of the messages from the brain.'

She trained in the UK, in Hull, as a nurse. Not a place she would want to return to, she has told you at some time or other.

'Anyway, we have to write something down in your passport for your place of birth, and your wife told us where you were from. You are from Caterham in Kent,' she says. 'Your new passport photo will not look like the old you, though.'

That's OK, you type.

'I know I say this every day, but you are so lucky to be alive.'

YOU TRY YOUR VOICE again two days later. It is stranger than you thought. At first you hear the hissing, like that of fire-crackers before they explode. This turns into a guttural crackle, like central heating coming on. Then you astonish even yourself. It is monstrous, huge, frightening, like a roar from a cave. The snorers gasp and bark aloud in their half-asleep dreams.

You are trying to say *my name is Greg*.

But you stop when you say *my*.

THE OPERATION IS A SUCCESS. You speak! You are not that bad after all. Firstly, you do not much resemble a werewolf when the bandages came off. This is true and the nurses have confirmed it.

They are used to all sorts of patients, injuries and scarring. They do not notice it as they do not notice bums, genitalia and the adult nappies that they have to change.

But the voice. You are not used to this voice. You have to get used to it and you have to put the tablet down. No more typing. There is no internet access anyway, so why bother using the tablet.

With each growl, you are transformed, a monstrous voice that is more like a howl or a bellow, deep like the night, unmusical and beast-like.

Today your wife will arrive and you are beside yourself with excitement. You will be leaving this place and beginning your new life. You need to say goodbye to Saadiya, the doctors, the inspector, the gay guy and the others.

Saadiya is smiling. You know that is a good thing.

'She's here! I can't believe it after all this time.'

You say 'I can't—,' your voice thundering, frightening even yourself. It's like you are in a rock concert and the volume, reverb, everything is wrong. You pick up your tablet again.

I don't even know what she looks like, you type.

'You will. She is so anxious to see you. Here's a photo we took outside this morning. She used my phone and she wrote her name on it the photo.'

You read it. Your wife. Phoebe. Ah, that explains Po-ebay. A petite Chinese woman with a ponytail.

She is tired-looking, without a hint of glamour or vanity. Your radar tells you that she would be better-looking had it not been for all this family stress she is under.

'She's just doing the insurance and visitor forms now. Won't be long.'

The door opens.

Your wife's eyes widen in horror. Saadiya is saying, 'are you OK are you OK', and putting her arm around Phoebe's shoulders. She says nothing. She just looks at you, curious yet calm.

You try to say her name. The two syllables come out completely wrong, like two claps of thunder. NO, you cry, because you don't want this to happen, yet all she hears is your animalistic roar, an earth shattering explosion.

Phoebe looks pale and starts to tremble. She is shaking her head slowly. You think she will pass out but her mouth breaks into a scream. She is hysterical. And when she starts she cannot stop.

Her hands search wildly for something to cover her mouth; she wants a pillow or something. She shakes her head vigorously and her hands are in the air.

You have never seen such a huge mouth, her teeth are bared and you can see the insides of her throat. The sound is continuous and ear-splitting.

A storm has entered this very hospital.

14

DOMINIQUE

O N THE PLANE AT around 3 am UK time, she had already been worrying which shade of paint she'd confirmed to the interior designer.

She might have forgotten as it might easily have been the last thing on her mind but *the team are waiting for confirmation*, said Lorraine's Whatsapp. All this was her new "project" when she got home, which would help her take her mind off things.

Had she chosen Serpentine or Urbane from Little Greene's 28 shade palette?

They looked very similar to her on screen, at least, and she needed the samples ready to go through. Or was it Plummett or Pigeon from Farrow and Ball? There was also Ganymede or Feather Quill by Valspar. Altogether there had been more than 50 shades of grey.

'Not an inspiring colour,' said Andreia, in textbook interior designer spiel, 'but designer, *de rigueur* and de-staying. From Alexa Chung to Zadie Smith, it's been grey.'

There was plenty of time on the 12-hour flight to think

about James. Once, a million years ago when James and Dominique had gone out for dinner it ended with a row. They were young then, too. Younger, at least. She had bought theatre tickets then.

It was raining heavily. They rowed over very stupid crazy things the kind no one can ever remember what they were. Or they did not speak to each other for months. A career that left not a second for imagination, or freedom or innocence. They never made it to watch Chicago.

Daphne was born a year later. She was named after the author of *Rebecca*, one of her favourite classic gothic novels. Now she was already in Year 8 at the Roedean in Brighton, where she had been boarding since she was 11, costing £37,440 a year in fees, as James once casually mentioned.

Of course, she missed seeing Daphne grow up every day but it was a family rite of passage. Pain hit her like the waves in a strong tide. Education was what we were here on earth for, they'd both agreed. It was transformative and empowering.

Both Dominique and James had boarded, their own parents' generation before them too and Daphne's future children would board, naturally. There was one thing stronger than family ties, and that was old school ties.

James and Dominique still believed boarding had been the best choice as no schools in London had what they wanted: the best for Daphne, which was a club, a family, a home all in one.

Roedean fitted their criteria perfectly, the campus being on a cliff near the Sussex Downs overlooking Brighton Marina. For an adult or a child, it was simply a haven.

Every child's possible interest had been considered, from dance studios, music rooms, a 320-seat theatre, a heated indoor swimming pool, a golf course, a private tunnel to the beach, a farm *and* a chapel to workshops, studios, laboratories and sports pitches.

There was nothing which Daphne could have loved more and she loved musical theatre and dance. Never mind that she'd never make a living doing anything like that. Why did she need to make a living?

Dominique was beginning to question this very idea about "making a living". James was dead. He was no longer earning. Would it be vile and vulgar to think about the inheritance?

THE FLIGHT FROM CHANGI had been OK. Lorraine had booked her a car to pick her up at Heathrow. Dominique had waited for the special item to be delivered, the FRAGILE item which was the Gibson Les Paul that could not be hand-carried *because she wasn't a rock star.*

She had been away for 14 days, she calculated, including transfers and time changes. And it was the strangest trip she had ever done.

Dominique arrived back in Holland Villas Road at half past six on a Sunday morning. She sighed when she saw her double-fronted bay window property.

Ellie opened the door and gave her a hand with the luggage. 'Lorraine will be here at around 8 to make sure everything is as it should be,' said Ellie.

Now, what does that mean, thought Dominique. She entered the reception room. On the left, was the pool table room-cum-library. The oak bookshelves and the pool table had been taped up and covered due to the ongoing works.

She had been in the middle of her refurbishment project when the waves of bad news arrived. First her redundancy then James's demise. There was a stag's head on the chimney breast over the carved stone fireplace, wrapped up in cling film like it was frozen food.

The carved oak yellow-felted pool table stood on an antique Oriental silk rug. No one but Daphne and James played pool, under the orange Art Nouveau glass shades.

Dominique sat in her 'comfy seat' which was the built-in banquette seating in the front bay window with matching yellow velvet cushion. Here the natural light was good for her to check her mail.

There were bills, letters, statements and so on, all demanding her attention as she had been away two weeks.

She felt drained and awaited the inevitable barrage of questions from everyone — her mum, Lorraine, Ellie, Daphne, Lucy and more — following the dreaded phone call to James's mother.

So many messages on her landline voicemail from her interior designer but she'd already signed off on the design process so that the works could progress.

She did not return these calls. For what? Nothing would be important. What she was doing was the most important thing already. Death. Taxes. The two certainties of life.

At around 8 o'clock, Lorraine rang the door bell. She went and sat down with Dominique in the same yellow velvet seating area. 'You're having a meeting with her today,' Lorraine said, pulling out an iPad from her handbag.

'Shall we go into the kitchen?' said Dominique, getting up. 'Who?'

'Andreia.'

'Oh yes, Andreia.'

Dominique called her Andreia because she had such a long unpronounceable name. They went into the kitchen and Lorraine put her iPad down to make coffee.

Dominique looked at the card pinned to the corkboard next to the Fischer and Paykel fridge. That had to go. The corkboard not the fridge. Patokobalahalandriea Tulawe-doboyavalarieava, Indo-Afro-Madagascar in origin and tipped to be of the the top twenty designers hot and trending right now.

Apparently the name meant she was unmarried (lucky her). If she was married, her name would be even longer as she had to take on the regional surname of the husband too.

If no one had heard of her, that was probably because of the long unpronounceable name, and that was good. The buzz should be kept to an elite few. She listened to the last of the messages.

Hi are you back yet? Please could you confirm the meeting. Visions of Jo Malone candles, shearling cushions, Venetian mirrors appeared before her like a smorgasbord of a glamorous, sumptuous and even fulfilling meal that she had no appetite for.

'FFS,' she thought.

And she was the one who'd engaged an interior designer. It now felt like the interior designer had engaged *her*. She did want the place sorted. Death by design. She did not want any trace of James left in this place. Something in her had also died with him.

She picked up his guitar and went downstairs to the lower ground floor. It was the room directly under the library and so also had a bay window, the room that was James's den to which he returned when he was in London for a few times a year.

It was like a teenager had left home. Every room needed

a designer, not a decorator. Scents, not smells. Shades, not colours. Dominique knew she tended to be possessive. She already had the entire first floor; the master bedroom, bathroom, office and dressing room.

The interior designer knew who wrote the cheques now.

She put the caddy of his ashes on the bay window. She wondered where to put his guitar that she had lugged back. Not to mention all the others which were coming by air freight.

Dominique and James had used to like the same music; The Cure, Joy Division, New Order, Grateful Dead, Violent Femmes. She did not even know what was popular now.

She decided to lean the Gibson in its hardcase against the bookshelves until Andreia sorted out storage of musical instruments. Of course she would like to sell them all but she really ought to let Daphne to have first say.

She felt lost in her own house. She went across the corridor from James's den to have avocado on toast for breakfast with the English tea that she had missed so much. No more Starbucks.

She looked through the images sent by Andreia on her iPhone. *Regarding the diamante headboard, would she like it studded or unstudded, marble console table – to have creamy gold marble but with black veining or grey and white marble with less obvious veining.*

This was too much for her to take in. Dominique forced herself to not think about James but he was beginning to, could she use the word, haunt her? He did not live here permanently but his was still a huge presence, he filled every room and everything that she thought of.

A cufflink on a bedside table. A plectrum on a shelf. Half-read thrillers abandoned under an armchair.

She started to type her reply.

Andreia, actually, I am changing the palette completely from neutral and classic and Kelly Hoppen to rustic, eclectic, world, that kind of thing. I know it's not too late because I can see that the stripping out has barely started. Just protection of the rooms only. Now that I have begun world travel starting with an embalming and funereal journey, my fascination for global cultures has begun.

No diamante. And forget marble. It's tomb-like and actually very significantly morbid for me right now. I'd much prefer great big slab of vintage rough hewn reclaimed oak for the console table. Much warmer. On industrial-looking steel X frame legs reclaimed from some shut down post-apocalyptic factory in Sheffield. And antique enamel metal sewing machinist's chairs for the bar area.

Also we need to look at those charts again. The colours are far too grey. I know I said grey before but now I think they will clash with the rustic look. Think barn, decaying 'thirties colonial quarters, think Catherine Deneuve in Indochine. Any chance you could re-visit that film and check out the scene I mean, the one in the internal courtyard, where it's raining and it's at night? I think you'll find it was indigo blues and Persian yellows.

Thank you.

Kind regards, D.

Andreia would not be happy that this was the third time she had changed her mind, but as far as the email was concerned, she felt satisfied with what she had typed, that she had very clearly given direction. She was her own client.

She needed to stop dwelling on James's death and focus on Andreia and the works, even if it meant she had to iron out their differences. Who was controlling who, anyway? She hit *send.*

Another email had come in with the lab report. Unsurprisingly, the DNA samples she couriered matched the deceased's. She did not reply. She saw the voicemail button was still lit red on her phone.

She must have received a call when she was typing the email to Andreia. She pressed play. *Hi Dominique. It's Martin. I just wanted to make sure you got home OK and that you did positively identify James's body?*

It was that Martin again. Sunday morning in London meant it was late afternoon the same day in Singapore. James had never mentioned him. Should she be pleased that he seemed "concerned" about her well-being?

She replayed the message. She noticed that now she was being referred to as Dominique and not Mrs Laney-Sambrooke any more.

Every now and then she had stop herself when she felt the palpitations and cold sweat coming on. She had to reach for her tablets or her drink, whichever was nearer.

She slid open James's desk top drawer to find medication. She rummaged through his clutter of stationery. She found a pencil and post-it notes. A guitar tuner. And something else.

A beautiful leather and stainless steel Porsche key chain, new and still in its original luxury case. It must have been an unopened gift from some promotional thing when James had a Porsche.

She tossed it into her handbag to be taken upstairs later and be joined with his ring and watch. She rubbed her temples with the hand span of her thumb and middle finger. She gave up looking and found painkillers in the kitchen drawer instead.

Dominique's pilates instructor arrived at 9 am and thus

gave her a reason to postpone seeing Daphne and her mum who were already on their way to London.

She had time to arrange the funeral after that with Lorraine. 'Christiana is here,' said Lorraine. Christiana was Danish, blonde and very into the whole hygge thing. The pilates was an hour long session and Dominique had paid for ten sessions in bulk for a good discount.

The Pilates instructor left at 10am. 'Can we talk now,' said Lorraine 'about the funeral arrangements?'

'Yes?' said Dominique, as though she was questioning it. Tears came, which surprised her. She now realised she had loved him. If she had not, she would not be in pain each time she thought of him. She had to sit down on the balancing ball.

'I'd like a humanist ceremony,' she finally said. 'I don't want anything fancy. A band, with two guitars. James would like that.'

'What about the venue?'

'How about somewhere in Notting Hill? You pick. Remember, just keep costs down. We have a lot of lawyers' fees coming up. And there is no hurry. Anytime within the next six weeks is fine. Let's try for July. It's more a celebration of his life. Let's not dwell on the word funeral. It's a memorial service. We're remembering James's life, and his achievements, his ups and his downs-'

Funerals were like weddings. They knew you were weak. Due to love or loss. They could name a price knowing your brain was confused and stupid and you had to just sign.

Just then the soon-to-be-upgraded video entry system chime went. It did not have cloud storage and what was the point of a security system which could not record anything?

According to the screen display, it was Daphne, arriving

in the B-Class Mercedes Benz Lorraine had booked. She was weeping as she got out of the car and didn't stop as she walked up the stone path through the clipped front lawns. Dominique was waiting to hug her.

'I missed you, missed you to pieces, mummy.' Dominique had missed her daughter too. She was looking so sweet still in her H&M unicorn leggings and her top with a kitten on it, still innocent and child-like even though she was getting very tall.

Whenever she came home, it upset Dominique that she had grown so much. It brought home how much time she spent away at school. She liked stickers, puppies and key-rings because somehow, girls liked "cute" things for longer than boys did.

There was even a Japanese word for it, the adoration of cuteness, people said. She didn't know anyone Japanese to check if this were true and if so what the word for it was.

Thinking of Japanese, Dominique decided to take Daphne to Itsu for lunch. It was time to break the breaking news and no one could do a better job in the world at this point, thought Dominique.

'Daphne. Daddy has passed away.'

'What do you mean?' said Daphne with a blank expression.

'Daddy is gone. Daphne, Daphne. No. He's not coming back. Calm down. Team hugs? Daphne, please.'

Daphne's head shook from side to side. She put her hands up as though in self-defence.

'We are going to go a memorial service. You see this jar?'

Daphne had no reply. She was panting and gasping for breath. The hands she put up were now balled up in fists.

'Gross!' Daphne finally screamed. 'You burned dad to

pieces and put him in there? No! No! I want Daddy! I want Daddy back!' She shouted and cried hysterically while Dominique tried to calm her down. She was like a beast that could not be soothed.

After several more terrifying howls, Daphne went mute, just looking down for a while. Then she burst into tears and wept silently.

'Daph, Daph, please. It's hard for me too. You need to stop crying. I was going to take you to Itsu.'

Daphne shook her head.

'I. Don't. Want. To!' she screamed. 'Fuck Itsu.'

This surprised Dominique as she thought they were over the tantrum stage. It did come back occasionally for a visit, like a screeching bat in the attic.

'My God, your language, Daph! I am not paying 37-grand a year for you to learn to swear.' Dominique looked at her daughter, feeling the stab of guilt and wonder. How could she have missed all this?

Daphne was growing up. She looked like a child, acted like a toddler, cried like a teenager and swore like an adult.

'You're not paying. You never paid. You just bought your shoes and handbags. Daddy paid for everything! You did this to him!'

'How?' Dominique felt light-headed. They could not be having this conversation, surely? 'I did not kill him!'

'Yes. Yes, you drove him away!'

'No! He went because he wanted this great job and we would not move with him. You would not be in Roedean today.'

Daphne was quiet. She looked at her bare feet, then at the ashes.

'Why is he...? Is he...? In the jar...?' she said, in a calmer voice at last.

'I didn't have much choice. Burial meant that he would not be here with us now, he would be in the ground in a foreign land. I didn't want to bring him back in a coffin; what would have been the point of that? 5,000 pounds to see him brought back and you can't see him anyway, it's all sealed.'

For a few minutes, Dominique just held her daughter tightly like she was a baby girl again.

'But he's not here with us now. I didn't get to see Daddy.'

Dominique found it hard to reply with a lump in her throat. She took a deep breath, bit her lip and tears came.

'He was not burned, they put him in this building, and whoosh he's gone,' she said. She wiped her tears. 'I pressed the OK button myself. I said goodbye to Daddy. You can be sure he lived a fulfilled and full life. He loved you and you loved him. He came back every term holiday to be with you. I would be so honoured if you can do me a favour and write a little something for the service. You could write a song for him. He'd love that, you know he would. Here. Something of his for you. I brought this back. His watch. It still works. You can even wear it when you are bigger. Look. His panther ring. You don't have to wear either of them, if you don't want.'

'I'll wear it now,' Daphne said, grabbing the watch. She seemed uninterested in the ring so Dominique put it back in her handbag.

Dominique's phone started ringing. She could see that it was the interior designer Andreia, so she hit ignore on the phone. Unable to stand it any more, she picked it up and texted back:

Yes. Exotic rustic not Danish now.

She hoped that answered the question as they were supposed to have a meeting that day but Dominique had finally cancelled it in the light of everything that had happened.

Normally, Daphne absolutely adored Itsu so whenever she was back in London, Dominique had made it a point of going to the nearest Itsu which was at Notting Hill Gate. This time Daphne took no more than two sips of her usual 'beauty smoothie'.

Dominique, now completely drained by all this like an opened can of tunafish, made herself prod at a few humps of octopus. It was called making an effort.

After Itsu, Dominique drove to the Waitrose in Kensington High Street to pick up stuff for dinner. She bought some salad, a bottle of Pinot Noir, lentils, Waitrose curry paste, a bunch of coriander, a bag of organic prawns.

Dominique called Martha in her 2.2M euro 'retirement' villa overlooking the Gulf of Saint-Tropez in Grimaud. She was blissfully shielded by senile dementia, and also being prevented from enjoying the Côte D'Azur views and the villa's Belle Époque architecture.

'Is this about Jules?' said Martha. 'Who is this? Who?'

She had no idea who Dominique was talking about. She was confused and thought that it was Jules, her own husband, who was being referred to.

Martha then started speaking French thinking that Dominique was actually from France. There was no point talking any further or repeating anything.

It was unlikely she understood the message that her son was also gone, and before that, Jules ten years ago. Both in accidents.

Jules had been back in London in the summer of 2008 in

their Sloane Square 'pied-à-terre'. He had drowned in the bath; drunk, asleep or both.

It was unbearable to think about at the time but now she had dementia, there was nothing else to think about any more. Jules's heart had always been on the Kings Road.

They'd gone back for what they called treats and treatments — appointments, IV therapies at Harvey Nichols and the usual medical checkups - for a couple of months.

It was in fact then when Dominique first learned of kick-starting one's wellness by injection or even intravenously – vitamins, CoQ10+, Hydramax, Megaboost and all the other magic bullets. He would never really, and truly and fully leave Chelsea.

It was always unbearably hot in the south of France during the summer. Martha always said it was good to 'escape' France for a change, to London where 'the shopping is good, the theatre even better and the healthcare unparalleled'.

DOMINIQUE THOUGHT OF THE UNPACKING. It was best to get it done after the call to Martha. Dominique was watching some items on-line, namely guitars on Ebay.

Meanwhile, she also emailed a couple of dealers in vintage guitars. She was feeling the jetlag now, and needed to lie down immediately, if not sooner. The bottle of Pinot Noir was still on the kitchen worktop, unopened, when she went upstairs.

It was late when she heard a sound at her bedroom door. It was Daphne coming to say goodnight. 'Come in, sweetie.' She said cheerfully. 'Let's have a team hug.'

Daphne lay down with her eyes open. She had been

crying. Her eyes were red and bulging. 'Mummy,' she said. 'Who is going to do daddy's job now he's gone?'

'Oh.' She hadn't thought of that. 'Someone. Don't worry about his job, darling. Good night. I love you.' She said. She thought, 'Martin Pelland'.

15

PHOEBE

THEY PUT HER DOWN, she had no idea how, as it seemed to happen in slow motion, but they sedated her.

She could not remember what happened after her screaming. Glass-shattering, ear-splitting screams which she had not even known were inside her. She shut her eyes tightly to stop thinking. She was in a hospital. She'd had a few seconds of looking around, the blue walls, green curtains, drawn.

'Blue and green must never be seen' went the saying. But that must only apply to clothes, surely no colour rules applied in this cold, clinical space. She wanted to tell Trish but she was tired. Her lids felt heavy.

When Phoebe woke up again, it was dark. She had never been good at waking up in the dark, for it could be morning dark, in which case should she stay up now for twelve hours? Or if it was night, she should return to sleep?

She could see shadows in the room. Someone had left the night light on near the doorway. The shadows moved. They were long and grotesque, she was imagining monsters, before she realised the blinds were open and the shadows were cast by trees outside.

She was used to London hospitals such as Tooting St George's where there were no trees outside any window and if you even had a view, it was a view of the next block.

Even the carpark was valuable, limited real estate which earned hefty carpark charges and naturally had no trees. But here there were trees. A lot of them. She looked at each one in terror. She picked up her phone, which was at her bedside, and switched it on.

She waited for the roaming signal, the wheel that went round and round searching like a beacon for hope. Roaming, in all senses of the word, was expensive. Look at where roaming got her (that was what her mother would and did say).

She got up and left the room in search of a stronger signal. The corridor was long but well-lit. You could not see the end or start of it. She kept walking until she heard voices from a room off the corridor.

She could ask someone where she could get a phone signal. She was about to knock but she heard something which made her stop. She strained to hear.

The heated conversation was audible but in Thai. She heard the two words in English, *Chelsea tattoo*. They were talking about Greg. They had to be. How many patients were there with this specific tattoo?

There were two voices. Male. She quickly found the phone's voice memo app and recorded the conversation. Of all the people who ought to know what they were saying about Greg, it should be her.

She heard the squeal of chairs being pulled out. The voices trailed off and stopped. Phoebe switched the voice memo recording off. She had 1 min 34 s of audio.

Footsteps. She dashed down the corridor and hid in a disabled toilet and turned the lights off. Then she peeked out, her face in shadow. The door into the corridor opened. She saw the backs of two men and they could have been anyone. She was too far away to see.

She crept back to her dimmed room. A few minutes later, the door opened, flooding the room with light from the corridor. A tall Muslim nurse entered bearing a tray of the most amazing smelling food.

She set down the tray on the nightstand and Phoebe now saw it was Thai food. Her stomach was growling.

'Feeling any better?' The nurse said. Phoebe ignored the question.

'You shouldn't have sedated me, I am pregnant,' Phoebe said. She could not say any more as the words did not come, they were stuck in her gullet like pieces of stone.

'My dear! Poor thing. You are in shock.'

The nurse's words came out like a surf of seawater with pebbles dredged up from the seabed and Phoebe had to hold her breath to not gulp it down. She was handed a plastic shot glass of pills.

Why did she need to take anything? She was not ill. Phoebe threw the pills on the floor. She turned on her phone, ignoring the nurse, who then picked up the pills and left the room.

Judging from the giant shadows, it must be night as Phoebe was feeling terribly hungry. The food was delicious and hot. Its fragrant aroma filled the room.

Massaman curry. Cauliflower. Beans. Lentils. Tom yam soup. It was better than a restaurant. It was like eating in a Thai family home, only with no toothless grandparents in the corner. She took big mouthfuls. She had been rude to the nurse and felt bad now.

~

'GREG.' SHE FOUND THE courage to say his name but her voice was trembling. She was in his room. She had left her ward and was ready to go if he was. The nurse left them alone for a while. Phoebe forced her eyes open. She was weeping openly.

She saw that he twitched and frowned. His thighs trembled. His eyes squeezed shut every few seconds from pain. She could not speak any more, and she was feeling sweaty and queasy. For a long minute, she held his hands in hers and felt better. Her tears fell on their hands.

'I spent the whole morning doing the insurance documents and forms for what's happened to you,' finally she opened her eyes and spoke. 'You know I had to get the police report and statement in order to file an insurance claim.

'The bill is astronomical. Luckily it's covered. We need to decide what we are doing, where we are going. If you are coming back to Battambang with me, I mean.'

I need to have my voice back and I can't trust the doctors here. They came in last night and told me that they will have another shot. He typed.

'I'll go back, pack up our stuff in Battambang and say good bye to the volunteers first. Then I'll be back for you, after the surgeons have one more go at you.'

'Thank you,' he said in his new, explosive way. *I am looking forward to our baby so much,* he typed. *I am going to be a dad. I can't wait. I am really sorry I am so ill. I cannot be of much support to you.*

'No, no. Please do not say that.' She fell onto his chest and the tablet, shut her eyes. She pulled him close. 'We are a family now. We support each other. We just need to go home. My mum will be a great help.'

OK, he typed. She held him tight to avoid looking at him. Equally she was horrified that he was looking at her, every detail, her hands, face, mouth.

She knew she looked like a homeless person. She had huge purple bags under her eyes — and over. She had been screaming, crying, sedated, awake, nauseous and to top that she was greasy, sweaty and unwashed.

Luckily, he did not remember the looker that she usually was. That's a relief, she thought with grim humour. They were both united in their circumstances. Growing a baby was empowering. A miracle. She was stronger for it.

In a month the morning sickness would pass. The accident and pregnancy had brought Greg and her closer. They considered being parents once, but spent nothing on IVF, just went on their Groggy and now their old dream was coming true, in spite of all that. It was happening. The reality hit her – they *would* have a child.

16

YOU

THIS IS LIKE THE opposite of cosmetic surgery. It's disfigurement surgery.

This morning it is raining and the room seems as overcast even with the ceiling lights on.

'Where is Phoebe now?' you say, though it is more like a volatile roar.

'She is safe; she is in another ward.'

You shake your head vigorously. She senses your panic and hands you the tablet.

Help me, please, you type. No wonder Phoebe is in shock. You are frustrated that you want to be ready for the baby and be the best first-time dad ever, yet you are trapped here, a howling animal.

You want to say all this to the nurse but even Saadiya, though your friend and confidante is, ultimately, just a professional doing her job, and wearing ear muffs.

Your voice is as thundering and raw as an engine. It's hopeless. How long have you been here? Are they at all competent?

Another medical intervention may be required. What is the procedure to get another procedure?

The doctor has arrived.

'Yes, we need to operate again. But there is great news, at least you can speak!' He cries, as though it's a Eureka moment of an experiment he's carried out.

'It is miraculous. Before the cords were all severed, and it was only 30-70 that you could speak again, so you are fortunate that you speak. You had a very serious accident, Greg. All the doctors in the world would have had to do the same for you. The surgeon will be here in a minute to explain everything to you. What he has done.'

'No more,' you blast. Saadiya covers her already muff-protected ears. Can they not see what has happened?

You are a limping monster with a face so disfigured your wife does not know it's you. She's having a baby, your baby. You can't bear that she's doing all this alone because you are so ill.

First the infection, then the circumcision, then this. 'I want out.' You speak calmly and slowly, still each word crashes like cymbals. You type: *home me Phoebe baby.*

You are too tired for punctuation or sentences. Since you saw yourself the first time they took the bandages off, you have become afraid.

You hold the tablet up for them to read. They look at each other without a trace of reaction.

You throw the tablet at the door and it shatters. It is a tiny satisfying elegant crunch. Saadiya picks it up and leaves the room.

∾

You HAVE HAD YOUR second throat procedure. They have

lowered the volume but your voice is hard, grating, mechanical, like a broken machine, which you are sort of, rather than thunder claps. For now, you remind yourself not to ask for anything more.

Every day is a mini miracle.

You are a howling monster and shunned by even your own wife. Why don't they just slit your throat? This is becoming routine now. Like the physio, the food, everything is familiar as though you were born and had grown up here.

Now that the insurance has taken over the case, thanks to Phoebe coming to do the paperwork and the calls, you can have a party. Have all the treatments, procedures, medication required to make you well again. And if you are not well again, have more.

Saadiya says 'this is how things are done here.' She does not know what things are like back in your country nowadays. You don't either. All of it is a mystery to you.

'You had a boating accident. Do you remember any more? How did you save yourself? Or did someone save you?'

You frown. Each day you lie down and look up at the stainless steel cables. The staff keep mentioning the yacht wreck. Achara. They are fascinated by luxury, by fantasy life, glamour, travel, girls. It makes your brain hurt. Sighing, you type *Seeing Phoebe helped*.

'What is she like?'

Kind. Funny. You type on a new tablet to replace the one you have smashed.

You have to make things up now. You know you are winging it. Forcing memories is forming memories.

We— you start to type. You press backspace and do not show the tablet to her.

YOUR DENTURES ARE MADE, your passport has arrived, Phoebe has too. The passport and Phoebe go hand-in-hand. They both mean that escape is near.

You will leave the hospital, Saadiya and the rest of them, begin your new life back home in London.

Phoebe has packed up and sent her belongings home already. She has booked your tickets. She shows you the printed itinerary:

Bangkok Suvarnabhumi International by coach
  TG910 leaving at 0055
  arriving at Heathrow, 0715 the next day.

You are not living in this hospital forever, nothing is forever. You take down Saadiya's email, phone, Whatsapp. Not that it is of any use, you have no phone. You have no money.

Your passport shows your new photo, a burns victim, carefully reconstructed. They say there was an explosion in the engine room.

You look like you have been crudely made of wood from a thousand-year-old forest, a full bust of the legendary Green Man and the perpetual shocked expression to match.

Seeing yourself a few times in the mirror has seemed less traumatic than the photo. A mirror shows you as 3D, alive. Mirrors are magic. A passport photo, however, is flat and dead, even you weep at your own image.

'The clothes,' Saadiya says. 'Your clothes.' She shows you. The local people in her village have donated a couple of T shirts in your size, a couple of pairs of pants and jeans shorts.

They are not to your taste. Wait! What was your taste? All you know is that there and then you take an instant dislike to the clothes. The doctor says the mind is amazing at unravelling a ball of tangled memories and thoughts. It can do this on its own.

'You will be better in your home country,' he says. 'Psychotherapy treatment will help you recover. An NHS is something we aspire to have here.'

You have, quite possibly, your last Thai meal when Saadiya comes with the trolley. You chat about the food you will eat back home. From her training in Hull, she reminds you what British food is.

Bangers and mash, roast chicken, lamb or beef, Yorkshire pudding, fish and chips, bread and butter pudding, orange and poppy seed cake. Curry. Sandwiches.

Not in that order and not all together of course! You laugh your sizzling, hissing laugh like the sound of pebbles being stir-fried.

None of those were your favourite food, you are sure.

PHOEBE ARRIVES AND YOU have a quick look at her belly, she is not showing yet. She will not show for a long time anyway as a sack dress is all she seems to like wearing. She frowns as she put her hands over her belly.

She has told you the number of weeks but you have forgotten. 15 or 20, what difference does it make to you? She manages a bright false smile that only someone brought up in the UK can do.

You have already had to endure the embarrassment of such a smile when you went for your dentures fitting yesterday.

It is your mind that needs filling not your teeth.

Phoebe has brought some new clothes for you – from Battambang market. They are even worse than what you've got on; the clothes from Saadiya's village.

She shows them to you with a look that almost says: 'Let's get this over and done with. It will be cold when we get back. Cold. Grey. There is Italian food too. There's English food,' she says with vicarious new mum pride, since she is not even English.

A pregnant woman in that perpetual state of smug – mums know best.

She's hiding something, she won't look at you. It's something you must have done. Her jaw is clamped. You are not blind. Your sight, touch and sense of smell have heightened, far from being depleted.

A stranger. She is trying to show you a grain of kindness but it turns into a beach of bitterness.

17

DOMINIQUE

OMINIQUE WOKE UP AT 3 am each night. Her forehead, neck and chest were damp, as though she was feverish. A strong presentiment, like a voice, told her the paint colours.

She had to switch on her bedside lamp, wake up fully and write them down in her white leather Smythson notebook, sort of like her project diary.

She felt uncomfortable doing this because a familiar feeling returned, that someone was overlooking her while she wrote. She needed to do it quickly and get the lights switched off again.

During the day, it was very noisy upstairs. The builders were taking down some panelling in the attic. Ironically, Dominique found James's basement den a sanctuary. Warm, dark — a womb.

It was the only room in the whole house untouched by the overbearing force that was interior design. She could not face Andreia's constant calls and meetings so it was nice to escape here. She opened the Rockcase of the guitar she'd brought home with her.

She played a chord, remembering that was how they'd met. He'd come to see her play in her band, when they were both students. It was out of tune.

She opened his desk drawer where she remembered seeing the electronic tuner. It reminded her that they had both existed once. She switched the tuner on and clipped it to the guitar's head.

It still worked. She plucked the same notes again, hearing the sliding pitches until it was in tune. She had no interest in playing any more. The instant it was in tune, she held it like a corpse for a second.

Then she re-interred in in the coffin-hard velvet-lined Rockcase. She snapped the catches, all 7 of them, to lock it in.

Since she'd got back from Singapore, the house had been giving her the creeps. Having the ashes here was probably not a good idea. The memorial service date was set.

An obituary and funeral announcement notice for the Sunday Times was ordered. Dominique planned a ceremonial scattering of his ashes near his parents' home in Grimaud.

Daphne had his ties and his band T shirts, his ring and his watch which she was looking after like holy relics.

Dominique was still having second and third thoughts, usually in the middle of the night. Two interior schemes were on the cards: Thai drug-dealer's den or Shanghai vintage industrial, according to the visuals and moodboards that Andreia had prepared.

Rustic-exotic, she wished she'd never uttered the words. Gold, emerald buddhas, silk cushions. It felt like it had gone naturally this way, a big whoosh of force, a strong sense that something else was pushing her around in the house.

Why didn't the house take on a Nordic calm, white and

light-blue whoosh? Both Andreia and her had felt it. The Shanghai Vintage Industrial possessed them and the house, like a fog lowering over two junks in the Bund.

Like a feeling that someone was watching you from behind a door but when you looked up, there was no one there. She did not know if interior design had caused that feeling or it had been there all along, only appearing in the light of the recent tragedies.

IN THE MORNING, SHE rubbed her eyes. It was 9:05. When the phone rang, she knew it was Andreia and eventually she did answer.

'Why this rustic *but* opulent Shanghai theme?' Dominique flagged up her main concern. Andreia then suggested,

'You could visit some 1920s Speakeasy or Claridges Art Deco Wing or some Belle Époque cities to get ideas. Yes, even Shanghai, why not?'

'I've done enough flights for a while.'

'You know costs and fees will increase due to changes to the budget, drawings, samples, specs and spreadsheets. Works have to stall while we re-design.'

'I'm not sure myself why I've gone down this Shanghai private club route,' Dominique said, ignoring Andreia's comment about costs.

She pressed and pinched the space between her eyebrows hard to get some relief from that tight, closed feeling every woman knows.

There was a board-like hardness in her chest and head from shouldering Daphne's stress and grief on top of her own. The house was oppressive and sticky.

'Dominique, you need to get away,' said Andreia. 'I think you need a break. You are not thinking clearly, Dominique, which is unlike you.'

It was already the start of the summer holidays and Daphne would be home in two days. How quickly the year had gone!

After she hung up on Andreia, Dominique looked up places to go for an activity week, a place for a parent and a child, not couples. A treat. A place to for both to catch up and to act, sing, read, enjoy, relax, unwind. All the things they said in the brochure.

She found the Kalliope Epic Musical Theatre Workshop and Retreat package. She chose something they could do together because Daphne was crazy about the performing arts. Drama queen since she was three. Dominique thought both of them would give it a go.

She planned to rediscover her daughter while looking for an investment property. She was undecided about looking for work but while the insurance payout was in hand, she would not fritter it away. Unlike James, she would not do something as stupid as blow it all on a boat, car or a drug and drink-fuelled weekend.

The mother-and-daughter week that Dominique had booked would include day singing workshops, learning and performing songs from musical theatre. This would be very cathartic and help release the tightened sinews of their family crises, she hoped.

Grief. Not exactly a big hole in their hearts, more an intermittent needle-like pressure, scratching like a stylus on a record. When the music ran out, it ran out, leaving the audible sigh of the wheel of life still turning.

Dominique was amazed that there were such diversions

to help repair mother-daughter or father-son relationships which the trials of modern life had soured.

People could not fix themselves. Someone else had to, and with such sophistication. Dominique could not resist. Those marketing strategies, they worked. She couldn't wait to sign on the dotted line, or as they said nowadays, to read out the three-digit number on the back of the card.

In the evenings there would be 1920s murder mystery parties or parlour games or vintage-themed entertainment. On the final evening, guests would perform a finale of a medley of songs they had been rehearsing from day one. Very empowering. Dominique could see this.

All those years of taking Daphne to the West End theatres, ever since she could sit up and watch a show. All those songs and plays they had watched and listened to together. Now they could be on stage. Together. Nothing too incredible – she had used to sing before it all got put away for the corporate life.

She could see herself as Maria doing "Tonight" from *West Side Story*. She would wow, even astound (was wow of greater intensity than astound?) the audience. She'd make those dads and sons well up. Why not?

Ooh! She started raiding her wardrobe to find out what could she possibly wear to the 1920s Speakeasy. She had a child with her so it had to be understated and cool not risqué. What was even risqué these days? She was totally out of touch with what was current.

She would get hold of Lucy who had at least five figures of Twitter followers and probably tweeted five hundred times an hour, faster than you could say salted caramel Primo-sized skinny organic soy latte. Lucy would probably have the entire kit ready.

And Daphne? There was nothing that she could not

wear. She was at that awkward age when she didn't know if she was an old lady or a child. She was into The League of Seven series by the YA author Alan Gratz where seven young heroes had to save humanity from giant monsters. She was also keen on traditional crafts like knitting and baking. Watching an old episode of Poirot had got her into vintage. That was no longer an adjective, darling, it was a noun.

When she got back home she would go full force into shopping for an investment property. She already had all the Mulberry bags one needed, ie. one. She wasn't one of those women with a bank account that never dried up, who blew it all on bags, shoes and cars.

A flat or an apartment was a cash cow. She would do James proud. He'd married her because she was good with her money, his money, their money.

Finding common ground with Daphne was important for Dominique. They hadn't done anything together for a long time. Like James she worked long hours. She had been acting like a man in lipstick and a skirt. Feminine feminist femster.

How fortunate that she had chosen the start of the summer holidays. Should it not be called an advance, not a retreat?

Dominique had her heart set on "Tonight" from *West Side Story* for the final night revue. Pierre, vocal coach to both Dominique and Daphne, half an hour every day for the week, said no. How did he put it?

'It is for a young girl. You need a song that's for a jaded, woman who is full of regrets, who is and may be past it.'

'What?' Dominique was speechless, but she accepted "I don't know how to love him", Mary Magdalen's song in *Jesus*

Christ Superstar. Mind you, if that wasn't a slap in the face she didn't know what was.

He did preface his supposedly delicately put opinion with 'Not meaning to sound rude,' but, in Dominique's books, anybody who said that was about to be very rude indeed.

Pierre was French Canadian from Montreal. A top coach, Pierre had turned Hollywood clothes-horses into Fred Astaire and Ginger Rogers, from Broadway to Birmingham.

He gave her a flyer which listed the places or clubs doing open mic sessions that she could attend in the next month. She and Daphne could go together to follow up on the great work they'd have done bonding during the week. Some were over-18 only though.

Her heart fluttered at the thought of flapper dresses, fringes, tassels, fezs, candlelit tables, mob bosses, cigars, intimate yet raucous music. Gin? Of course. Cocktails, yes. Chinese underworld, divine. Descending staircases through unmarked doors in Limehouse or Wapping. Thanks to Lucy she could even dream in hashtags. Words were a waste.

Pierre had encouraged Daphne to perform "There is a Castle in the Sky" from *Les Misérables*, a young girl's song, of course he would suggest that. Or even "Tonight" from *West Side Story* at which point Dominique simply had to step in and disagree openly. That was her song, she chose it, and he could not give it to someone else, especially not Daphne.

'Why not,' he said.

'Because I am her mum and I said no.'

To all this Daphne simply rolled her eyes, something she was quite good at doing, having practised it since she was born.

'I thought this was a parent-child bonding week,' said Dominique.

To which he replied, 'how are you bonding?'

'We are sharing the experience of performing.'

'But seriously, how is that bonding if you do not wish her to take a song and run with it?'

'*FFS*', Dominique said under her breath. 'Daphne can have the final say,' said Pierre. 'This is ridiculous.'

For the first time Dominique was jealous of her daughter. How could she be? She felt a bit guilty, perhaps. Guilty that she didn't know which was worse – suffering the shock of James's death AND finding out he had all these hidden assets in a mysterious private offshore company by the name of *Achara* - or being termed past it by a vocal coach?

If only he knew, before Pierre was born, Dominique had been in an acid grunge band in her Uni days. She was rocking it now! She could do more than sing. She'd like to have seen Pierre play a single note on the bass.

First undesired effect — jealousy.

Second — shift in perspective. When she was indeed young, she'd pursued nothing more than her career, she was a lawyer, a wife, a mother. Not a note sung, a string plucked. How many lives were we to live in a single life? Music had ceased to exist once she qualified as a lawyer. It was a profession. It was not like being a car mechanic where you had the evenings left for carousing and messing about in a band in some rented garage space. The profession was all-consuming and you couldn't go for it half-arsed.

Third undesired effect — strong urge to fancy someone and she didn't mean all the dads at the bonding session. Amazing what aphrodisiacs massages, yoga, karaoke, walking in the countryside, cycling, games, teamwork, quizzes were – who would have thought it? Bonding exercises. 'Bonding, darling, not bondage,' she remembered telling Lucy before her phone was confiscated. 'Phones. Tablets. They are the chisel that breaks the family,' said Pierre to those (parent or children) who did not abide by the rules. 'The thin end of wedge.'

Then there was the organic food, vegan, zero alcohol craft beer, gluten free, halal, dairy free – any thing that could be catered for was catered for.

But not a drop of alcohol, and no nasty things like Costa, Harvester, Greggs, Sweet n Treats newsagents or Tesco Extra, Krispy Kreme or anywhere that would tempt you away from the straight and narrow. And this was in the nearest village three miles away.

There were only useless shops selling farming parts and medical aid. A week of indulgences; massages, carers, coaches, singing. For normal people worried about paying the gas bill, this kind of retreat was on the other side of winning the lottery.

Even in a week Dominique felt she was turning into her younger self. It might have been "that time of life", it might have been the week of indulgence itself, or it might even have been James's death being a source of rejuvenation.

She was slimmer, had glowing skin and thicker hair. Thanks to the new Energy Booster Shots craze, REVIV's certified medical staff would travel anywhere you said and injected into you B12, Slimboost, glutathione and CoQ10+.

When she was at her most exhausted, she had the Royal Flush Deluxe for £349, the Rolls Royce of IV therapy. Ultra-viv, Megaboost and Vitaglow, in 2 litres of fluid of vitamins, antioxidants, minerals, electrolytes and high dosage glutathione.

That was an unexpected digression. She was having a second wind, she was discovering herself, not her daughter.

A child was naturally on the path of discovery anyway, but a middle-class middle-aged woman?

They *were* both rabbits in the pen, but she was the rabbit that had got out. Daphne was still in the pen. That would come. It was a matter of time. Most rabbits got out of the pen, the others stayed there until they died.

Fourth undesirable effect – outfit or wardrobe crises. Like, every day. Dominique did not like to choose outfits. It was much easier at work. You wore work outfits which looked similar or the same. Summer and winter were different versions of the same thing. Dominique did not like the outfit that the wardrobe mistress Roisin chose for her song, "I don't know how to love him".

'Well, I don't know how to love the outfit,' she said. 'What makes you think that I'm going to wear a veil and a navy blue cloak like some frumpy dumpy old Albanian beggar?'

'Actually she was Jewish, not Albanian,' corrected Roisin, 'and she was not old, she was a prostitute. She might even have been young.'

'Great! Yes, I know,' she replied impatiently, 'but I said *like* some Albanian, not that she *was* or I *am* Albanian.'

'That is the costume for Mary Magdalen.'

I am being bullied into this, first the song, now the costume, she thought. She had been eyeing up proper costumes, waif-like from Les Misérables. She wasn't doing all this organic low carb diet, HIIT cardio and yoga just to wear a veiled cloak on what would be her opening night. It should be called her closing night.

During these minutes, hours, days of self-transformation, her own house was being transformed by Andreia. Property agents with listings which might interest her would also be contacting her. There was some kind of Grade II-listed cottage in Maida Vale she was toying with. That or a swanky flat in Southwark for rental investment.

The cottage was just a fanciable fancy. There was still the house in France which they went to every year. That needed renovation. She didn't spend too long thinking about these properties. You had only your mind to consult with when there was no wifi. You didn't need WiFi if you didn't have a phone. QED.

The CEO had addressed them on day two. Petronella van der Waal, a petite brunette in a grey hoodie, said,

'I was just like you when I realised I did not know my own daughter. I did not know my son either but that is another story. I was working 60 hour weeks in as a TV exec in Southwark. I was totally lost one day and woke up not knowing even who I was. I realised my passion is really in my family and in showbiz. Somehow I had to find a special way to unite the two and that is how Kalliope Epic Musical Theatre Workshop and Retreat was born.

It's really inspired by a play Tales of Olympus. Kalliope, the goddess of eloquence and epic poetry, also known as the goddess of all Muses, descends from the mountaintop to enlist the help of an 11-year-old mortal, Jason. But does Jason have the guts to overcome his stagefright and become the next bard?

When I started this company, there were only four families interested. They were all my friends who needed this, you know, this intense, meaningful family time. And as you know, music naturally brings people together. It's something we already share. And we don't even need to be musical or play an instrument. We just want to spend time with our children. Most dads, let's face it, are not theatre ticket buyers. They have no idea about any songs outside of We Will Rock You. But eventually that changed and...'

Dominique lost interest in the marketing spiel. She'd heard it and knew what was coming. Some discount off the next course, or that loyalty thing where you had to give a friend's email address and receive a gift...

Zzzzz.

Without WiFi or her phone, her mind drifted. The flyer in her hand drew her in. Squinting at it, she read about the speakeasy bars. Chicago cabaret numbers she would be good at. She even had a black glitter clip-on baby top hat. She wasn't going to be belting out show tunes dressed as a nun-cum-beggar prostitute.

Daphne could do drama on her own in school. This week was not about herself, it was about them. She didn't mind the get-up, she would be a sport for the family. Was this what they called playing the merry widow? Or a midult? A merry window into the midlife?

18

PHOEBE

PHOEBE HAD SUDDENLY BECOME aware that being pregnant was like joining some kind of cult. That's why there were jokes about mumzillas, slummy mummies and so on. There was a set of rules of what you could or could not do now that you were pregnant.

For example, riding on the Norrie would probably be considered a no-no unless you were a local. Why? Because the locals took risks no white person would take unless the white person was under the influence of alcohol, drugs or madness. If a white person rode around on a 125cc moped in an Asian city but would not consider riding on a bicycle in central London - that was just risk assessment.

Even the Norrie had a system of rules that it followed, anarchic though they might be. No anarchy was completely without rules. The Norrie was the casual name for the Bamboo Train.

The local mode of transport was unique, cutting through the middle of lush countryside. It was a crude small motorised platform following a narrow gauge railway that linked Battambang with Phnom Penh. Phoebe thought the centre of gravity was so low it gave you an alarming sense of speed when, actually, it was only travelling at a measly 15 km/h.

And the noise was so loud you had to travel with ear plugs. Normally none of these discomforts would have affected her decision. But discomforts had turned into plain risks. What about the baby? How would this impact on the baby?

Every thought was followed by the mental postscript, 'the baby'. Not what she or would Greg think. No one and nothing else mattered other than this unnamed person called 'the baby'.

Suddenly she saw her phone flashing and felt its vibration. It was her mother. When she did not answer, her mother rang again. She picked it up but the Norrie braked suddenly.

The jolt made her lose balance and her phone too, almost. She held tightly with her one free hand, realising it was not safe. 'Mum, I can't talk,' she shouted. 'No. I can't. I am on a train'.

'Why you can't talk when you are on train?' her mum shouted back.

She decided to disconnect. She couldn't help being rude.

Phoebe knew she had turned into someone else. The transformation was not yet complete, would never be. Parenthood. The great leveller, a burden spared from the childless.

When the journey was over, she found a quiet WiFi spot under a shop canopy where she could Skype her mother back.

'The passenger crew list is out,' said her mother. 'Did you see news?'

'No. No I did not.'

'There were 4 of them. Two young Thai women and one other Englishman. All identified already. And Greg, the only survivor. There are photos, if you want to see the article. I send you link later.'

Phoebe didn't answer because her jaw was clenched. She started imagining who these women were, what they looked like. She could not help thinking that one of these women was Greg's squeeze.

He always *had* had an eye for the ladies. It was not impossible. Now that she had to be a parent to him too, she had to put the thought — no, her suspicion — aside. He could not provide any support to her when he needed support himself.

'OK, I see you not replying,' Phoebe's mother went on, 'so you must be busy. What about maternity clothes? Are you buying them there? Very cheap there compared with London.'

'Yes, mum. Yes.' She came to her senses as soon as her mother changed the subject.

'In Phnom Penh there's a big market. I am going there with Trish now. That's why I was on the Norrie train when you called.'

'OK I let you go.'

'OK. Bye.'

On the way to Central Market Trish asked Phoebe, how she was feeling. Phoebe said she was fine; once she'd had a big breakfast, she did not feel sick at all. They passed the triangular green in the centre of Road No 3. There were kiosks, stalls, mopeds, even a French style statue and fountain.

You wouldn't know that Battambang was founded in the eleventh century. There were no traces of the Khmer Empire left except for glint of distant temple spires. French colonial architecture from the turn of the nineteenth century decorated the grand tree-lined avenues.

Locals sat on the long pointed narrowboats in the Sangkae River, eventually connecting to Tonle Sap Lake. Phoebe and Trish observed floating villages and protected wetland in the Sangkae.

'It's like a dream,' Phoebe said.

'What is?' said Trish.

'It is. This whole Greg thing. I won't use the word nightmare. People describe accidentally smearing their phone screen with wasabi as a nightmare. But I *am* actually living a nightmare. They have identified the passengers on the boat. Two were Thai women. You know what that means!'

'Don't be silly. Do you really think that he-? '

'Yes I do.' her voice was cold, flat. 'It's just my instincts, I know. But as he is not well at the moment, I can hardly confront him now. If it *is* true and even if he does remember all about it, he is bound to deny it.'

'Don't you trust him?'

'I did but now I'm not so sure. How can you be sure?'

'Probably nothing happened. Maybe they were working on the boat too. Don't be racist. You're Asian yourself!'

'No. It's not that. I'm fed up and frustrated with not knowing enough about him even though I thought I did.'

'He will get better. He will be thrilled when the baby comes. Everything will come back to him, then, I bet.'

Everything when *the baby comes, when the baby comes.* Phoebe was sick of hearing it, especially when she caught herself saying it too. Like all this was not worth thinking about. You didn't think of the present, what you had, but only of the future, what you didn't have.

She remembered that dream-like nightmare state described in 'The Lover' by Marguerite Duras. She had re-

read it before they travelled abroad a year ago. The beauty of the landscape and the people. Everyone and everything was thin and beautiful.

It was so French, romantic and unrecognisable from what she was living today. She imagined herself a latter-day Jane March, a waif with a bob hairstyle and man's shoes. Slim and slight. In fact she was just a middle-aged mum with a ponytail and men's hiking shoes.

There was no point in discussing all that with Trish as she was young and would have no valid insight into the matter, the matter that was growing inside her, anyway.

Back in Phsar Bocung Chhoek Market looking for vegetables, seeing names and signboards everywhere reminded Phoebe that she would very much like to have a Cambodian name for the baby. After all it was conceived here.

Seems odd there was always someone else. Even when she was in the toilet or anywhere alone with her own thoughts, there was someone else there all the time. A ghostly presence, made even more spectral because it was a part of her, inside her.

If it was a girl, she'd like Jorani or Rangsei; who wouldn't love a name that meant radiant jewel or one meaning ray of light? If it was a boy, he would be Charya, meaning of good character. Secretly, she would prefer a girl.

AT BANGKOK SUVARNABHUMI INTERNATIONAL, Phoebe and Greg were seated on the TG910, Phoebe in the window seat. It was already 0055H but the plane was still taxiing on the runway though they were supposed to be taking off now.

The fasten seatbelt signs had just donked on. She was

half asleep as it was way past her bedtime in her current state. Even so, she could not settle until the plane took off because that was the way she was.

She thought about Trish, sad that she had to up and leave her friend and Cambodia so suddenly. She had only just gotten used to the pitch-thick syrupy coffee.

There was not enough leg room on Thai Airways especially not for itching legs. She disliked flying. She had only ever flown because she'd wanted to volunteer abroad and live cheaply. She was only a spoilt lonely Londoner. They both were.

There had not been an ounce of charity or generosity in them before they went to Cambodia. It was like they were saving their human kindness only for those who were as far from home as possible.

She could not stop thinking of the two Thai girls who'd perished on the yacht. From just being a slightly annoying husband, just like anyone's husband, Greg had become a stranger. Could she trust him?

She looked over at him and she stopped her tears by blinking rapidly and looking away, through the cabin window. Complete strangers gave him a few hard, or pitiful glances before quickly looking away to make it less obvious.

The truth about volunteering was that it did not equip you with any more skills than you already had, especially with regards to empathy for your own loved ones. He would be well soon, she reminded herself.

He was not even in a wheelchair. He was burned, reconstructed and could not speak properly, that was all. All the broken bones had almost healed. A bit of hydrotherapy and physio and he would be back to his usual self.

How much easier it was volunteering for someone else, for charity, for climbing Mount Everest, for so-and-so, for people you'd never met and would never meet again, ever. You only needed to appeal to someone's weakness and sympathy for your cause, whatever it was.

She noticed herself frowning at her reflection in the porthole window during take-off.

In the terminal, she'd typed into her blog on her tablet her very last Cambodia post, "Goodbye Battambang". Just after that she'd rolled on her oh-so-flattering anti-DVT flight socks.

And now her legs were itching like crazy. It was the last place on earth she was expecting it. What she was really itching for was the truth. The only way to the truth was to strip him. Crude, but it would work.

She did not know how this could be done as he seemed quite capable of dressing and washing himself. The safest time would be when he was asleep. Fewer than 24 hours had passed since they'd left hospital. Soon they would be sharing a bedroom and even a bed back in London.

The thought was frightening as she did not know this man. What if he sleepwalked or hurt her because he could not remember her? She had to make sure no harm came to the unborn child, and if that went well, the born child too.

Ironically, she had volunteered to gain confidence. She was in a position of power now, caring for herself, her crippled husband and her unborn child. Yet how come she felt weak? The moment she'd laid eyes on him there was a shift in her perception, like when a meal which you were about to eat had a fly land on it, instantly changing your view of the meal from edible to soiled.

More importantly, she had to look up how to get him classified as disabled on the NHS. She would use the hospital file and the letters from the consultants, that was all she could go by. She would take them to the GP as soon as they arrived back in London.

The A380 aircraft flew over Kazakhstan. Only then did Phoebe manage to speak to Greg. It seemed time. They were in Europe now. The time zone and the continent.

'Greg?' her voice wavered.

'Yes?' he exploded.

She knew better than to ask him any more. She wanted to but was aware that he could not really speak with the whole aircraft hearing him, including the flight deck. She squeezed his hand instead.

It felt like a rubber glove for doing the washing up.

SHE BIT HER NAILS on the ride home. Their arrival time in Heathrow was 0715. Phoebe had had to take into account the prerequisite 2-and-a-quarter hours - one hour for immigration and customs plus the hour and fifteen minute drive - before informing her mother of their ETA.

Phoebe did not get the "pleasure" of hearing her say 'this is what you get when you go on a gap year' at the airport itself because her mother did not meet them at Heathrow. Phoebe had no SIM on her card that worked in the UK any more.

She had no income and no accommodation. Having intended to give notice to the tenants in their Balham flat and turf them out sooner than planned, she now considered that this would be unwise.

She knew it was selfish of her because she'd rather have a break clause with her mother than with her tenants. She swallowed her pride. And now she would find herself back in Bishops Road, Fulham, where she grew up, breaking every clause there was to be broken, except now, she was back with her dependents. This was a welcome change. And at age 41.

'This is the problem,' her father Robert had once said to Phoebe, not even that long ago. 'You make all this money but the children are penniless.' Asians felt you could say anything to their children. Shut up. Be resilient. Deserve it. Go. Go. Cry. Scream. Run to your room.

Phoebe took a deep breath. She exhaled slowly, through her mouth. The Uber driver stopped outside the double-fronted three-bedroom end terrace house in Fulham. Her childhood home.

There was as usual no parking space in that particular area of Fulham, with its tight roads and bumper to bumper parallel parking. The driver had to half block the road so that they could unload the luggage. There were a suitcase and a backpack each.

They didn't need to find cash to pay the driver, she thought with relief as payment would be deducted from her mother's card.

Two window bays in perfect symmetry protruded from each side of the front door. A Christopher Wray lantern hung above the entrance door, and though Phoebe had liked to check for dead insects and cobwebs since she was a child, to her disappointment there were none.

Even the insects did not want to come to Fulham. She knew the lantern was Christopher Wray because her mother kept repeating the name every week for about three weeks: *I've got to go back to Christopher Wray* or *I've got to ring Christopher Wray*. Or *I wonder if Christopher Wray is open yet.* Phoebe did not know who Christopher Wray was until she was an adult, but for her Balham flat she knew she wanted Ikea lighting, frames from Wilko, trays from

Paperchase and nothing else that reminded her of her childhood home.

White rambling 'Claire Austin' English roses clung onto the porch arches over the entrance doorway like round puff pastry shells. When she saw the rambling rose she remembered that it was July. Her heart raced.

When in Asia she'd been unaware of the passage of time because there were no seasons, or rather, all 4 came every day– hot, hotter, hottest, and rainy.

She saw the stone steps leading up to the front door. As a child she had never even sat on them or played on them.

The step nosing of the Victorian house had worn down to a shallower, less defined profile, like icing on a cake sagging at the edges from heat. This was Fulham. You did not play on the streets or at the front door unless you were an urchin waiting to be run over.

She paused to admire how well-kept the house had been while she was away. There were new white plantation shutters on every front window, *de rigueur* in any self-respecting London home, no doubt. The front had been painted some Farrow and Ball standard, but classy, grey.

The wonderful thing about Fulham was that it never really changed. It changed but never changed. You could still walk to Fulham Broadway or Parsons Green tube.

There were still exceptional schools in the area, both fee-paying like Phoebe's had been, and London Borough of Hammersmith and Fulham schools. The grey paint had been Sloane palette uniform since a few hundred years ago. It was just new grey paint.

There was now an award-winning gastro pub at the end of the road called the Mitre. The pub had always been there since Fulham existed. Just the gastro bit was new.

Phoebe would never find it hard to slot back into her old

way of life. Home was somewhere that bugged you in a way that felt familiar.

Balham had almost been a holiday. There was nothing familiar about this house. Cambodia was not a holiday. It was more like work. Every day, all that struggle with the language the moment you left the apartment, every meal strange and new, including fried bugs.

She recalled growing up in this comfortably numb London house, a memory tainted by the premature death of her sister Bethany from heart failure at only 31.

She died after contracting Lupus. Latin for wolf. The imagery, the very mention of the word 'wolf' still conjured nightmarish terror to Phoebe. It had always been taboo to even mention the word in the household due to its connotations, the fairytales, old wives' tales, wolf at the door, the big bad wolf, wolf in sheep's clothing and now, Bethany too.

The thirteenth century physician Rogerius, had named it because of the disease's most horrific symptom; erosive facial lesions that were reminiscent of a wolf's bite.

There were only sad memories in this house that was so perfectly kept and decorated. She remembered nannies, nursery, school, piano lessons, eventual escape to Uni, and Bethany's passing.

Someone had departed but someone else was arriving, she rubbed her swollen belly. Her heart sank, and she sighed. Phoebe found the courage to push the black gloss-painted wrought iron gate open.

As a child it had towered over her. The fleur de lys spiked rails had imprisoned her in the garden with no hope of escape. Now she could see it was only about three-foot high. It could not possibly keep out any intruders, not even uninvited cats.

Eva opened the door and hugged her. 'Welcome back,

Feebs.' Her mother had tears in her eyes as she stepped back to check Phoebe's tummy bump.

'Ten weeks to go,' she said. 'I have the third trimester look.'

'Welcome home,' whispered Eva.

She hugged Greg without hesitation. It was not like she had not seen his disfigurement. Phoebe had sent her photos by Whatsapp. She just had not heard his voice. 'Eva,' he said, the sound loud and jarring as a wolfhound's bark.

They moved the luggage in. Greg limped in but Phoebe's mother either ignored it or didn't notice.

19

PRZEMEK

E HAD HANDED IN his final assignments to Kingston College. It was a cause for celebration and he would do this in style.

But first, a Sidecar. He'd always liked to make himself a quick one at home before venturing out. He'd have a meal, all old fashioned, 20s style, a cocktail, a clip or two on YouTube to get himself in the mood.

It was a warm July night. He'd make himself a Waldorf salad, watch Fletcher Henderson and his orchestra doing the Shanghai shuffle from 1924: Louis Armstrong was on cornet, you could hear he was going to be a big star one day.

He enjoyed the thrilling soar of the muted trumpets, the orchestral swells at the end and the tinny drums through-out, like the whirr of machines. The occasional stab of an oboe. It was fast-paced and slightly frenetic. This was as different as it could get from the irregular gurgling and clanking of central heating pipes and the sharp hissing of boilers.

The cheese was ready-grated and came in a plastic resealable bag from Marks and Spencer Food Hall. It was not authentic but if the taste could fool him, it would fool anybody. Andreia was out once again but no longer did he wait, worry or wonder.

It did not bother him any more that she was spending so much time on work or clients or fun — or all of the above. He had been spending all his waking moments on his studies too. All were all-consuming. That was the nature of consumption. There could only be more and never less.

He looked forward to Oysters Rockefeller at the unnamed Shanghai style speakeasy in Limehouse. They knew what he wanted, so he never ate until he was too full.

You entered through an unmarked door, down a steep wooden staircase with a single lightbulb. He'd found the place through hearsay, word of mouth recommendation. It was the best way. He got many jobs through word of mouth, and Andreia, whose words were as beautiful as her mouth.

The waiters were of all races, black, white, Hispanic and some even had pigtails, Manchu style. They were wearing the traditional starched white samfoo tops with frog buttons, mandarin collars and black satin trousers. And some kind of black Kungfu shoes, observed Przemek.

They hurried about, bearing trays of drink and food. Once inside the lobby, the music from the five-piece ensemble was deafening. It was den-like, dark, lit by candles and crystal chandeliers. The intoxicating smell of perfume, irises, orchids, and peonies filled the air.

In the old days before cigarettes were banned it would have been cigar smoke and, of course, in the even older days, the sweet stench of opium. Someone took his coat off him to store in the coat room. He was given a ticket. He swanned towards the central circular fountain, tier stood upon tier, tiled exquisitely in a Chinese design, decorated with a magnificent golden firebird at the pinnacle.

He entered the main club. It opened up before his eyes like Aladdin's cave.

Przemek had never really been anywhere, save Poland and England, but the world was right here, in Shanghai, Limehouse, London. Despite his enchanted state, he wondered where the pipework was laid for the fountain. It would be just a cold feed, no hot, if the mains pressure was sufficient. And where would the pump be in a totally subterranean internal space?

Once he had the skeletal map of the place clearly visualised, it was time to move on to the bar. He ordered what he had been waiting for – half-a-dozen Oysters Rockefeller — while he perched on the chrome and ostrich leather bar stool to admire the rattan ceiling fans and the ornately carved timber screens. They were probably made of some cheap pine stained dark. Or someone was breaking the law, if they were real mahogany. Antique screens were out of the question, even for a place like this.

Or perhaps they were real antiques – he could not tell in this dim lighting. Even so he would not be satisfied until he found out for himself. A delicate porcelain tray with scalloped gold edges was slid in front of him, complimentary roasted nuts.

The golden boy was proud, really in the moment and in the time. The band stopped playing and took a break.

'Hey. You've been here before?' A voice said from behind him.

He turned around. 'Yes,' he said.

It was a heavily made-up woman with the tiniest glittery top hat pinned to her waved dark hair.

Her jewellery looked expensive, maybe Art Deco. It all matched: teardrop earrings, necklace and bracelet. The stones were black, hexagonal and set in chrome like a machine. She looked like a middle-aged showgirl.

He had never seen her before. She was attractive but not obviously so.

'Mind if I sit here?' She gestured to the bar stool next to him. 'Waiter,' she called out, 'I'll have what he's having.' She turned to Przemek,

'Oysters! I love oysters! Would you share a bottle of Dom Perignon with me?'

'No, no. I'm fine. I will stick with my Sidecar.'

'Sidecar?' She repeated, as though he had said Zombiehands or something. 'That sounds fun. I'll have one with you.'

He noticed that her bracelet was actually a FitBit activity tracker. Was that what you would call a continuity — or maybe timeline — error? He wasn't sure. He had seen that kind of thing before on YouTube amateur films. Or films about films. 'The Making of the Titanic' and so on. Przemek was momentarily sidetracked.

'Sidecar.' Przemek explained. 'It's cognac, triple sec and lemon juice. That is the English version.'

'Oh yes? What other versions are there?'

'The original version. From Paris.'

'Fascinating! You're a walking Wikipedia!'

'Thank you.'

'And may I ask where are you from?'

'You may ask, yes.'

'And?' She persisted. 'Where are you from?'

'I am from Poland.'

'You are a prince or something.'

Przemek laughed, dare he say it, too heartily. His ears burned. He couldn't even look at her. And had the lady not bought him another Sidecar he would have got up.

There was something about her that looked familiar and he could not put his finger on it. There must be a reason why he wanted to get up. He wanted to. He really did. But he could not think why. And she seemed harmless enough, just wanting a chat.

Another dish of roasted nuts slid from one end of the bar to where they were sitting.

'I am sure you get people saying you look like Leonardo di Caprio, you know the film? The Great Gatsby.'

'No,' he lied. 'No. No one ever said that.'

'Your English is very good,' she said draining her Sidecar.

'Thank you.' *I learnt it from YouTube* he wanted to say but stopped himself. It was not true anyway.

Suddenly, the lady slid all the oysters down her throat. 'It's my turn!'

Before he could ask what she meant, to his astonishment, the lady jumped off the stool and walked onto the stage and into the limelight.

20

DOMINIQUE

S EEING THE EMAIL FROM Andreia brought dread to her face. Each change was chargeable and she had only just paid the last invoice.

The jobs were still not finished though she did say it would be very soon. Andreia would be here in half-an-hour and she had to go through the agenda for the meeting.

She was still living in a building site. She was fed up that Andreia was taking so long, despite her being away for a whole week to give her free rein of the entire property. Now she was back, the house looked the same.

Dominique went through the list of changes even though she was feeling very rough from having been out last night. When she'd done "Stormy Weather" on stage, that Leonardo guy had looked impressed.

He hadn't taken his eyes off her once. There was no rejuvenating spa in this world which could compete with knowing someone wasn't able to take his eyes off you.

Her voice was clear, moving, *young*. None of that nonstop vibrato they did on that godawful X factor — or any of that modern oversinging with added and meaningless orgasmic croaks. Hers was an old-fashioned voice, one that spoke rather than sang. Who knew? She'd surprised herself too!

All those years she'd given to the corporate world and to family life. Not a note. When she'd come off stage, she noticed that he was gone. Fans had to leave a gig. And maybe she would not see him again. She did not know his name and the place didn't even have one.

It was getting hard to focus. Andreia was writing really long emails and they were not divided into point form, because she was French-speaking, Dominique supposed. They just could not keep it brief.

And Dominique had not made some of those changes, the lights which she'd wanted were not available Andreia said, and so some even more expensive light fittings had been specified for her approval.

Twenty-two thousand for the chandelier. That just seemed fair but unfair at the same time. Some changes had been approved from before but were mentioned again.

Some redundant gas pipes were found. They had to be cut off but she had to get them tested first by the boiler engineer. The boiler had already been moved and survived.

Now they were sourcing a limescale inhibitor or remover or a water softener – which would Dominique prefer? Couldn't Andreia make an informed decision and inform her? She really needed this place finished so that she could get back to life and then start looking for work or new properties.

The week before she'd gone away, she'd given Andreia the brochure for a flat she was toying with in Southwark. She seemed keen enough now, anyway. Two bedrooms, needed total gutting, had a side garage — very unusual in flats so central to the city.

She wanted to turn the garage into a bedroom or move the kitchen into there, so she asked if Andreia would help her put in the application to Southwark council, get the plans done and so on, no extension, just internal alterations. 'Anyway, she had only just made the offer so it was still early days, she typed.

Dominique went to her coffee machine. She needed a coffee, just thinking about that Southwark flat gave her the heebie jeebies.

She was beside herself with excitement, but had to keep cool because she didn't want Andreia to see she was excited and quote her high. She had to play hard to get. It was called anti-flirting. If they knew you were desperate, they charged more.

She also had to keep her excitement from Daphne, for a quite different reason. She did not want her daughter to grow up with any sense of entitlement, thinking that assets like these would drop into her lap like plums from a tree.

Dominique had learned from her own upbringing. It sounded good. A holiday home in France. Parents whose conversation revolved around antiques and theatre-theatre, the kind without singing and the new red quinoa in Waitrose. Wine from her mum's friend's chateau vineyard. All that could really screw you up.

Dominique dressed up, gulped cocktails and slurped oysters but she was only entertaining herself, a rebellion against her own sensibilities.

The number of times she had already had to do that for corporate events, Christmas parties, functions. They had big budgets too. Nobody had just two cocktails a night. She laughed at the memory of it. They were good days. She did not hate that world she had left. It was just that better days were coming. And how.

Hiring her interior designer was no big deal. The business of law was hard, but not that hard. She was not a scaffolder or a roofer, spitting and wiping her chin with her sleeves.

All she'd done was carry on her family tradition. From making coffee to running million pound cases, it was all about strategy.

~

DOMINIQUE LEARNED FROM WORKING with financiers, not from her parents, that closed-end funds were long-term investments of at least five years, offering big returns and high yields while keeping her assets safe.

She already had her Crowmobile and her getting-to-High-Street-Kensington-Waitrose silver Merc. And anyway, not exactly Ferraris or Porsches. And how many women had you seen driving those? It was all unctuous young Arabs or soft-looking elderly white men with tans.

Tim Fazackerly, though, reckoned that the brochure was "bollocks". As her estate agent, or sales negotiator as they liked to call themselves, he did say property was the game for long-term high yields.

That was why she had decided to go through with the deal with that flat in Southwark. She would be paying cash; it would not require a mortgage. That vineyard in France though...

Dominique was making plans to visit France again. That was what happened when you had property around the world. Instead of holidays you visited your properties and paid some attention to them even if it was only to make sure they were still there.

If you could not make sure they were still there yourself,

you hired people who could do this, property managers/consultants, personal assistants, antique dealers, whatever fancy names they liked to call themselves. She'd keep an eye on them and they'd keep an eye on your assets.

The person she had had an eye on for some time was Andreia. She did not know anyone more hardworking or trustworthy than Andreia and already she had quite a few recommendations and larger contracts through Dominique.

Andreia was still young, just starting out and did not have the usual excuses of too many jobs, children or illness or children's illnesses. She had nothing to take away her time, focus and drive from answering Dominique's emails, calls and Whatsapps 24/7.

Dominique had been a lawyer and she'd had her own clients before, so she knew that clients only did it to test you. Those who passed the test naturally would be able to handle the assault of communication, now that she was a client herself. She had given Andreia the responsibility of following up the leads which Dominique had dangled in front of her.

Andreia was running at least four West End interior design contracts, a few more Holland Park homes and so forth. She could hardly keep track of Andreia's portfolio when she had to keep track of her own.

She had her diary in front of her with the school term dates, her wallet with all the cards protruding. Her notebook, pen and mouse were ready.

She was fully-equipped. Lorraine had kept several tabs open for her to look at. She felt like she'd been offered multiple menus in a restaurant. The choice was immense, but Lorraine wanted Dominique to look through the options.

She was in the middle of scrolling for flights that

Lorraine had pre-highlighted on the Easyjet bookings page, when an email came in from her solicitor. She saw the subject heading and minimised the email browser. She was sure all that stuff was well under way.

The nice thing about France was being able to leave at anytime and not worry about accommodation. She always stayed at her own villa.

The solicitor was Henry Tummings and with a name like that you'd assume quite a large midriff from all those lunches and launches. The firm was based in Pimlico. She made an appointment with him as soon as she could after she'd booked flights to Bordeaux for Andreia, Daphne and herself. Poor Daphne. She had complained on so many occasions about to going to France and each time she thought it would be last time.

And the next time would be the first time she could bring a friend. Hashtag bring a friend, said Daphne. Hashtag why even. Her daughter had turned into some Snapchatter who spoke another language, hashtaguese, a sardonic lingo peppered with grim sarcasm. This must be what the current generation was like. Sometimes Dominique laughed but mostly her daughter's hashtags fell on deaf ears or, as her daughter would say it, deaf yeahs. Mos def.

SHE DROVE TO PIMLICO the next day.

'So what is so important that you could not say to me on email,' she said to him. 'You know I do not like coming in if I don't have to.'

'Well, it's about the Will.'

'I know it is. What about it? I thought it was all in hand'.

'It is complicated.'

'What is?'

'The Will.'

'Well, please get on with it.'

'James has more assets than originally perceived.' He took out a sheaf of papers, but Dominique was not threatened by pieces of paper, she was a lawyer herself.

'OK I am listening,' she said, not looking at the paper but at him.

'There is the villa in Surin, Phuket near a golf resort, only 5 minutes' drive to the beach. Pool, jacuzzi, fully landscaped garden. '

Dominique started to picture it and welcomed the villa like a prodigal daughter. Of course she would add the villa to the ever-growing list of properties that she was taking care of. Could she fit Thailand into this year's jam-packed travel and renovation itinerary? Could Andreia foreseeably take on another interior design contract a little further from home?

'Chanote title.'

'And what is that?' she said. 'Pardon my ignorance.'

'Not at all. How would you know? It's a Thai legal term.' Tummings picked up a sheet of paper, '"Freehold Title Deed (*Chanote* or Nor Sor 4). This type of title grants the holder of this document full rights over the land, to deal with or to use it to the exclusion of others"'. Thus, if you are planning to buy land in Thailand, this type of title deed is the best and most credible title deed to hold.'

'Is it vacant?'

'Yes. According to the estate agent, and I can give you his mobile if you want, only James used the place. It is not rented out.'

'Yes I will have the agent's number, no harm there. I will need access to the place anyway.'

'But six bedrooms?'

'Who—?'

'Your guess is as good as mine.'

'And what else, you said more assets than we knew about.'

'The yacht which you did already know about.'

'The insurance is taking care of that. It was destroyed in the storm.'

'There is the house in France.'

'We knew about that. Daphne and I are booked to go there during half-term.' Dominique did not mention Andreia. That had nothing to do with Henry Tummings.

'A vineyard in France. In Champagne.'

'A vineyard?'

'A vineyard, yes. Apparently James was investing in wine and bubbly too, the French agent said.'

'Understandably.' She said. So many agents, Dominique thought.

'The agent also said that it was James's retirement dream to learn winemaking.'

It was the first she'd heard of it. Dominique bit her lip, listening hard. She tried to imagine James surrounded by vines. He was at the peak of his earning capacity, the top of the ladder, the apex of his career, before the accident. How cruel life had been.

'Well there are people to hold your hand all the way now – whether you're hobbyists or serious businessmen. France now has specialist notaries fluent in English, Spanish and even Mandarin, to make vineyard purchases as painless as possible.' Tummings sounded like he'd been reading up on the subject.

'Sure,' she said. 'I don't doubt it.'

'Do you know anything about making champagne?'

'No. I have to say I only know how to consume it. Like most people.'

'He has bought it with someone else. So if you sell James's half, you may not need to learn winemaking and you can continue to consume it. Like most people.'

Dominique did not smile. He was not saying what he should be saying. It was just feeble chitchat.

'Coming back to the villa.'

'Yes?'

Henry started to shift about looking cagey. He read out from the sheaf of papers.

'It is one of Phuket's most luxurious, ultra-private estates nestled on the top of the island's chic Surin Beach hillside. The elegant six-bedroom pool villa, whose name is-' he pointed out the script font in the documents (Willā h̄æng khwām rạk læa s̄ængdæd) and then carried on reading, 'meaning "villa of love and sunshine". Views over the white sands of Surin Beach, also known as the Thai Riviera, with Phuket's most upscale international shopping, bistros and lounges-'

'Henry, don't get carried away.'

'Looking over the Andaman Sea. 16-metre long infinity edge pool—'

'Henry. Please. Can I stop you there? What are you trying to say?'

'What do you mean?'

'Henry, just cut to it. What is going on?'

'Well, this is it. Why I had to ask you to come in. James had it down that it should go to Achara.'

'And what or who is that?'

'I do not know, really. It is a company we are looking

into. As the executioners of his Will we are in the process of finding out now through another of our departments, Dominique. We have a team who solely track down beneficiaries of any Will we deal with.'

'Oh, well, it's all news to me!' Dominique kept her lawyer-face on, she'd had plenty of shocks back in the day. No reason to give anything away, just because she was on the other side of the desk now.

'Indeed.'

Henry found nothing more to say, though he was the type of solicitor to keep it to himself if even he *did* have something to say.

'What was the name again?'

He ignored her and continued to peer through his varifocals at some particularly interesting page from the stack of papers.

'And that was all it said in the documents?', she changed her question.

'Yes that was all, Dominique. I wish there was more. We are spending an awful lot of time on this case. It's complicated and it's a ...' he searched for the word but never completed the sentence.

'Mess,' she found herself muttering.

After about half a minute she gathered her thoughts.

'Who is the co-owner of the vineyard?'

Henry rustled again, riffling the pages of the sheaf of paper. 'Petitemort Holdings Ltd,' he said.

'And what might that be?'

'An offshore company registered in the British Virgin Islands. We can easily get more details. There is nothing for you to do there. They are directors in name only. They are not entitled to anything financial in the deeds.'

'What about Tom?'

'What about him?'

'Well? What's on the menu for him?'

'I am certain that there is nothing in James's Will for his brother. That is why I have not mentioned him.'

That explained the chill in the air that was always between James and his brother. That, and the fact that, after their father Jules had died, Tom had inherited the Sloane Square apartment and the cottage in Dorset. He had a few thousand in his account every month for him to 'live it up', as James said at the time. Whenever Dominique had asked how much it was, on the few occasions that they ever spoke, invariably about money, James had replied 'don't worry, it will never, ever run out.'

21

YOU

YOU STUDY EVERY ROOM. You remember so very much more than the day before on the plane.

Coming home has been helpful to you. Is there anything more disorienting than having a major accident and multiple injuries in a foreign country?

Each room is narrow but simply and smartly decorated in several shades of grey or bluish white as if time had stood still in a townhouse somewhere in Malmø or Uppsala. It has no past or present, just like you.

You go into the kitchen directly from the hall after the luggage is put down.

'Sit down, sit down,' says Eva. Lunch is lentil soup which Phoebe's mother has prepared and some designer Roman bread with organic butter. 'I thought you might be sick of Asian food. Try something new. OK? Must try.'

Phoebe is hungry. She eats fast. She is eating for one and a half.

'The bread is from Marks and Spencer's,' says Eva. 'They have such good choice these days.'

You already know that it's not what you had in mind

because of your false teeth. How you crunch through the thick crusts depends on how you can manage what feels like someone else's mouth. Beggars can not choose and you are now possibly more hideous than a Phnom Penh leper. You are a deformed beggar.

Through the dining room you can see that the front and back room have been knocked through to form one large long space. The floor is bare pine floorboards, sanded and polished to a satin clear sheen.

In the middle of the room is a Persian rug and the white fabric-covered sofas with turned wooden legs look very comfortable either side of it. A flat screen TV stands, like a wide, low scarecrow in the alcove of the front room, incongruous with the backdrop of Penguin Classics on alcove shelving with fluted classical detailing, a mini Greek temple of books.

Under the plantation shutters you first saw from outside are gothic flower patterned perforated sheet panels to hide the ugliness of radiators. Already you can tell there are many periods of art history and architectural languages being spoken in this Victorian terraced house in Fulham. Roman, Scandinavian, Greek, Penguin, Sloane, Gothic and lentil.

You surprise yourself with your own strength. Despite the limp, you take the luggage two at a time upstairs into what's going to be your bedroom.

Phoebe can not lift anything as she is pregnant. You understand that you are still a man and there are expectations of you. These traditions stick. After all, you are not in a wheelchair so you must still have some upper arm coordination and strength. Sympathy turns to pity with just one glance at you. Men lift luggage.

You feel lethargic and you are worn out by your illness

and the travel. You feel the urge to ask her mother to do the job of a bellboy but that really *would* be pushing it.

The bed is a small wrought iron double covered in a cream coloured waffle weave bedspread. Teddy bears, too many to count, sit on the bed lined up like a stepped city skyline, tall to small, like they're ready for their studio photoshoot.

The sheets are light grey. Everything is white or grey. But you remember the colours differently, you are glad you remember something, even if it's only that it was once not grey.

Each alcove has built-in wardrobes, also grey, with panelled doors and red and white padded gingham heart door charms suspended by silk ribbons. It's like a tweenie girl's room.

Phoebe stays downstairs chatting with her mother but within minutes you know it is bad news. She is weeping. She is trying to keep it down. The sound is like a tyre deflating or an out of tune violin which someone is trying to play softly because the player knows it is. You think it is probably about you. This is understandable. Either that or it is about the baby or the volunteering being cut short or some other crisis. Maybe it is her mother, upsetting her, as usual.

Whatever it is, it makes you feel exhausted. You see a mirror over the bedhead. It is in a beaten silver frame. You think it might be from Morocco. Your eyes really, really hurt from all these things you are looking at and feel you have to look at. They are bloodshot and you frighten yourself again because every time you see yourself you are reminded you've turned into a monster.

You think back on the nurse who was so kind to you.

You've already forgotten her name because you haven't heard it in the last few days.

All the memories from the hospital you are fighting so hard to retain are leaving. You can feel it. They are dimming like a torchlight with its battery running out. Phoebe is crying because you must have upset her.

Yet you can only lie down. You want not to look at a mirror ever again. Your head spins. You can not look at the bedroom any more.

You creep onto the cream-coloured waffle bedspread without taking off your trainers and you fall into a deep sleep. You dream of Thai food.

You HEAR THEM SHOUTING A WORD, repeatedly. You wake up. It takes you a few moments to realise. It's your name. You struggle to your feet.

YOUR FAVOURITE THING is exploring the house whenever the two women are out; taking walks, coffee, Pilates, going to Sainsbury's or Waitrose. They talk about it like a rotating programme of weekly activities. Why would you want to go with them anyway? Not only are you hideous, it's not like you are going to buy anything or do anything. They have organised physio for you and that is the only exercise you will get for now.

After your memory game every morning, you are left in the house alone for a short while. It was only about half an hour at first, but now they feel comfortable leaving you for up to two hours. You seem to know things when you sit for your 'tests' each morning. Every day you repeat your name and their names to them. They are your family and your first teachers. They have tested you on the items you read in the Guardian.

'So what did you read? Name three stories that stood out.'

They test you on what you've watched on telly and whether you can tell the whole story in a nutshell. You watch *Claimed and Shamed* and *Caught Red-handed* in the morning and in the afternoons you tend to go for *Flog It!* or *Pointless*. Idiots claiming for the loss of the phone they're calling on. Incompetent burglars grinning at CCTV cameras. Greedy relatives selling Granny's knick-knacks. Two blokes making fools of game show contestants. You narrate the gist of each one at your usual deafening volume.

'What are you waiting for?' They ask.

You are waiting for your NHS letter, you answer. It will take a while to get a consultant appointment, you know.

'Good,' they reply in unison. 'Improvement. Can increase number of questions,' says Eva to Phoebe. 'And the speed,' adds Phoebe.

'Yes, speed of asking you,' Eva agrees, looking at you.

As they are out again, you decide to explore the back bedroom on the first floor. There is no reason other than you feel most familiar with this floor. The top floor has been converted into a large master bedroom suite with dressing room and en suite bathroom for Eva and her husband.

You do not feel comfortable ascending the stairs to the top floor. You instinctively feel that it is out of bounds. So you stay on the first floor. Not just any of the first floor bedrooms but as you look towards the back of the house from the landing, it is the right hand side bedroom, the one with the chimney breast. It is now a spare bedroom-cum-office for Phoebe's dad.

You take in everything that is in the room. On other occasions you have explored the kitchen and utility room downstairs and they must be new renovations, because you do not find anything familiar about them at all.

The front room *is* familiar, which you realised on your first day here. However, today is your first time in this smaller back bedroom. The door is usually shut as it is Robert's home office. You know an important man like him needs an office everywhere. He already has an office in his office at his office, but he also *has* to have a room at home as an office.

Before you go into the room, you already know there will be two dark lime green alcove cupboards on either side of the chimney breast. You are half correct. When you open the room door, there are the alcove cupboards but they are not lime green. They are like everything in this house, a satin grey. You stare at them in disbelief. Without opening the doors, you already know there are four shelves in each, quite high ones.

When you open the cupboard door, you stagger. You are right. The cupboards are old and have been repainted several times so the mouldings of the panels on the cupboard doors have lost their crispness, they look like slightly melted icing on once sharp edges.

You run your fingers over the smooth grey satin finish of the paint. You notice that it is no longer in good condition now from all the opening and shutting. The paint has chipped where the roller ball catches the frame. You see glimpses of previous paint colours in layers, like some kind of gloss paint striptease. You see that amongst the three visible colours, one is the exact dark lime green you saw in your mind.

You are changed, confident. You do not really care what this room is or why you have seen it, but the appearance of your memory is becoming tangible, in layers, just like the paint.

You pick up a bronzed plaque on the middle shelf. It means nothing to you. It's just something to show that Robert attended a medical conference in Bali in 2016 sponsored by a drug company, BioCore Meditech. You just like the mirrored bronze finish of the plaque where you can see your hideous self, and your greasy fingerprints forming. You use your t-shirt to rub at and polish off the marks you have made. Holding just the wooden edge of the plaque, you manage to put it back without leaving any more fingerprints.

You sit in Rob's office chair, daydreaming. Nothing comes. You have to daydream, Phoebe has advised. You *do* try on a daily basis but nothing comes. Either you just can't let your imagination run free or you have none. Some people recover quickly, said Eva, some...

You lose your train of thought. It still happens suddenly, as though someone has pressed a remote control somewhere repeatedly and your brain is stuck between channels.

You hear a rattling sound, a clank. You try to remember what it is, exactly. Chains? Something to do with a buckle, you visualise a shiny rope and buckle, you half-remember a heavy metallic clunk. Where is this chain and buckle? You do not know but that's the image that appears.

You look at your watch to start timing the time involved in remembering what you are trying to remember. How long it takes the electrical message to go from the brain to your ears and back. It takes you another two seconds to remember that it is the sound of Eva and Phoebe coming back.

You panic slightly as you know you should not be here in Robert's office. The sound is the front door and its various locks to keep you in and away from mischief. When they are in, they do the whole thing again in reverse. The double locks, the keys that they hang up away from your sight, or keep in their nifty little handbags.

You rearrange yourself, quickly leave the home office-cum-spare bedroom and you shut the door very quietly. It is important in your memory game that you leave things as you find them. The fewer things you change or move, the fewer things you have to change or move back.

You stop at the landing again, where you saw your wedding photo in a frame earlier. You listen.

'You're going to need a bigger bag than that soon, Feebs,' you can hear Eva speak from the entrance hall downstairs. 'Yup,' says Phoebe, 'I am looking at different nappy changing bags, the kind that don't look like nappy changing bags. Yes, I saw a white Storksak one a while ago, not sure where, it was online.'

'Oh yes?' Eva then says something in Chinese and you cannot understand. She often does this. She switches to her Chinese mum mode the moment she comes indoors. Home. The safe place to speak your own language. Phoebe thinks it must have still been about the bag so she replies.

'It was on sale; I'll look for it again.'

In such a short time, Phoebe had changed from Gap year volunteer with no makeup, to a yummy mummy darling with tan Chelsea boots and several bags. She must always have been a yummy mummy. She has changed, but not really changed, just like Fulham. Your shift in weight on the landing makes it creak. They stop and listen.

'Greg? Greg?' you hear Phoebe call out. 'Is that you?'

You are feeling terribly guilty as you descend the stairs because you should not have been sitting in someone else's office. You feel so at home in an office, *anybody's* office.

But you must not do it again.

22

PHOEBE

I N HER OLD BEDROOM, now with a grown-up's double bed but still with her childhood teddy bears and soft toys, Phoebe lay in the dark.

Because she was jetlagged, she'd had dinner at five and gone to bed at seven by which time she could hardly keep her eyes open. It was still light.

It was dark when she woke up with the clock showing 4:23 am. At first she did not know where she was.

She grabbed one of her old teddies – Ridzwan. He was her favourite. He had gone grey now, just as an old teddy should. She went through a right on and political phase in her late childhood and most of her toys had had to be given new Muslim, Hindu or African names. It must have been some kind of Commonwealth perversion, the Judæo-Christian names from storybooks. Out they went.

She remembered her childhood with an inane pride. She had always been quietly rebellious but she did not actually know how to rebel, so ended up feeling repressed. Perhaps most people did.

In the darkness she used her fingertips to feel for the

smooth finish of Ridzwan's glass eyes, just as she did as a child, but now it brought no respite or enlightenment, as it used to.

Her heart was pounding. Her forehead and the back of her neck were covered in cold sweat, like she'd just been caught in some autumn drizzle. Her reluctance to strip search Greg had come from the knowledge that it was exactly what she felt she had to do.

As she had not seen him naked for months, how could she be totally certain they were her husband's genitalia? This was a weird question and after she had set up her phone on her mum's WiFi, she searched for an answer. There was no answer, or not one she was looking for. They were all links to send you off on an adventure to tell if your spouse was cheating, or, from the NHS, if your spouse had genital warts, or how to gently hint to your spouse that he or she had poor genital hygiene.

It was a terrible accident, she reminded herself. Phoebe's heart raced. Hadn't he been through enough? She was wide awake. 4:39 am. She put Ridzwan down on her pillow, as though it was his bed and he needed to sleep. She would wait until 5 am. If Greg was not still awake, she would pull his shorts down. She tested her iPhone's torch. On. Off. One. Two. Three. It worked.

She rubbed her protruding belly. It was kicking. It was a comforting feeling, like being massaged from the inside. She felt its foot move from top to bottom, side to side, in light flutters. Babies, when they started moving, kicked around midnight when you were trying to sleep or in the early hours, when you were still trying to sleep, she had read somewhere.

Unlike the baby, Greg was sleeping deeply. Yes, there were now three of them in this room. Even when she was testing the torch, he did not move at all. She was also in a child-like state again, napping while her father Robert came home from work. At 68, he was still working, as a consultant neurologist with UCL. His area of research was B cell Depletion Therapy in SLE. It became his obsession after Bethany passed away.

Phoebe knew he was a revered figure. It had been rammed down her throat growing up in this house. He was always in the limelight because he was the longtime chair of neurology at UCL; there was a room and a series of lectures named after him.

On the one occasion she attended a UCL function a few years ago, she and her mother were treated as dignitaries, VIPs. Specially decorated rooms, champagne reception and sushi, while everybody else had to make do with stale sandwiches. He'd tried to retire but couldn't cope with having nothing to do and anyway, he had to keep working to avoid his wife Eva. There was always tension in the house as Phoebe was growing up.

The previous evening, they had had dinner as a family for the first time in years, since well before Phoebe went to Cambodia. The accident had brought them together. They'd had a lovely chicken pie dinner that her mother had made two days earlier. There was salad from the fridge. They'd made small talk and by 7 pm Greg was also exhausted, though you couldn't tell from his face since it no longer had any expression at all.

She studied his face. It was less grotesque by torchlight. It looked like some sinewy and fatty piece of raw pork, marinated and ready to roast. Children had screamed when he'd arrived at Heathrow, scattering, running, burying their faces in their parents' thighs and crying.

In Cambodia there was less romanticised fear. They had

been through actual atrocities of war. Their own demons were much more fearsome. Their lives harder on every level. A deformed, disabled man was just that. They looked at him with wonder, curiosity, pity. Occasionally, she and Greg would even get a smile from a child, the friendly smile of empathy.

For his reconstructive surgery she would make an appointment with the GP to get a referral as soon as possible. After all, this was not like the old days when no one knew what you looked like before an accident. They had so many photographs of Greg before, too many, maybe thousands on his SD cards alone. A surgeon would be able to work from those easily.

She felt sorry for him and she was even afraid of him. How could this man cause her so much terror? She counted down from 10. When the analogue bedside clock read 5 o'clock, she yanked down his boxer shorts gently but quickly. She had to know. The time was now. She wanted to be neither right or wrong. She just had to know.

But her plan backfired. He screamed.

She was so shocked, she cried out herself. Her heart was pounding. When she looked at him in alarm, she thought he was still asleep. His eyes had been and were still shut.

Was he dreaming? He did not actually wake up at all. He screamed, 'don't kill me!' Don't kill me? His voice was as loud as a car crash, a deafening groan, then another cry, a long painful cry.

This time he did wake up. His fissured face was marked with tears, big streams of tears. He thrashed about. His tears wet Ridzwan and the pillow. She could feel his tears and snot flying off, like salt spray.

She saw the lights come on in the corridor outside from the gap under the door.

'What's going on, is everything OK?' it was Eva, who always slept lightly.

'He's had a bad dream, mum. He is OK, he is OK.' Phoebe found herself chanting meaninglessly, though it must have been true in some sense.

He calmed down, still moaning and weeping audibly, like a child after a nightmare. She stroked his head and what was left of his hairline gently. She did it so rhythmically it sent her back into her own sleep-wake state and she decided to leave the strip-search for another night. She must rest and not try again. What was he dreaming about?

'Don't kill me.' He'd begged in his pitiful voice.

THE SHIPMENT HAD ARRIVED from Battambang. It was fully insured. Phoebe knew that Greg's camera equipment was safe. His Fujifilm X-T2 Mirrorless digital camera with 18-55mm lens alone was worth £1,300. Not to mention the various lenses, wide angle telephoto, three tripods, tripics, filters, cases, lens hoods, accessories, memory cards, filter kits, grips and dollies. There was a second camera, a Canon XF100HD camcorder worth £1,400. Altogether there was £10,000 worth of equipment here.

If it could bring Greg back, then it was worth every penny. She handed him his favourite, the Fuji, but he did not even know where the on/off switch was. He carried it like a flowerpot. He studied the dials, the controls. He put it down and picked it up again, turning it this way and that, as if looking for something. So far he would not pass the test of Photography for Beginners.

'Let's put that down carefully. There's lots of other things we have to look at. We're doing this together, Greg, look,' she said, as though speaking to a child. He put it down again. 'It's like Christmas.' She felt sheepish as of course he knew what Christmas was, he could read, he could write, even do maths. He just could not remember himself or what had happened to him or any particular Christmases. 'Isn't it exciting?' She said in the dullest voice.

It might have been exciting, if you liked unwrapping presents, layer by layer. And Phoebe did not. Surprise now came with a sense of quiet doom.

Phoebe took out some photos and paintings in frames that Greg had taken, printed and framed very cheaply, or at a tiny fraction of what it would cost to get done here. A photo of ruins. A jungle. A well. Village children. He only did commercial work. He was not supposed to be artistic. 'A little cliché-d, but they were new and unclichéd at the time you took them,' she joked. She was trying too hard to be humorous, and she knew that he knew that she knew.

He did not smile. He did not appear very interested in any of it, his *own* photos, there was no glimmer of recognition or excitement for the life that was once his.

'Look, our wedding photos.'

'Yes.' Suddenly, his eyes widened. 'The suit. It's grey.'

'Yes.' She confirmed.

'I changed after the service?'

'No. We chose that one together.'

He frowned and looked away.

'What's wrong?' she asked.

He shook his head.

She picked up the photo of her sister and her when they were children which she'd taken all the way to Cambodia and back. She felt her throat tighten and tears forming. She turned the photo around and put it back in the box.

Greg and Bethany had both been working as video and

film editors through an agency in Hammersmith and they'd met in a BBC cutting room. They had a laugh and they'd got on well. Bethany had introduced Phoebe to Greg at an art fair one evening a few months later.

'It was a magical time,' Phoebe said to Greg. 'Working in the West End, in design, in the 1990s, Friday nights in the Dog and Duck followed by a Chinatown meal. Occasionally a drag show at Madame JoJo's when it was someone's birthday. Fabulous.'

He looked completely blank, like she was speaking Chinese. Next was a painting, an original by Leang Seckon, Cambodia's first contemporary artist. 'Now, this was your favourite painting,' she said. 'This would be worth quite a tidy sum now.'

She picked up one of the gallery's brochure cards out of the crate and read it aloud. 'He combines ancient Khmer narratives with modern-day concerns, such as rapid development, environmental degradation and Cambodia's violent past. He arrived in Phnom Penh in 1992 to enrol in a painting class at the Royal University of Fine Arts and since then has made multimedia work that draws heavily on personal experience. Having sold his first painting at the riverbank for \$350, his most valuable work is now being sold for \$20,000.'

Greg seemed to be listening. *We are living in parallel universes,* Phoebe thought. They had spent £2,000 on two medium-sized originals. She would not mind having them valued and selling them as she didn't want to be reminded of that period.

She made a mental note to look up art galleries specialising in contemporary Asian Art. She would need to hire some technician to hack into and unlock the passwords of his Mac and MacBook. At one point he had been a total whizz at photo and video editing providing e-commerce visuals when he was freelancing for Sephora, with the South East Asian production team based in Singapore. He could still do all of it if he could remember the skills.

Phoebe kept pulling stuff out of the crate. Cards. Fabrics. Decorations. Books. Art books. Photographs. SD cards and other unidentified paraphernalia to do with Greg's profession. She would have to decipher them and sort them out as she went along. She would copy out the files from the memory cards. She cringed at the irony, feeling tightness in her throat and tears coming to her. They were called *memory* cards.

Phoebe lifted out carved, lidded Khmer vases, 8 or 10 lbs each she remembered from the weighing-in. Greg and she had chosen them after an hour at an art fair. They were delicate and perfect at the time, one for each of them. As she cuddled the vases in her arms like twin babies, she remembered the early days in Battambang were the best time she and Greg had had together.

They seemed heavier than she remembered. She put them down. She opened the lids. Inside were small flattened bubblewrap packages with something soft and white inside. Impossible to tell how many unless she took them all out to count.

She removed the topmost, peeled the tape before she realised what it was. The vase was filled to the brim with these packages of a white powdery substance. She shot a sideways glance at Greg. He was looking at the art books.

Before he noticed, she re-taped it shut. The packers must have packed the vases as they were. She hadn't packed anything. Greg or someone else must have filled the vases. All this time, and she hadn't known. Ironically they'd helped to keep the vases intact in the journey home by sea.

She shoved the package back, and, with care, put both vases into the crate. She shut the crate lid and asked him to take it upstairs to the office-cum-store-cum-spare-room where she could unpack and hide the contents later without him knowing.

'Sorry, you know I can't lift anything.'

'Sure,' he barked. As he lifted the crate, a yellow post-it note flew out and stuck to the floor. It must have been on the inside lid of one of the vases. She thought it must be just another label from the crate's contents. She picked it up and was about to crumple it to throw away, when she caught sight of what was written on it.

Just a single number: 5.

23

DOMINIQUE

I T WAS THE WEEKEND of *Play!* She had now signed up for 6 weekends of summer performance art – singing, dancing and acting.

This place was recommended by Pierre and Dominique wanted to join in with Daphne. It was the only thing that was keeping her daughter and her together. The guilt, the grief and the drama, literally the drama.

She could see Daphne was a natural performer, someone who was better at escaping reality than she thought. They might even be in a play together. So far she had been learning and rehearsing songs from *The Greatest Showman*. This was a step up from *West Side Story*'s "Tonight."

Play! was in a minimalist, architect-designed glass extension type church hall in Kensington.

Daphne was improving but, if she could stomach the thought, Dominique sensed there was somewhat of a rivalry, although her daughter was much worse at this drama lark than she was.

Although Dominique was not in competition with Daphne, any mother-daughter rivalry remained unspoken — and ironic — as they were supposed to be doing this together, for the sake of the family and to patch over the hole that James had carved in it. From the moment Daphne was born and she first held her in her arms, when she looked at the shrivelled face and skin, she had only managed to take things a day at a time.

As a parent, if you could predict the next 24 hours you were winning.

She had always welcomed the idea that Daphne would be far superior in anything, looks, achievements, boyfriends, and far more successful than her to boot. But she had not taken well to the death of her father. Only now had she seen some improvement.

When she saw her daughter, Dominique saw only James and although James had always been a handsome devil and Dominique the envy of her friends at Cambridge, it was she who was elegant as a dancer.

She was petite, she had athletic limbs, whilst Daphne was tall and skinny, although her eyes were soft, down-turned and lady-like. They were her grandma's eyes, Dominique's mum's. She had thick brown hair that was straight and hung down like a stage curtain. She had refused to get it cut since the tragedy happened.

Since then Daphne had become even more like her father, though she was not sure if this was hereditary or contrived.

She had become vain, not in the sense of teenage girls, but in a recalcitrant and proud way, the way she spoke Hashtaguese, the way she wore expensive clothes which looked drab and baggy which she bought with her own pocket money. She had more backpacks than a schoolroom. She did not save and Dominique did not know where the money went. Dominique had had to cut her pocket money from £300 to £150 per week. Did she think it would never run out?

When Dominique last saw James, he had seemed like a panther, when, in London, he had been a little grey mouse. They had told him not to underestimate the power of the white man in Asia.

Singapore had turned him into an ageing rock star, grey haired, with a half-dozen Rolexes and a single diamond earring. He got away with it in the corporate world, in banking, because he was James. He was vain, unconventional and everybody wanted to be him. He gained respect this way.

There was nothing similar in appearance or character-wise between Daphne and Dominique. The only thing that kept them together was sushi and drama. After *Play!* It was the trip to the ubiquitous *Yo! Sushi* or Itsu in High Street Kensington. That was where Daphne liked to hang out now that she had preference for green juice rather than Coke. Hashtag healthyliving. Hashtag selfie. Hashtag YOLO.

Daphne had no interest in France any more, making it;

a) cheaper as Dominique could go during term time,

b) she could get all her admin and the building works done without thinking about how to entertain Daphne

and

c) Andreia and her could really crunch through some design decisions and have more intense meetings.

Now that she had discovered James's additional assets, no time must be wasted and she knew she had to track down the mysterious owner of the vineyard in Champagne. Before it became a drink, it was a place. Before James became a corpse, he was her estranged husband. The process of finding the person or the company called Achara must also be started straightaway. She sent Henry Tummings an email to that effect.

24

PRZEMEK

PRZEMEK FOUND HIMSELF BACK at the Friday night Speakeasy in Borough Open Air Festival when Andreia was away in Kazakhstan.

It was a bugger to get to. He had to Uber it. But it was Cuban night and in London it was boiling. Through the pollution you could not see a single star. The sky was red. The city was lit up and the only stars were in his eyes.

This was the night he had been waiting for now he had his gladrags from Poland. He had been listening to the music on YouTube and learning his moves. He would totally be in the moment.

He had a golden tan. The music was all going to be 30s and 40s mambo, son, cha-cha and conga. It would be a feverish thrill to dance the Cuban salsa, or the mambo. He felt distracted all day since he was in Screwfix at half past seven in the morning queueing up for a Grundfos UPS2 15-50/60 3-speed central heating pump and pump head which he did not know came separately so he had to queue again. With desire on his face and his mind in the clouds he handed over cash for the pump and pump head.

He was already humming familiar Cuban *son* tunes, with their anticipated bass just before a downbeat and distinctive rhythm that gave rise to salsa. Przemek had planned to wear his African shirt, Havana white peaked cap, Cuban heels (naturally), pleated voluminous red bowling trousers with turn-ups.

A deep excitement burned inside him, his core, his hips. He did not know if he could handle it, this explosive feeling. His heart banged, leapt and hammered about like a tumbadoras drum. He felt like a rebellious dockworker of Havana and Matanzas, one who formed the *cabildos*, a form of social club among African slaves brought to the island by the Spanish conquistadors to work on the sugar plantations. He felt spontaneous, improvised and lively.

He checked his appearance in the full-length mirror at home and he was pleased. This summer holiday was indeed looking good, and he was not just saying that because he was an eternal student.

He would have loved to have had records and a record-player but there was no room for them and Andreia would not be pleased. It was either Montse or the records. He searched for party music and he found rumba music on his Spotify. Then he changed to YouTube instead because he wanted to hear the narrative history behind it too. 'The word rumba comes for the verb *rumbear* which mean to have a good time, to party'. His reverie was interrupted when his Uber arrived.

～

THE WHOLE PLACE WAS decked out to be like La Tropicana, the infamous Havana nightclub, playing Cacho Lopez's Mambo from 1938, the first mambo ever written.

There were gyrating hips, twisting, pelvic thrusting, and that was just the lean, muscular guys. Latinos, blacks, whites. Asians too. All the peoples of the world brought together by music and dancing. Hips were swaying; to percussive music and the magic of the palitos drumsticks rattled out a cascara rhythm. A dance troupe called the Young Thugs were performing on the stage. Laughter, dance and songs made him a part of London and London a part of him

'Hey,' he heard a voice call out to him. 'You.'

He was not sure where the voice was coming from as the whole place was really buzzing and when you heard someone call out in a foreign country, you were never too sure they were actually calling you. A noisy environment made your own language difficult never mind a second. He turned around.

'Yes, you.'

He did not recognise her at first. He glanced and saw that it was the dark-haired lady he'd first met at the Speakeasy in Wapping.

'Oh, yes, hi!' He was pleased to see her though a little surprised as it was so unexpected.

'Have you seen the original Tropicana?' she said.

'No, no.' Always, the double-no in case the first one was misheard. How could he have? He wasn't alive in 1939, and most of all he wasn't alive in Havana in 1939. What did she mean?

'In 1939 it must have been heaven,' she said. 'Six acres of lush tropical gardens in a suburb of Marianao.'

He became excited by the imagery. He knew what she was talking about. Entering another world, the fantasy one, the one in the past. Time travel. 'I cannot hear you,' was all he managed to say in response.

'Let's go somewhere quieter.' She said. He followed her to Cahoots, a black and white striped 1940s style champagne kiosk with rose gold foot rails. He wanted to hear more. She bought two flutes of Mimosa and passed one to him automatically, without asking if he wanted one. He shook his head.

'OK, double trouble for me,' she said. She sipped from both to mark her property.

'Now. Let's see, where were we? Ah yes. The spectacular showplace that became the Tropicana evolved out of a Depression era bohemian nightclub called Eden Concert, operated by Cuban impresario Victor de Correa.'

'This sounds good.'

'Yes. Yes, it does. So one day, two casino operators approached Correa about opening a combination casino and cabaret on a property on the outskirts of Havana rented from this heiress called Guillermina Perez Chaumont. Known as Mina.' She sipped her champagne elegantly, like she was a bird.

'Wait. How do you know all this?'

'Just listen first. Thereafter, it became an outdoor cabaret. Singers, dancers, musicians, food and entertainment. Chandeliered dining room. The works. El Beau Site was original name. But it was changed to Tropicana.'

'So now you will tell me how you know all this?'

'Yes. In my mind I have been there. I am living in 1939 or maybe 1942. I am hoping to transform myself into someone with taste.'

He laughed. 'I love your story.'

'It's all fact.' She threw her head back and finished the second flute. Granted, they were very small, child's play. In London you did not get much for your money. And that was a fact, not a story. He looked at her perfect throat, and remembered her magical singing voice.

He knew so much about dance, the rumba, cha-cha, mambo and so on, but he didn't want to show off his knowledge right now. He did not think he was capable of articulating all that information in English anyway. Seemed like hard work when he was trying to enjoy himself.

'Let's go.' He said. 'Shall we dance?' He noticed the next act had gone on stage – a Brazilian percussion and all-woman cabaret band.

His eyes locked with hers and they embraced. They broke their connection and bowed. The music started and they were dancing the guaganco. She was a wonderful dancer. It was hard to tell under the heavy makeup and intense coloured lighting, but she could be twice his age. He thought of his mother who was such a brilliant dancer back home but he thought better of mentioning his mother.

'Do you remember me?' She said tentatively.

'Of course,' he said.

'I remember you,' she said. 'You are the Polish prince.'

He laughed again. 'No,' he shook his head feverishly like a cartoon character. Then as he looked all serious, he corrected her in a fake Spanish accent. 'I am Arturo Sanchez. The greatest mambo dancer you will ever know.' She laughed with him. He hadn't laughed in a long time. It actually hurt his six-pack muscles, as they were so unaccustomed to laughing.

He feared what he was feeling as they danced the Thugs' guaganco. All the other couples were dancing too. They were not even on the stage. It was an open air ballroom and the atmosphere was magical. Chandeliers dangled from each tree and his heart soared with the pain of joy. He could not keep his eyes off her. His mouth melted onto hers. He was drawn to her. She was a magnet for his desire.

To think he was queueing for the Grundfos pump and the wrong part only that morning in Screwfix. Now he was in Paradise, or maybe the Tropicana in 1939. He did not even know if she was married, divorced or single. He did not think of Andreia for a second. He just wanted to kiss this spider woman. And she kissed him back. At first with a closed lips and then they both had their mouths open.

He was lost. It was her, the music, the night. It was 1939. They did not speak. They danced one dance after another until the sexiest dance music came from the band, the Cuban salsa, not Spanish or South American. The real salsa.

Przemek forgot everything, his name, his country of origin, his job, Andreia. He just danced. She was slim and petite and her dress and leggings were all lace. He kissed her again, deeply and he felt his own erection straining inside his Calvin Klein boxers. He might not even see his spider woman again, but he did not want to think about that. 'The golden boy of dance', he thought to himself as he tried to hide his hard-on.

25

DOMINIQUE

WHEN SHE WOKE UP, she remembered it all with a thrill. She was young again.

No anti-ageing facial spa treatment had the same effect as the electricity passing from a kiss. She was detonating from her excitement and she wasn't even drunk or hungover. Those who blamed their follies on alcohol were clearly that, foolish.

It was Saturday. She would celebrate with Lucy. First, she would have a shower and get ready to take Daphne drama and dance at *Play!*.

She'd already *had* enough drama and dance for the entire weekend but it was only a summer's worth of Saturday mornings and a promise was a promise – as no doubt Daphne would remind her.

She looked for her tap shoes in her wardrobe's bottom drawer. She needed to take it easy and tap was easy - for her. She got ready; leggings, vest top and socks. It was like any other Saturday except for being the best Saturday of her life. All the pain she had suffered dissolved like fizzy drops.

After James moved to Singapore, whenever he came

back he stayed like a guest in the basement office-suite with his guitar mausoleum. She remembered with sadness how he had looked on that chilly stainless steel slab, half-eaten by fish and decomposing.

It *was* like a dream, especially since Przemek was no longer there. She'd known he would have to leave because there was no way the neighbours or God forbid, the neighbours' staff, were going to see him, accidentally or otherwise.

It was so damaging when you were proud of something yet ashamed of it at the same time. She floated like a ghost, making coffee whilst still hearing the Cuban music in her mind, loud, clear and percussive. She replayed his moves and what an amazingly natural and sexy dancer he was, and if he hadn't said he was Polish she would have thought him a Latino. "Gringos" didn't have that kind of rhythm.

Every single detail came back to her. And with each, she wanted him again. The dancing, the silent trip back in the Uber and the looks from the driver in his rear view mirror. *What is this cougar doing with that toy boy?* 'Everything boils down to money', she imagined the Uber driver thinking. It could as easily have been, 'hey, he's lucky, she's rich and they're getting laid'. She'd finally placed Przemek when they entered the house. He'd found the alarm so quickly in the dark. He was her heating and plumbing contractor.

The phone rang, interrupting her thoughts. 'Lucy.' She squealed.

'Thank you for texting with with your news earlier. I know you were giving me a pre-warning. I don't know if I should be happy for you.'

'Of course you should be, why should you not be? If it were you, I would be thrilled for you.'

'Why?'

'To have done something new. To have done something crazy for the first time. I was, am, a lawyer, don't forget. We do not do anything crazy, at least not without a contract first. I made that mistake when I got married. I had no plans for that day so I thought why not get married-'

'Dominique! It's no laughing matter! And you're joking about it?'

'I am joking, yes I am. Why can't I joke? I am feeling very cheerful today!'

'You're off your head.'

'You knew I was never happy when I was married if you can call it being married.' She did not want to say more. About how Przemek had worshipped her. 'Listen, let's meet for dinner tonight. I've got to go to tap now with Daphne. I really must go. OK?'

'Rocco's Wine Bar?'

'Rocco's Wine Bar it is. At 7.'

She could not say more, but she replayed every moment in detail. When she was in his arms and he looked at her, she had everything she could ever want in life all at once. It was only for a few moments, yet it had proven to her that it was all possible. You could have someone who really *was* just super into you, who could not take his eyes off you. And there was no turn-on stronger than that.

James had not even looked at her for years, maybe since Daphne was born. Not properly. She suspected he may not actually even have liked her very much. Someone to be ignored, not adored.

Marriage had a shelf-life. Why did you think mortgages were 25 years? That was the shelf-life. It started to get used up around the 20-year mark. That day would never come now.

Since one woman's good news was another woman's

bad, Lucy was already there when Dominique arrived at Rocco's that night. She fully expected the moral and social disapproval stare.

Instead, Lucy broke into a big grin.

'Oh, so you are happy to see me?', said Dominique nervously.

'Of course I am happy to see you. Look. A wine list.'

'Let me get my glasses.'

They ordered a glass of Italian Pinot Grigio Blush each.

'A woman wanting to be adored, a middle aged woman, is seen as having some kind of perversion, a narcissistic disease,' Dominique said. 'Is this how you see me?'

It was difficult to want to feel empowered when no one else wanted you to be empowered, except social media. And that was only to sell you stuff. 'Be great. Be yourself. Conquer yourself, not the world', said Rene Descartes. Why did they call women domestic goddesses when there was nothing further from the truth? They were not goddesses, they were wives and mothers. Heroines of the mundane.

'Well, it's-' Lucy sighed.

'What are you trying to say?'

'It's just a one-off. You're having a midlife crisis.'

'No. I'm just another existentialist. It takes one to know one.'

'No, I am not shagging a plumber. He's your plumber, Nikki! I am so in shock. I cannot believe it.

'Nothing happened.'

'What do you mean nothing happened?'

'I mean I did not hurt anyone and no one hurt me.'

'Is he married? Single?'

'I do not know.'

'You've really got to be careful. How could you do this?'

'Because I need someone to love me, physically.'

'Then it's just lust!'

'Yes, and so? Kill me.'

She thought maybe Lucy was jealous. That was entirely possible of course. Lucy sipped her wine with smiling lips but her face was frowning and certainly not calm. She was trying hard to be happy, and Dominique could see that. She wished she had not told Lucy now. She obviously had nothing else to worry about except social media, clothes and films.

'You know you are my best friend,' Lucy said. 'I am so thrilled for you to have found someone to love you. And of course I'm jealous! He sounds wonderful, even if he's made you happy for just one night,'

'Well, you're saying that, but I'm not sure it is for one night. You see, we have a deep connection.'

'Plumbing.'

Dominique laughed. 'No. I don't know what. Some "meaning of life"-type connection. He's very clever. Don't be fooled. He is only a plumber because he is poor and his English is not great. He is not a plumber because he was born into it.'

'Born into pipework.'

Dominique roared with laughter again. She threw her head back, aware that Lucy could see her fillings from all those Curly Wurly bars in primary school. 'Lucy, you are good to me.'

They celebrated with a wonderful dinner, breaded chicken with Provençale sauce, rocket and lemon and a baby spinach salad, just the way Dominique liked it. What was so special about food? She had had every type of fancy food in the world. Your food should be like yourself. Her favourite foods would be like herself: small-sized but smart, with a bite.

'I don't feel guilty. I am actually empowered. I feel on top of the world. It was so intense and mind blowing. I never knew that sex could be this great.'

'Ok enough now. Could you stop it, please? On second thoughts, don't. Spill the beans. Did he use a condom?'

'No. I am beyond having children. Oh, Lucy! The way he could not stop looking at me! Every woman wants to be adored, now and forever.'

'Describe him.'

'He's cute, about 5' 8". I told you already. He is Leonardo di Caprio in Titanic.'

'Yes, well, you are definitely on a sinking ship.'

Dominique smiled. 'Who knew that I'd be empowered by passion? I thought it would weaken me, turn me into a worm. No backbone, needy.'

'Please. You will never turn into a worm. Maybe an intellectual.'

They laughed again and again and, it seemed, at anything.

WHEN SHE WOKE UP the next morning, she was no longer in a good mood.

She was feeling at best neutral, or even a bit sad that she'd never see him again. Or that she'd screwed up or that he was just an opportunist and was not that into her. And what of it? Should she even care? How could she imagine that there could be anything more between them?

It was unlikely that they would meet again. She lay in bed clutching her Smythson leather diary and was just about to open it to her to-do list page, when she had an attack of cold shivers. She was concerned about her own moral judgement. It was out of character. What had made her think it was a great idea to go out two nights ago and come home with a Polish plumber? She had intended being cautious because there were complications with James's Will. She must have been actually certifiably insane, drunk or both. It was a bad idea. Bad, bad, bad.

But now, two days later, by the cold glare of the bluish — not even warm or yellow — morning light, she saw her own stupidity. It did take a while to sink in. She did not know herself as well as she'd thought. Only the French would do something so uninhibited and brash.

She acknowledged that only a desire so strong could make a mature woman take such risks.

She rummaged in her bedside table to look for a couple of Paracetamol. The drawer was already open. She remembered that she'd wanted to give Przemek a little something, but he did not want anything. She'd found the Porsche key-ring in its box and wanted Przemek to have it as he could certainly use one. It even had a free tracker app and he'd only need to activate it. It would be so useful if he misplaced his keys. She could see that he thought this was a good idea. He accepted the gift after some hesitation, just the key-ring. He declined the box.

Now she held it and looked at the emptiness within, its slick velvety padding, with a deep vagina-like slot into which the key-ring was once inserted.

26

YOU

A FTER THE GOOD MORNINGS and introducing each other correctly, it is time for new words and a quick revision of old words from the flash cards.

It is the day of your pre-op consultation. It seems neverending but this is your life now, appointments. After all there is nothing else you can or could do.

After the last GP appointment, you have managed to get a consultation with a specialist at Charing Cross Hospital. Despite scarce availability on the NHS, local clinical commissioning groups have successfully lobbied for your eligibility. After all, you do have such extensive diesel burns that even your vocal cords are damaged.

Every day you take strong painkillers, without which you can not function. You have to listen to the consultant drone on about skin grafts, skin flaps and tissue expansion. After telling you what they will be doing, they tell you why they don't really like to do it but have to. There are risks. Pain of course, as if you have not endured enough. Infection, scarring, the repaired skin rejecting the grafts due to restricted blood supply, even bleeding. The complications number well more than the procedures. If any skin graft does not 'take', it will have to be removed before any more surgery could be carried out.

They have done all the scans, diagrams, photographs. You are being referred back to the GP who will receive all this information by letter. You sit down with Phoebe to watch some educational videos on the before and after while they prepare your notes.

'Some well-known celebrities were in there,' said Phoebe who rattles off their names but you do not know them anyway. 'Names of famous people are not in your list of words to learn but you would be doing it soon,' says Phoebe, who reads you the papers every day and patiently, too.

She explains what is happening in each country. She is getting bigger now and in three weeks you'll be a parent and looking like a new person, or rather, the old Greg or the new old Greg. As to exactly how it might affect your appearance, you are unsure but you like the idea of it.

Anything would be an improvement from this and you might be able to speak normally again. You have not enjoyed being a monster or the strange looks it has brought. You'll never look exactly the same as before, but there are lots of photos from the USB key which Phoebe gave the consultants to work from. The real Greg, they keep saying.

When you get back, it is time for Phoebe and her mum to go out. They have told you they are going to Waitrose. 'We have to pick up some food,' Eva says, even though you already know what Waitrose is as they go there twice a week. They have not been speaking to each other for days. This is less worrying to you than to them. Although you *are* supposed to be listening to family members speaking to regain your memory.

This is one of the activities supposed to help you remember. However, it is not your memory you are afraid of, it is the two women. They need not be concerned whether you are listening in or not. You have not the faintest idea what they are talking about.

Saying 'we have to go to Waitrose' is the code for, 'we need to take our arguments outside'.

This is your favourite time. You'll return to that room that you seem to feel comfortable in. You are about to do a quick re-cap of what you found four days ago, when you're drawn to the cupboard's peeling paint.

As you reach to open the door, suddenly you hear a loud tune. What? What is that? What is the tune and the sound? It is bell-like chiming, but it plays at least 6 notes and you are surprised that you even know the notes because Phoebe has told you that you do not play any instruments, nor are you into bands though she has been playing you the radio every day to give you some idea of the 'shite being played these days': her *exact* words.

You follow it, the bell-like melody, and you are in the hall. You see a box light up and you follow the sound. Now you realise it is the doorbell.

'Hello, hello!' A voice calls out. Who is that?

You ask who it is in your inimitable hideous voice.

'Przemek.'

'What?'

'Przemek. Plumber. You called. Boiler not working?'

You open the door. As it slowly swings like a vampire's coffin lid, you see him reel in horror. You are used to this reaction now. Who would not jump back in fright? Even Phoebe and her mum have not got used to it, you yourself cannot look in the mirror at the beast looking back at you.

'What do you want?' You growl inadvertently.

'You called about boiler.'

You stare blankly at each other. You want to remember if Phoebe has said anything about this man turning up or if her mother has mentioned it in passing. You shut the door first. You look for messages. They write things down if it is important. There are two places:

One – behind the front door there is small spiral bound notepad and you have to read what they have remembered to write down. There is nothing in it.

Two – there is a job diary lying around on the worktop near the cordless telephone in the kitchen for busy people like them. You go into the kitchen to look for it and you cannot remember where it was put.

The man is left waiting and you can hear that he is calling Phoebe. You stand on the other side of the door, still shut. You listen at the door. You are a child again. This is how it could be for a while. You know your name and your age, but none of it rings true. Only the fact that you are a hideous monster, a child who is literate but with no responsibilities, is true. You open the door again when he knocks.

The man hands his phone to you. You listen.

'Listen, Greg, I am so, so sorry. I forgot that Przemek the plumber was coming. It was booked, then cancelled and then it was uncancelled and now his other job was cancelled so he is earlier than expected. Would you please be so kind as to let him in? He's done work for Mummy before. I won't be long.'

You are not listening because you are distracted by the man's keys. 'I'm going put money for parking,' he says. 'I leave tools, bag, here first. OK?'

You growl. You undo the chain and let him in. He brings his tools and a bucket full of tubes. It is like a doctor's bag but in plastic. It has many compartments – you can see because the lid is translucent and the kit is on wheels, like luggage. He takes his bunch of keys with him to move his car and put money in the meter.

He comes back in and winces again at the sight of you. When he is in the kitchen, you have to write his name down not because you want to remember him, but because the next time you see him, Phoebe would test you as to what his name is. She is very patient and would not show her annoyance if you do not remember, but you feel a terrible need to not disappoint her. You want her to know you are getting better. You got your Paperchase notebook diary out of your back pocket with its integral little pen and write down the word Przemek best as you could understand. Puh Jray Meck. Doesn't matter if it is right or wrong, you want to make Phoebe proud. All you want is for her to be happy.

He wheels his trolley into the kitchen, without needing to ask where the boiler is.

'I think it's pressure again,' you hear him call someone and speak in English, probably Phoebe or Eva. 'It's valve. What? Another day. No just valve. Boiler is old. Yes. I have parts but... yes another day. I don't have time to drain system now. What? We need couple hours at least. Yes.'

You spot his bunch of keys on the radiator cabinet cover in the hall, under the coats. You pick it up while he is on the phone and had the boiler cover is off. There are tools on the floor which he is picking out like they are pieces of art.

You see the word Porsche on the bunch of keys. It is a gold key-ring with a slim black stitched leather tab that has a crest.

The logo design on it attracts you. You pick up your new reading glasses — also on the top of the radiator cabinet — conveniently situated for occasions like these. In the centre of the crest is a black horse raising its front hoofs. In each opposite corner of the crest are black and red horizontal stripes. There is a word on top of the horse. *Stuttgart*. In each of the two other opposite corners of the crest is a strange symbol, it seems to be three curved eyelashes or waves.

He is still busy, now there are humming and clanking sounds. You limp to the kitchen; you see he is trying to put the boiler front cover back. You return to the hall. You flip the key-ring around. On the back side are the initials

JLS

You check your notebook. They are not the plumber's initials. But still you write them down. They may be the plumbing and heating company's initials.

He is coming back. You hear the trolley's wheels rotating, and getting louder as the plumber leaves the kitchen and heads to the hall. You put the bunch of keys back on the radiator cabinet and see him out. With time, everybody who looks after the house and you — the cleaner, the plumber, the meter reader, the Amazon delivery van driver, the regular postman — will all get used to your appearance or rather, get used to averting their gaze and pretending they haven't seen you.

27

DOMINIQUE

THREE DAYS AFTER DINNER with Lucy at Rocco's Wine Bar, Dominique started going through mail regarding James's estate.

Firstly, money had been transferred from the car mart agency. It was good and bad news.

According to them, James's 2012 ocean blue Ferrari California 4.3A in Singapore was supposed to fetch S$338,000. The mileage was slightly high at 56,000 km. Though it had new tyres, recent servicing, road tax and had been fully maintained, it could still have got a hundred more if it had had half the mileage.

After fees, tax, commission, transfer duties and so on, Dominique had received only £165,560.65. C'est la pits. She'd lost more than twenty to charges and duties. However, she was relieved to get any funds turning up in the account at all amongst the current run of surprises.

Secondly, Dominique received another email from Henry Tummings about Achara, and about the vineyard. Just to jog her memory, he mentioned again that the part owner of the villa in Thailand was a company called Achara.

The part owner of the vineyard was Petitemort Holdings Ltd, an offshore company registered in British Virgin Islands.

Dominique was trying to remember James's father's portfolio. All she knew was that his father had started his own hedge fund in 1998 with 8 million, developed it into an outfit with 200 staff. When he'd passed on, Tom got the flat and the cottage.

James being the favourite son had everything else including the second house in France near his parents' place in Côte d'Azur. However, the yacht, the Phuket villa, the Ferrari and the vineyard seemed to have nothing to do with James's father. It was all James's doing.

The last thing he'd wanted to do was work for his dad and the first chance he got he ran away as far as possible. This was the full extent of his rebellion, he kept doing what he did best – gambling, same as his father. That was all investment was, basically. The investor took the risks but it was the hedge fund manager that acquired billions of dollars' worth of stock.

Instead of replying to Henry's email, she called him.

'Henry,' she said. 'I got your email.'

'We have had to do some detective work for you, Dominique.

'I'm sure your fees will reflect this *extra* extra work.'

'Executing a Will is a complex process.'

'Of course.'

'Well, all we know is that Achara is a wine import company in Thailand. You don't need to look that up.'

'I remember seeing the receipts when I cleared out his flat. But why a vineyard? Was James even into wine?'

'Are you, Dominique?

'No! Wine is into me. I only know how to drink it.'

'So both companies, Petitemort and Achara, seem to be about wine.' Tummings read from a printed sheet, 'Achara has been supplying hotels and restaurants with the finest luxury beverages in Thailand since 2007 from eleven countries: France, NZ, Australia, USA, Chile, Argentina, Spain, Italy, South Africa, Germany, Japan. They supply sake, wines, liqueurs—'

'Please stop.'

'There is an address here, we are in contact. Phone numbers, email, Instagram, everything.'

'I am left with the Holland Park house and I simply don't agree.'

'And the car.'

'Oh please, Henry. The car? You mean the two-year old Mer—'

'Both. Both Mer—'

'No. I don't agree. Both are depreciating assets, so they're not assets at all.'

'You'll have to contest it. It's in James's Will. Anyone who has a beneficial interest, or potential beneficial interest in the deceased's estate, can contest a will if they believe they have a valid claim. Typically, those who contest a Will are the surviving spouse, children, cohabitee or other dependents, such as adult children who were being financial supported by the deceased, and children who are treated as a child of the family.'

Dominique exhaled. 'His mother's dementia is deteriorating and requires round the clock care,' she said. 'He has a brother who gets nothing. Not to mention he has a daughter who is still a minor. You know what school fees cost. I know what is happening in his family and you don't.' She did not mention the flat she had just bought in Southwark.

'The villa in Phuket, the house in France, half the vineyard,' he replied. 'Any of these could have been used to pay for Daphne's education, right up to university, and her accommodation and living expenses.'

'Quite right.' This Henry Tummings could be so ambivalent, so spineless, she thought.

Dominique looked down at her dark polished nails. 'What should an individual do if they believe they have a claim?'

'If someone believes the Will is invalid, or believes they have a valid claim against the estate, they should take the first step to protect their interests which is to apply for a 'caveat' which prevents the assets of the estate being distributed pending the outcome of the dispute.'

'How long will this caveat last?'

'Six months, although it can be renewed. Often, the dispute will be resolved before it reaches court.'

'Hmm.'

'Indeed.'

James was in her life more when he was dead than when he was alive. If everything had been well, why had she to find out *now* about these companies? Yet she felt an intangible affection for him. She knew intimate details of his habits such as what coffee he *liked* at which time of day but she did not know what he *wanted* in any sense or at any time.

'What happens if an agreement cannot be reached during the caveat stage?'

'If an agreement cannot be reached during the caveat stage, and the dispute cannot be resolved, a formal claim may be made to court. Claims against an estate involving a Will typically fall into two categories: The Will is invalid or the Will did not make sufficient (or any) provision for the claimant. The first one doesn't apply as it is valid. There were two witnesses. You can contend the second.'

'But how will the court assess a dependency claim?'

'The court will consider various factors including the age of the dependents and any responsibility for young children.'

'I want to make the claim.'

'Well, you have six months as that is the length of the caveat to protect the assets. You only have one child. His brother Tom has income forever. Your case may not be as... as... strong... as you'd like it to be. Just think about it first, Dominique.'

'I don't want to think about it.' Although she was a lawyer, inheritance was not her field. She could not be expected to have this information at her fingertips.

Dominique wept after she hung up. She had started to miss Przemek as though he was a childhood friend, someone you confided in and did dumb things with. They did not seem so dumb now. Even so, she felt a tenderness towards James. She did not feel angry. She wanted to get to know him through these companies that he'd set up. If he was so brilliant, why had James given so much of his own hard-earned wealth to them?

28

PHOEBE

I T WAS STILL DARK. Her eyes shot open wide. She had a brainwave. The way to 'check' Greg intimately would be to give him a sexual experience.

She switched on her phone. 06:18. She slid up to switch on the torch mode on her phone. She reached over to his boxer shorts and gently tugged them down.

She used her torch again to see his cock clearly but it now seemed obvious that no one really looked at a limp cock very often unless it was the owner or if it was not, it was the spouse accidentally seeing the owner getting changed or standing at the toilet. Anyone else's cock wasn't something you saw every day, at least not for Phoebe.

Phoebe honestly could only be 75-95% (depending on the angle and lighting) sure it was Greg's member. Can a woman truly know her husband? How could she be so sure? What if she had not seen him naked for a while? What would qualify a long time? She also questioned her own memory and sensations.

There was no choice but to get him hard. She held it and methodically massaged, using her thumb and fingers. He started to wake, moaning appreciatively. His cock was hardening, but she still could not be sure. How could this be? She was his wife. Surely any wife could tell if it was her husband or not.

Were most men very similar indeed? Unless you were a hardworking prostitute, you would never know the answer. Phoebe felt the irony land on her like a slap. She only had fewer than 2 or 3 minutes to look carefully. He was close to coming. His moans became words. He was whispering and gasping. With a grim expression, she still helped him achieve orgasm. He was now awake.

She looked at him and sighed. He would be thinking, *this is great, she really still finds me attractive.*

But Phoebe was thinking of the Thai women on the yacht. It was a turn-off. She pulled off tissues from the box and handed them to him. She lay back on two pillows, glared at the ceiling then turned away from him and towards the wall.

It's today, he growled. I love you.

She did not reply. It was the day of the surgery. The first of four procedures. It was really important. If she could not be 100% sure from such intimacy, then she required more medical intervention. Her dad Robert had been talking to the consultant as they took his feedback seriously and although surgery was not his expertise, he *was* a neurologist.

They'd already told Robert they would fix his voice box first. This was based on several recordings on YouTube and countless raw files on his hard disk, of Greg's voice. They would do their best at reconstructing Greg's original voice and accent. A human voice was as unique as a fingerprint. It was more important to get his voice back than his appearance. Phoebe knew that it was the key to getting Greg back, if not his heart, soul or mind, then at least his voice. This was a security issue too. A voice is more secure than a password or passcode. Soon, when he was better, he could have his bank account back and use Alexa.

Now, if he asked: '*Alexa, who am I?*' she would not be able to answer him. However, for other applications of speech technology, computer algorithms were increasingly able to discriminate, recognise and identify individuals from voice recordings.

But how well could Phoebe do this herself? She was beginning to doubt her own abilities. She thought she had a normal sense of hearing. She'd never damaged her ears or anything like that with loud rock music or concerts. When it came to recognising her closest family and friends, she was probably quite good.

But would she able to recognise the voice of her first primary school teacher if she heard her again today? No, she did not think so. It was impossible, surely. How about Greg's voice from a year ago, from five years ago? She was not confident that anyone could recognise her voice from five years ago either. For a girl to feel confident, she felt being attractive was far more advantageous than being clever. That certainly worked for Bethany. She wondered what Greg saw in *her*. He must have pitied her, as she pitied him now.

'Everything else is still up to Greg's own recovery efforts. Yes, especially his accent and the way he spoke. Voice identity perception could be extremely challenging, he may never sound the same, or he may sound the same as someone else,' said the consultant looking at his screen.

'The idea is for Greg to be able to use Alexa,' said Phoebe. 'It would be nice, but I know it's an ideal case scenario.'

'Fine. Let's talk about the surgery then. His speaking voice will be quite tight or effortful after the surgery and will possibly become worse for a few days to a week until swelling starts to subside. Discomfort will last for a few days and include difficulty with swallowing and a feeling like you've got a sore throat. He is still very lucky to not have had his throat severed by the accident. These procedures are carried out from the mouth to not be too invasive.'

'So could you now go through what you're actually doing?'

'There are two procedures to be carried out. Web glotto-plasty removes the upper portion of the thyroid cartilage and raises the larynx in the neck,' he pointed to a digital email of a scan on his screen.

'In this technique we are going to suture the front of the vocal cords together to try and raise the comfortable speaking pitch.' He laced his fingers together to illustrate what he meant by suture.

'Following that we will do laser vocal cord tuning which means tuning the cords, just like a guitar's strings, to a person's comfortable speaking pitch — male or female — which can be raised a few semi-tones. This procedure is not too invasive,' he wriggled his fingers over his head as though entertaining a toddler, 'and can be done in the office. Now if that does not work, more aggressive variation on the proce-dure can be done in the operating room.'

To show aggression, he clenched his fists.

'Now let's just get on with it, as you probably have the gist already. Here is a print out of what you are supposed to be do after the op.'

He handed her a sheet of A4.

She read it quickly and then handed it to Greg.

Post-operative Instructions

Complete voice rest is very helpful for one week after the surgery. All kinds of verbal conversation must be avoided for one week, including whispering.

Just remember, there are very few sutures in there and until your body's own scar tissue helps support the procedure, the sutures could pull out.

Non-active work can be resumed in a few days. Speaking may begin increasingly after a week. You may resume aerobic activity after two weeks. Weight lifting should be deferred for a month.

Greg read it quickly too. He looked at her warmly and held her hand loosely.

She smiled a tight smile.

29

PRZEMEK

P RZEMEK STARTED WORK ON A new block of luxury flats in Camden.

They had commercial space on the ground floor instead of a car park entrance and concierge lobby. He had two plumbers working with him while they installed the underfloor heating system in the hard floor areas such as the bathroom, kitchen and living rooms. He'd squeezed in a bigger job this time because it was still summer and he had to get more income before starting the course again in September. He was under pressure of increasing his income over a short time.

He was doing all this to avoid thinking about Dominique. Every day thinking about her made it better, yet worse. Like an addiction. At first it was all sexy, mind-numbing and tingly but the more she came into his thoughts regularly the more freaked out he was. It was like being drunk at sunset each time he pictured her. He fanta-sised about coming on her face, in her loose fist, in her hair, inside her when she faced away, his hand on the headboard.

Either he would get the sack or more jobs from her. This

would not go well. It seemed unprofessional so it must be, mustn't it?

He spent the entire morning calling the underfloor heating supplier because the zones were incorrectly speci- fied and consequently the wrong control pack was sent. The 3kW control pack was delivered instead of 14kW, 6 bar short of providing the right pressure. He called the architect and the main contractor who would appeared on site like ghosts at certain times of the week only. The sightings were not guaranteed, so the only way to get it right was by phone. As somebody who hated talking anyway, he was *really* sick of talking, talking, talking, by the time he'd finished.

The shock came that night. He did not know it was her until they both arrived outside her home. There was no gradual impact or time for it to sink in. After all, he never met the "client" when he was working on site. There was a split second when he had to decide to tell the Uber to turn around and take him away, or to go in with her and he did the latter. He'd never lost his mind for an instant, over a woman, only over her. He even briefly remembered "if it's still in your mind, it's worth taking the risk." Descartes. Or was it Celine Dion?

It confirmed a profound, genuine and instinctive connection. She wasn't like Andreia, she was available but he knew it would not lead to anything as she was twice his age, about a hundred gazillion times as rich and...

However, she *did* seem to be quite taken with him. Hadn't she offered him a Porsche key-ring which he never once assumed to have meant he would be given a Porsche next and anyway, Porsche was German and he was Polish. He could not believe his ears, when she offered to put him through University.

They stayed up all night, not just having sex, his

favourite thing, but also talking, his least favourite thing. But it was through talking that she was engaged by his desire to be educated. He remembered with guilt it was the best sex he ever had since the last sex he ever had. Every other experience had disappeared from his memory, only to be replaced by the most recent and spectacular.

He was terribly foolish, he thought. Luckily she did not appear to have a husband. This was what saved him from going insane with fear over that weekend.

'How did you end up here,' she'd asked him.

'I was half-educated back in Poland and on some relatives' pressure, decided to come to London to train as plumber and make good living.'

'OK,' she said but he thought she meant 'OK?' In English there was often an upper inflexion at the end of a sentence which meant you were not totally certain if it was a question or not. It depended on the cultural context and there was no context he could refer to right now except the bedroom.

'I am OK, yes,' he said. 'OK as skilled vocational person but I can't see myself doing it all my life.' After he started going to the Speakeasy, he'd decided that actually he did want to live like a handsome mysterious 1930s film star. He couldn't do that *and* be a plumber.

'So what *do* you want to do?' She had asked.

'To be educated.'

'What exactly do you mean by *educated*?'

'You do not know what *educated* means?' He asked.

'Well, only what I know to be educated means.'

'That's it, then. It is what you think educated means, mate.'

'You called me mate!' She laughed. 'That's cute!' He did not know what to say so he took her into his arms and held her. They kissed again, long, hard, deep. You had to be good at kissing if you weren't great at talking and he'd just been subjected to talking at length.

There was a blank space in which that word *educated* bounced around while they dozed. When they woke up, Dominique said he *would* be educated. She had thought it out.

'Now you just have to think it out what exactly do you want to be educated in.'

'I came to UK to better myself but I am exactly same.' He said. '*The* UK. *The* same.' He corrected himself automatically. In Polish there were no articles.

'I get that. You want to change yourself.'

'No, no, not just change. Make myself someone else.'

'That's change isn't it?'

'No. Is not change. Change means similar but different like change hairstyle. But I really want big change. How you say, *transformed*.'

She was thinking about it, he could see. She thought about it a lot more than Andreia ever did. Andreia was solipsistic, only thinking of her own career, her profession, her development, her future. There was no space in her life for Przemek except as someone who fixed things and took her out to swanky places. Even those opportunities had dwindled.

'I am interested in BSc in Physics and Philosophy, joint degree at Kings College.'

'Oh darling,' she burst into a hefty laugh like he'd just delivered a punchline in front of a stand up comedy audience. His thought made him chuckle.

'L – O – L,' he said. He liked humour in the bedroom, especially bedroom humour.

'Yes, lols indeed. Why on earth did you think of that?

Surely that is very hard to get into. You have to do the A levels here, have you even done A levels back home?'

'No.'

'And your English, if you don't mind me saying. Are you going to be able to even write the essays? You don't know what you're getting yourself into.'

'I do: three years, full time, joint honours, Strand campus.'

'I don't mean that. What are you getting yourself into? You don't want to be out of your depth even if you *could* get in. Which you may not.'

'Are you playing devil's advocate, mate?'

She laughed again and she was pretty when she laughed. It made his heart soar like a puppy after a ball. 'I don't think I even told you I was a lawyer,' she finally said. 'But not an advocate.'

'No,' he agreed. 'Not the devil's anyway.'

She leant down and wiped her tears with the tips of the pillowcases. 'I have not laughed so much since 1922.'

'Me too,' he said. 'It was a long time ago. I am sure we met then.'

They dozed a bit more in spoon mode. He was wrapped around his lover. It might have been four minutes; it might have been forty. When he opened his eyes, he continued. 'I have been studying already. I have little time but I just fill it all up. I did the ESOL course when I first arrived. 8 hours a week for 10 weeks while I was studying to do the exams for Level 2 qualifications—'

'Which means?'

'Which means GCSE Grade C/4 or above in English Language and Mathematics.'

'OK...' Again, he thought she could have meant *OK*?

'Yes, OK,' he said. 'Now I am doing the IELTS in

September. Which I will taking at the same time as my Access to HE Diploma in Science. So in 2 months I will be back at Kingston College.

'Is that even A levels? I do not understand any of that.'

'Never mind. Whatever it is, I have to get As! Especially in maths.'

'So how long is it?' she said. She rubbed his arms and felt their muscular weight around her.

'It's a year.'

'Will you be working? How many hours a week is it?'

'Yes I will be working. It's three days a week. It's for a year. Approximately 15 hours a week including a one-hour tutorial. I have to study 15 hours also on top of that. I apply for Kings College during that time. And hopefully I will get in. So I can start the BSc in 2019.'

She sighed again. She could not take her eyes off him.

He realised the time when he looked over her head at the bedside clock. 'I must go now,' he said.

'Why? Where are you going?'

'To my own home.'

'But it's a Sunday.

'I still have a home on a Sunday.'

'What? OK, then, *mate*,' she emphasised the word. 'This is... well, I wish you well.' She had chuckled, not wishing to sound negative or pessimistic. He kissed her again. He looked at her for maybe a minute, a long time for looking at someone.

'Thank you for most remarkable evening,' he said as he closed her bedroom door so quietly she might not have heard him. He knew all the codes and he let himself out into Holland Villas Road, a street that was both so familiar and yet so alien it might as well have been from a novel he was reading.

30

YOU

YOU ARE NOT SPEAKING for a week.

It is back to writing on the tablet or in a ring-binder journalist's notebook from Poundland — 3 for a pound.

You would hardly speak anyway. You are not allowed to exercise and you are on strong painkillers which Phoebe or her mum are administering to you at six-hourly intervals. It feels like a very bad sore throat. It is nothing like what you have already been through.

It is August. Hot and sticky. You don't want to be out in this heat. They tell you they are going to the midwife appointment and then Lillie Road. This is where the Poundland is. It is the great leveller, Phoebe says, without irony. They need to get cleaning stuff.

You have nothing, not a pound. You cannot even go to Poundland. There is income in the joint account from the rental of the flat, but you cannot access it, no PIN, no three-digit code on the back of a card, no signature. Everything needs to be learnt.

After breakfast, you practise names and the five things

which have happened or which you remember in the week. For a week you'll have to use the iPad to to do this. They can be in any order and you can use the family diary or calendar to check if you are correct or incorrect. Then you repeat your life history, from your birthday, the names of your schools, the jobs that you did or were doing right up to the accident. You write it out on the tablet as if it is poetry and Phoebe watches with interest. She is motionless until her mother says, 'come on, stop it.'

'Stop what?' She wipes at her eyes and snaps at her mother. Phoebe is emotionally both strengthened and weakened by your condition and is often moved to tears when you display any improvement.

'Stop. It,' says Eva, like she is addressing a toddler having a tantrum. 'We need to go now.'

Eva tells you where they are going. This means it does not include you. They remind you each day that you live in Bishops Road. They tell you what happens at the end of the road when you turn left or when you turn right. In your mind you now already know the area very well. You can picture every fire hydrant, every corner. You can identify houses. You have a knack for directions. You do not know why this is.

Although you have not done any walking about on your own, soon you will be able to. In fact, right after you have recovered from the vocal cord surgery.

In a week you will be increasing to ten things. You have to talk about your favourite food. You scribble on the tablet *Thai food*. 'You can forget about Thai for now,' she said sharply, then she softened. 'But if you can remember how to speak it at all that would be amazing.'

You can't. You are unable to speak a word of it. 'OK nevermind, when we come back, we can go for a walk around.' She speaks to you like you are a pet, which needs walking everyday to familiarise you with your immediate environment.

Your time alone has increased to three hours. They remind you what you are supposed to do. Nothing strenuous. You can watch telly or read something. You should rest. You retreat to your favourite room. Sometimes you will pick up any book from Robert's shelf. They are either medical academic books or non-fiction of no interest to you as you can remember that you did not like to read much, let alone Robert's dull books about wine, fishing, golf and trains. The psychologists have concurred that reading is really quite a good exercise for your mind.

You force yourself to read the spines on the bookshelves and you shut your eyes and recall their titles in your mind silently. First you recall three, then five. That's enough. It is mentally exhausting. When you get to the last one, it surprises you. Not that you have remembered the title from the exercise, but it seems familiar. You open your eyes. *The Sailing Handbook: A Complete Guide for Beginners* by Halsey C. Herreshoff. You open it. It was published in 1996. You turn the page to where the title is.

To Robert. Read this first, then we're going to do it. Merry Christmas. J.

You replace the book. Next to it is a photo album. Phoebe has shown you photo albums before. Family albums. Pretty quickly you got bored as you didn't know any of the people in them. You had to feign interest and you forced yourself to remember the names and to retrieve them when she tested you.

This photo album has a vinyl snazzy cover meant to look

like leather. You sniff it. It is not leather. It must from the 1980s or before. The photography is not as sharp as digital and no one prints photos now, so it must be from negatives film that the photos were developed.

On one of the early pages, someone has handwritten the label 'France'. It is in a handwriting you do not recognise. It is not Phoebe's or Eva's anyway. Maybe it is Robert's which you have not seen.

People hardly see anyone's handwriting these days. Everything is typed. Text messaging, Whatsapp, email. What is handwritten? Nothing except the communication between you and your wife and her mother. You are the only person having to handwrite everything. And they tell you your handwriting has changed so much.

They struggle to show you what your handwriting was. They have nothing. Your parents may have something you wrote as a young person maybe. But you have no parents now. Phoebe says that both died of terminal illnesses one after the other which led you to go on the Groggy.

You keep turning the pages and it goes further and further into the past as the photos are even more degraded. You see Phoebe as a child. You know it is her as it says Phoebe, aged 1. Bethany, aged 3. Who is Bethany?

You look through the photos; they are of green fields. Nothing spectacular. There are stone buildings, ruins of a castle or something. What are these buildings called in France? There are actually very few buildings. Every photo is of fields. But on some close-ups you see that they are not fields. They are vines. There are green grapes, purple grapes. They are vineyards.

Towards the back of the album, here are photos of barrels in some underground vault, photos of bottles of wines. The labels. You read the labels. They make no sense.

There are some guys in photos. You don't know any of them. They might even be workers in the vineyards or the bosses or just tourists. There are 2 children, 2 boys and 2 girls. The girls are Phoebe and Bethany as per the photos before. The boys are older than the girls. They have not appeared, not yet, in the family albums that Phoebe had introduced you to. You shut the album and put it back.

You find a pack of cards on the shelf. You do not know why but you put it into the pocket of your track suit bottoms. You know exactly what they are without opening the flaps on the box.

As an afterthought you remove the album again, returning to the page with the 4 children. You study the boys. You had the exact same navy jumper as the boy. You know this because it was very itchy and you did not like it. You turn to the page with the wine labels. La Petite Mort.

31

PHOEBE

G REG HELD THEIR DAUGHTER, Jorani, for the longest time. She really was a radiant jewel.

She had only recently seen him weep, despite what he had gone through. He could speak, he could cry.

At last they had the family they wanted. Parenthood had arrived late though not that late. There was a baby girl in his arms. Now there were three of them.

Eva was in the corridor. She held the baby for just a few seconds before handing it back to Greg. They passed the child to and fro like it was a game. They held it and thought of something to say. Then they passed it on. Whisperings of *she's beautiful, she's beautiful* were uttered like a prayer. Her hair was very dark and there was a lot of it. In fact, it was almost black. You could hardly see what she really looked like since she had the crumpled features of most newborns.

AFTER TWO WEEKS THE baby was not latching on. Phoebe felt like she might die of exhaustion from the stress of childcare.

They all said *it won't last long, dear. The first 25 years are the hardest.* And so on. She had taken her attention fully away from Greg. She could not even grill him every day on his memory tests. Those were in the BC days. There were the days BC and AD. Before Child and After Delirium.

She could not put Jorani down. If she did, the baby would scream and scream and once in her obsessiveness she'd timed it and the screams did not stop after 22 minutes at which point she gave up and carried the baby again. She'd strained too hard when giving birth and now her eyes were still bloodshot.

Two miracles in a short time. A child for them. A voice for Greg. Yet something else also happened. The voice itself was close to what he sounded like, yet he had a new public school posh accent. He was from such humble working class beginnings in Kent.

'But you know you were a chav, don't you?' She said.

'Ab-suh-loot-leh', he'd joke back.

'GREG, YOU NEED TO look through this when you have the time,' she said, knowing full well he had too much time, not too little. The MacBook Pro technician had unlocked his computers and tablets.

'I will download the photos so you can view them on the iPad, if you get a chance.' Phoebe went on.

Only he would know what was on the memory cards. She wanted any work he recognised to be billable.

Greg avoided looking at the photos on the memory cards that she had painstakingly downloaded. He showed no interest at all.

But what she wanted to bring up with his doctors would

impress them. She'd observed that he had found books from Robert's office to read. They were in French. She hadn't known he was bilingual.

One night, Phoebe had been woken up so many times by Jorani she could not sleep, she left Greg sleeping and got up. She crept downstairs and opened Greg's MacBook Pro. She had to find answers on Mumsnet with Jorani cradled in her left hand. She was desperate for help or some kind of new mother support system. She did it with one hand as the other arm was cradling Jorani.

Just then an unread Whatsapp message popped up with a bing, originally sent to Greg's phone but he had the desktop app too. *Looking forward to the trip. Martin.* The date was in May, a few days before his accident. Not only his phone number, but all of Greg's Whatsapp contacts were available now. She looked at the conversation before that one last message.

Greg: Do you have it?
Martin: I will.

What was "it"? There were only those lines. Other messages must have been deleted. There was no photo of Martin, but his "profile avatar" was the Chelsea logo.

32

PRZEMEK

I T WAS A HOT summer Friday night and still light. He'd been sitting in the garden with his rifle waiting for squirrels.

He heard her come in to the kitchen. He put away the rifle. It was 9 pm and she wasn't out for drinks or whatever networking thing she was up to. She looked stressed and did not say hello. He came straight in from the garden. She seemed to be looking for something in the fridge. 'Andreia, I have something to tell you,' he said. 'I have to leave.'

'Leave where?' she shut the fridge door and looked vacant and glassy.

He swallowed and tried to think how to do this as directly as possible. 'Move out.'

'Why?' she seemed dazed, and not really looking at anything, as she put her laptop bag down on the dining chair.

He opened his mouth but stopped himself.

She shut her ears with her hands, blinked and shook her head rapidly. She fell into the chair next to the one with the laptop on it and buried her head in her hands.

'I'm very sorry.' He whispered. He figured as there was no good time to break the news to her, he should pick a moment when she was already stressed, because there was no point in spoiling any good mood moment she might have.

'Don't *sorry* me,' she mimicked his pleading voice. 'Are you crazy?' She screamed after a minute of silence, whilst she was taking it in. He could not and did not answer.

'Get out. Get out.' She screamed again. 'I got you the job there.'

'No! I got myself the jobs,' he said helplessly. There was no point in talking about the jobs themselves. This was not about the jobs. It never was.

'I hate you,' she hissed. She jumped up from the dining chair. Her beautiful Rihanna green eyes were wild with confusion. 'You are a complete bastard. I got you that job.'

'I got all my jobs. I price for them all. I prepare all quotes and submit blind. They don't even know who I am.'

'You're scum. You just used me-' She came towards him, hand on hips.

'No. I did not. *You* used me.' He decided to defend himself after all but his heart was sinking. Already his mind was made up, yet maybe his strong mind was his weakness.

'For what? What did I use you for?' She stopped to think, gasping just like she used to when they had sex. Her eyes darted about the room, like she was taking it in for the first time.

'You know what. Fixing shit.' Przemek spoke quietly, knowing she was beyond comprehension, or conversation. It was better that he kept calm and left. He became aware that his fists were clenched. Don't panic, he told himself. Always stay or look cool.

'You fixed nothing,' She was hyperventilating between

each word. 'You just wanted to fuck me so you can meet rich people. Rich women. It's pathetic.'

'You never want to fuck. You are too busy.' Przemek regretted it as soon as it slipped out. He'd done what he hated, speaking before thinking. He was as low as her.

'Get out. Get out. I hate you. Fuck off.' She screamed and shook her fists in the air. She reached for something. He could see she would not hesitate to destroy the flat.

'Andreia. Andreia. It was over a long time ago,' he started coming towards her. He put his hands out in front of him to protect himself. 'You would not even look at me for the last half a year.'

She picked up the River Cottage cookbook on the worktop and flung it at him.

'How many times do I have to look at you?' She looked for something else. Her eyes were like an animal's. There was no logic. Just instinct. 'Are you so vain and pathetic? I am busy. I am working.'

'So am I!' He dodged the book and he knew he should just leave the room immediately. It fell next to him with a flap of the pages and a cracking thud where its spine broke.

'Yeah. You're real busy. You're busy fucking that woman. I hate you.' She turned ugly, baring her fangs. He had no idea her jaw could drop like a reptile's. She looked worse than Montse when feeding. Her hands swam in the air looking for something else. She picked up a huge grey glass vase from the worktop. It was probably two feet high.

'Don't, Andreia. Please. That's the Alvar Aalto from Harrods. You love it.' She heard the magic words and it stopped her. She replaced it heavily. It sounded like a rock being set down. She sobbed, burying her eyes in her elbow pits like a child, her shoulders rising and falling. He felt truly sorry seeing her this way, so vulnerable and terrified of her own fury. He was filled with pity.

'Goodbye, Andreia.' He said quietly and left the kitchen. He wanted to look for the things he wanted to take with him.

'Good.' She sobbed. 'Cos I don't ever want to see you again. Fuck off.' She could not even say it all at once because of the severity of her crying. The peaks and troughs came in waves and took her breath away.

He sighed. There was no more to say. He couldn't look at her. It was impossible. Yet looking at someone was the most important thing to Przemek. Think how much we looked at children. You did not take your eyes off them. They amazed you and you could not stop looking at them. That was how you showed someone any kind of affection. Looking.

It had been the most ear-splitting row he'd ever had. Not long ago, they'd seemed like the perfect couple, the golden boy and girl of Battersea. He hastily packed all his possessions into a JD Sports bag and the ten-or-so boxes collected from the cages in Homebase earlier that morning. He moved Montse and the tank, the heater, the kit.

Seeing the things he was not taking, their joint stuff and her things, he remembered with fondness how much she'd wanted these rose gold and marble luxury accessories. The vintage industrial rusty-looking lighting. The Chinese black geometric shelving. The antique prints of tropical palm trees from Paris. All of it was hers.

He could hardly think through the chaos and volume of Andreia's voice. She really was taking this badly. He'd thought he would have time to move out gradually. Obviously this was now a crazy idea. He started to think maybe she was just mental. Anybody who could not calm down had to be. He took his frozen squirrels out of the freezer and placed them in an insulated chiller picnic bag.

Meanwhile, she repeated the same insults, full of expletives, over and over. His ears buzzed. Her hysteria was mounting and seemed to gain more momentum and energy, not less. She was not like this at work or on her jobs. He did not even know where he was going. But he had to go that night. He managed to move all the items. including Montse, her tank, lights and heater, into his van. As soon as he slammed the door shut, he knew she was gone from his life forever. He considered once again the Cartesian saying: *I am amazed how weak my mind is and how prone to error.*

He sat in his van in the dark, shutting his eyes, waiting for the first rays of daylight.

33

YOU

YOU'RE READING AND LEARNING in Robert's study when you hear the baby crying in her cot.

It is your first time alone with your own child. So technically it isn't babysitting. It is called parenting. Phoebe is out for lunch.

'What are you doing?' He gasped. Suddenly, a man has come into the room and Jorani is still shrieking. It's feeding time. Phoebe pumped out the milk earlier and it's in the fridge. There is no need to write these things down any more. They are part of the every day voices that you hear, the things you have to do and how to do them. You stumble out of the chair like Goldilocks.

'What- are- you- doing, I- said-' he growls like the bear.

'I— I am reading.' You stammer.

'What? What are you reading?' He demanded.

'Books.' The answer tumbles out.

'Don't ever come into my office,' he said. The S sound of *office* came long and sharp like a snake's hiss. 'How long have you been in here for?'

'I don't know.' It is the truthful answer.

'You know,' he snaps. Robert lunges. 'You pest. You absolute pest.' He goes at you with full force. You step aside. He misses and falls over. How is he so powerful when he is an elderly man? Ah yes, he is a Kungfu expert. He trains twice a week.

You tear out of the room to escape him. The milk. Downstairs to the fridge. You even know how to warm it up using the Avent bottle warmer. Never the microwave—

Robert shouts after you. 'It's because of you.' He steps in front of and blocks you.

What is because of you? What have you done except not given your daughter the milk? You rip at your hair, in a dilemma. You want to go back into your bedroom to pick her up. He appears to not even notice that there is a baby yelling. It is like a fire alarm which rings and rings. An alarm. It's a sound that you know.

'Get back! I am not finished with you!' He reaches out and grabs you by the collar. 'I am going to kill you.'

'What? Why? Why?'

'You just pretend to be some retard.'

Ugh. Egh. You struggle to say anything, while your hands grip his to pull him away.

'Yes, you. A fuckwit I am about to deal with. You have no right to go through my study. No right.'

Robert is foaming at the mouth. Momentarily he is distracted when you bare your teeth. You push him off, use your good leg to kick him. You suddenly tear yourself away from him, limping and shuffling one step at a time, to the bedroom on the top floor. Jorani is yelling. Your baby. But Robert is strong.

You call your daughter. Jorani, you say, Daddy's here, I am coming, OK.

She knows your voice yet she does not stop screaming. It is even more intense now.

He follows after you in big strides. Two steps at a time. He grabs your already injured calves. He is right, you are a retard. You can barely get up the stairs quickly enough to pick your baby up. You are not fit to be a parent at all.

Isn't this guy a doctor? Maybe it is a thug, it's a robbery, it's not Robert at all. You have issues trusting your own judgement. You fear losing your memory again, having to start the day every day with tests. Trapped. Can't run away downstairs and out of the house because you must take your daughter with you first. You almost reach the top of the stairs. He grabs your ankles and yanks hard. He pulls you down. He rains great blows on you.

You lose your balance and you fall headlong, you hope all that skin graft survives. There is still one last procedure as soon as it heals.

You land.

You hit your head on the newel post. It must be quite hard because you hear a terrible thud. Numbness fills your skull like a liquid, immobilising you, buzzing inside your head. You have been really getting better until you got into this mess. Not for the first time, you pass out. Everything is so white, it's black. The sound of the crying finally stops.

34

DOMINIQUE

S HE WOKE UP IN the night with the burning sensation and feverish chills.

Pain in the ass and in the front.

It was inevitable and she would have to tell the GP like she was a young woman who had no idea how she caught it. Cystitis. Common name: TMS — too much sex. She googled the quick treatments but knew she probably required antibiotics as it had spread to being a kidney infection already.

Looking through G in her contact list for her GP surgery's number, she saw H which was after G and Henry Tummings came up, bringing up awkward thoughts. Temporarily he had been pushed out of her mind due to recent epic bedroom marathons.

In front of Henry, Dominique hesitated, not wanting to bring up the fact that apart from these people who were dependents, there was also Przemek to care of. She did not have to. Przemek would not hear of it. He would rather have a loan from a bank like any other student but she would like to help him. She wanted to. She was double his age, she was both his mother and his lover. He was a project, a pet, a toy, she thought, with a prick of guilt and pain.

She reached for the paracetamol in her bedside drawer. She popped two out of the blister pack. She swore gently when she saw that there was no water in the glass on the bedside table. In no way did she see her altruism as demeaning. In what way was it insulting to help someone like him get ahead? She got up to go and refill with water from the bathroom. Above all, she thought she did love him. It was not so much romantic love but a sense of duty towards erotic love.

She felt sick. She was weak and had to flop down again when she came back from the sink. She had lost many years, decades, to being unloved, unromantic and unerotic. She wanted him. It was powerful and overwhelming. She wanted to die. The enormity of her desire terrified her. It must alarm him too. She would and could spread her talons, arms, thighs for him at any time. She used to think men were the same and rejected her like James did when the novelty wore off. Now she was not sure.

Desire was both an illness and a drug.

'You're making a fool of yourself, Dominique. You know I only want you to be happy but you may not be happy,' she heard Lucy saying in an imaginary, but plausible conversation. 'You stole him from another woman. You are playing with fire. You're a mature person. Don't do stupid, naïve things.'

Dominique knew the drill. Who had not seen the cliché of an old or middle-aged chubby man with a young girl-friend or wife? You would assume she was gold-digging and he did not care. So shocking and sexist at the time and now. What about when it was the other way round? The cougar was the derogatory term for someone like her. A terrifying predator, she was also shocking and sexist.

He was not after a merry widow or a pot of gold. It was desire that made her do things she did not want, that she was ashamed of, because she knew she must or she'd die.

Przemek was in her life now and she lost her trusted interior designer. She had to choose between him and Andreia and she had chosen him. She could not blame Andreia. She received her final invoice, some jaw dropping £47,000, not just for works to this house, but the trips to France and the flat in Southwark. Furniture and fittings for all these places for which she had been charged a holding or administrative fee.

She figured you could always hire another interior designer because there was a glut of them in London eager to take on anything, but you could not get another lover. Not easily, not ever. She was nearing 50. If she had in the past, she would not have been in this situation now. James might even have consented to a divorce. She had remained committed to James until his death. She had thought she loved him and could not let go. But now she knew she had been depriving him of his freedom, and he of hers, that was all.

Yearning was strong, but patience was the antidote. Desire came in waves, like grief. But as with all biochemical waves, hunger pangs, sugar cravings, rage, if you waited just 10 minutes, they passed.

She was on her second week of being in feverish pain, on and off, and she did not want her mother, Przemek or Daphne to know. She told Lucy. And Lorraine and Ellie knew what was going on anyway because they'd have to be blind not to. She wanted care from no one. Lucy came

round anyway with some goodies in a Harvey Nicks box –
candles, flowers, organic chocolates.

'So what have you done now, Nikki Nik.'

'What do you think? Sex. May cause irritation from
prolonged use. Seek medical attention if symptoms
persist.'

Lucy smiled. 'You poor thing. Are you drinking enough?'

'H two O to alcohol, one-nil, home game.'

'That's good. So what are we up to these days?'

'Let's see. Where were we? I emailed Achara customer
services in Bangkok and even filled in the online form. It
was all useless. No one replied. They were either too busy or
had very poor customer service or both.'

'OK.'

'James really had been caught up in something bigger
than he thought. In the process, I am also now caught up in
it, as usual. He always was greedy and put too much on his
plate without the intention of ever eating it. That was how
he was brought up. He wanted and needed everything and
everyone but actually he did not want anything or even
anyone.'

'Was James's Will witnessed by anyone?'

'It was signed in the presence of two witnesses therefore
I could not claim that it was invalid. I couldn't claim he was
mentally incapable.'

'No. He was living a 150 miles per hour life.'

'He was capable with a capital C.'

'Let's call Bangkok now,' said Lucy suddenly. 'Yeah, do it.
I am here, I can help you.'

Dominique reached for the phone next to the bed,
called the number in Bangkok and pressed the Speaker icon
so that Lucy could listen in. It rang and rang. Then it was
answered, presumably in Thai, so she had to do the tourist

thing of speaking in very slow English. 'Hello! Hello! Yes. Do. You. Speak. English.'

The female voice said 'a little.'

'I need to talk to the owner,' she said. 'Achara.'

Then it turned out the voice could not speak that much English after all, and asked her to wait. She was put through to at least 3 other people until one spoke English. He did rattle off some long Thai name. She wanted to discuss the Will, she said. They already had been informed of this and would be expecting not a big cheque but the deeds. The lawyers would be doing that now. They needed a lawyer themselves if they had not already got one.

'I want to talk about James's Will.'

'I am sorry. You can't just ring up. We don't even know who you are.'

'I am his wife.'

'You can't be. We know his wife.'

'What?'

'You need to go through our lawyers now. They are dealing with it. Please don't call again.'

'Wait. What? Wh- who is his *wife?*'

'Bye.'

'...'

He'd put the phone down, whoever he was.

'Are you OK?' said Lucy.

'Wife.' Dominique gasped. '*Wife.* Wife.'

'Nikki. Please,' Lucy put her arm around Dominique. 'I have heard of this,' said Lucy. 'If the Thais say *wife*, it could be a mistress or a girlfriend, not a legal wife.'

'But still he said *wife*,' Dominique said. 'You heard him Lucy. And now *I'm* saying it.'

'Don't worry, Nikki,' Lucy said. 'We can listen to it again. I've recorded it-'

'You have?'

'On my voice memo phone app. No idea what for, but you might find it useful.'

Dominique could not even thank Lucy. She groaned, and buried her head in her hands. 'What am I doing,' she sighed, 'tell me what is happening,' she said to herself more than to Lucy.

Whoever *they* were, not only did they stand to own the condo in Phuket but half the vineyard. If only Przemek knew what on earth was going on, not just in her kidneys but her mind. Dominique groaned and grunted, dabbing at her eyes with a tissue.

'Calm down, Dominique,' said Lucy. 'You've got an infection and a fever. You're in pain. Nothing will happen between now and tomorrow. Just rest first. I've got to go. I will come back tomorrow to see how you are getting on.' She gave her a hug and departed.

Dominique turned over and tried to sleep but could not. Lucy's e-mail with the voice memo file arrived in her inbox. She did not want to listen to it. Was James married again or was it a mistress? Did he love her? She did not want it to be true. That word kept jumping out at her every few minutes waking her up from her feverish state. *Wife.*

35

YOU

A TINKLING, SLOPPY SOUND wakes you up. It sounds like you are near water.

Are you on the boat again? What is that sound? You are in a lot of pain and you groan. When you open your eyes, you are not on the boat. Your father-in-law is in front of you with a glass of water and two white tablets. You gasp, reeling, cowering. You retract in your bed like an animal.

'You are back in your bed,' he says, 'take this.'

You don't know if you should. You look at his hand and you are completely still. Thinking, thinking.

'What is it,' you ask.

'Tramadol. It's time for your medication.'

You are resigned to it. You do not want to take it. He shows you not a tongue depressor but a 1" by 2" softwood offcut that the plumber had left behind. 'Do you want me to force this down your throat?'

You shake your head, shrivelling again under the duvet.

Your wounds have been dressed. There are bandages on

your knees, even the cuts on your head have been dressed. You look clean. Made up. So it can't be poison.

'Just fucking swallow it,' he snarls as if reading your mind. 'It's not poison. What is the point of poisoning you? You who's cost the NHS tens of thousands. And still counting. I am an old man and I dragged you all the way to your bed. Why did I save you? Why not kick you down the stairs?'

'What?'

'You will not tell anyone what happened. If you do, I will break you. I swear I will.'

'What?'

'Don't what. You know what I am talking about.'

'I don't.'

'Greg,' he says. 'I am at the end of my patience. You are pretending. I am warning you. Don't think I am an old man and you can fool me.'

You shake your head vigorously. You don't like him calling you Greg but you have no strength, no energy, to respond and now you also may be addicted to Tramadol as you have been on and off it for so long for all your injuries and surgeries. You head hurts so much. You absolutely have to take the medication. You have no will to fight it. Without it you cannot function. They have all turned you into an addict.

'You know what I am talking about,' your assailant says. 'How dare you go through my office?'

Everything has come back to you in such precise detail, right up to the instant he slammed your forehead on the newel post. Everything that happened on the boat. This is not what he is saying. This is about something else.

'You scum.' he yelled. 'You left her and she died.'

'What? I did not!' you yell. 'Lies! No way!'

'You went on to a party when you couldn't find her in the

pub. She went looking for you. She was mugged in an alley-way,' he whispered.

'No! I don't know what or who you are talking about.'

'STOP! She went back to the pub and had a heart attack. The whole pub knew what happened. And you don't? They caught the muggers.'

'No! None of this is true,' you insisted.

'You fucking deny it? You deny it?'

'I deny it! I wasn't me-'

He ignored you. 'SHUT UP! When she was diagnosed, she told you about it. The funding deal that I was involved in. She told you! You knew all along!'

'No! What funding? This is all wrong!'

'She died in a toilet! In some shithole of a pub in Peck-ham,' he hissed. 'With. No. Money. No phone, no purse. I had to stomach you coming back to the UK and living in my fucking house. I had to get you well and kick you out as soon as I could. And now I know what you are looking for in my office. You will see I have removed all the evidence. France, the boat, vineyards, everything.'

You've seen those photos but you don't want him to know you'd seen them as since he is already accusing you of snooping and, furthermore, he wants to kick you out. In another era, someone was paying him in gifts. Something Meditech. You are just an addict now, a penniless dependent.

'My baby girl,' he says with tears rolling from his wrin-kled hooded eyes. 'If you had been... If she could...' he stopped to get his breath back. 'Every day we think about her. Every single day. Not a minute's peace.' You feel sorry. You too are almost moved to tears. An elderly man still mourns the death of a child, always a child.

A few moments silence while you watch him wiping his tears. Then suddenly he gets up.

'When they come back you will tell them you fell down the stairs,' he says, in his doctor voice.

36

PRZEMEK

H E WOKE UP IN his van. His neck and head hurt. It felt like he'd been beaten up.

His bloodshot eyes watered when he yawned. When he remembered with a shudder the row and Andreia's expletives, he shook the thoughts away like they were flies.

He started the van and went to the nearest MacDonald's at the huge roundabout of the Wandsworth Gyratory. Whilst having his big breakfast there, he used the WiFi to message and call as many estate agents as he could. He had money for the deposit and for a night's accommodation at the York Road Travelodge.

The next day he moved into a studio flat in Mount Avenue, Ealing, a very similar place to the one he was in before he moved in with Andreia. The estate agent had blinked when he said he was looking for a bedsit. There was no such word, she'd said. A few years ago, that word had disappeared and become studio. It cost £875 per calendar month. It was close to North of Haven Green on the second floor of a large, early Victorian, split-level end-of-terrace house.

It was a bright studio room with its original fireplace and an open plan kitchen with a vinyl floor which was printed like it was a farmhouse stone floor. The whole place had been painted that colour that all rental flats were: Gardenia by Dulux. It was full of mismatched landlord furniture in pine or white melamine which was great as it was as far from Andreia's style as you could get and, besides he needed bookshelves and a desk for his studies. He was unsure if his air gun skills could be used to hunt squirrels for Montse. He did not dare check out the shared garden yet.

With a sharp pain, he remembered that he'd left the air gun behind anyway. It was still in the shed. After he settled in, he would have to go back to retrieve it. He still had the keys.

Once moved in, he filled the freezer with Montse's meals before they thawed. He worked day and night on his reading up and self-preparations. He had checked the garden, he realised that it was too small, too overlooked and, in fact, not even a shared garden. He wandered in from the side alleyway and realised then it belonged to the other flats, there was no access from his studio.

He missed the Battersea garden and the squirrels. His own wildlife park had existed just for him. Just him, the hunter, and his prey. Now he was not a hunter. He was Dominique's prey and she his muse. With shame came pride too. He started his preparations for the start date of the Access to HE Diploma (Science). Only a week to go before he started at Kingston.

It was a most important academic year ahead as he needed to get *that* score to get into Kings and he felt he could do it with her support and her adoration. It was doing wonders for his testosterone and his confidence, for they went together, hand in hand. He wanted that feeling of ambition. He craved it. It was what he was born to do.

He was young, tanned with a strong build and he knew machines inside and out. He'd become a plumber because someone said there were shedloads of plumbing jobs in the UK. But when he came here, he'd changed. Life changed him and the UK changed him. He no longer wanted to do what he came here to do – plumbing.

He had always been a thinker, but leaving home had made him a dreamer, he became what he wanted to become, part of the Polonia – people of Polish descent living outside Poland. He did not dream of being back home. He just thought about it sometimes. They were two different things. English people daydreamed all the time. The lottery, living in Spain, Christmas bonanzas. It was part of their culture to daydream.

His thinking became like Montse's. Hardly any. Just food, sleep. He'd told Dominique he wanted to turn into someone else. It was time to dream.

For two months he was settling in to his new studio flat, filling any spare time with daydreams, and he felt quite comfortable, at ease at last. He could call it home. It was his. There were no women controlling the moneybelt or his activities. It could actually be called a mini paradise.

But one day, Montse went missing. She was not in her tank, fondly referred to as Pałac – Polish for palace. Could it be too small for a Burmese? He checked the dimensions and did a quick search online for what size it should be. He had been overfeeding her the squirrels in the old flat in Battersea because there were simply too many squirrels.

Now she was back on the rat diet from the online pet shop suppliers. He realised it was not enough. Snakes only ran away – if a snake could even be said to run anywhere – when they were starving. An escaped snake was a sign of animal abuse.

Przemek could barely breathe. Someone or something was bound to get hurt and he needed to act fast. He had to find Montse, starting in his own tiny studio. It should not take long.

First he checked that all the sash windows were locked shut and the back and front doors were fully sealed when shut, without any gaps. He checked all the kitchen units. Any doors which could not shut with a click or a snap tight closure, had to be checked as snakes had muscles which could help them 'open' or rather 'push away' doors which were not tightly fitted enough.

THE EXTRACT DUCT GRILLE was missing. She'd got out. Although he wanted to he could not report it because he could be done by the Policja.

Przemek spent a good two weeks clearing the freezer of Montse's food, the tank, lights, heater, everything. He did not want anyone to know. He was living in cold reptilian fear. Sick with anxiety. Every day guilt crawled over him, and every night sleeplessness. What if they found her? He imagined himself in the national newspapers and blowing his chances of getting into Kings.

Przemek had on many an occasion enjoyed eating a shiny blood red apple while looking straight at Montse. There was always something magical and biblical about snakes. The serpent was traditionally symbolic of renewal, transformation and rebirth due to its constant shedding of skin. Of course it was also symbolic of the original sin and the temptation of Eve.

Montse's escape brought about a grief he had not felt or expressed before. He found himself weeping without any warning which surprised him as Montse seemed like a good choice for a low maintenance pet requiring minimal or no emotional input such as affection. A terrible ache ripped him apart. He must have been in a one-sided relationship. He spent so much time thinking and reading while Montse was in the room that somehow he felt Montse was part of his subconsciousness.

Now that he had started his course, he could not see past the next exams. He forced himself to think of the two women in his life to take his mind off Montse.

Immaculate, feminine Dominique of the old world. Fantasies. Hot penetrative sex, baths, chandeliers, lace stockings, cherry red lipstick, no TVs, phones, alerts. She even smelled luxurious, intense, of Persian roses. He wanted to live it, love it, breathe in and be revived by a decadent and dying world, a world where there was nothing else but human thought, ideas and form.

Przemek felt it was necessary to disengage with social media if one was keen to be purified of modern life. Dominique was not his stepping stone nor someone to be "stepped on" while he got through his classes and worked fewer hours. He could not accept a penny from her.

Andreia was from the new world. Neat, no-makeup makeup, over-sized dresses from obscure Scandinavian or Japanese designer labels in grey which looked like architectural origami. He experienced a mixture of shame and tenderness towards Andreia, like the thought of a warmed-up pie gone cold. He remembered only the good things about her, the boxy outfits, her matching rose gold pair of candelabras, sports bras and Sweaty Betty leggings, her assortment of social media platforms which he'd watched her cycle through with her fingers swiping right. He was never going to be good enough for her, for she was someone who moved with the times, moving fast and right now. She didn't waste time.

Reading fiction was "wasting time", as was staring at Montse for 40 minutes while sipping Polish lager. All activities had to be directed towards something, as they could not be complete in themselves. If she was reading, it would be to write a blog post, to give a talk or to research the best phone camera or the best phone or five ways to increase traffic through content marketing. It would be to achieve a professional or health and fitness goal. It was impossible to entertain Andreia.

Not once did she ask or talk about his course or about Montse. The only time they were to go back to Krakow she could not make it. Thankfully she did not, for she would have been in the way of his vintage shopping spree and absinthe bar crawl. The milestone big events interested her the most. Birthdays, Valentine's, Christmas. She was a walking Google calendar. What would happen to these events, shows and talks, all lined up, timed and alarmed like targets to shoot?

Andreia did not know about his rifle so he'd had to keep it out of sight. If she'd ever known, she'd have freaked out. And not because it was a rifle. Because it was ugly. At best, she'd put up with living with Montse who she referred to as *it* and not *she*. Like Frida Kahlo, she was her own muse. He listed the now redundant air gun on eBay.

After three weeks there had been no news and no arrests.

No one came to his door to search. He concluded that

Montse was dead. How could she go for three weeks without food? If she had been eating humans or pets everybody would already know by now. With cold and trembling fingers, he went to bus stops and tube stations like a fugitive, furtively picking up the Metro and Evening Standard every day without fail, hunting for any news on reptiles found and caught.

37

DOMINIQUE

THE VIDEO ENTRY SYSTEM rang and rang.

If you didn't answer the door within 5 chimes, and it knew that you were in, it would get diverted and your phone would also start ringing like mad.

Dominique felt very frail when she woke up and dragged herself to the door within the 5 chimes. The two enormous grey velvet sofas had arrived from Toast or Loaf or some nonsensical one syllable name like it was breakfast but was actually £16,000 worth of sofa.

They were ordered about ten or twelve weeks previously and were supposedly ethical and sustainably made in Nicaragua. Not great for the air miles but there *was* an entire village there making ethical sofas. She had forgotten ordering them and now thought they looked incongruous. Yet she'd approved the fabric samples and signed them off for Andreia, but still, they seemed huge and wrong now.

Dominique had been happy that there was no one else to care for or to care for her and nothing to take care of, that was, until the sofas arrived.

After they were dumped onto the reception room floor

like two loaves of bread dropped from a shopping bag, she signed for them. She went into her office, switched on her laptop and looked up a previous email. She found the long undecipherable Thai name for Achara's lawyer.

The other name on the vineyard title deed was straight-forward, another company. A UK company that James was a joint director of. 'Petitemort Holdings Ltd'. Now there were a few of them in this. They would all get a share of the vine-yard. Such a charming and ironic cliché of a French name, Petite Mort or Little Death or orgasm to the rest of us, but it was a British company. Naturally to have a name like that you would have to appreciate English whimsy. It would not take long now to track them down and negotiate all this, before she made a claim.

AN HOUR LATER, THE entry system chimed and chimed. This time it was the delivery of the wallpaper. Both for the house and for the house in France. It was handblocked Chinois-erie; a scene with bridges and birdcages on a black back-ground. It cost £200 a roll. There were 76 rolls. She'd got very obsessed when she first saw it at the Chelsea Harbour Design Centre. You could not find this anywhere else; in the UK or on the continent. Now it did not make any sense. The house in France might not even be hers any more. She must find a way of returning them. She might even have to re-sell them to get some money back at least.

Sitting on the plastic covering of one of the sofas, she called Henry. 'Contesting Will,' she said.

He repeated there was no basis for doing so. 'Dominique, James was of sound mind and there was a witness, his senior colleague at the time.'

Dominique's eyes darted around the room. She had no idea what all this stuff was that surrounded her. She had lost interest in interior design and Andreia, just when everything was coming together and being finished.

When he was alive she could not communicate with James. And now he was dead she was communicating with him via lawyers. They were like spirit mediums, only speaking in legalese, devoid of any emotion. She only had to say the words, 'But I—' to be interrupted by the usual nonsense, 'I understand completely'. They didn't understand anything. They had to reply with disclaimers woven into every exchange of information, either spoken or written. Not a single response had been thought through, how could it be?

Her mind was spinning. There was nothing worse than a spiralling, unravelling mind when you were surrounded by things you supposedly loved and desired. Just then something occurred to her.

'Dominique? Are you there? Dominique?' Tummings had noticed her silence.

'Yes.' She replied. 'Yes I am. And who is this senior colleague?'

'Martin Pelland.'

'Thank you.'

38

YOU

TODAY IT IS MILD. After breakfast mind training, which Eva has to do because Phoebe has been up all night, and is still up, trying to feed the baby, you rush outside.

You want to be in the garden as soon as possible so they are out of your hair. It is increasingly difficult to do any research because Eva and Phoebe are often in now, after your "fall". They no longer trust you with your own daughter, and that is a fucking annoyance since you have been working so hard at it. You sit in the garden, scratch at your scabs and scars.

This inconvenience will be turned around shortly. You clench your jaws. Only five days to go to the last of the skin grafts. The day of escape is imminent. No bank account or internet access still. Once you are good with the PIN then they say you can have a bank account. They meaning those in charge of your body and mind and soul. The goddesses of your domestication.

You have changed a nappy. You know a lot more now: where the tape is, which is front and which is back, there are girl's nappies and boy's but not at the newborn stage. There are different sizes according to weight. You have new memory games – the name of your daughter, her weight at birth, 3.4kg. You wait for a chance to change the nappy but it never comes. You know about breastfeeding and that a newborn has to be fed every two hours. None of this matters because now they don't trust you. You look at your tight fists. What are they capable of?

You establish the entire compact garden in your mind by sitting out in it. Squarish. Fulham houses do not have large gardens.

You have already looked at the A to Z from Robert's office, as you can only look at the iPad when you are allowed to, such as when you are doing your brain training or when you are learning the roads around here, since you don't know the password.

But when the others are not around, you have to make use of the old ways of looking up things, which has to be done in Robert's office when he is not in. You have lifted the navy blue vinyl-covered A to Z hardback and have it with you in the garden. Although it is not to scale, you can see proportion. Your pre-internet memory functions let you read a street directory or map and transfer it into your mind without having to refer to it again and again.

In a kitchen drawer, you find the measuring tape. While in the kitchen, you spot Eva's and Phoebe's purses, keys, lipstick holders and phones.

They are upstairs trying to soothe your daughter. You act before the yelling stops. You take two pounds each from each purse and put it in your pocket, which you'll empty and hide later. You cannot take a lot at once or it will raise suspicion. Just a tiny amount per day. Soon you will have enough cash. You take the tape, a pencil and the A to Z back into the garden.

The garden is only 7.5m wide by 8.3 m long when measured. You stand on a stepladder you find in the shed and look over the fences at everybody else's gardens as far as your eye can see. The houses with extensions, without, with loft conversions, without. With gates and rear alleyway access.

You mark them in pencil on the A to Z and the number of the houses that you count up. You know it does not matter that you mark in pen or pencil because no one ever looks at the A to Z any more because of phones. You are just a relic, a burden to this family, as redundant as this A to Z. You plan on taking it with you when you leave.

You have no evidence yet. You have time. Time is all you have. Time is not like money. You can waste all the time you want. More simply arrives the next day.

It is getting hot now, and you start to perspire. You start to flick at your own scabs and scratches. They often feel like ants, covering you in a tingly numbness. You begin slapping at your own injuries, face, torso, limbs, increasing the intensity with each slap to stop the itching and irritation, killing those imaginary ants. It brings relief and tears to your eyes, to know you can do this without any damage, to feel it, that you are — and because you are — alive. *No scratching if you are to improve, no long nails, no excuses or no last procedure.*

You want to punch the timber fences that surround you. Lunging at them, panting, you stop only when you think of that escape day. You must be a good patient, as good as can be with your teeth gritted, and hands clutching your own head, tearing at your hair.

39

PHOEBE

FTER DINNER AND JORANI was down for her deepest sleep of the day. A long nap from 7 to 9 pm, thank God.

Phoebe opened the last folder in the iPad labelled Greg 2018 to let him watch the final file. 8:05pm according to the kitchen clock.

This period was when she was most tired. Giving Greg activities was like work - a continuation of the morning's training.

She opened a folder of the most recent files, April 2018, a month before his accident. They were shot on a yacht, though she did not know if it was the same yacht that he had his accident on. They were mostly interior shots of each cabin. Greg did a lot of photography and videography for corporate hospitality clients. He could have been filming for those real estate or holiday promo programmes for Sky. Greg stared at the footage.

'Look Greg! This was the beautiful boat you were working on...'

He said nothing. There was no one on the boat, and it was immaculate.

'I am sorry; I know you don't want to do more mind training. Morning is your best time, I've noticed.'

He smiled at her and said 'sure' in his new 'posh' voice. Though it was not the same as it was, it would never be and she was happy that he had any voice.

There was always a quiet time after dinner and before the baby started yelling, so it was a good time to relax, drink wine or just chat.

Phoebe saw that he had his hand in the pocket of his grey tracksuit.

'What have you got in there, Greg?'

'Nothing!' He gave his false smile again, creasing his scarred and disjointed facial expression, which made him appear grotesque.

'Come. On. I can see you have something. Show me.'

'Why?'

'I just want to know,' she said. She had not been cheerful for a long time, not since she last saw her baby smile at her and kick her legs. 'Because the more you don't want me to see it, the more I want to.'

'OK.' He said. 'But promise me, you won't laugh or get cross.'

'Of course not. Why would I? Why should I?'

Slowly, he pulled the pack of cards from his pocket.

'Wow! Where did you get them from?'

'Don't worry, I didn't rob anybody.'

'Oh Greg, I sure hope that you'd rob somebody for their Rolex and not a pack of cards.'

'Play?' he asked without a trace of fun or invitation.

'Play?'

'You know. Cards. Play cards. A card game.'

'Can you even play any games?'

He didn't answer. He frowned and looked away, like she'd asked something embarrassing.

'Of course! I would love to.'

'Before that, I need help loading the dishwasher,' called out Eva from the kitchen.

'OK, mum,' said Phoebe, with a sigh. She looked at Greg and he just nodded. He pointed to himself with his thumbs to show her that he did not want to call out or reply to Eva and that he and Phoebe were partners in this together. Things had improved so much since he got his voice back, or rather his new voice. They were a couple again.

Phoebe knew that Eva did not like to see them enjoying themselves. After Bethany there could be no more fun. A sad little chuckle was fine. Proper hearty laughter was unheard of. Greg slipped the cards back into his pocket. He loaded the dishwasher in five minutes because it was something that he had learned and practised. He knew where to put every item.

He came back and retrieved the cards again. Before he could say anything, she said, 'Guess what? I don't know any games. I can't teach you. We never played card games in all the time I knew you.'

'That's OK.' He said without looking at her. He sat with her at the sofa, their thighs touching. Phoebe checked the time and glanced at the baby monitor. The lights were green, not orange and blinking and there was no sound from upstairs. They might actually be able to play a game in this short window before Jorani woke up for her feed.

They heard front door lock and Robert coming in. The door slammed and he double bolted it on the inside. No one was going out again, then.

Robert had been looking haggard and in a foul mood

recently. In a Chinese family you could not bring up something if it was wrong. The person who had something to bring up would do that themselves – and no one did. The repression had gone on for generations and that was how Phoebe had been brought up. If they were visibly in a bad mood, you left them alone. Anyway he was still working at his age, and she was pissed off and exhausted too, so they were even.

Robert's eyes darted over the dinner table, already cleared of cutlery and crockery. His dead and lifeless eyes became transfixed by something. Greg was just about to lay the cards on the glass coffee table.

'You want dinner,' said Eva, in Chinese, from the kitchen. It was not a question; it was a statement. Phoebe could hear the microwave whirring. Robert had light meals nowadays. But he did not reply. He was too busy looking at the cards being dealt.

GREG SHUFFLED. HE DEALT the cards clockwise - five downward facing cards. Four sets. He assumed that they'd want to play and they'd be offended if not invited. So instead of asking he dealt four hands on the coffee table, although Eva and Robert were not even sitting there. He put the rest of the deck in the middle of the table.

'I think so,' said Greg. Phoebe did not know what he was saying 'I think so' to. 'We can just write down each of us has put in a pound, for argument's sake.'

Phoebe got a pen from a drawer and a flyer from a cleaning service. 'This is interesting. What are we playing? No, don't tell me, the winner takes it all.'

'Yes,' he said. 'Correct. Look at your cards now. This is

the time to evaluate how strong your hand is. Beginners show their tell. Tells include shallow breathing, lack of — or too much — eye contact, facial muscles flexing-'

Poker face. That was it. She noticed that indeed he wore the same expression most of the time now.

'Where did you learn this, Greg?' asked Phoebe 'We never played card games.'

'Poker,' said Robert. 'The ante is one pound per player. Deal or be dealt with.'

Phoebe laughed but her hands twitched. 'Am I seeing right? You play poker?' She leaned over and kissed him on the temple.

'From never playing,' said Robert, 'to dealing.' He glared at Greg.

'Dad, please.'

He did not stop to look at Phoebe at all. He kept his hooded eyes on Greg, frowning as though thinking.

'Well, there is a first time for everything,' said Eva. Always helpful with the clichés.

'You first,' Greg said to Robert. 'You have to make a call which means open or check. Place first bet or pass on it to the next person.'

Robert remained stony faced, his jaw clamped shut. The vein in his temple throbbed. He said nothing at first. 'They look like my cards.' said Robert. 'Where did you find them?'

The door bell rang suddenly. 'Who is it?' Phoebe called. Robert jumped up and opened the door, leaving the chain on.

'We are from the NCA,' said the first of two men in quilted jackets which Phoebe could see through the gap in the door. He flashed his badge. The second man also flashed his badge. It was hard to see as it was dark outside. She could not even tell what the badges were.

'Could we ask you to remove the chain, please?' One of them said.

'What is this about?'

'Dr Robert Wong?'

'Yes?'

'Please remove the chain.'

Robert sighed and removed the chain. Phoebe felt bad for her father, award-winning brilliant doctor and scientist. Now elderly and exhausted.

'Dr Wong,' said the first man. 'We have a warrant.'

YOU ARE IN BANDAGES again. At least it's the last time.

You are told that they can come off in 5 days. What's 5 days compared to your time in this lost state? You have finished with the last of the skin grafts. You are completely back to yourself, or as much as you can be, says the doctor. But you can't even yawn.

After seeing the consultant, you go back into the lift, she holds the lift open, as though you are heavily pregnant or someone overweight who needs the lift doors fully open.

Phoebe takes your hand and guides you. You enter the lobby.

You can only see through the slots in the bandages. You're in the hospital cafeteria. You just want to go home and lie down, but you feel you don't even have the strength to say it.

You know she will test you as it hasn't been done this morning yet. First you recite your profile biography in one paragraph like it's a morning prayer. You suppose it is now. You say your name and address, your wife's name, the names of everybody in your immediate family. You do not even need the photos now.

'What is the date?' Says Phoebe, looking pleased. She is not asking you, she is testing you.

You tell her. 'December 4th. 2018. It is Tuesday.'

'What is in 3 days?'

'Your birthday.'

'What shall we do? It's a joint celebration.'

'Joint with who?'

It isn't you, you know that. You have been made to repeat that your birthday is 19th August so many times.

'No,' she smiles and frowns at the same time, an expression only a Chinese person is capable of. 'I mean we are celebrating the end of all your medical interventions.'

Even if you do do badly in a test, Phoebe has never said a negative thing. She has always lied for your pride. You look forward every day to her voice, her tests, the sight of her lying, expressive eyes, her warm hands as she hands you your drink.

Neither of you will ever know what the other is thinking. 'Your reward,' she says, handing you the worst cup of coffee you've ever had, but it will help you think clearly. It has been twelve days since Robert's arrest. Nine since he came out on bail.

'WHAT? WHAT FOR?' PHOEBE had demanded when the National Crime Agency came round.

'You are under arrest on suspicion of supplying confidential pharmaceutical research results to the developer BioCore Meditech,' the officer said to Robert, ignoring Phoebe.

'You do not have to say anything, but it may harm your defence if you do not mention when questioned something which you later rely on in court. Anything you do or say may be given in evidence.'

BioCore Meditech is the name on the photos in Robert's office, sponsor of his 2016 Bali conference and other 'gifts', sailing trips, the vineyard too. You said nothing while Eva and Phoebe let out peals of incessant whys, what-fors and who-are-yous, like bells in a tower. You watched Robert being taken away, not even by force. There was no need. He wasn't the type to struggle or fight back.

'Suspicion doesn't mean anything, right? Is that right?' Phoebe called after them but they had already entered the black car. 'What about dad's coat or a jacket?' Phoebe cried. 'Where is he going?' It was pointless. Phoebe and her mother hugged each other, weeping and gasping.

You did not cry. You were immobile, speechless. 'He did not even eat his dinner,' Eva pointed at the kitchen. The first and last thing that occurs to a Chinese person is food.

'You should not have started him on that stupid game!' She turned on you after she disengaged from her daughter's embrace. 'You must have known he likes poker!'

You didn't answer.

'He plays online.' Eva was hyperventilating and weeping. 'He's crazy about it!'

The baby then started crying as she was sleeping lightly now that it was nearly time for her to wake up for her feed and nappy change.

You'd bring the baby down, you said. They stared at you limp up the stairs.

∽

SINCE THEN YOU'VE BEEN WAITING for the last of the procedures to be over, and anything to do with Robert's arrest has been unmentionable. With some difficulty, you try to drink the coffee. Phoebe stops you. She fetches more milk and a straw from the cashier's counter. Milk added and straw in the lid, you drink deeply. You have no idea why you are so thirsty and so drained.

Another operation over. You have been living like this for so long you cannot remember a time when you weren't having operations. Could you have been well once? It seems impossible.

She watches you suck and by gosh you could still suck and suck so well. It seems to be a skill unaffected by the tragedy that is now yours. You see it as yours and yours alone. No one can take it away nor can you. It is so part of you you do not want to think what life would be without the tragedy. It is more real than any of these words she makes you recite. She holds your free hand like a child while you use your other hand to hold the cup you are sucking from.

She lets go of your hand. Her eyes cloud over and she is thinking of something else.

Not long to go now, you tell yourself.

DOMINIQUE

'I HAD NO INTENTION of going back to Asia yet here I am again,' she said to Lucy.

They were on the 21:20 EVA Air flight from Heathrow headed for Phuket via Bangkok.

'You're doing fine. I'm here with you this time and God knows I should have come with you last time.'

'How do I know I am doing fine?'

'You found the offshore shelf company Petitemort and now Achara Wine Imports. Progress.'

'After this, no more. Tracking down the assets has been a losing battle for me,' she said. It made her blood boil.

She wanted to give up but she could not. Because of one word. Wife. *Wife*. Losing James's millions to all these people made her throat tight.

She wanted to crush her drink and fling it into the plane aisle. If not for fear of getting arrested, she would have been smashing a lot more things than a plastic cup of gin and tonic. All these rôles didn't suit her: widow, mum, amateur detective, employer to all these people; cleaners, gardener, now-defunct interior designer, and her one-time plumber, now lover. 'That bloody Henry Tummings-' she swore, speaking her thoughts aloud.

'The lawyer?' said Lucy.

'—is not helping by saying he'll go to court but it will cost me. A lot. Probably half the assets. Or all of them.'

Legal fees were a bottomless pit. It was twenty to begin with. Every trip to court cost fifty. She'd already started using the proceeds from the insurance payout to pay Henry's fees. Money seemed to be cycled and recycled.

'Don't you long for the days when you had nothing, no one had anything and therefore everyone had an equal share of nothing?'

'No,' thought Dominique. She'd never had nothing. Now she needed to find James's everything. All of it just developed into more headaches. For her and Daphne she'd find this *wife*, recoup James's assets. If she was to be miserable and unlucky all her life, she had to know why.

'Well,' said Lucy with a sly smile. 'You already do have everything. Even a lover to screw.'

'Lucy!' she whispered. 'You do know there are other people on the plane?'

'I know. Sorry. Let's order the snacks now, shall we? Where is the menu? Ahh here.'

She found the menu card in the seat pocket. Dominique sighed and shook her head when she was offered it. She brushed away hot tears with the serviette that came with the free nuts. No wiping or rubbing, that would encourage wrinkles.

'What time do we get in?' Asked Lucy although Dominique had already told her when, before they took off.

'Five to seven, tomorrow evening.'

Dominique was finding it hard to concentrate on anything because she finally understood the crude phrase 'to fuck your brains out'. She had no brains now. They were porridge, a non-moving muscle. How was she going to get to the bottom of the mess James had left behind in this state? It was like being ill. Sick with desire.

During the fourteen-and-a-half-hour flight she had plenty of time for reflection interspersed with little golden daydreams of Przemek's tight muscles clasping her entire back, her thighs gripping his. She had to brush these away like cobwebs the moment they came to her because they made it impossible to think.

As time had gone by, it got worse and worse because she was hardly seeing him now. He lived in his own bedsit, or studio or whatever he liked to call it, and she did not have the guts to contact him.

If she sent him a text or email, as she would have done twenty-odd years ago, she'd have no idea — and would be unable to see — if he had read it or even retrieved the message. But if he replied, she'd be grinning like a fool for half a day, a junkie given a fix. On Whatsapp you saw two blue ticks. It was actually a verb now, "to be blue ticked". According to Daphne, it meant "to have had your messages read and acknowledged". On Messenger you got the photo of the person next to the message. These indicators that she was 'checked on' and that they had 'checked in' showed her that she was needed.

Upon arrival after a peaceful, yet still sleepless, night and a half, Dominique and Lucy were picked up by a car that Lorraine had organised. They checked in at the Bangkok Marriott Sukhumvit. 'Have anything,' Dominique said. 'It's on me.' Lucy craved the rare and expensive crispy fried golden carp and so had insisted on dinner at the Siam Tea Room. Despite its dull name, it was a regular haunt for high-rollers from the finance district.

The next morning, they slept in until 11:30, jet-lagged, missing breakfast completely. Lucy checked on her phone the place they had to get to.

'This is a bit like detective work, Nikki Nik.'

'It's definitely work,' said Dominique. 'Not sure about the detective bit.'

A driver had been organised and turned up at 12 noon to take them to the family-friendly suburb of Thonglor. Not far from the hotel, it was an Islington-ish suburb with urban playgrounds, massage kiosks and yoga huts. And of course, Achara Wine.

Achara Wine PLC was a cavernous space with a standard glass cabin as its entry lobby. Outside it was 35 deg heat but inside it was air conditioned to subzero temperature and dimly lit. You would have thought you were in a wine cellar in the middle of a Bulgarian winter. Shapely bottles stood on the worktop for the evening tastings. She noticed Lucy reading the noticeboard to check out the tasting schedule. How pleasant it was for these tasting people, and lucky Lucy, while she was suffering. Dominique developed a sudden dislike for wine, although it had once been her closest friend. Where once she'd once drunk it with so much gusto and delight, it revolted her now, a bitter testament to her fate.

'Good afternoon. May I see the director, please?' Dominique said to the receptionist. 'I did call and email from London many times.'

'Sorry? You did or you did not?'

'Did. Did.' Dominique repeated it, so firmly articulating the Ds that her incisors ached.

She waited while the receptionist went to find the manager from the back offices somewhere. This place was strangely reminiscent of the mortuary she'd had to identify

James in. Andreia could have turned these chic dumps from meh to yeah.

The manager was a tall and well-dressed Thai by the name of 'Eddy'. With a fitted European designer shirt and ruby-coloured cuff links, he must have been well-paid too. Dominique thought he was eager to assist because she was white, so there was no doubt that she would be a wine drinker.

'How can I help you?' He said.

'Thank you for seeing me. Who is in charge of the company?'

'Achara. She is the director. Was.'

'I need to see her. She has a joint partnership with my husband and I need to see her.'

'She is gone.'

'What?' said Lucy. 'What do you mean?'

'She was on the yacht,' Eddy continued. 'Did you not read the news at the time? They never found her. She was probably eaten by fish.'

'Calm down, Nikki Nik,' said Lucy. You OK?' She put her hand on Dominique's which was resting on the reception counter.

'I- I don't – I have come all this way to be told this? Why did you not say it on the phone?'

'You never asked. You never mentioned Achara. My brother is the new director now and he can't speak to you. This is a family business; you understand? Yes, we are share-holders now and this was James's Will. He gave her the company. He bought this place.' He waved airily around at the wine cave. Thais had at least five nicknames, all official. Even the name in a passport could be a nickname.

'But- who- is she?'

'Achara is my sister. And James's wife.'

That word again. *Wife*.

'But-' she grabbed at words. She choked. 'but- *I* am-' her throat was dry. Her head spun. She couldn't breathe. What was happening to her? She felt herself unravelling like a reel of thread and gasped.

'Nikki,' said Lucy. 'Nikki.'

'Do you want to sit down? Can I get you water?' Eddy said. But Dominique shook her head, clutching at Lucy for support. She looked down at the floor. She was wavering.

'It has been so difficult for us. I hope you feel better soon.' Eddy said.

'It's been difficult for us too,' said Lucy, placating. 'Dominique is James's wife.'

'So you said. He was my sister's husband.' He was visibly upset and he started to clam up.

'We've come all this way from London.' The cultural differences were vast. Neither Dominique nor Eddy had any experience of this kind of conversation. He was not even using his first language.

'I can't help you. I- I am very sorry.' He wiped a tear away with a used crumpled tissue, retrieved from his pocket. He turned his head left and right in order not to rub at his eyes. On the plane Dominique did not rub her eyes either. And now she could see why. The Thais were meticulous about such things. No wonder their beauty industry was one of the most exemplary in the world, thought Dominique, distracted by this butterfly thought. She could not share his grief. What about hers? Did they grieve for her?

'She's gone from our lives. I don't know what to say.'

Dominique croaked to Lucy, finally, 'Let's go.' She did not thank him. What would she be thanking him for? The sight of all these bottles that James had invested in, while she was working hard in London and Daphne was locked away in boarding school, simply revolted her. She could not wait to get back out into the car park.

'That was not great, to say the least,' said Lucy. 'I'm so, so sorry Nikki Nik.'

Dominique hung her head and wept silently in the car park until the driver said they should get in the car. She was a mess and might as well have been a tramp being dragged away, unable to find any strength to protest. Everything was stained and crumpled, including herself. 'At least it's a Lexus and air-conditioned,' said Lucy, 'Come on babes, the engine is on. The driver wants us to hop in. Come on. Let me help you, darling.'

Lucy placed a comforting arm around her friend and pulled out tissues from her secondhand Chloe handbag, once Dominique's. She opened the car door. Dominique slumped into the seat like a heavy bag of laundry. Her tears made dark spots on her already dark Marc Jacobs top which she had brought to look smart. Not so smart now.

'I am just left with the house in London. All his millions have gone to others. Even the house in France, his parents' wedding present to us. I have nothing but his life insurance payout and the Holland Villas Road house.'

'I wouldn't call that nothing,' said Lucy.

Suddenly, there was a tap on the window. It was a Thai girl, carrying an umbrella to keep off the sun.

'Who is that?' said Dominique, looking blank.

'No idea.'

She pressed the button to wind down the window. The girl had enormous sunglasses on and therefore would not be easily identifiable.

'I work here. I am a wine intern. My name is Noi.'

'What does that mean?'

'My name?'

'No,' Dominique stopped herself short. Her voice was already very shaky. She gritted her teeth. 'What... is... a... wine... intern... and... what... do... you... want?' Each word squeezed out like a drop of blood.

'I'm on a 12-month work experience here. I know her.'

'Who?' said Lucy.

'Achara.'

YOU

W HEN YOU WAKE UP it is later. You check the flip-calendar and clock that Phoebe bought when you first came back from Cambodia.

It is Saturday, December 8th, 2018, 08:32.

You're still wearing bandages from your last skin graft operation. Two more days 'til they come off. It is time for your morning dose of painkillers. Phoebe has put them by your bedside with a plastic bottle of water. This means she is not in. You swallow. You know they will keep you on the meds. You've had so much treatment they probably need a building just to store your medical history files. Without the painkillers you cannot keep going, not even for a day.

You hear Eva's voice. Also an incessant drilling sound. She is talking to someone. Somebody repeating the word 'pressure'. What pressure? You are in pain. Robert has said to you not to tell anybody or he'd kill you anyway. Maybe he has a Jekyll and Hyde personality. He seemed to be himself yet someone else, a monster. Now he has been detained for some insider trading. It is what you think of every day when you wake up now, even before you take your painkillers.

Suddenly, a young blond man with a golden tan appears in your bedroom. You take a dislike to him. He is like a little god. Dazzling, young and perfect, all of which you'd notice whether you were a man or a woman.

'I have to bleed radiator. I am sorry to disturb.'

No articles. That means he's Eastern European. You remember, he's the plumber. His massive bunch of keys are sticking out of his pocket. You have been waiting for days, weeks, for him to come back and now he has returned. You stay calm.

'Hi.'

'Hey. You OK?' he says. You ignore it.

'Tell me, where did you get that key-ring. Porsche.'

'What? What key-ring?'

'Porsche.'

'Oh!' He looks down at his right pocket of his overalls, completely unaware of what it is that he is being asked. It has nothing to do with plumbing and he appears astonished that he even has keys dangling out of his pocket.

'Someone give it. Why? You like Porsche?'

'Oh yes. I love them. I used to have one,' you say.

'Oh yes?'

'Yes.' You repeat.

'And now?' he asks. 'Do you have Porsche?'

'No, I don't,' you shake your head slowly, still focusing on him.

Astounded, he starts to look suspicious. He does not reply.

'Do *you* have a Porsche?' you ask.

He knows something is going on. 'Excuse me,' he says with a frown. 'I have to work in here.'

'I had a bang on the head,' that's all you can say. You don't want him to go without telling him.

'Sorry, I don't understand this,' he is shaking his head, backing off, putting his hands in front of him. 'Sorry, I don't know what you are talking about.'

'The key-ring,' you ask again. 'Is it yours?'

'Yes!' he looks at you directly. 'Is mine!'

'No!' You shake your head. This can't be true.

'Goodbye.'

'Where did you get the key-ring?'

The plumber shakes his head, he is speechless, blank. You don't even know his name. It is written down but it is in the notebook downstairs. He goes red. He stares. Either he can not understand that much English or he really does not have an idea what is going on.

'I gonna get the lady. Eva.'

'No! Please don't! Forget I asked you anything.'

'Calm. You calm. You stay. I get your wife's mother now.'

'No!'

It is useless. You just know it. You are a whizz at poker but now you may have screwed up. You have money but it's less than twenty pounds as you have been pilfering two pounds and small change: not every day, but irregularly, so as not to arouse suspicion. You don't even know where your passport is and you cannot apply for anything, let alone leave the country. You cannot be *anything* with nothing. You are as good as homeless even though you've got somewhere to live, it's here and it's no home at all.

You have and are nothing but the clothes and shoes you have on. At least you know the address you are at. It does not matter that they do not let you use the internet except for learning words and skills. They have no idea you have learned the nearest interconnected 4 pages of the A to Z from Robert's study. You *know* London within 3 miles of this house you are living in. You have had his entire library to learn from. You've read an entire book with a fitness plan for cardio, yoga, meditation. You've learned about sailing, golf, 18th Century French literature. You've been reading his books about illnesses, medical financing, self help, fencing, history.

The plumber has transport, money, cards, phone, clothes, shoes.

And the key-ring.

43

DOMINIQUE

'S HE WAS MY BEST friend,' said the girl with the huge sunglasses. 'But we need to go somewhere else. We cannot talk about this here.' she pointed at the Achara Wine cave as Dominique did earlier, 'I will meet you this evening. In your hotel lobby.'

'What time?' asked Dominique.

'7pm? Can I have your address?'

Lucy handed her a card from the hotel, one of several they'd picked up from reception.

As the driver pulled away from the car park, Lucy said, 'We seem to be getting somewhere at last.'

'I am not so sure. Not even sure if we should meet her. Or if we should even have come to Thailand. Why are we here? Could you remind me as I really am losing my mind?'

'Nik. You wanted to come to find out what happened to James, didn't you?'

'And?'

'And to know why he wanted what he wanted in his Will. Because Henry Tummings is useless.'

'That's true. He is useless. I should know. I was a lawyer.'

'You still are. And not a useless one.'

'Then I should be more logical than I am.'

'You can't. Your mind has gone since fucking your plumber. This is why I am here to help you.'

'OK.'

'For Daphne's sake you must sort all this out. Didn't Elizabeth Taylor say put on some lipstick and pull yourself together?'

'Pass me my Chanel Rouge Noir.'

'Anyway, regarding tonight. No harm done. We'll be meeting somewhere public. If you are worried about kidnapping and all that Thai crazy violent drug cartel stuff.'

'I wasn't. But now you've brought it up...'

'Don't be ridiculous, Nik. I am trying to cheer you up. We're on a mission after all.'

That afternoon, Lucy went to the pool. Dominique collapsed into a deep sleep in the hotel suite, feeling overwhelmed by everything. Usually she would masturbate in order to relax or de-stress. It was free and better than Dr. Yannis Alexandrides's III Celestial Edit Black Diamond masks costing £395 a go. Just take my money, she'd used to say. But who needed a mask now when she had to wear one all the time? Her new mask of shame. Whenever she had 10 minutes, she fantasised about Przemek doing things to her, not being able to keep those strong, tanned, masculine hands, or his intense blue eyes off her. That usually helped her achieve satisfaction. But recently, she was truly unable to focus, not even on masturbating.

LUCY WOKE HER UP at 6 pm. 'I think you should have a shower and get ready,' she said. Dominique put on some fresh clothes: a Donna Karan top, earrings and Citizens of Humanity jeans. She slipped back on the same Chanel flats she'd had on in the morning. She felt very groggy and needed to wake up quickly.

'Have an espresso martini. Let's get downstairs early and be prepared for when she comes.'

Dominique ignored her martini suggestion. 'Let's go,' she said, looking down at some imaginary spot on the carpet floor. 'I am ready.'

Noi arrived at 7 pm in what seemed to be real designer clothes — last season Stella McCartney, thought Dominique — and Fendi shoes. Dominique didn't even say hello, nor did she offer her a drink. Why should she do anybody any favours?

'What are you going to tell me?' she snapped.

'Madam,' she nodded at Dominique, who finally gave her a grudging 'Hello.' She went on. 'Please. Tell me what you need to tell me or I am going back upstairs.'

Noi opened her mouth as if about to say something but she said nothing, her eyes widened in surprise. She was young, maybe in her twenties, though Dominique found it hard to tell the age of Asians without causing offence.

'She was a sugar baby,' Noi finally said. 'Achara means pretty angel.'

'What does that mean?' This was new to Dominique. First Achara was referred to as James's wife, and now she was a sugar baby. 'They said *wife*. I need to know if she is.'

'Yes, *wife*. A wife is a sugar baby. I am also James's sugar baby. He does not mind. We both were signed up to a website called Bowl of Sugar.'

'Did you both get married to James?' said Dominique.

'No. At present I'm seeing two sugar daddies — one in Malaysia, and the other in Singapore. They know about each other. The Malaysian sugar daddy is 53 and pays for my rent and car instalments, while the Singaporean one is 48 and flies me there from time to time for shopping and fun. We are not prostitutes, please.'

'I didn't ask that but thank you for the clarification,' said Dominique.

'We are educated. We are fluent in English. We have all our own teeth. Real prostitutes have their teeth taken out so they can give better blow jobs. And they are also in pimp-slave chains for like three generations.'

Dominique winced. Her eyes were getting bleary. She bit her lips. She could not believe what the girl was saying and yet she kept listening. She had been rudely awakened from her afternoon stupor.

'Achara was a pharmacy student, second year and I am still a second year student in business. We are doing this for fun, treats and gifts-'

'You have *got* to be kidding,' said Lucy.

Dominique wanted to know what had happened to Achara so she forced herself to listen. She could not even look at the girl-woman who carried on despite Dominique's humiliation. Lucy put a hand on her shoulder to say *are you OK* but Dominique could barely feel it. The hand on her was like someone had touched her with a leaflet.

The girl-woman went blank for a minute while she gathered her thoughts.

'OK,' she spoke. 'You wanted to know who she was and what happened on the boat. They are still looking for her. It's now been 10 months. The family won't give up. They totally blame James. It wasn't his fault there was a storm that night and his boat capsized.'

Dominique thought that maybe the girl-woman was trying to tell her to get lost and leave the family in peace.

There was the 6-bedroom villa in Surin, Phuket, belonging to this wine company now, too. Dominique could not see how she could retrieve any of it. This was James's Will. He was the daddy of these *wives*, his sugar babes.

Now I need a drink, thought Dominique. Not wine. Fuck wine. It was the cause of all this. *Something stronger.* Talking to the girl-woman was like talking to an alien.

'Achara and I were friends, like I said. James paid my rent and bought me a car. He bought her clothes, shoes, handbags, whatever she wanted for a trip. He took her on trips on his yacht or his golfing trips to Phuket. Achara was his favourite. Men like beauty and women like intelligence. She was definitely the prettiest girl in the entire college. So she got a much better deal.'

'Why do you do this? Why do you need these guys to give you income?' Dominique thought about her and James's daughter. Daphne would never be in this situation because the girls who did this stuff could not possibly be feminists or care that they were paid by men for sex and companionship. Were even high-end escorts sisters too?

Henry had advised her not to meet the wine company in person. Still she'd wanted to. She was a lawyer. She had negotiated difficult cases with difficult clients.

But these were neither cases nor clients. To make them budge she would have to hire even more lawyers, a local specialist in addition to an international one. Dominique hadn't the stamina for it. She felt drained by the process, by her sex, by her own confusion over the amount of stuff that James had had and lost.

'Well,' Noi replied without a trace of shame, 'I got into sugar dating because I prefer to date men who aren't concerned about spending money. I've dated men who expected me to pay for my own McDonald's meal and movie ticket, and I don't want to date those types any more.'

Dominique had nothing to say. She just stared at her folded hands in her lap. The room started to go round and round slowly like a carousel.

'The success of daddies like James inspires me. Their monetary support allows me to pursue my career but they also give career guidance to help me find my way in this world. I have a lot of respect for James.'

When she got up and left, Dominique noticed the waft of her perfume. They were wearing the same perfume. Chanel Chance Eau Tendre. All his women must wear the same perfume. Dominique imagined that Achara did too. It was soothing and nauseating at once. He wanted them to wear it for him. She sighed.

They watched Noi leave the hotel lobby and porte cochère until she was out of sight. Dominique dragged herself from the chair. Her head lolled and she was not herself. She staggered back upstairs to the executive suite with Lucy.

Dominique felt light-headed, strange, almost like she was drugged. She said to Lucy, 'I am cancelling the Phuket leg of our trip. We're not going there.'

'We're not?'

'No. Not the villa,' Dominique gasped. 'I hate him!' She saw her own reflection in the dressing table mirror. She looked strange, wild. 'All that belongs to them! Them!'

She started screaming; wordless roars with her eyes squeezed shut and clenched fists. She threw pillows, books, shoes, clothes. She picked up any objects lying around, the hairdryer, the bottles in the bathroom, smashing them against the walls. She found her suitcase on a little table and threw that too. It opened and sent more clothes flying.

She was about to smash the flatscreen TV until Lucy shouted. 'Stop! Stop! Nikki. Nikki. Listen.' She grabbed Dominique's wrists hard to immobilise her.

'You're acting crazy. Stop it! Now!'

She wrenched herself free of Lucy's grip. She could not stop. All these things were as light as cotton wool. Her eyes darted about the room like butterflies looking for flowers. She could still hear Lucy's voice crying. *No, no, stop, stop it, please, now.* But the words sounded faint and fuzzy. She lifted the dressing table chair and hurled it at the wardrobe mirror, shattering it with a crash.

44

PHOEBE

I N THE LOBBY BEFORE they left the hospital, Phoebe spied the copies of Metro left lying around discarded on the seats.

Greg was bandaged up and did not notice the headlines: 'Drug Scandal Doctor'. Three words to link media with reality, for once.

She put a copy in her bag. Greg was oblivious.

She called an Uber to get them home as quickly as possible. He needed to rest. Besides, her mother was looking after Jorani. She guided him to the bed and helped him lie down.

While her mother was busy making the shopping list, Phoebe took the Metro out in the bathroom and read the article.

Dr Robert Wong, one of the most accomplished and prominent Lupus -Systemic lupus erythematosus (SLE) - researchers in the world, has been arrested on a charge of insider trading. Dr Wong is chair at University College London, one of the top universities in the world, and has been working on an experimental drug to treat lupus. His life's mission has been to find a cure for lupus or SLE. A lucrative sideline involved providing information about the pharmaceutical industry to researchers from hedge funds.

SLE is a heterogeneous disease that requires a customised treatment approach. Therapies range from non-steroidal anti-inflammatory drugs to one of any number of immunomodulators or biologics. However, the clinical community has yet to arrive at a perfect therapy or combination of therapies—

Just then she heard Jorani's cry. She was crying too. Dark spots-appeared on the paper as she was reading it. She replaced the paper in her bag. She did not want her mother to see it.

'I need to go out,' her mother called out in Chinese. 'Can you come down now, please.'

She tore off two sheets of toilet paper and wiped her tears. 'Always a maximum of three, don't be wasteful', her mother used to say to her.

She picked up Jorani and went downstairs. When her mother had gone out, she switched on the TV in the living room, aware that she would have to switch off before her mother came back. The red screen banner read *Drug Scandal Doctor.*

'...someone approached Dr Wong one day allegedly offering him the opportunity to make extra sideline income as a consultant,'

said the reporter by the name of Jennifer Fairling, standing with an umbrella outside the UCL campus in Gower Street, Bloomsbury.

Phoebe gasped. Who was that someone?

'At first his golf partner, Jules Laney-Sambrooke sucked him into the luxury parallel life world of sailing.

Jules was a legendary trader. He made his billions completely on the basis of his ability to look at market screens, trusting his gut and his eyes. He had a 18,000-square-foot house in Hampshire with a cinema, a pool and a sizeable modern art collection. In later years he and his wife moved to south of France, where she still lives. Due to hospital appointments and treatments, he came back often to his summer home, a 3,000 square foot Sloane Square pied-a-terre apartment, until his tragic death in 2008.'

The camera panned across the street view of a red brick late Victorian 4-storey grand apartment building in Chelsea.

'Laney-Sambrooke grew up very middle-class in Hampshire. Surrounded by affluence in the Home Counties, and being an extremely competent poker player in school, he was motivated early on to make money. He studied economics and launched his hedge fund, JLS Capital, in the '90s with 5 million pounds. He was generating huge returns, at first 30, then 200 per cent, managing his own and other people's money. His son James, also a trader, died in a boating accident earlier this year.

A still of an elderly man getting into a limousine outside a hotel followed by a passport photo of his son, a middle-aged man. A Middle Eastern man in a suit then appeared in a split screen with the reporter.

Jennifer Fairling: We are now joined by Dr Wong's close colleague, Dr Seyed Khosravi. Dr Khosravi, you've worked with Dr Wong.

Dr K: Yes. I have known Robert for almost 8 years from the lab.

JF: Tell us a bit about Dr Wong's expertise and how he got involved with Laney-Sambrooke.

Dr K: JLS Capital was trying to figure out the outcome of a drug trial for a particular product in the lupus area. They were trying to make bets on these various things. Dr Wong started doing these consultations with hedge fund traders—

JF: You mention traders. What are they looking for?

Dr K: They are very, very focused on the kind of intelligence they wanted. They know that the newest research is still unknown except to those who have been in it decades. Almost every branch of the immune system is involved in the pathophysiology of SLE, including B cells and T cells. We try to block different cytokines, receptors and signal transduction pathways. Researchers have tried all the obvious.

JF: Dr Khosravi, thank you very much for joining us. We now welcome financial analyst and New York Times bestseller author, Richard F Eberhard. Richard?

The split screen now showed a bald man wearing a polo-neck fine knit T-shirt, surrounded by bookcases in the background.

R: Hi Jennifer-

JF: Richard, you've met Laney-Sambrooke.

R: Yes, I met Jules on the golf course in 2005. Since 1978 Jules got close to Robert, very good at flattering him and trying to get information out of him.

JF: How did he do that?

R: Oh. Over plenty of conversations, dinners, going to France on wine tasting tours, sailing. Jules had been to Robert's home with his boys, as though they were close friends or family.

The doctor had his first taste of what it meant to be beyond middle class, to be actually wealthy. It was called intellectual seduc—

Phoebe heard the door. She switched off the TV using the remote control.

45

PRZEMEK

P RZEMEK WAS SEEING DOMINIQUE that night after work. It was a Saturday night. He could relax. No leaving her at 5am to rush off to work.

She'd got in to London the day before. He'd got an an email from her before she left Bangkok. He was glad she didn't bug him about not doing Whatsapp or social media, like Andreia had.

Lorraine had organised an Addison Lee car which would drop Lucy off first in Chiswick, exit off the M4 near the brewery, then take the Westway up to Town, finally dropping her off after turning at the Holland Park round-about just after driving through Westfield. Przemek couldn't help laughing at her over-detailed email with the driver's entire route. Przemek replied with an 'OK'. He did miss her, and not just because she was cute, thought he didn't want to admit it.

He knew that when he met her she would be tired and require pampering, dinner at home and so on. And so on meaning wild sex. He had not seen her for ten days due to his Uni workload and some of the time she was in Thailand anyway tying up her late husband's business. He arrived at Holland Villas Road at 6pm, after work but not before going home, showering, changing into fresh, neat vintage clothes and doing his hair.

'You seem a bit strange,' she said.

'Yeah, so do you,' he said. She did look a little unwell, very pale and worn out for someone who had just been to Thailand. They both laughed, surprised as children who had just discovered joking. He embraced her tightly, until she couldn't breathe, the way he knew she liked it. They kissed, lightly at first, as though discovering someone new. Then she threw her throat back to deepen his kiss. He felt himself harden and stopped kissing her.

'Did you have good trip?' he asked, because he felt he should.

'Yes and no. I got my answers but I didn't get the answers I wanted.'

She hugged him tight. She shut her eyes. 'You're probably wondering what all that means.'

'I understand.' He smiled. 'Nothing makes sense.'

'You're right! I just needed someone to tell me that.'

He held her tight again, and pulled out her top. He explored her wetness between her legs with his fingers. They went downstairs to the room he thought of as the guitar room but knew was a study of some sort. It was just full of guitars. Expensive guitars. They took off their clothes. It was incredible to have such a big house with no one in it, he thought. They could have sex in any room. The choice was staggering.

He had sex with her on the sofa. It was the biggest revelation. The huge velvet sofa was as big as most double beds he'd had sex on. He did not like to use the word fuck. Fucking was sex without emotion and he had plenty of emotion but only for her. He did not even know her very well. He only needed to look at her tiny waist, those vintage classic red lipstick and satin 4 inch heels with their red soles and he was hard.

The enormity of her desire perplexed him as much as any physics or philosophy. She was wet for him. She lay with her legs intertwined with his. Her tanned, slim legs which had walked five continents of the world. His pale limbs which hadn't. He touched her bottom affectionately.

'Let me be your muse,' she said. 'Every fuckin' genius needs a muse.'

'You are a-mus-ing,' he laughed.

'And you're a genius at fucking.'

'I have this strange thing at work. One of my jobs. They changed one radiator to heated towel rail recently. That seemed to change pressure. So I had to do this job today and drain down the system. And guy asked me to help him.'

'And?'

'He's bit weird anyway. He's had accidents and corrective surgery. So he looks and sounds strange. He keeps asking where my key-ring came from and do I have Porsche—'

'Well just ignore him. Of course he'd keep asking. It's worth 200 pounds easy. Real gold-plated and real leather. He's probably a crook or crazy. Hope he's not the owner of the house? Did he pay?'

'No. I had to get his wife's mother and she paid.'

'Well. It's nice that today someone got paid and someone got laid.' She kissed him tenderly and put her arms around him, running her hands over his back, and finally anchoring her nails deeply into it.

46

PHOEBE

P HOEBE WAS DRIVING. THEY dropped Robert off in the Northfields pre-trial detention room at the remand centre for more questioning and interviews.

The baby was in the car seat at the back and Greg was home alone.

It was a sorry sight. They had not stopped weeping since. It was tragic to see him age a hundred years before their eyes, his tall frame crumpled like a paper doll. He was a broken man.

After giving the best years of his life to his adopted country and to medicine, they were repaying him with incarceration. They had said as much to Arvind Ramachandran, the lawyer representing her father. He'd said there was a good chance he would get off lightly.

They waited an hour for it to be over. Phoebe pushed the buggy around listlessly, killing time. An appointment was made for the next set of interviews and questions, so she switched on the voice memo app to record the date reminders hands-free.

She noticed the audio file of the Thai conversation in the

hospital corridor months ago. She had forgotten all about it, but now she knew she had to get it translated.

She drove back, using Google Maps on the phone. The round trip took 4 hours, allowing for including traffic delays, stopping to feed and so on. They had known it would take that long, and that they couldn't leave the baby with Greg for that amount of time. She needed the spare keys, usually on the hook, for the plumber to use and there was no "spare spare" set.

If Greg needed to get out, if there was a fire, say, he could always use the back door. Locking him in for just a few hours was necessary for her own peace of mind.

THEY GOT IN JUST before 1pm.

'Greg?'

No answer. The house was silent. Even when Greg was quiet he was not silent because of his aches and pains. Like an old dog, he was always shuffling, sighing, moaning and occasionally growling. Phoebe carried the baby seat into the kitchen and left it on floor while she searched the house. It wasn't as though it was big. She ran to the top floor, threw the sliding doors of the wardrobe open and ran downstairs again. Her eyes scanned each room in seconds.

'Greg?' She called again. Nothing. Not even the customary grunt or growl. She started to panic.

'Where are you, Greg? We're home.' Still no answer. A wild itch crawled over her like ants, turning her hands and face hot and numb. Where was he?

47

YOU

WHEN YOU WAKE UP, you hear nothing.

You gasp. Shit. What time is it? You check your bedside flippy clock and calendar. Wednesday December 14th. 10:55. It's so late already! They must be out.

You have been sleeping so much. You take your meds as usual which Phoebe has placed next to the bed. It's only two days since your bandages came off.

You run up to the loft storage space, two steps at a time, panting, trying not to trip. Here is the stolen money, hoarded and hidden in an old tennis shoe. You count it again to make sure. You consider £39.40 a lot nowadays. Oh fuck! Nearly forty quid! Recently you've had to find a used envelope to put it all in. It's hard to even find an envelope these days. Eva recycles everything straightaway and she crushes them up with such vehemence and passion you wonder what envelopes and junk mail have ever done to her.

You also discover a navy blue Sports Direct bag which looks new, unwanted and is possibly a freebie. Something here looks familiar. The two Cambodian lidded vases. You open the lid of one. The white packages, which Phoebe thought you didn't notice, are still there. You are just not interested in them, you never were.

Now for some clothes. In Eva and Robert's bedroom, on the same attic floor across the landing, you yank open the wardrobe doors. You flip through and remove items from hangers that you never see him wear.

You do not want him to think anything is missing when he comes back from his lawyer's appointment, questioning or whatever. Phoebe does not update you with every detail. Just what you need to know. "For now". You are not the same size as him, but he is tall for a Chinese man. The elderly man's dress sense is not ideal, but so what, you are scarred, disfigured, shiny-skinned. You have false teeth, a limp, a crisp upper class accent. Without looking too hard, you pick two smart shirts, two pairs of trousers, a jacket and a coat. You will wear one of the shirts and a pair of trousers, the jumper and the coat. You need to hurry. You have wasted time oversleeping.

You run to the main bathroom cabinet and grab a piece of soap, a new toothbrush and some toothpaste, the kind you get on a plane or in a hotel room, from a huge stash. On second thoughts you decide to take two each of these. The Chinese save these things wherever and whenever they travel until there is enough to last until World War V and beyond.

There's a sound. What is it? A rustling sound. You have been in the loft eaves storage space so have been unable to hear anything from downstairs. You stop. No. Nothing. It is the radio from next door. They have builders in. There is always rustling, sawing and tinny radio sounds.

You fill the navy blue Sports Direct bag with the stolen

toiletries which were in turn once stolen from hotels and planes. You're recycling or upcycling. It sounds better than theft. You thunder on downstairs.

You take as much food as you can from the fridge. Salad, tomatoes, carrots, cheese, fruit, yoghurt. The bag is fairly full now. One last thing. In the hall cupboard, you try on Robert's leather shoes. You do not fit them. He is a 9½ and you are a 10½. You have to wear your own £10.99 trainers from Decathlon. They look out of place but with a face like yours, as if anyone would be looking at the trainers. There is a tightness in your throat when you see the activity mat and the kicking arch with bells and mirrors. The sight jolts you to your senses, the present. You stop to look and your eyes fill with tears. A baby girl. How special is that? You should know because you once had a baby girl too.

You suddenly start to cry and drop the bag, unable to look any more. Your hands cover your face. Your heart is cracking like glass. You grab tissues and dab at your eyes. You know you must keep going or you will run out of time.

48

PRZEMEK

ONDAY. HE HAD GOT up at five to avoid the traffic but the queues in Screwfix were long.

Fulham Palace Road after the A4 Hammersmith junction was absolutely rammed. He thought about Montse for a few minutes while he was standing in the queue, looking at some old photos of her on his phone. Sometimes he thought he'd like to get another Burmese.

He picked up all the parts and fittings for the Bishop's Road job and loaded them in the van. It had to be done today. The customers had been waiting a while. The problem was intermittent with different error codes each time on the boiler. A boiler problem in winter was no joke. He turned left at the Tesco Express on Wardo Avenue, right at Munster Road and finally left at the Bishop's Road arriving at about 8:55.

As his van was pulling into Bishop's Road, he saw Phoebe and Eva getting in the car, Phoebe's bum was sticking out in the road while she was trying to strap in the Isofix baby seat. There was already a man's figure inside the car. It had to be Phoebe's husband. Eva was trying to cram a large Sainsbury's bag and the baby's changing bag in the car, too.

There was a lot of loading and unloading and they both looked miserable. If they were all going to be out, this was a perfect chance for him to work on the central heating. He parked his van, not exactly nearby. Maybe 100m away. It *was* Fulham, which meant narrow single lane roads and tight bumper-to-bumper parking, night or day. He was lucky to even get a space. Eva got out of the car and came over to see him.

'Good, you are here, take a set of keys,' Eva said. 'Just leave them in the house when you leave or call me. We were waiting for you to get here. We have to leave now.'

'I'm sorry. Traffic very bad.'

'That's OK. Bye.'

'Bye.'

He unloaded his tools and went in. When he put his tool trolley and his keys down in the hall, he heard a sound. A rustling, scratching sound from the eaves. 'Hello? Hello?' he called out. But there was no reply. He called again. He listened. Nothing. He decided it was next door's ongoing painting and decorating works. There was always a tinny radio, they seemed to like Capital FM, the pinging, scraping sound of filling knives stripping wallpaper and the scratchy noises of sandpaper on old plaster.

He set himself up in the kitchen. Turned on his phone's playlist on his bluetooth portable speakers. He detested the radio. He had Spotify. Showtunes and big band music from the 1930s and 1940s. Benny Goodman. *Stomping at the Savoy* being the first track. This was more like it.

When he went back into the hall to retrieve the radiator key from the bunch in his toolbox he noticed a pair of man's leather shoes. He'd almost nearly tripped over them. He frowned. He could have had an accident. What were they doing there? He bent down and grabbed the shoes with one hand. With the other hand he flung open the hall cupboard doors and threw them in without a glance.

49

YOU

YOU ARE IN THE hall cupboard, behind the coats.

The coat cupboard opens, daylight pours in. The man dumps a pair of leather shoes at your feet. They hit your feet and it hurts like hell despite you having concealed yourself under layers of coats and winter boots. You have managed to strip off his key-ring from his bunch of keys while he has been in the kitchen meddling with his music playback system and setting up his speakers. You leave the rest of the bunch — his own house keys, his van keys and some other.

The plumber's arrival has saved you from having to leave via the back door and garden so there won't be any clambering of walls and fences to get to the road after all. This is your lucky day.

You leave via the front door. You have no keys because they have given the spare to him. But now you notice that there is a wallet AND a bunch of your house keys that he's left on the radiator cabinet top where Phoebe leaves your Oyster card and any messages for you in your daily to-do notebook. There is handwritten message for you:

Back by lunch time. Help yourself and make yourself food from the fridge. Do not wait for us. P x

You scoop up your navy blue Sports Direct bag. You grab the house keys and the Oyster card. On second thoughts, you swipe the wallet too. It's surely all the plumber's stuff as none of it was there earlier when you came downstairs to try on shoes. You open the Chubb night latch lever as carefully and slowly as you can and use the key to shut it by turning it in the lock rather than slamming. You shove the Oyster, wallet and the house keys into your trousers, or, in fact, Robert's.

You turn right out of the house. You have been studying the A to Z for weeks now so you have the route by heart. You walk on Bishop's Road until you reach Clonmel. You turn right and keep going, crossing the A304 Fulham Road. You carry on Epple until you reach Parsons Green. There is a direct tube to Victoria. You tap the Oyster.

You're in. Or rather, you're out.

50

DOMINIQUE

'Y OU'RE NOT GOING TO believe it, Dominique.'

She loved the way he called her by the full first name with a long *neek* emphasis rather than how everybody else said it.: Dominic. He sounded so sophisticated and... European.

'I'm calling you very quickly. I lost my wallet and I lost their house keys.'

'Oh no! What happened?'

'They gave to me but I don't know where I put them so I cannot even lock up after me. I have to just leave and slam door behind me. They will be so mad at me.'

'No! They won't. Let me talk to them. I know how to handle these things.'

'You? They don't even know who are you.'

'I am a lawyer remember?'

'I thought you were showgirl.'

'Very funny. We can suggest paying for another set. Or changing the locks.'

'It's that guy.'

'Which guy?'

'The guy. The husband guy. You see I was about to drive off. But now I am in van. And the guy took key-ring. It must be him because he is only one who even seen it.'

'Oh you don't need it. It's just a key-ring. It's not important.'

'*Tak*, but you see, I personalised it!'

'How do you mean?'

'I put GPS tracker app onto key-ring like you said. Is Spy Tec STI GL300 Mini Portable Real Time Personal and Vehicle GPS Tracker. Now it works anywhere is reception. Up to France!'

'You're a fucking genius. I knew it.'

'No, I am not. You are. You said to activate the app that come with key-ring. I must go. I will find thief. He took my wallet, the house keys, my Porsche key-ring. I have to come back to borrow money from you. Sorry. Otherwise I cannot get to college this afternoon.'

'Come quickly.' She said. 'I miss you.' Dominique rushed upstairs to put three coats of Lancôme's Hypnose Waterproof mascara on.

Y OU ARE ON THE tube.

You wait on the platform until an Upminster bound train comes along, not an Edgware Road service.

The District line train arrives. You get on it.

There are many seats at this time of day but you sit next to someone in a high visibility yellow jacket with a guide dog also wearing a matching high visibility vest. You don't know how long it will take since you have no GoogleMaps or anything to help you check stuff. You only can do it the old way. Count 3 minutes per stop. 7 stops, therefore 21 minutes.

You pass Gloucester Road station. You look at the public art covering the tunnel walls of the platform.

3 more stops. 9 minutes to go.

You are at Victoria. You get out of the station and look for the signs saying Victoria Coach Station. It is quite confusing. You spend about 10 minutes lost in the station before you can find an exit and it is the wrong one anyway.

You still have another 15 minutes walk. But as soon as

you see the Apollo Theatre with its golden ballerina on the dome, you know you are heading in the right direction. You turn left at the junction where you see a tiny triangular park with a horse statue on a pedestal, pigeons, pigeon shit and face-tattooed drunks. It's 'London'. It's not like Fulham and not like Asia. You pass some shops and cafes. You pass Starbucks and Body Shop.

Suddenly, someone stops you, grabs you by the arm. ''Scuse me,' he says. You know that voice. ''Scuse me.' Who is it? You yank your arm away and you turn to look around.

'What are you doing here?' You say. It's the Polish plumber.

'No. I should be asking you what you doing here.' He looks angry, perplexed but kind. He is curious.

'I—' you cannot find a thing to say. Where do you start?

'You have *stolen* my key-ring,' he growls. 'Where are you going?'

'Oh, that.' You say. 'Have it back.'

You fish out the whole bunch from your pocket, or Robert's pocket, rather. You try to detach the Porsche key-ring.

'No!' he says taking your wrist again. 'Why did you take it, and where are you going?'

'I—'

Suddenly, you break into a run without ever intending to.

'Hey!' He shouts. 'Stop!' He yells, but you keep running, you think you can still do it, didn't you use to run 10km every week and never ever get tired, or sick, or see a doctor or dentist, not even once? But you are running like a chicken. You have a limp now. No, you are not running very well at all.

'You are thief!'

He is taken by surprise. And so are you. But he is young and fit. Not an ounce of oldness, illness or fatness on him. His face has round high rosy cheekbones, like a little blond angel. So cute he even has a kiss-curl on his forehead where he has forgotten to gel it up to look cool.

You start running again. He reacts, you see it in his blue eyes, he starts to run too. Instead of going down Buckingham Palace Road like you have planned to, you suddenly take a hard left and disappear into a building. You don't know what building it is. There are signs saying it is Victoria Place, and you have not noticed it on those ancient A to Z street directories. There are crowds here in which you can get lost and he won't find you.

'Stop him!' You hear.

You are drenched in sweat and you see Next, Boots, The Excess Baggage Company. You don't even know whether you should go right or left. You are disoriented. Claire's Accessories. The Perfume Shop. Holland and Barrett. Where? Where? You take the escalator over Isle of Flowers, two steps at a time, weaving through the people standing on both sides of the escalator like they shouldn't but do, threading through them like a needle through a densely woven blanket.

'Thief! Stop him!' He calls out, and now he is on the escalator too.

Where, where to next? Your mind is blank. You see Tortilla, KFC across the atrium, Costa, Café Rouge. You spin round and jump back onto the down escalator. You do not have the mental or physical capacity to do any more than just keep going. You're just a penniless, disabled thief. He follows you.

You are failing. You will black out. You know you will. You are in so much pain as you dodge and disappear behind

columns, pedestals. You see the sign to Victoria Coach
Station. You check your pocket. His wallet. Your money.
£39.40. *Hey! Hey!* People hear the plumber shouting and
start to put their arms out to block your path. Your escape is
failing. You see Leon, but the very last thing you see is Sainsbury's. To think you almost manage to leave the building!
You are ill. You fall over. You collapse from the pressure.

I got him! I got him. Someone grabs you. A huge black
security guard. His hands must be the size of a pair of gates.
He is half in uniform. He has a fleece top on and jeans and
some clunky boots which look like they could do actual
building demolition. The fleece top says Ace Security
Management Services Ltd.

'He's trying to make a run for it! I got him!' He says to the
others. He grabs you so hard your weak arm muscles almost
pop out of your skin like when you press edamame pods to
squeeze the beans out.

The plumber has caught up. 'Why you have taken my
wallet and keys? Where are you going?'

Your head is throbbing from the running and the adren-
alin, you need your meds, they are in your Sports Direct bag
together with a bottle of water, and all these people are
looking over you, they block the daylight. There are so many
of them it's dark suddenly. Your eyes shut. You are wet with
tears and sweat. You can't move while they pin you down.
They, the plumber and all these people whom you don't
know.

You feel their hands in your pocket, or Robert's pockets,
searching, emptying them. They find the Porsche key-ring
with the house keys, his wallet, your Oyster card and unbe-
lievably, to them, a mini pocket-sized A to Z.

52

PHOEBE

'MUM! MUM!' SHE CALLED and called. 'Greg is gone.'

'Where?'

'I don't know where. If I knew where, why would I shout out that he is GONE!?'

'Well,' Eva said, supporting Robert going up the stairs to his study, 'do you think he has gone for a walk?' Eva was not calm, it was simply her usual repressed behaviour, expressed via a numb and robotic response.

'No, no, no!' Phoebe yelled from the bottom of the stairs. 'He has just had his bandages off two days ago. He had a fall only a couple of weeks ago. He should not be out on his own.'

Her mother paused to think. 'Did he take his clothes with him?' asked Eva.

'No.' Phoebe said. 'Mum?'

There was no reply. Her mother was not paying attention or had lost interest already. She was talking to her father in hushed tones, trying to make him eat something. Her father's room where he slept night and day was now his study on the sofa bed. Her father would be tried at the end of the month. He might or might not go to jail, according to Arvind Ramachandran his lawyer. If he even survived all the stress, at the age of 68. How could they do this to him? She buried her face in her hands and wept.

Her priority was finding Greg. Somebody would help Greg. She sat down and pressed her hands together as if she was praying. She tried to do her breathing exercise. 7 in. 7 out. Greg. Greg. He was ill again. He must be. She hung her head.

Phoebe remembered Jorani was still in the car seat. She took her hands off her face. She went back downstairs, took her out of the car seat and put her under the activity mobile for some kicking time on the playmat. She looked at her watch again, her phone, her watch. She heard a loud clunk from the pipework, a little gurgle, like laughter in the pipes. The hot water was on. The keys. The plumber. He had been here but may not have seen Greg.

Greg could have left straightaway when she'd left. He could have forgotten where he'd gone, he wasn't right mentally yet. He'd fallen and hadn't been able to say how or where it had happened. She heard a ding on her phone.

An e-mail had come in from Fiverr with an invoice for the Thai translation and the transcript attached.

53

PRZEMEK

THE THIEF HAD BLACKED out.

'You want to call the cops?' Asked the security guard. 'They're right here. It wouldn't take long.'

The man was ill and weak, he was out of condition. He could not run. Anyone could see that. He was malnourished and had a limp. Przemek just wanted to get his wallet back and turn the thief in to the police. But it would take a while and he did not want any more delays. He'd made reports before, when he was burgled. There were at least three statements to be taken by different officers. They would only take the thief away. But he was Phoebe's posh sick husband.

'No, I don't,' he said, at last.

The security guard went back to the management office to get the first aid kit.

The bystanders dispersed after the security guard did not come back after 3 minutes. Rubberneckers had no patience. What did they want? A performance?

Przemek worried about parking. Because he had lost his wallet, but not his phone, he'd had to use Ringo to pay for parking. When you lived in London, all you worried about was parking and traffic fines. They could do you in if you were living on a rock-bottom budget. He considered himself a rock-bottom kind of guy, with his hefty student loan to pay for and a job where he had to chase clients daily for payment. The security guard came back after 10 minutes with a blanket, a hot cup of coffee and a first aid kit.

The man came to and was horrified. First he had a spasm, then tried to get up and escape again, though he'd never have made it. He scrabbled around feebly like an old dog getting up.

'Stop it, please, could you calm down,' said the security guard, holding him down like a toddler, pinning both arms.

'Let me go,' he pleaded. 'I have to go somewhere.'

'Would you mind kindly tell me why you have my wallet?' said Przemek. 'And my key-ring.'

'Help... me... please,' He gasped and panted, his eyes shut. 'I need my medication. Please. In the bag. I can explain, but don't call the police. I am in so much pain.'

Przemek thought about it. He *really* wanted this thief arrested but he *could* take him back to Phoebe.

'*Dobrze.* I help you.' He said finally.

The man fell back, his eyes shut and he was quiet.

'I take you home,' said Przemek, handing him the pill blister pack and noting the name of the drug.

'No!' The man opened his eyes. 'Don't, please! Don't take me— not home— I...it's not my home,' he gawped. He took a gulp of the coffee to swallow his meds. 'Help me... get where I... am going.'

'But where? I pay to park with Ringo. Let's go to van to stop parking. I have my wallet back now but I am not made of money. This parking here costing 9 pounds an hour for me to just running around all over place to find you.'

'Good,' the man whispered.

'What? No.' said Przemek. 'No good.'

'No, no,' he panted. 'Good... you can help me... thank you. I will tell you everything. From the start...'

Przemek sent a text straightaway to Dominique. He never called her by her name, or nickname or darling, hi, X or dear, and any term of endearment was out of the question. Never ended any message either with miss you or X or lotsoflove like she did. His messages started and ended with the point. Brevity was the whole point of texting, wasn't it?

Listen, I got to help this guy. Can't come back today. I will be back tonight.

He thought about it for a minute. 'Should we not tell Phoebe?' he asked the man.

'Yes... we must—' said Przemek. 'And... you sure you are not go back there?'

'We are not. It's not my home. They are having a family crisis now. And I... .' He huddled and collapsed back onto the blanket. He shut his eyes again.

'I'll take care of him,' said Przemek to the security guard. He turned back to the man in the blanket.

'OK. I will tell Phoebe,' said Przemek, 'that I am with- with- what is your name? I don't even know. What is your name?'

54

YOU

YOU STAGGER TO THE van parked on Victoria Street. The plumber helps you, supporting you with his arm around your shoulder. He is strong and young. You feel like you are being carried, like you are on a cloud. You lean on him all the way. You are weak and in pain. The painkillers are not working yet but you *have* over-strained every joint and muscle. You can imagine it is not a good sight.

He wasn't able to park in the car park, he says, because of what you did, which was steal his wallet. To park in a car park, you need a credit card or cash and he only has his phone with the Ringo app. In the car you tell him your name.

Then you tell him everything.

A LIGHTNING BOLT SPLIT the night sky. For a few seconds it looked like daytime.

It was 01:22 am on your Rolex. There were humps on the

horizon but you set sail anyway because you just wanted to go away on your pleasure craft with her namesake. Your two Acharas. Both pretty angels. You ignored warnings of unstable weather. You did lower the radio antenna as it would be a lightning rod.

You stopped for a moment on the jetty to take in Achara, your Supermarine Swordfish 36 Sportscruiser. Commonly called a 36 footer. GBP 125,000! Should have been BGP - Bloody Great Pounds. The result of Chinese New Year bonus five years ago. Christmas was no biggie in Asia. The CNY thirteenth month bonus was the annual highlight. You were getting ready to sell her. You will get something bigger and better. Your promotion meant that you might be transferred to the Bangkok office soon and you wouldn't need this piece of junk.

You glimpsed your fellow passenger, a silhouette in the dark but you recognised his outline and voice.

YOU SNEAK A LOOK AT PRZEMEK, he's listening, though his eyes are on the road. You go on.

'What are you doing up?' you asked.

'What are you doing?' he echoed.

'I am putting away the antenna and the canopy,' you said. 'Can't you hear the wind?'

'Can I talk to you?'

'Let's do it tomorrow,' you snapped. He'd been tanking up on coke earlier. 'You should have a rest. You had a long day doing the shoot. Look. Can't you see I am busy now?'

'Give me your ring. I'll give it back.'

'What?'

You must have heard wrongly. Your Cartier wedding ring was worth 22K.

'The leopard one with green eyes.'

'Panther,' you corrected him. 'This is outrageous. Are you... robbing... me?'

'No. Borrowing from. Just to tide me over.'

You said nothing.

'Where's Martin?' he demanded. 'He was supposed to be here. With the funds. I have instructions.'

'He does not have the funds and he says he couldn't make it.'

He lunged at your throat, surprising you.

'He's just using you,' you gasped. 'Just as he did to the oth-'

'Fuck that. Your ring, please,' he growled. 'You give about ten times that to your whores.'

'H-he just used you to take some excess baggage for him-' You wanted to say they were not whores. Sugar babes were your confectionery. You'd bought him sweets too. But there was no chance you'd give him that ring.

'No. Martin would never.' He shook his head fast, frowning, teeth bared.

'You're a fool,' you said. 'Where's the missing 5 kilos?'

He threw his head back and laughed. He started choking you. You could not speak. He was strong from lugging equipment around. Rigging, big shows, stadium entertainment. You thought you might pass out. You felt your eyeballs bulging out from the pressure, you shut your eyes because the lids could not stay open. You clamped your fingers onto his and tried to pull them off but he kept his grip tight. Even your nails made no difference. As soon as he saw you lift your foot, he knew you were going to kick him. You both spun round in drunkard's dance while you tried to shake him off. A punch flew out at you and winded you. The winds were getting too strong for the autopilot. You were losing control of the boat.

He could not smell the imminent storm. The fool. He was in another world. He rained more blows onto you. The Rolex and the ring were torn off you, and put on his own wrist and finger.

You could not get up. Each time you tried to move, he kicked your stomach to stop you. He was going to kill you.

He kicked you hard and you felt a rib, or maybe several, crack. The pain lit the sky white. You shut your eyes and you saw only black. You were lying on the deck. You put your right hand in your pocket. It was there. With your thumbnail, you felt for the groove in your Victorinox Swiss army knife. To open it with one hand, you remembered what to do from learning it when you first sailed. You were just a boy then. Your father taught you. And now you had to use that skill.

You look at Przemek.

He lets out a whistle and shakes his head.

55

DOMINIQUE

'P̄RZEMEK, COULD YOU SPEAK clearly?'

'I am in Brighton. It took one hour and quarter—'

'Why? Say everything again.'

'You got to calm down first.'

'I can't fucking keep calm,' she said as calmly as a white upper middle class perimenopausal woman could.

'Just let me hand you over, then.'

'No. You're driving me crazy,' Her tears leaked like a faulty tap. 'Just tell me where you are and what you are doing.'

'The thief. He's called James. He says he is your husband. Now I help him. He has no money. I drove him to Brighton. We are — (where are we?) — yes we are outside Roedean-'

'That's Daphne's school.' How could he speak so plainly about this? Had he gone mad too?

'You need to talk to them. We need your help. Dominique, please. OK. You are not calm. I will call you back.'

She was hyperventilating and she was shaking. She could not even stop shaking to get her meds out from the kitchen drawer.

She threw the phone at the nearest wall. She waited for it to shatter but thanks to its silicone protective cover, it did not.

She reached into the glass cabinet where the phone had landed. She found single malt whisky and took a glug.

Przemek was with a thief, an impostor after her money, and who had found a young, naïve and gullible victim like Przemek to trick.

She was trying hard to remember what he'd said: that they were "outside the Roedean trying to see Daphne".

As if he could hand over the phone so that she'd talk to the impostor. She wanted to call the police. Przemek had been scammed. The impostor had also found out everything about Dominique and her family.

He even knew where Daphne went to school.

He knew where she lived.

And her late husband's name.

Y OU GO ON.

A wave knocked the Victorinox Swiss Army knife from your hand and it disappeared. You saw Greg's body tip and slide off into the darkness like an unfinished sandwich from a plate into a bin. You could not tell the noises of the boat, your dear boat, from the sounds that her namesake, your sugar baby was making. The two Acharas, the boat and the doll-sized woman. You could hear her screaming but where was the sound coming from? All the noises became deafening. She was staggering in the salon, heading for the deck. You saw her. She saw you. At that point the eight-foot, L-shaped, leather sofa broke loose, flew across the salon interior like a paper plane and smashed Achara into silence. One of the screams stopped and another began. Yours. She was immobile. You wanted to run to her. You wanted to save her. You could not. She would not have survived the impact of a 100kg force travelling at that speed. You said goodbye. To the woman you wanted to kiss and fuck and overwhelm with luxury the instant you met her.

You lost something else – an outrigger. Two windows smashed. It was almost instant. Water came in. The reefer door tore off and dumped its contents. The battery box broke loose and shifted into an engine alternator, knocking out the DC system onto its side. All the time the boat was soaring like a magical pirate ship into the night sky. It hadn't been the sofa that was flying, it was the boat. The sofa had merely come apart.

The boat hull could be on a huge hump of a wave and the hump would disappear so the boat was left in mid-air and then she dropped like a stone. It was like being on a roller coaster without the rollers. Without the coasters. You were freestyling.

57

PRZEMEK

THE MAN FINISHED TELLING his story. Przemek turned into London Road, down Marina Drive, along the B2066 and finally into Roedean Way where he parked up.

The man lifted the left leg of his elderly-man trousers to show the Chelsea calf tattoo, the only feature still well-preserved and intact.

'Ever since I first met him, he wanted to be me,' he said. 'He even had my tattoo copied onto his calf. We were both Chelsea fans. Eventually he had my ring and watch too.'

Przemek had spent a disproportionate amount of time looking at his pet reptile and aiming at grey squirrels, neither of which were exactly attractive in the conventional sense of the word. Yet they were shiny treasures compared to this man's disfigurement, so hideous it made his eyes water.

Dominique was probably the most beautiful thing he had ever stared at. It was a fine line between beauty and vulgarity. In the van the lighting was so good, too good. It showed up every imperfection. Andreia used to do her makeup in her car. She didn't like how the vanity mirror on the passenger side of the van made her look.

Przemek stacked the paper cups from the A23 services Costa. He had stopped to give the man a break from telling the whole story from shipwreck to South-West London breakout. Przemek had needed a break too. Everybody had stared at him at the Services but tried not to look like it.

It was still only Monday and yet Przemek felt many weeks had passed. He sighed. The man's tears fell and he wept. He used his damaged hands to bury his face. Przemek was not good at this. He rummaged in his glove compartment and found some old serviettes from Wagamama. He handed them over. They'd just stay in the van until he was ready to get out.

'She won't believe me. My own little girl. If she doesn't believe me, I'll kill myself.'

'Let's think of at least 6 things about her. That only *you* know.'

'This is like a road movie. Thank you. I just want to— to see Daphne.'

This was a good distraction. Przemek was not ready to think about Dominique. He never was. He did not want to live in that big house in Holland Park. For a start, it was too big. Secondly, he was not sure he loved her. She was like Montse. A pet you felt affection or fondness for. Was it love?

Studying philosophy did not get you answers, just more questions.

THE MAN WAS READY at last. Przemek collected the rubbish from the car; Marks and Spencer sandwich wrappers and the coffee cups. Meanwhile, the man put on his jacket.

'You sure it's here?' said Przemek.

'Of course I am sure. I have been here so many times.'

'Just checking.'

'I am sure of everything that happened to me. I am just not sure if they will believe me.'

'Well, I did. And if they don't, you need to act ill.'

'Act ill?'

It was a cream-coloured, and rather grand, late Victorian Gothic building with one of those perfect lawns. They rang the bell and waited. The receptionist showed them into a waiting area while they filled in visitor forms to get passes. Patiently, Przemek filled in the form and assisted the man who could not even write very well.

'I am her father.' he said to the receptionist.

'And who are you?'

'I'm his plumber.'

'You're his *plumber*.' Her eyebrows almost reached her hairline. 'What are you doing here?'

'I gave him lift,' said Przemek.

She did not reply, just blanked them out with a stare. James had tears in his eyes again. 'I feel very weak,' he said to the receptionist, following Przemek's advice. 'I need my tablets, Przemek. I am in so much pain. I need to sit down.'

'He is ill; can you help at all?' said Przemek. 'Some water, please? Can you not tell he has been in bad accident and now he is not OK?'

The receptionist weakened at that point. She'd have had to have had a heart of marble not to have felt sorry for James.

'Let me check with the headmaster. And find out where Daphne is right now.' She glanced at the gigantic railway-style clock and her computer screen. 'They are all at Lunch in the Main Dining Room now. They'll be finished in about 5 minutes if you would like to wait here. After lunch she should go back to her House to pick up her kit for Drama. She's doing Musical Theatre this term and preparing for a show right now, so she'll be needing her lyrics.'

It was the longest 5 minutes that Przemek had ever had to endure but it meant there was enough time to sit James down and give him his medication. He appeared calm, but tired, clutching the white plastic cup from the water cooler.

Eventually, a smartly-dressed grey-haired man and a teenage girl appeared in the reception hall. James broke down in tears. He was unable to stand up. He was shaking. Przemek put his arm around him. He buried his face in his hands, aware that he was so horrifying. A monster. The grey-haired headmaster turned to the teenage girl and said, 'Daphne, is this your dad?'

The girl went white. Her jaw dropped and she started screaming hysterically. She ignored Przemek completely.

'Daphne, listen, sorry, I am sorry, it's me, Daddy.'

She kept screaming at an inhuman pitch and volume, covering her ears and shutting her eyes tight. The headmaster had to sit her down to stop her.

'Stop it, Daphne, calm down, look at me. Daphne. Look. At. Me.'

The girl stared at the headmaster. She began panting fast, but at least she had stopped screaming. A torrent of vomit ensued and the receptionist had to grab a box of tissues and a plastic bag from her desk at lightning speed.

'Get her some water, please, Becky. Quickly.' The headmaster said.

The receptionist rushed off, as soon as she'd cleaned up the girl. By the time a plastic cup of water arrived, Daphne had already blacked out. The headmaster sighed.

'Daphne's father had an accident at sea. His ashes were brought back and his funeral was in J—'

'No. I am not dead. I am here.'

'We won't go.' Said Przemek. 'We need to talk to Daphne.'

'We have to call security.'

'No. Call her mum first,' said Przemek. 'Call Dominique, if you don't believe us. Can't you see he is very weak and ill? He's had accident and so many operations.'

The headmaster did not reply.

When the girl came to, she shook her head, slowly at first and then fast. She wore a big frown. She was unable to speak.

The headmaster looked away and fiddled with his cuff links.

'Come with me please, this way,' he said, finally. 'Let's do this in my office. I have Speakerphone.'

58

YOU

'Y OU DIDN'T DIE, DADDY?'

'No. I survived.' You look at her for a long time, and she at you.

'You are the same Daddy.'

'I know.'

You are silent again. She holds your damaged hand. No words are possible, or necessary. Until you start to speak.

'You were 3. The roads were icy. I was taking you to your nursery in Notting Hill, you know, up the steep hill. We had to get out of the car, get down on all fours and climb up the hill. You made it to breakfast at school, and daddy made it to work.'

'They asked me, did you really crawl to nursery today and I said yes.'

Just to hear and see each other was enough for you.

'You were 5, I made you this sandwich of two choc chip biscuits and butter. And you cried and made me promise that we would not tell Mummy and I said it was a secret.'

'I miss that sandwich.'

'I know 6 things only a dad would know. I've told you 2 and now I'll tell you the rest'.

'You have more?'

'When you were 7, I came home from work very late every night. One weekend you handed me all these broken dolls to fix. I was very cross you did not allow me to lie in as it was a Sunday. I was so exhausted but I woke up to fix them and it took hours. You admitted that you broke them on purpose so we could fix them together.'

'When you were 9, you you found out what April Fools' Day was. You woke up one morning and told me there was no school today. I said is it because it's April Fools' Day? And you said how did you know!'

'Daddy that is so funny! That I thought I could fool you.'

'When you were 11, you started boarding at Roedean. You were very upset to leave and I said you could take your favourite ripped jeans with you, it would be like a permanent sleepover, the longest camping trip with no parents, all ripped jeans, windsurfing and horseriding. What you always wanted.'

'Ripped jeans? That was what Mummy said I'd be sick of in about 3 days.'

'You loved them for a week.'

'The rips got bigger!'

'They don't usually get smaller.'

She smiled. 'I just knew you weren't dead, Daddy. We hung onto all your guitars.'

'You didn't!'

'Mummy didn't want to but I thought there would be time for me to play them one day.'

She hugs you, surprising you how quickly it has happened, that you are her daddy and it hasn't been so hard to prove after all.

Your faces are wet with tears. So is Przemek's. He has been quietly sitting and listening. Only the headmaster is dry-eyed. The receptionist is typing up the conversation. You are unable to tell her any more memories even though you remember them all. There's time, there is plenty of time.

Przemek pats you on the shoulder.

'You have to go now, Daphne is rehearsing for her end of year show,' says the headmaster. 'She has Drama now.'

There has been enough Drama for one day, you think.

59

DOMINIQUE

T HE INSTANT SHE HEARD Daphne's voice, she knew it was true.

No DNA testing would have been required. It did not matter that James was alive. She wanted Przemek back. Not James. Przemek was Prozac. He was her drug, her Cuban Pete, her king of the beat. What she wouldn't give to hear an opening percussive groove, a Latin bass, the stab of three muted trumpets right now, a rumba or tango, be pierced with his blue-eyed gaze, impaled by him.

It was what she was born to do, what she wanted, what every woman wants, to be adored, now and forever in that instant.

TWO HOURS LATER, PRZEMEK sent a text: *Sorry. Goodbye.* No dear, no X, no best wishes, no miss you. All these things she had surrounded herself with; the luxury stuff, from IV therapies, to rock-star cars, none of it meant anything to her now. She thought of the handblocked wallpaper from France, with its gold bird cages on a black background. *She* was the bird in the gilt prison, surrounded by blackness, her own vanity and greed.

60

PHOEBE

'I DON'T KNOW WHERE Greg is but Przemek has just texted.'

'Who?'

'Przemek. The plumber.'

'Wh-where is he?'

'I don't know. I have to open this email. It may be important, Mum.'

It was the translated audio file from Fiverr now the task, or 'gig' as they liked to call it, was completed. It was the snippet of Thai conversation she'd overheard in the hospital corridor. She checked that her mum had left the room before opening the file to read the transcript.

For ease of reference, they had been named Speaker 1 and Speaker 2. Speaker 1, male, native Thai speaker. Speaker 2, male, non-native Thai speaker. Possibly white or European in origin.

[START OF TRANSCRIPT]

    1: Chelsea

    2: ... (inaudible)

1: ... identified ...Chelsea tattoo missing.

2: That's good.

1: No, sir. That just means that his legs were badly bitten, decayed or destroyed.

2: ... (inaudible)

1: The survivor is here. Do you wish to see him?

2: No. I know who he is.

1: Who? We can run more investigations-

2: What investigations?

1: Dental records, DNA-

2: What is your price?

1: Price?

2: Price to skip more investigations. I know his wife. She'll say if it's him all right.

1: If she is not certain... then she'll want it done.

2: [sighs] I know you well, Chief Inspector. We go back years. You've helped me move those fishing vessels more than once. To the right place, the right people. I've learned Thai. I know the culture. I helped you build your second home. Your children go to university abroad. Your wife wears the world's top designers. You know what to do.

1: But Martin, sir-

2: Don't call me that.

1: Sorry. You say you know the dead man. Who- who is he?

2: An idiot. Just like you'll be if you don't shut up, with due respect, dear Chief Inspector. We're short. He did not have the additional 5kg. Do you know anything?

1: No.

2: God knows where he's hidden it. Once again I ask you, Chief Inspector. Name your price. Wait. Do you hear a sound outside?

1: Let me see, sir. A moment, please.

[END OF TRANSCRIPT]

61

PRZEMEK

H E DROVE FAST BACK to London because he was thinking of college and the lectures he'd missed. Phoebe was waiting. He headed for Fulham.

When he arrived he sent Dominique the text. His angst and guilt disappeared like dew. He stopped feeling that anything was wrong. She was strong. You had to be to live in a house like hers, have no job and still be in it. There was nothing a middle-aged wealthy white woman could not face. Alone or otherwise. She seemed built for it and money helped build her for it. Her weakness was him. And now he had removed that weakness.

'What? What?' said Przemek.

'I have been talking to you,' said James. 'Did you hear a word?'

'No. Sorry. What did you say?'

'What will I do after I see Phoebe?'

Przemek sighed. 'You can say goodbye to her. Or you can stay with her until you find job and leave. I am going to get very busy. Sorry, I am not sure I can help you very much after today. I am already on this course and have to study night and day. And still working.'

'Plumbing?'

'Don't be so shocked. There is plenty work. Is job that robots cannot do. No worries, will not be replaced by AI.'

'This Christmas will be the best one in all my life. If get to see Daphne.'

'You will.'

62

YOU

'WHY? WHY DID YOU not say this before? What do you think you are doing to me?' Phoebe demands. You have not seen her like this before.

'I am saying sorry, please forgive—'

'Don't even say that,' She sobs. 'You have known for so long. How could you do this to me, and Jorani. Feeding, playing family.'

'I know but can't you see? I—'

'Stop. I can't listen to this—'

You remain quiet. You hand her a serviette from your pocket, the Wagamama one from Przemek's glove compartment. She snatches it. She calms down. You know her. She does not like to be cross for long. Her arms are folded, her eyes red. She appears fine one minute and the next she has tears in her eyes.

'I am not Jo-jo's dad. I am an imposter. Feebs—'

'Please don't call me- that- that name.'

'I have known since I knocked my head on the stairs. I could not say so because I was waiting for all the procedures to be completed. I needed a roof over my head, I needed a home. I am a liar. I am very sorry. Please forgive me.'

Phoebe swallows.

'Give me a chance to explain. I have known the inside of your dad's cupboards were green once, though at the time I didn't know why. I was in that room. It was 1978. I was 13. My brother Tom was 8. I came with my family to your house. You were 1 and Bethany was 3. You won't remember me at all.'

'No, I don't. Could you just leave—'

'Please listen. I went into your dad's office because... because I saw when the door was open that there was a sailing boat. A model. I was fascinated. Since then all I wanted was to have my own boat. To sail. My brother and my parents, you and your sister, were all downstairs, and did not know that I'd snuck away to study the model,' you say.

Phoebe does not reply. She clenches her jaw and shakes her head.

'I got married in a blue suit. I was the boy wearing that jumper in the photos. Our trips to France. All the photos are part of who I am now, how I became well. But now I know must go.'

'You have nowhere to go to. My parents will loan you money for your first month's rent somewhere.'

'Thank you. I will pay it back as soon as I can. I feel terrible about what my father was trying to do.'

Phoebe waves her hand and looks away. For a moment, you look at her, waiting.

'I lost... my sister... to SLE,' says Phoebe. 'My dad had to do what...what he did because he had nothing to look forward to. He wanted the drug to be a major breakthrough and your father provided the funding. I do not blame my dad's arrest on you.'

'Thank you.' You hug her.

'Bye.' She does not want a hug, she pulls away and folds her arms, reaching out only her knuckles to wipe her tears. You must say what is on your mind which now works.

'Feebs, I need to go back to being James Laney-Sambrooke. I need cards, a job, a phone—'

Phoebe buries her face in her hands. She nods.

'At least say goodbye to Jo-jo.' She whispers.

You look at the baby doing her tummy time on the playmat with her activity arch. Three months old. She is getting big now. In two months she will be eating mashed bananas and able to roll over. But you cannot look at her. You just can't. You too are clouded with tears.

'J-James,' Phoebe says, 'does the name Martin mean anything to you?'

You hesitate. 'Yes. I- He- he worked with me. My subordinate. Now he's been promoted. Why?'

'Does he have a Chelsea tattoo as well? Were you supposed to meet him on the yacht?'

'We all have it.'

'What?' She says. 'Who's we all?'

'The Chelsea tattoo, ' you say. 'I had it first. Your- your-Greg and Martin also had it done a year ago—'

'Why?'

'Well,' you sigh. 'They're fans... and- and they want to be me. But I got robbed. You do know Greg was dealing?'

She is silent and will not look at you.

'Hang on. What are you saying? Do you- do you- know something?'

'Maybe.' She gives a tiny pained smile. 'I recorded a conversation in Thai when you were in hospital. It may be helpful. Let me send it to you now you have a phone.'

63

DOMINIQUE

TUESDAY. I SEE HIM in colour on the screen of the world's greatest video entry and security system.

Seconds later, I open the door. I can barely look at him, his reptilian skin and eyes.

I have not slept all night. I am still in my black satin pyjamas. Nightmarish thoughts of the day kept replaying. The new James. He said goodbye to Phoebe yesterday. He has moved out. They have given him money to rent a flat. My late husband. Alive.

'Thank you for letting me see Daphne yesterday. Dominique I am sorry,' James says. 'I don't know what else to say. I can't-

He sounds different yet the same. The accent, the voice.

I cannot reply. Tears prick my eyes. I blink them away. He weeps too. We hug tightly. It is like our first hug, like when we were still in Uni. As students and just friends. I was an undergraduate and he was doing his Masters. Minutes pass, maybe 5, maybe 20. Time is still.

'Let's have a coffee. Please,' I say. 'Stay'.

It is all I can say. He breaks into a grotesque expression

but then I realise he is smiling. We go downstairs into the kitchen. He knows everything about this house, his home, ours.

'Everything looks different.'

'Not different enough,' I say. 'It's got to be completed by another company. I found a company: "The Finisher Offs. They are a construction team specialising in finishing off unfinished projects to proper finished-finished. They've valued the entire job based on items outstanding, so that's the entirety of Andreia's package, more or less... sorry, James. I *know* I talk too much. All the time. Why do you even care about all this?' I gesture at the space around me.

He laughs. Not a bitter laugh, just a laugh. 'You haven't changed at all,' he says, which cheers me up.

'Of course I have.' I reply. 'I'm much worse than before.'

He smiles.

'The same, sir?' I ask. He nods. The espresso machine does its thing. I put his coffee in front of him. I know what he drinks. Skinny double macchiato.

'We can have a look at your guitars...?' I say a little tentatively, not sure what he will say.

'Thank you. Daphne says you kept them all.'

In his old den, he looks at, picks up and puts down his guitars like they are guns. I tell him I am now not interested in design or being featured in House & Garden, I was only doing that to assist Andreia's portfolio. It is a relief to completely cut out design from my mind, the pursuit of beauty, things, luxury, real, imaginary. The Finisher Offs agree with me completely.

'Indeed you must be the perfect client. The kind who just wants the keys handed back and the work completed.'

After we chat like the old friends we are, I've only just

made this discovery: we uncoupled a long time ago. We could not be lovers then and not now.

I've always thought that sexual chemistry was imaginary, what actors on screen or characters in books did to make you think that was what happened. But I know now it is real, intense and powerful and it has blinded and paralysed me. And it's happened with someone I don't even know very well. It is pure physics, chemistry and biology with Przemek. I have never known passion or toe-curling orgasms like that before. Now that I am nearing 50, it is unlikely that I will experience true desire ever again.

Once he's finished his coffee, it's time for him to leave. He will make his way back to Brighton where he has chosen to find a flat. 'I have an Oyster card, Przemek's old phone, keys, a SIM card, £39.40 in cash. £2,000 in a new bank account for me to live on for a month. I am a person now, just so you know.'

I look at him, remembering something. 'Martin Pelland. Do you know that name?'

He hesitates, looking blank. For a second I think he hasn't the faintest idea what I'm talking about. But then he says. 'This is the second time I've heard this name recently. Of course. Scum. He was lucky to escape the boat trip and the storm.'

'He was the one who called me to identify a body. He seemed very concerned and even called to say he was coming to your funeral.'

'Because he wanted to make sure I was dead. He always wanted my job, and now he has it. But not for long.'

I raise my eyebrows. 'Oh yes. You know he must have intercepted the lab tests. Because they came back and the DNA on the hair matched the deceased. Now how did that happen?'

'Did you leave the samples with the concierge for the courier to pick up?'

'Yes, how did you know?'

'That's what you'd do if you lived at the serviced apartments. Martin picked your samples up and threw them away. Then he sent Greg's hair to the lab.'

'But how did he have Greg's hair?'

'Easy. They're close. At any point there would have been Greg's DNA in his penthouse suite. Cups, mugs, beer glasses. Even a toothbrush, come to think of it. Greg had met him and stayed there before the "gigs" that he was doing for Martin.'

I listen intently, thinking about every word.

'James,' I smile. 'Goodbye.'

'Dominique,' he says. 'Good to see you. Bye.'

We hug again for a long time.

He waves a small bunch of two keys at me, and I notice the Porsche key-ring that I once gave Przemek. He takes it off the keys and gives it to me. 'I don't want it,' I say but he says, 'I don't want it either.'

I sigh and accept it.

I THINK OF HIM every day. And it has been every single day since he first looked at me.

It has been hardest in the early mornings or late nights. They are the times when we send each other a text or two. The Porsche key-ring with the initials JLS is a curse to both of them and a souvenir to me. Scratched and battered from going to work with Przemek with his tools and equipment, it's the only thing left to remind me of him. I close it tight with my fist. I need it as much as he does not need me.

While my eyes are shut, I carry out pillow-biting and repeating affirmations and mantras in my head. They'll never fill the hole inside me.

Let the young discover for themselves that choices are an inconvenience, money a noose, morality a joke and all you have is the body and the brains you're born with. Use them.

Four months later

I AM AT MY newly-formed non-partnership law partnership, practising again, as is my fate, though not in a bank as before. "She loved working even when she was not working" is the phrase they used to sum me up at the office, as are "Working should feel like not working" and "being at home feels like working and being at work feels like not working".

I am helping James put Martin and the Chief Inspector where they should be – in jail. Being there for him, going through the documents, having a chat.

I was born to be hard nut to crack and I would rather be cracking other hard nuts. A woman who is resilient deserves admiration, attention and appreciation. I'm not going to get that at home. Maybe others do, those who are especially capable at home, cooking, cleaning, baking, home decorating, admin, booking holidays, filing, getting quotes.

I accept that I am not one of them. I have glittery, sweet and savoury memories into which I dip.

Someone did make me very happy once.

64

PRZEMEK

FIVE MONTHS LATER

H E PARKED IN THE 20-minute loading bay outside the Ealing Broadway tube station.

It was late and he hoped there was at least one copy of the Evening Standard left, which he still hadn't skipped since the day Montse went up the extract duct. There were none left, he had to pick up a copy dumped by a commuter in the see-through bin. His hands shook. He dashed back to his van and sat in it for the whole 20 minutes.

Montse was alive. His girl made the headlines. She was found in Ealing Common by joggers five months ago. They alerted The Royal Zoological Society who then came to get her. She was unchipped. They named her Hla, Burmese for 'she who is beautiful'. They set her up with the boy Burmese at London Zoo. Six weeks ago Hla laid 37 eggs. She had been pushing them together by coiling herself around them. She did not leave to do anything, not even to eat. Food had to be brought to her in the last six weeks. Her muscles vibrated which kept her eggs safe and warm. Her babies had now just hatched, each baby 20 inches long. He re-read it so many times it was seared into his mind. When he blinked, his tears rained down in big drops. Stains formed on the crumpled eighth-hand Evening Standard's front page, in larger and larger circles until they merged and covered the page and Montse's photograph until she was see-through and no longer visible. He put the paper down on the passenger seat. Hla. *Hla.* He pressed both palms into his eye sockets as he wiped his tears. He started the van.

HE SHOWED HIS TICKET and pushed the turnstile.

He saw her again.

Behind glass, as she always had been.

65

EVA

SIX MONTHS LATER

A SINGLE MUM WAS no longer taboo for a Chinese family.

My daughter was a widow, anyway. She would be applying for commercial work in graphic design and digital media again. Jorani was signed up at Balham Rainbow nursery. Phoebe had got her flat back from the tenants.

An immigrant was supposed to come to this country to succeed. It might not have worked out that way for her dad and me and now it wouldn't for her. Everything was a struggle for the most part. Robert had to work quadruply hard compared to British doctors. He was awaiting the second trial and his health had deteriorated again. He did not really care about the trial. He felt dead already. Certainly without his Western medications and the Chinese traditional soups that I brewed, he would have starved to death already. Luckily his lawyers had more verve than he, my daughter and I did put together.

Phoebe and Jorani were all I had now. Phoebe had invested so much in that man who was not even Greg. We'd become very tight, the four of us. Baby, Phoebe, "Greg" and me. We were a unit. There was nothing we did not know about each other. We all depended on each other. He was there for her and she for him. But I understood he had to go his own way, to being who he was. James.

Do not feel sorry for me, I, who had had very high expectations of coming to the West, living like a tai-tai, giving up work and becoming a lady of leisure. If I did not work, I ended up thinking of Bethany. Work was the remedy for grief which never went away. I worked 12 hour shifts as a nurse in geriatric care until I was 60 after which I left the NHS and became a contract nurse for private agencies.

My last assignment was "caring" for a patient called Jules Laney-Sambrooke in Sloane Square in the summer of 2008. It was such an easy commute for me from Fulham. It was hard to say no to a contract like that.

He knew me and I him, since the time he came round with his boys for lunch a few times. But either he did not care, remember me or genuinely could not tell "us" apart. Or, he did not want to know me now that Robert was of no use to him, the drug had failed and was withdrawn. Who was I to him but just another carer? He had so many. Round the clock.

He was in the bath and his wife was out shopping at Harvey Nichols. His eyes were shut. I brought him his towel which I left balanced on the hand basin. He was massaging himself. I knew he should not.

He was placing pressure using his two fingers on the baroreceptors of his carotid sinuses, carotid sheaths, and the carotid body in the internal carotid artery just above the bifurcation of common carotid artery. This caused an increase in blood pressure in these sinuses with resultant slowing of the heart rate, dilatation of blood vessels and a fall in blood pressure. From his history, I knew he had ventricular arrhythmias which caused hypersensitivity of the carotid sinuses. He thought he was in for a good massage. It was quite good except that it did not last long.

In two minutes he died of heart failure, with no symptoms of vagal inhibition.

A good wife, mother (and grandmother) does not boast or reveal what she has done for her family, the sacrifices that she has had to make. No one knew that I did not help him. Not Robert, not Phoebe. I am now already 70 years old. I deserve my dignity. I worked for it. I gave my family 200% and I did it for Bethany. If I was happy, they were happy. All immigrants and children of immigrants had secrets. If you did not, then you were not an immigrant. A secret redeemed me.

I kept mine in the caves of my heart, a tiny jewel that glowed, which no one could touch or take away.

66

YOU

EIGHT MONTHS LATER

Y OU ARE AWAKE BUT lying in bed aching.

You look at your flippy clock; it is a Saturday. August 10th, 2019.

You are 54 years old. You are waiting to hear back from the lawyer. You have been able to retrieve most of assets as you contested the Will, now invalid. Half the vineyard. Achara Wine Import which they're trying to buy off you now. The villa in Phuket. Greg's vases, Whatsapp messages and the post-it note with the number 5 (for 5kg) helped you to put Martin and the Chief Inspector where they belong – in hell. You paid back Phoebe's parents for the loan almost straightaway.

You live 5 minutes from Daphne so you can see her nearly every weekend. You have no view, unless you consider that of a car park and some bins a view. But you are near the sea, where your heart had always been.

Surviving the accident and your monstrous appearance has proved it. You were a skipper all along. Sometimes you thought about the two Acharas as you would remember a dream. You are helping Przemek and his colleagues to to set up a sideline: a business providing a subcontracting service to the construction industry, so that he won't ever have to work as a plumber again. He can focus on his University studies now.

Half of the vineyard profit has gone towards buying your 3-bedroom flat in Brighton, where you live alone. The other half of the vineyard was owned by La Petite Mort, whose director was Dr Robert Wong, and though he had been only a director with no financial control, you have made sure that's changed. Half of the profits go to Phoebe. You have your guitars back. Your mother will pass on soon and you will inherit the earth and its dirt, the stain of wealth.

You have not seen Phoebe since the day you left London. It seems like so many years ago when you held her tight after your first operation, the worst one, when no one could look at you and she did, for a long time.

There is time. Time is all we have in this life. You can waste it. More simply arrives. You think of your baby girl, Jorani, now 11 months. Once not long ago you were as helpless and penniless as Jo-jo. What you thought of as claustrophobia was family life. How you longed to escape when you first knew who you were. How long and impenetrable the hours were. Every day in the cage was like a month. And home is an anchor that feels crushing on your heart.

It was special, wasn't it? It must have been because now you are in pain.

There are very poor families in Cambodia, you only know this from Phoebe. It is not your memory, but you know enough about it now.

What is memory but an inkling of what you know? Those villages in Battambang need a generous donation to the school that Phoebe taught in. You've got that. You get out of your bed and get dressed. Phoebe and Jo-jo, your best teachers.

They don't know you are coming, nor your desire to take them back. It would be your first time seeing the village. The cry of gulls, long and low, is drowned out by city traffic, people, children, the drone of what you always thought you could hear from your bedroom in Fulham.

Leaving the marina, you start walking uphill to the train station, the sea behind you.

You hear the tinkling sounds of boats fade.

IF YOU ENJOYED THIS BOOK

... I would be thrilled if you could also help others enjoy it. Reviews are gems which help persuade others to give my books a shot. If I have more readers, I will be more motivated to write which means more books. Please leave me a review.

AUTHOR'S NOTE

FOR BOOK CLUB DISCUSSION

Themes

I hope you enjoyed this multiple narrative novel about desire and survival. If a man wakes up in a foreign hospital badly disfigured and amnesiac, is it more important that he survives or that he remembers everything?

At first I wanted to write a novel about memory and identity: is what we are being formed and transformed all the time by our memory and our identity? What if it is not? After I wrote this book, I realised that nothing matters except our desire and our will to survive, without which there would be absolutely no use for our memory and/or our identity.

Settings

I am sure that you, like me, love to be transported to other places and times. That's why we read. I read and I write to escape. As with my others novels, *Overboard* is set internationally, in real places, with diverse characters.

It is set in Thailand, Cambodia, Singapore and London. It is about modern people, mobility, unease. It kicks off in an unnamed hospital on the south coast of Thailand, somewhere idyllic, transgressive yet meaningless to someone who is badly injured. I thought of *The Beach* (1996), the novel by Alex Garland made into a movie (2000).

It all seems perfect at first, and even the food is perfect. The main character (the patient) knows that Thai food is his favourite food the moment it comes in on a tray, yet realising at the same time, that it is all hopeless when he is ill and in terrible pain.

Characters

Many years ago when I first completed my MA in Writing in Middlesex University, I identified a gap in the market. There were very few novels with diverse characters but they interested me and Middlesex recognised that. It made me the writer that I am. It brought out the international flavour in my writing as something to be celebrated and not sculpted and filed to fit into the mass market. With the encouragement of my Uni, I bravely wanted to tackle culture and diversity in creative writing. I already had decided I was not going to follow the lead of modern Malaysian writing which appeal to the Western market, predominantly romantic novels set during WWII.

Smashing the Stereotypes

I write about modern Asians and I use fiction as my medium. I was and am still inventing my own new genre. I cannot find enough quirky, eclectic and dark novels about modern Asians who are not Crazy or Rich. My characters are uneducated underdogs like Li-an in *Heart of Glass* or Minos AKA Luke in *Cry of the Flying Rhino*, or middle-class professionals like Phoebe Wong in *Overboard* who struggles with being bland and dull in the shadow of her hard-working brilliant parents, and Dr Benjie Lee in *Cry of the Flying Rhino*, well-educated but weak and brash. Above all, there is an element of transgression and fun, and Asians are not supposed to be having fun. These are anti-heroes, not what "immigrants" are supposed to be in fiction.

The five viewpoints of You, Phoebe, Dominique, Przemek and occasionally Eva at first run in parallel through the main plot and subplot but arcs soon intersect. The main character You is the patient, the unidentified man who has survived the shipwreck. Phoebe's character is closest to my understanding of the basis of middle-class immigrant life in London. She's a graphic designer of Malaysian Chinese origin on a grown-up gap year ("grog-gy"), volunteering in Cambodia. She is a child of immigrants. Her father is a top neurosurgeon and her mother a retired nurse specialising in geriatric care.

Dominique is the most fascinating character to me because she is the "professional, intelligent, bad woman". Her parents named her after the main character in Ayn Rand's *The Fountainhead*. As she grew up, she became more and more like her fictional namesake, never giving people what they want. She gave herself what she wanted, which had to be something she also despised. Luxury. Love. She is a contradiction, like Li-an of *Heart of Glass*.

Przemek is a philosophical Polish plumber working on Dominique's London mansion. He has a pet python called Montse.

And now I will let you in on a secret code. The serpent is a recurrent motif in all my novels. It is silent and symbolises the darkness in human nature. The shedding of its skin is a universal sign of renewals, that things will turn, and move to another phase.

The serpent itself is a character.

That's another story for another evening.

ABOUT THE AUTHOR

Ivy Ngeow was born and raised in Johor Bahru, Malaysia. A graduate of the Middlesex University Writing MA programme, Ivy won the 2005 Middlesex University Literary Prize out of almost 1500 entrants worldwide. She has written non-fiction for Marie Claire, The Star, The New Straits Times, South London Society of Architects' Newsletter and Wimbledon magazine.

Her fiction has appeared in 'Silverfish New Writing' anthologies twice, 'The New Writer' and on the BBC World Service. Her story *Funny Mountain* was published by Fixi Novo in the 'Hungry in Ipoh' (2015) anthology and *The Accidental* was published by Fixi Novo in the '2020' anthology. Ivy won first prize in the Commonwealth Essay Writing Competition 1994, first prize in the Barnes and Noble Career Essay Writing competition 1998 and was shortlisted for the David T K Wong Fellowship 1998 and the Ian St James Award 1999.

Overboard is her third novel. Her debut *Cry of the Flying Rhino* (2017) won the 2016 International Proverse Prize and *Heart of Glass* (2018) was her second novel. She lives in London.

You can find her here:

writengeow (www.writengeow.com)
Twitter (twitter.com/ivyngeow)
Facebook (facebook.com/ivyngeowwriter)
Instagram (www.instagram.com/ivyngeow)
Email: ivy_ngeow AT yahoo DOT com

ALSO BY IVY NGEOW

FICTION

Overboard

Cry of the Flying Rhino

Heart of Glass

The Power Ballads and Other Stories

NON-FICTION

Amazing at 50: 10-day Flat Tummy Challenge

Awesome at 50: Body Reboot in 6 weeks

30 Chinese Dinners: Healthy Easy Homemade Family Meals for the Time-Poor (coming soon)

EXCERPTS FROM REVIEWS

Cry of the Flying Rhino

What readers have said

"This is a beautifully written and cleverly structured novel, and for a first novel it demonstrates a maturity of technique that is impressive." - Anthony Eden

"A terrific read. Ivy Ngeow's debut novel is like nothing I've read before. Cry of the Flying Rhino tells a story of defeat, struggle and an eventual coming to terms with reality." - L

"A must read! It transports to a vast place of history and tormented human journeys, with a fast pace, often funny, and enjoyable writing style." - Isabelle Roux

"A well-crafted literary novel with a great sense of place, a plot that moves along briskly and a cast of compelling characters. I can see why it was awarded the Proverse Prize." - Helen MK

"A rich and thoroughly captivating read. This fast paced novel is incredible and had me hooked from start to finish." - Ljk97

Heart of Glass

What readers have said

"I read this in 3 days...The pace of the action, the complications of the plot itself, and the language of the hip age delivered in machine-gun style had me totally engaged on a level very few stories can... Get this book, it's a very good read. Just make sure you have no urgent appointments before starting it." - Induna

"What a ride! I won't hesitate to give another Ivy Ngeow novel a try. If you like suspense, drama, and the like, you can't go wrong with Heart of Glass." – Michael K. Eidson

"Lose yourself in a GREAT novel. I can't say enough how much this novel means to me. It gives a real insight for me into a woman's life. I am so looking forward to Ivy's next novel, treat yourself to a brilliant mind and enjoy the journey." – John H. Lease

"Ngeow gives Li-an musical chops, talent, the gift of gab, some hard-boiled actions and places her on the slick road to Noir and Greek Tragedy "- Dr GMK

"An exciting read. A great book which was fast paced and very hard to put down."- Happy Traveler

"Blondie, Call Me! Ms. Ngeow's descriptive prose and her amazing ability to capture dialects create an enchanting experience for the reader. Highly recommended." – Jonathan L. Wesner

"I loved the high speed pace of the story and the minute Macau and Hong Kong details that were spot on. I really miss the good old days and Ngeow perfectly brings that back."- Susan Blumberg-Kason

"Another exceptional work by Ivy! This book pushes into such an amazing world. Great language and very fun plot."- Zeromeo

"Brilliant literary thriller combining a classic plot and original voice. Yeah, I loved it." - Hamish

ACKNOWLEDGMENTS

I would like to thank:

My publisher, Leopard Print for being hands-on ("paws-on") and involving me in every step of the way, Phil Coleman for insight into the banking and the financial services industry during the writing process, Frances Fitzgerald of Frances Fitz Reads, for the developmental edit, Ewan Lawrie, author of No Good Deed and Gibbous House, for detailed edit, Jared of Alphavision for the minimalist, modern cover design.

Your hard work has brought this book into the world today.

To my readers, fellow authors and loyal followers on Twitter, Instagram and Facebook, my family and friends for your help, time and support. You helped me start, write and finish *Overboard*. You cheer me up every day, and you have given me encouragement, motivation and the reason to write.

To all of you, my heartfelt thanks.

SNEAK PREVIEW

OF THE NEW PREQUEL TO 'HEART OF GLASS'

1971

HE PUSHED THE RUSTY wrought iron gate. Its creak was loud as a cat's cry. The front yard and path were overgrown, dark with shadows. But when he looked up, he saw it. 3 stories high, in Indiana limestone as smooth and creamy as his own young face. "Oh my," he whispered. It had turrets and wings and its slate roof gleamed like scales, the steep slope of which was pierced with round-eyed porthole windows. If this mansion was a monster, it would fly.

About 50 yards away, he parked his '65 red Rambler which, when he was 18, his Grandpops bought him. He wasn't sure if it was good enough to be seen. Not yet. Not until he got used to the place. Well, after he'd walked short distance up the grand tree-lined N Lakeshore Drive, he already knew that he could get used to living here. No, working here, he corrected himself. He walked tall, straighter, his chest expanded, shoulders risen. The path was covered with strangling weeds, thorny bushes from which insects seemed to swarm out of when he disturbed the prickly undergrowth. The paving, which he could see was once ornate, colorful, geometric, were missing or cracked.

He knocked and waited. He noticed an old bell. A large nipple with an even larger areola. It said press so he did. He listened. But there was no sound. That'd be the first thing he'd fix around here, he said to himself.

The door opened.

"Well, hello and good morning," said the old man. The 'well' made him seem friendly. The frail man had very sparse fine white hair, a little stoop and his voice was thin. He was wearing clothes from at least a hundred years ago, no, maybe thirty. But at least he was well-dressed. At least he was even dressed. You heard of old people who wore what they slept in all year round.

"How do you do? You must be-"

"Jerry. Jerome Francis Siracuse. You can call me Jay Jay. Everybody do. I mean, does."

Jay Jay felt awkward, like he was losing the ability to speak, not that he was at all a great speaker in the first place. He had always been the quiet type. Lord knew how many got into trouble for opening their cake cave.

"Well which do you prefer?"

"Jerry, Sir."

"Alfred Sutton." He held his hand out. Jay Jay took it with a firm shake. You can call me Alfred.

"Yessir."

"The Professor sent you."

"Yes. No. My girlfriend, *fiancee*," he tripped over the word. *Fiyonsay,* she told him. "Not fiyonsee, hon. It's for'n." And small talk was for'n to him too. He left all that to Dallas. The art world and so on.

"She told me about the job."

"You ever done anything like this before?"

"A little," he lied. "I am good with electrics, plumbing, carpentry, gardening. I can fix most things." That was a bigger lie but he would learn pretty quick as he was only 22 years old and he'd learnt so much already. He had no choice. Since they shut the factory, he had to take anything. Odd jobs. Temporary jobs. This was the big one. A permanent gig. Dallas was gonna have her fancy wedding. They'd talked about it enough and Jay Jay was tired of listening to her. All the girls at Marshall Field's departmental store where she worked were excited, she said. It was always the wedding the wedding the wedding. He knew that she loved him but now he felt like a wallet. An open wallet.

"Jerry? Jerry?"

"Yessir."

Mr Alfred's voice interrupted him. "Come on in. Let me show you around."

I have my resume here, Sir. Jay Jay reached into his black briefcase which now felt redundant. It was brand new and Dallas had bought it for him from Marshall Field's. Mr Alfred smiled, showing his false teeth, white and straight, and then he shook his head and waved as though waving an insect away.

Dallas said he could easily return it to get a refund since he'd never use it again if Mr Alfred did not want to see his resume or if by some insane chance, Jay Jay didn't get the job. The old man already trusted him. Dallas only knew of the job through the Professor at the art school she was modelling for. The Professor, she'd said, trusted her in return. He was probably sweet on her. They all were. Dallas was a pretty little tomato. Actually, she was a work of art.

He went in and slightly bowed his head. He shuffled and cleaned his shoes on the door mat. He did not know what to do with the briefcase. It was awkward as a dog who didn't want to go somewhere and he decided to put it down in the hall on a very long hall table covered with paper, tins, jars, so much stuff Jay Jay's eyes could not take it in. "This is the hallway," said Alfred. The dark mahogany staircase was carved and sweeping, the stair carpet, once blood red, was now worn and faded. Wallpaper, once grand and in dark alternating stripes, was torn and peeling, stained at the top where there must have been a leak once. This was a grand home, thought Jay Jay as he stared at the huge monkey's tail handrail starter at the bottom step.

"As you can see, there are things to fix in every room," said Mr Alfred. He did not stop at all. He continued to wander around the rooms through the heavy oak polished doors which were open. He opened and shut the doors which weren't and Jay Jay was already swimming in the information he had to take it. He didn't even write anything down. How was he going to remember all this? Should he go back to the briefcase? Dallas had packed a notebook in there the night before. A smart black hardback one from the art school.

"Don't think too much. This is just to give you an overview," Mr Alfred said, as if answering Jay Jay's worried thoughts. "I don't want to go into a home. My family want me to. They want to sell it. But I was born and raised in this house. Your job as a handyman and caretaker is to help me fix everything here so that they can see I am capable of living here on my own."

"Yes, I understand, Sir."

"Basically I just need your help to fix this damn place up and we haven't even got to the garden yet. Are you good? Have you got green fingers?"

Jay Jay looked at his hands.

Mr Alfred laughed, a thin but loud squeak which sounded like an old basement door's hinge. Jay Jay noticed that everything was covered in dust. Some had joined hands and become sheaths. The enormous front sitting room had its couches and chairs covered in white fabric. The chandeliers were coated in cobwebs like it was icing on the cake. You could hardly tell that they were made of crystal drops. The dust was opaque. This joint would need a good clean. Maybe it was all that was needed first.

Jay Jay realised he said that aloud.

Mr Alfred replied, "I like that. I know you are being straight with me and I like that. If you need me to hire a roofing guy or a cleaning team you just let me know and you get them in. I'll pay them. You will find the right people for the right job. I am sure you are well-connected."

Jay Jay wasn't but he sure ain't gonna let that on. He could find a directory, he would check their references, he would ask around. The girls at Dallas' work would know someone. No way did he want to screw this up. No one he knew could be trusted. Not after the kinda things he'd been up to.

They toured the kitchen, various rooms, including a large room which looked like a library with floor to ceiling oak bookcases and in the middle of the room an old-fashioned banker's desk which was double-sided as on one side sat the banker with access to all the drawers, cigars, drinks, ledgers and so on, and on the opposite side the customer, the layman asking for a loan with nothing but the cap in hand. The desk was the only spotless thing in the entire house so it must be in use. The top was still covered in green leather and it was smooth, dust-free, polished.

They headed out of the library, and there was a piano room with a bar, the bathroom and then the upstairs stories.

The bedrooms began to blur together. He had not even any idea what each room was. "This was my mother's room, also the room I was born in," Mr Alfred said. Each bedroom looked similar, all with the same problems of torn and stained wallpaper, cracked ceilings, rotting floorboards, broken lights. "It's good it's the morning, Jerry, most of these rooms have no working lights. At night it is pretty much pitch black. I just live in one room at the top. It is the smallest room."

With that Mr Alfred waved to the narrow staircase. Jay Jay was impressed that such an old man was still able to climb the stairs, though not for long. Once he had done up these bedrooms on the second story real good, Mr Alfred could move downstairs to be in a more comfortable surroundings. It ain't right for him to live the last remaining few years of his life in this grand home in an attic room crammed with dirt and clutter, a sink and a toilet like a prisoner. He deserved way more.

"I know what you're thinking but I can still do this and I can still do this because I did it everyday. I climbed these stairs since I was born and I have kept my health going. That is what poor people in Greece, China, Russia and so on, do. Every day they are up and down mountains and hills. If you sit around all day, you're gonna turn old. I am not old. It's this house that's old. I'm not hiring you to care for me."

Jay Jay nodded. He disagreed as the man was vulnerable but he kept that to himself. How could he say he was not old? Did he mean he was not ill? But illness could hit suddenly. At any age. He'd seen it. Papa Moriarty. One minute he was eating a wafflewich. Next minute, bam. On the floor. Cardiac failure and he didn't even know it. He thought it was bad indigestion. The pain was not even in his heart. It was way deep in his guts. And that's the body for you. The mind had nothing to do with it.

They went out through the grand and enormous French doors with arched tops to the back garden terrace. There must have unbelievable parties here. Mr Alfred said so as much. He wanted to have them again. He was tired of living like this. A hobo, prisoner, in a near-derelict cage infested with roaches, mice, poison ivy and other pests. They wouldn't go so he might as well be friends with them until now. It was time to call in help.

"Someone like you."

That was how he referred to Jay Jay.

Jay Jay knew that it meant someone not quite qualified but is trustworthy, keen, hardworking. Young. Not even confident. Someone who would stop Mr Alfred's family from kicking him out, whoever his family was. Surely it would be a big family and Jay Jay knew he might even get to meet them if they came round. After all he'd be in charge of this entire property five days a week.

"Let me show you your office, work room," Mr Alfred chuckled.

"I have an office?"

"Of course. You're gonna be working here, aren't ya?"

"Yessir."

They crossed the terrace and headed down the sweeping Indiana stone staircase in the garden with a far-fetching views of Lake Michigan, beaches and the navy pier. An overgrown old wooden cabin sat quite squarely and at ease at the end of the garden. "Well, we had a gardener and a caretaker once. Oh and a driver too. I don't know how they lived here but they did."

Jay Jay could well see how they did. The cabin was way bigger than his entire apartment that he shared with Dallas.

It had two rooms. The main work room and the office which was once also an office of some kind. It still had a desk. Everything was like a mini version of the house. Dusty, mouldy, rotted. Jay Jay could see that a lot of work was required to get this place going again and he could not wait to start.

"You could start in here. If you have any equipment you could leave them in here. I am sure there are actually already tools here, but I can't say if you could still use them."

"Probably rusty or broken by now."

"If you want to buy new tools, I'd pay you back for them."

Jay Jay could see that everything would work out fine, and that Mr Alfred was a reasonable man and despite his age (Jay Jay didn't even know the exact figure) was still sharp and quick.

Jay Jay was born in the spring of '49 in Beecher on a pond farm less than an hour's drive away. Far as he knew his father was still alive, though he had no idea where. His grandfather raised and spoiled him, but not too much, hence the '65 Rambler, secondhand but pretty much perfect. Jay Jay decided he didn't want to be a farmer. His buddy Ty convinced him to go to the city. After all it was only about 40 miles away. He could come back to Grandpops anytime he'd like to, said Ty.

Now Ty became a cop. And that was a bad move.

Jay Jay stared at the contents of the cabin, and walked around for a few minutes. When he turned around, the old man had seemed to vanish. He was alone. He left the cabin and shut the stiff door. He wandered back to the arched French window but it was now shut. It was the kind which could not be opened from the outside. It had no knob to turn, just a keyhole.

WANT MORE?

Thank you for reading *Overboard*. If you'd like to receive a free short story collection, *The Power Ballads & Other Stories,* please download it here. Join my VIP fan club and be among the first to know about future books. If you have comments or would like to write to me, please use my online form. You can also email me:

ivy_ngeow AT yahoo DOT com

You will not receive spam. I know. I hate spam too. I will only keep in touch with you about new books, gifts and deals. I would love to hear from you.